ALSO BY DOUGLAS BAUER
Prairie City, Iowa

Dexterity

a novel

DOUGLAS BAUER

SIMON AND SCHUSTER   NEW YORK   LONDON   TORONTO   SYDNEY   TOKYO

Simon and Schuster
Simon & Schuster Building
Rockefeller Center
1230 Avenue of the Americas
New York, New York 10020

Simon and Schuster and colophon are registered trademarks of Simon & Schuster Inc.

Designed by Barbara Marks Graphic Design
Manufactured in the United States of America

10 9 8 7 6 5 4 3 2 1

Library of Congress Cataloging-in-Publication Data

Bauer, Douglas.
  Dexterity.
  I. Title.
PS3552.A8358D4   1989   813'.54   88-35641

ISBN 0-671-64997-3

Portions of this novel appeared in very different form in *Epoch*. Chapter Fourteen appeared in *Hot Type*, a fiction anthology published by Collier's, under the title "Lore."

Acknowledgments

I'm very grateful to Bill Appell for his singular insight and long friendship. I owe thanks, too, to Dr. Leon D. Eron of the University of Illinois at Chicago, for sharing his research on intellectual functioning and aggression, and to Dennis Amtower and Amtower Biokinetics. Also, Sally Bottiggi of the Columbia County New York Historical Society provided much necessary information. And I'm especially thankful to Judy Karasik and Sven Birkerts for their careful reading and superb criticism of the manuscript at various stages.

*For
Sue and
for
Bill K.*

The reader should know that, while the events in this novel take place in and around Columbia County, New York, I have freely re-arranged its geography, and invented places that do not to my knowledge exist.

Dexterity

One

On a Saturday in spring when Ramona was sixteen, she stood with her friends in the bright new heat and watched Ed King move away from her toward Luther Sherrill's pickup truck, sitting fueled and ready in the gas station's driveway. Ed was shirtless. The sun whitened his always pale flesh to a ghostly translucence. But as Ramona watched him, the slide of his shoulder blades, mean as angled implements as they pushed against his skin; as she watched his long, skinny body moving with an anomalously feminine grace toward the pickup, she saw Ed as anything but spectral. She saw him as sensual life itself.

This was the spring before the extraordinary fire. The crumbling brick building with its intricate turrets still stood on Summit Street, the textile mill long closed. But a portion of the building was being used that spring, filled with the fumes and craftless work of a rubber-processing plant. In the spring before

the fire, there were not yet the wide gaps of empty lots on Summit, through which you would be able to look directly past the valley's sweep beyond the town of Myles, to the gray-blue rise of the Catskills.

As Ed reached for the handle of the passenger door the pickup came to life, its motor exploding richly. From where she stood with her two friends in the doorway of the station, Ramona heard Luther Sherrill shout, "Let's move it, King. Let's go." He raced the pickup's motor. Old blue smoke plumed from the exhaust and made a brief low sky. But Ed was in no hurry; he knew the moment's pace was his to make. He placed his can of beer on the roof of the truck and turned to speak to her and when he faced her again she saw his slanted smile, the thing in the world she needed most to receive. She stepped past her friends toward him. The sun was full and lambent on her face and as she squinted into it she heard him say, with a fine, theatrical threat in his voice, "You stay right there, you hear me? I'm comin' back for you and you better be right there."

"Oh, yeah?" she shouted back. She drew on her cigarette and threw it down on the driveway. "What makes you think I will?" Her voice was low and rich, noticeably so for a girl so small and young. She ground the cigarette into the asphalt as she gave him an extravagant glare. "Who the fuck you think you're talkin' to?" She was his match, theatrically, and the source of her energy was the thrill of being owned.

Still smiling, Ed simply pointed at her, then reached for his beer and climbed into the cab. And as the truck pulled away, he leaned through the window and pointed again. "You better be there!"

"Maybe I will!" Ramona shouted. *"Maybe."*

"Fifteen minutes," Ed shouted back as the pickup waited to pull out onto Summit. "I'm comin' for you!"

"We'll see!" She tried to say something else, but the pickup's tires screeched and its motor roared like war as it raced away, and still Ed leaned out the window, looking back at her, aiming

his finger and his smile, until the truck reached the turn at the end of the street.

She watched, then walked back to Lovilla and Wilma Jean, her two best friends. *"Shit,"* she said. "Who's he think he is, tellin' me to stay here and wait for his ass?" She couldn't keep her happiness from jiggling her words. She walked a tight full circle in the driveway, stomping her feet a couple of times.

"You gonna stay?" asked Wilma Jean.

"What're you gonna do?" asked Lovilla. They watched her tantrum eagerly, pleased to be helping in their secondary roles.

Ramona reached for a cigarette from Wilma Jean's pack. Wilma Jean shook one free and handed it to her.

"I don't know," Ramona said. She shook her head and looked into their faces. Like her, they were garishly made-up, their mouths the shape and shade of red paraffin lips. They wore tight jeans that announced their future bodies. Ramona's tiny shapeliness. Wilma Jean's thinness. Lovilla's plump thighs straining the denim.

"I'll give him fifteen minutes," Ramona said and nodded. She looked out at Summit Street. "He said he'd be back in fifteen minutes. But I ain't waitin' one second more."

"I guess you should," said Wilma Jean.

"I guess," Lovilla said.

Ramona crossed her arms and cocked her hip, signaling that the wait had formally begun. Her friends shook their heads sympathetically. She felt light-headed with the pleasure of what love did to a day, supreme with the notion that others were living these same moments as ordinary life.

This Saturday in spring was two years before they were married; three years before her parents moved to mill jobs in North Carolina. She had loved Ed King for nearly six months, and for some time now almost every thought she'd had contained at least a strand of dream of how their life would be. In school, watching him, low-slouched and arrogant as he moved through the halls with the other boys in the senior class, she

wanted him so badly she imagined crawling down inside his jeans as if slithering into the mouth of a dangerous cave. In front of the mirror, as she drew her lavish lips, she whispered, "Mrs. Ed King. Mr. and Mrs. Ed King." She'd written "Ramona King" in thick purple scrawls, like serpentine tattoos, on the covers of her notebooks. With a nail file, she'd carved the name "Ramona King" into her desk tops, working as lovingly as a headstone carver beveling names into marble, and the care with which she worked inspired her to imagine a life of measureless bliss in which, as Ramona King, she would walk at Ed's side, gliding up and down the hills of Myles. She saw them living at the edge of the village in a new house trailer, saw the sun reflecting off its siding as if it had caught the cut of a diamond. She imagined herself inside the trailer, keeping it as gleamingly clean as its aluminum brilliance deserved, and, at night, in their bed, of fucking Ed until she'd milked nothing less than his soul up through his balls and into her.

She turned to Lovilla and Wilma Jean and said, "I guess you guys oughta go on."

They both nodded gravely, and Lovilla said, "Right." She watched her friends move slowly across the drive. When they reached the sidewalk Lovilla called back, "We'll be at Dee's if he don't show." She pointed toward the luncheonette, four doors down the street.

And Ramona shrugged her shoulders and called, unable any longer to keep the lilt of her expectancy from softening her voice, "He said he's comin'."

Years later—not very many years at all, but a few years after they were married—Ramona would more than once remember the instance of this Saturday, though it was nothing she tried to rekindle. Once, as she sat at a bar beside a man nicknamed Jesus Christ, the moment would suddenly flush up in her mind and when it did she would hear Ed's words, *I'm comin' for you*, as an

affectless prediction which seemed menacingly certain. And once, as she stood vertiginous with loneliness in a room above a flower shop, she would hear them again, and see his smile and pointing finger, and then his words, *You stay right there . . . I'm comin' for you,* would sound to her like an invitation to surrender, like the hope of blessed rescue. But never, in recalling them, would she relive the moment as she did when it occurred; when Ed first told her to wait where she was until he came to get her, and her heart was stopped by the perfection of it all.

Two

hile Ed waited on the curb in the humid dawn for his ride to work, Ramona paced through the rooms of their tiny, sagging house. The morning's heat was already so wet that her bare feet made soft sucking sounds on the curled linoleum floors. She moved from the kitchen to the living room, catching glimpses of Ed through the windows, through the rust-edged hole in the screen door, as he stood with his back to her at the end of their grassless yard. He looked lazily into the air, seeming to assess the breaking sky as if he'd ordered it. His posture was easy and pliant.

Inside, Ramona's pacing grew more and more impatient. She stopped abruptly near the living-room window, thinking she'd heard her baby in his crib upstairs, and was relieved to receive the quiet of the house. Cautiously, she cracked the door so that Ed wouldn't hear it and looked out for any sign of the big orange truck. Seeing the two of them, Ed at the end of the walk,

Ramona peeking out the door, one might think of a mother watching with her son for his morning school bus.

At last she heard the truck's motor, a huge high whine, and watched it pull to a stop. Ed was the last of the crew to be picked up. He moved to the rear of the flatbed and deliberately climbed the slatted tailgate.

"Goddam, King," Ramona heard one of the workers say to Ed. "You take that long to fuck at night, your old lady must say, 'Now, what was your name, again?' "

Inside the cab, two other workers laughed loudly.

"Adams," Ramona heard Ed say to the first worker, "just eat my asshole and pretend it's a doughnut."

Ramona heard their laughter and saw Ed's smile break, a harsher source of light against the early haze of sun, as he made a spot for himself at the front among the rakes and shovels.

Ed's fist gave the roof of the truck a quick signaling blow. The engine revved, and as the truck pulled away, Ramona's eyes narrowed on the circular seal of Columbia County, New York, painted on its door. She waited until she could no longer hear the engine, fading very gradually, the only sound in Myles, then she hurried to the kitchen table where she'd begun to sit every morning as soon as Ed had gone.

Because she was small, she had to straighten in her chair for the back of her neck to meet the line of the sun. It shone for a few precious minutes at this time of summer with a precisely beneficial heat through the window above the sink and Ramona moved her neck in exaggerated feline motions, spreading the sun into her nape and through her shoulders.

From childhood, she'd been drawn to rituals. As a young girl, she'd sat at supper with her parents and her younger brother, James, and pretended that the passing of food—mashed potatoes and canned vegetables and a high stack of white bread—was a mystical rite following an undeviating order. When she'd dressed for school in the morning she'd imagined she was a

queen, not actually dressing herself at all but standing indiffer-
ently while an attendant slipped her garments over her head.
And at the heart of her fantasies, beyond the customary secrecy
of a child's inner world, had been an instinct to enrich the
dulling poverty of her young life in Myles; to live obliviously
above it in an orderly thrill.

As she sat now, receiving the sun at the table, it would be
easy to assume that little had changed. Her face, at twenty-one,
was a very young girl's. You could immediately see it as the face
of the child who'd passed the bread plate to her brother.
Leaning forward on the chair, her toes resting on its rung, she
was the same delicate size as she'd been at thirteen.

And her impulse toward ceremony was nearly undiminished.

She had begun to think of her early mornings at the kitchen
table almost as an adulteress anticipates the instant of her
lover's touch. Part of her impatience for Ed to leave was the
pull of illicitness, her fear that the sun would arrive while he
was still waiting outside for the truck, that he might come back
inside for something he'd forgotten. She knew that if Ed caught
her at the table, suppliant in the heat, he would call her a fool
for believing that the sun through her body was as a drug in
her blood, one that often numbed the pain. Pain which was not
often overwhelming anymore, but, more regularly, a low
steady pulsation. Or which was sometimes an elusive, floating
pain which refused to remain where it more logically belonged,
where it had begun: at the base of her wrist where her right
hand had been.

Several things had influenced the accident which took Ramona's hand. She'd always driven inattentively, her mind wandering at the wheel, somehow never quite accepting that the way
she steered the car had much to do with how it behaved. And
she'd been particularly careless that night at the moment she
approached the turn, reaching awkwardly with her right hand—
perhaps because her left hand held a cigarette—to close a
flapping window vent whose edge had lost its rubber seal.

There was also the curve itself, a notorious, nearly ninety-degree bend in the gravel road south of town, which was radiant with ice in the January cold. And finally there was her frame of mind, even more distracted than usual, racing thoughtlessly as the car left the road at the turn, skimmed a shallow ditch, and glided with the abrasionless grace of a sleigh into an enormous elm. The collision threw Ramona forward while the vent's naked metal edge collapsed like a guillotine on her wrist. She was wildly spun, turned nearly upside down, and the heel of her boot kicked through the windshield while her hand was immaculately severed.

News of Ramona's accident had moved through Myles with a small town's efficiency. By the following morning, word of it had reached the oldest resident of the nursing home on the northern edge of the village. It was being traded among children at the old grade school on Court Street. Its speed was further helped by the particular intrigue of the accident's details. The car, a long-finned Dodge, had struck the tree at an angle that destroyed only its driver's-side door. And Ramona's injuries were also fastidiously brutal—she was otherwise only bruised and swollen, her seven-month pregnancy miraculously saved. But even more, the spread of the story was hurried by reports that the Dodge had held Ramona's belongings and that, as her cries had made clear to those who'd found her, she'd been leaving her house and Ed King for good. In shock, the pain of her injuries not yet alive, she had been screaming for her mother and her father; or screaming *to* them, people said, that she was coming with her baby to be with them again.

At the kitchen table, Ramona lowered her head and held herself still. She moved her hair off her neck, lifting it like a skirt, letting the sun enter her, and felt it warming the coldness that she often imagined was inside her spine. Breathing deeply, she reached to push the neck of her blouse farther down and

exhaled, hastening the heat through her limbs. She smiled from a long distance.

Her baby's sudden cries from upstairs were raw and full. Ramona jumped at the table, opened her eyes, and sat dumbly for a moment, returning. After five months, she was still regularly shocked by Jonas's waking sounds, strong whoops certain of themselves at the moment of utterance. Although they'd changed from an infant's piercing cries to looser, broader noises getting closer to speech, they remained instantly full-throated in their new modulations.

Ramona hadn't known at first whether the strength of Jonas's crying was something she should be proud of or worried about. So she'd asked other young mothers in Myles if their babies also woke so rudely.

Wilma Jean Robertson told her, "My William is, what? . . . March-to-May younger than Jonas? And he sleeps so good I can hardly hear him. Sometimes I sneak into his room and lean down to his face and I have to put my hand over his mouth to make sure he's even breathin'."

Something in the image of Wilma Jean bending to her child, her long, skinny palm above his mouth, impressed Ramona deeply. Perhaps it was the idea that she found such a check necessary. In any case, she frequently imagined Wilma Jean hovering over William in his crib, and sometimes in Ramona's picture her friend's maternal hand became a slowly lowering lid.

Her closest friend, Lovilla—who'd married Raymond Adams, the worker who'd greeted Ed on the truck—had assured her that there was nothing unusual about Jonas's waking sounds. She'd told Ramona that her own son, now almost a year old, had often cried from the bottom of his lungs while opening his eyes.

"It's just, he sounds so goddam *mad*," Ramona had said.

Lovilla had shrugged. "He's either hungry or he's shit his pants, or both. Other than that, what's he got to be mad about?"

"Mad at *me*, I mean," Ramona had said.

Lovilla had smiled and waved her hand dismissively. "You the one that put the shit in his pants?"

Ramona's long fall of unhappiness had begun soon after her marriage and had steadily continued through its three years. When she thought now of Ed, amazed herself at how her feelings had turned, she held no clear serial of individual abuses in her mind. Instead, she thought of his life as a pattern of habits she despised.

She thought of hearing the door slam as he returned from work after stopping at the Hill Top Tap, its fermented stench on his breath and in his clothes. He was rarely completely drunk, more often he was happily dulled, and she sensed that when he moved past her to the refrigerator for a beer, he looked at her through the distracted glaze of his more pressing concern to keep that pleasurable dullness at the same steady level.

She thought of him at the supper table after finishing his meal, leaning back on his chair and telling her what he'd said or done to Adams at work that day. And while Ed spoke he shaved his cigarette ash against the sharp-edged opening of his empty beer can, the ashes hissing softly as they fell.

She thought of him sprawled in his chair in front of the television, his long legs crossed, his white feet bared, and of watching his big toe move to the music of commercials. And when Ramona thought of these acts, she resented each component of them. She hated the sudden slamming of the door, the sound itself, as much as she resented his beery ignorance of her. The innocent hiss of his ashes dropped in beer, the thought of it alone, angered her as much as his indifference to anything but the details of his day. The sight of his twitching toe revulsed her as much as his weekend laziness or the heat of his temper.

But the truer cause of her disillusion was not so much the things he did as what he had not done. For, in marrying Ramona, Ed had not helped her stay above the common

moments of the desolate village, as she'd been certain he would do when she was sixteen and watched him stroll away from her in the driveway of a gas station; when she was seventeen and eighteen, watching him and touching him and always wanting him, and sensing his invulnerable air as the thing that allied him with her. She had waited expectantly through the first months of marriage for that even greater sense of altitude she'd known would come, but he had not given it to her. He had given her, instead, the daily life of Myles. Every day, all the time, he had given her Myles.

Growing up, a girl in Myles, she'd been struck most of all by the fact that the day was a thing of aching length. She'd had so much *time*; and after a point, with all that time every day to love Ed from the vast distance of not being married to him, the routine ugliness of Myles was nothing she truly saw. And then all the things that had shielded her—life as a daughter, the febrile shapelessness of a day, the distance of longing—had been abruptly stripped away when she'd married Ed. Life suddenly seemed somehow familiar in ways she couldn't quite place. It was hardly the life she'd believed she'd have. So Ed's assuredness began to seem to Ramona a kind of stupid rigidity, and she grew to believe that he'd betrayed her and lied to her; that he'd perversely changed.

In the kitchen, Ramona heard Jonas crying again. She rose slowly, then suddenly hurried up the short set of stairs. By the time she reached him he was making longer, calmer noises, although his wiry body was flapping energetically, full of spastic task.

Jonas's crib filled the side of their bedroom where the ceiling angled sharply downward, keeping the area in shadow. His face was busy with expression and appeared against the sheet to shine up through gray light like a moving-surfaced moon.

Looking down at Jonas, Ramona watched his hands rhyth-

mically open and close as he tried to wad the air, and she imagined his palms—flat and spread, then tightly fisted—as mouths alternately screaming and shutting. She'd become obsessed with the shapes of others' hands, the way they lay and moved, and she'd noticed Jonas's fingers spidering constantly now.

He frowned at Ramona and gave a strong cry. She knew he was hungry and needing to be changed. He cried again, almost a sound of syllables. Ramona felt sure he was ordering her to move, to pick him up. She continued to look down at him and perhaps thirty seconds passed. She was not angry or particularly sad; simply very far away. She stared at Jonas, his cries sounding thin and watery from behind her numbness.

Then she reached down, her left hand sliding under him, and lifted him to her chest. She felt and smelled the fullness of his diaper.

While she held him she looked out the window where an angled stretch of highway leading from Myles toward Mellenville filled a lower corner. It was a scene that mesmerized her. The twisting gravel road south of town which she'd started down last winter eventually met the highway, and if she'd made the curve that night and driven on she'd have come to the highway at the intersection she was now staring at, framed in her bedroom window. From this distance the gravel strip appeared an insignificant curl, the highway's frayed strand.

"Well, ol' Joe," Ramona said to her baby, "if I could just figure out how to do this . . ." Her surprisingly deep voice had an unlikely tranquillity that Jonas seemed to hear, for he squirmed in her arms, trying to burrow into her. Terrified that he might fall, Ramona instinctively squeezed him and he yelped as his breath escaped.

"Jesus," Ramona said, "I was just tryin' to keep you from fallin' on your head."

She felt Jonas's hands pawing her blouse. Trying to see around her, he flopped in her arms like a broken-backed doll.

His strength had been increasing incredibly in the last month or so, his spine growing stronger by the day. As she carried him down the steps she felt his drooling mouth on her chest, wetness spreading on her blouse. Back in the kitchen, she laid him on the table and peeled away his diaper. She saw that the sun had moved, making a square of unreachable light on the wall.

When Ramona had dreamed of a life with Ed in the gleaming silver trailer at the pastured edge of Myles, she'd never once seen herself as a mother. As vividly as she'd pictured the future, as detailed as she'd made their days (she'd known the lemon-wax smell of the trailer's surfaces), she thought only of the two of them together. Unlike other girls her age, who looked at the young mothers in the village, looked at their babies perched on their hips, and yearned for motherhood themselves as a life of status and romance, Ramona had given the notion little thought. So, through the first two startling years of her marriage, it had not seemed to her that pregnancy was yet another lovely thing that hadn't come to her as she'd expected it would. In fact, when she suddenly noticed her small breasts swelling and began to wake every morning with a thin nausea, she perceived in these signs her body's betrayal, the dimensions of a more elaborate trap.

The day she'd driven home from the county clinic, her certainty confirmed, she'd gone immediately into the bathroom and turned to face the door, where a long, smoky mirror was mounted. In a kind of daze, she'd taken off her clothes and stood completely naked. She began to inspect herself, feeling her breasts, smoothing her hands over her stomach, as though she might find some contradictory evidence. She tried to imagine a life beginning inside her. She repeated aloud the words of the doctor at the clinic, mimicking his happy emphases. She stared, loudly congratulating her body as the doctor had, for a quarter of an hour until the false play of her voice began to sound to her like a mindless warbling.

*   *   *

In her kitchen, after changing and feeding Jonas, she stoppered the sink to run some water for his bath. Beside the sink, she kept two smoothly curved pieces of wood that Ed had made to fit around Jonas so he wouldn't slip out of her grasp and into the bathwater. She hadn't needed to use them since Jonas had grown strong enough to sit up fairly steadily, but she kept them beside the sink anyway. She felt inexplicably fond of them; they seemed souvenirs.

At her feet, Jonas lay on his stomach on the linoleum. He saw a spot of light on the floor ahead of him and struggled to crawl toward it, but he'd only learned to move laboriously backward. His head bobbed wildly as he tried to keep his eyes on the spot ahead of him where he wanted to go, but the more effortfully he worked to reach it, the farther away from it he moved, his body inching in reverse. He wailed, maddeningly frustrated.

Ramona stepped past him to the table and sat down to wait for his bathwater to cool a bit in the sink. She watched him grunting on the floor. Again he reached for a tuft of dust and shrieked as his effort to go toward it sent him backward.

At the table, Ramona slowly began to unbutton her wet and food-stained blouse. She continued to watch Jonas, smiling down at him as she finished her buttons. Then, after she'd slipped the blouse off, she spontaneously undid the Dacron straps around her shoulders and let the plastic shell that held the hand slide away from her forearm. And as though she felt it weightless with its freedom, she let her arm rise in a slow, levitating motion until it stopped, a salute, above her far-focused eyes.

Ed stepped out of the Hill Top Tap into the air of Summit Street. Although it was late afternoon, the day was still shimmeringly hot, and his time inside the air-conditioned darkness

of the bar had made him forget the heat he'd been working in until an hour ago.

He headed down Summit toward Tommy Beener's garage, his lunch pail in his hand, a six-pack of beer in a sack under his arm. As he passed Sampson's Grocery, Dee's Luncheonette, the other shabby storefronts, he watched his reflection float slowly across their windows.

Although he was a young man, his movements—while loose and fluid—suggested the carefully dispensed energy of old age. His shoulders slouched noticeably, as well, and if you didn't know him it would be hard to believe he was only twenty-four. Even as a boy, he had moved deliberately and at the age of eleven, twelve, people had called him Gramps. A few still did, and Ed didn't mind, heard the name as friendly, but it had seemed to people less applicable as they'd come to understand his uncommon strength and his week-long taste for manual labor. And as they'd also learned to feel the force of his mood quickening the pace of any room he entered, a kind of nervous alertness to what he might say, whose past foolishness he might decide to remember out loud.

He walked under the raised door of Beener's garage and again into a darkness, not as cool as the Hill Top's. He stopped beneath a car held high in the air on a hydraulic lift and peered up into its rusted underbelly. Farther back in the darkness he heard the anvil clang of a tool being flung to the concrete floor.

He heard Tommy Beener yell, "Fuck!"

Ed laughed as he saw an old blue Chevrolet in the corner of the garage, its front end raised off the floor. He saw Tommy Beener slithering on his back from under it. Next to the car, two other men sat on battered metal folding chairs, chuckling.

"This fucking *fuck!*" said Beener.

"Easy," Ed said, reaching him. He knelt and set his six-pack on the floor beside Beener. "Have a beer. Cool yourself."

"Fucking piece of shit," Beener said. He wiped his hands on

a rag and opened Ed's sack. His greasy overalls were erratically mapped with ink-blue sweat. "Don't ever buy a Chevrolet," Beener said, pronouncing it "Cheverlay." He flexed his lips to drink. He had a gap, three top teeth wide, near the front of his mouth.

"Shit, Tom," Ed said, "what difference does it make? You fuck 'em all up just as bad." He looked past Beener to wink at Ewel Chesley and Marvin Broder on the folding chairs. Everyone laughed, even Beener, the gap in his smile flashing blackly. Ed pulled two more beers from their plastic circles and offered them to Chesley and Broder.

"Obliged, Ed," Broder said.

Chesley raised his palm in refusal, as though taking an oath. "I'm goin' in a minute, Ed."

"Drink it or wear it, Chesley," Ed said, smiling.

"You twisted my arm," Chesley said and took the beer. Ed opened one for himself, set the last two on the floor, and eased himself up onto an old oil barrel.

Beener sat on the floor, his formidable belly resting in the cradle of his crossed legs. "Yours won't be done till tomorrow," he said to Ed. "Thanks to this piece of fuck." He nodded at the Chevrolet.

Ed looked out the back window to the Dodge, parked with half a dozen other ailing cars behind the garage. It had begun to make loud clanking noises the day before while he was climbing the long hill from his house to Summit Street.

Ed shook his head, pretending despair. "I swear to God, Tom, I don't know why I keep comin' here." There were two garages in town, the division of customers a matter of age. The older men took their business to Squeaky Frye at his Sunoco station. Tommy Beener, who'd been in Ed's class, held the loyalty of almost everyone in Myles under forty. "It sure ain't the service." He glanced around the garage. "It must be the romantic atmosphere." He looked at Marvin Broder. "It *sure* as

fuck ain't the quality of the company, is it, Marv?" His smile
now a tight smirk, Ed held his eyes hard on Broder, hoping to
make him unsure of what to say.

Broder shrugged and smiled stiffly. "I don't know, Ed," he
said. "I guess."

In his mind, Ed cursed Broder as he watched him take a swig
of the beer he'd given him. "At least you can't complain about
the price of the drinks, can you, Marv. You cheap son of a
bitch." His pursed smile and his eyes did not relax. "You know,
you're old enough now, you can actually buy beer for yourself,
legal. You probably didn't know that, since you never have."

"Is that right?" Broder said. He was looking at a spot in the
air between Ed and Beener. "Thanks for the tip."

Ed felt his anger rising and decided he was too tired to follow it.

They all sat in silence, then complained for quite a while
about the heat. They talked of the new girl from Mellenville
working at Dee's Luncheonette, whose tits strained impressively
her lime-green waitress uniform and who also seemed capable
of keeping food orders straight.

"She's got a real quick mind," Ewel Chesley said seriously.

"I like a chick with two and two makes four," said Tommy
Beener.

Beener finished his beer and reached for another one. He said
to Ed, "You need a car for the night, I can loan you one."

"Nah," Ed said, smiling genuinely at Beener. He shook his
head. "Tomorrow's fine." Again, he looked through the back
window. He felt a fondness as he saw the Dodge—its rust-
marked white finish gleaming falsely in the sun—though his
feelings were not so much for this car, particularly, as for the
pleasure of cars generally and the way he felt inside them.

Ed drove a car in town just as he moved on foot, with a
provocative slowness, and it gave the sense of the car being
strenuously reined. He'd driven this way since he was a

teenager, regardless of the car, which he kept lightly clutched on the brink of second gear. There was a flamboyance in these crawls up and down the streets of Myles, the car's rear end raked high and swaying on its springs with a concubine grace while the motor concussively whined. But treated so abusively, Ed's motors had always broken regularly, as the Dodge's had the day before.

He looked at Ewel Chesley, a short, stocky man with a bulldog's bunched rings of skin at the back of his neck. "That's yours," Ed said, pointing to the floor and the remaining can of beer.

"Thanks, Ed," Chesley said. "I'm still good." He jiggled his half-empty can at Ed.

"What the hell, Ewel." Ed winked at Chesley. "You here to drink beer or just sit there bein' good-looking? 'Cause you ain't doin' worth a shit at either one." Then he chuckled and offered it to Broder with a small, sarcastic surrender. "I ain't taking it home with me, Marv."

Broder looked at the can of beer for a moment, then nodded in an odd, formal dip of acceptance and leaned down to pick it up.

"That's eight hundred thirty-seven beers you owe me, Broder."

He watched Broder's profile as he brought the beer to his lips. His face had bothered Ed when they were boys and it bothered him now. It seemed to Ed that it had barely changed; a kind of taunting; seemed still the wide, full face of a child, his cheeks unusually fat.

In truth, Broder was not especially cheap. He bought his share of rounds through a long night at the Hill Top, and Ed recognized this very well, but he habitually accused Broder, anyway, as a kind of easy focus of his more complex dislike.

"You heard about Moon's wife's sister?" Beener asked in general. Moon was the owner of the Hill Top and Ed had

learned in the bar an hour ago that Moon's wife's maiden sister, Evelyn, who'd lain in the Columbia County Hospital with cancer in her lungs, had died last night.

"She die?" Broder asked, leaning forward on his chair with interest.

"Last night," Beener said.

"Goddam, that was quick," said Ewel Chesley. "When'd she go in? Ten days ago? Two weeks?" He shook his head. "Damn, that was quick."

"What time did she die?" Broder asked, his curiosity giving him a kind of sudden animation. "Moon and his wife there, or did the hospital call 'em?"

Fuckin' typical, Ed thought. He also disliked Broder's bottomless appetite for the gossip of Myles. In this way, he reminded Ed of Waycross, an old man he worked with on the highway crew, who filled the air all day long with distorted local history and tales he'd heard third-hand. Ed sometimes called Broder "Waycross, Junior," an insult which Broder seemed not once to have heard.

But it was not simply Broder's love of gossip that irritated Ed, for more than nearly anyone in town Ed's mind was fed by the continuous undersong of its mundane life.

"This surprises me," Broder said, of the news that Moon's sister-in-law had died. "Moon was sayin' just last week she could lay there a long time."

"Well," Beener said, "he was wrong, and I say it's a lot better she went fast."

"Yeah," Broder said, "but Moon was sayin' they'd told him she might be months."

"Christ, Broder," Ed said. "Why don't you go to the hospital and check for yourself. If she's still layin' there, tell her not to worry, that the way *you* heard it she's got lots of time left."

Ed watched Broder shake his head, appearing still skeptical.

Although Ed had found several reasons to dislike Broder, his hatred really had to do with a particular moment, one night in

the Hill Top, a week after the accident that had taken Ramona's hand.

Coming out of the bathroom, Ed had been stopped by Broder's loudly slurred words, spoken to the other drinkers gathered along the bar. As he'd been about to step back into the room, Ed had heard Broder wondering happily to the others just how limply Ed must hang. "I mean, you figure," Broder had said. "He couldn't even keep that flat-titted wife of his satisfied enough that she tried to run off." And then he'd laughed sloppily, his wide face raised in invitation.

Ed had seen a few of the men, Raymond Adams among them, glancing wildly toward him as he stood in the bathroom's door, his eyes on Broder's back. It had taken him several moments to recover and by then Broder had sensed the nervousness in the room and looked behind him to see Ed standing in the bathroom's yellowish strand of light. He'd simply glanced silently at Ed and turned again to the bar.

By the time Ed had returned to his bar stool, he'd begun to feel a certain gratitude for having overheard Broder. His words had been a confirmation. For Ed had been sure since the night of the accident that people were talking about him with the quick-breathed excitement a local scandal always put in their voices. It had been eating at him deeply, for he'd never been the subject of the town's interest in a way he hadn't desired.

He'd paused a moment more, held by the complicated sense that acknowledging what he'd heard would somehow be making a confession. But pretending he hadn't heard Broder would be a display of another sort of weakness. And then he'd looked at Moon behind the bar, given him his angling grin, and slid dollar bills toward him while he said loudly for everyone to hear, "Give Broder another of whatever he's drinkin'."

In Beener's garage, Ed watched Broder glance at his watch and slowly stand.

"Gotta go," Broder said. He raised his second can of beer, still nearly full, to Ed. "I'll take this one for the ditch."

Ed nodded and smirked. "Sip it slow, Marv. It'll have to last you till you come to town tomorrow and find somebody to buy you a new one."

Beener and Ewel Chesley laughed. Broder merely smiled and nodded, then sauntered through the darkened garage and out the door.

Ed shook his head and smiled at the other two men. He pointed to a small jar lid filled with cigarette butts on the edge of Beener's cluttered workbench. Ed said, "Fucker's brains wouldn't fill that lid." They all laughed again.

"He means to please." Chesley smiled.

"So does a head of lettuce," Ed said.

Out of the corner of his eye, he saw Broder through the window of the garage. He watched him walking past the Dodge to his own car at the edge of the lot and his eyes followed him. Although he saw that Chesley was standing now, heard him saying that he, too, had to get home, Ed's mind was once again on Broder and a second night last winter.

In the weeks after Ramona's accident, Ed had driven a heaterless Plymouth which Beener loaned him while he repaired the damage to the Dodge. A few days had passed since he'd overheard Broder's accusation in the Hill Top, and Ed was driving cautiously one night over back roads still glassed with ice. He often drove the reticulate country lanes of the county. He loved to wander aimlessly over them at night, on Saturdays, letting the circuitous paths draw his route for him as he tried to anticipate where a road would eventually meet one he already knew. He was an obsessive cartographer of the three or four counties stacked atop one another along the east bank of the Hudson, kept in his head an increasingly detailed network of narrow highways and gravel lanes.

But on the night he was now recalling, Ed had been driving with a purpose, on the gravel lane leading south from Myles toward the curve and the elm where Ramona had left the road. He'd not really planned to, had begun his drive that night with

his habitual meandering in mind. But then he'd found himself driving the southern gravel road and once he'd started down it the notion came to him that if he visited the place of the accident he might possibly discover something, anything, that could help ease his mind; that might reveal to him somehow what was happening to his life. He'd no sense of what he'd see. He had not been near the scene. But his spirits were lifted as he'd felt the return of his long-held belief that, like a brilliant Indian scout, he possessed the ability to read revealing narratives in the lay of a road.

He'd guided the Plymouth carefully over the ice-rutted road. A snow, which had begun to fall casually an hour before, became suddenly heavy. Ed had glanced to his left, barely able to see the D&H railroad tracks paralleling the road.

The idea that his name was fueling the town's current gossip had only deepened in the days after he'd overheard Broder, and as he drove toward the curve and the field's massive elm, he wondered, as he had, what could be done to divert it.

For the several months before, Ramona's incandescent anger, her fits of brooding vacancy, had been a source of growing confusion to him, giving him no option of response he knew of but rage. But her attempt to run had left him shaken beyond rage, though rage was woven through it, and as he'd driven that night through the snow toward the elm tree, Ed had been thinking back to the beginning of their life together, when she'd given him the sense of being adored. When she'd made herself his. When he'd known she wanted to fuck him as one wants to breathe sweet air. And when he'd received what Ramona gave him with the instinct that it was only the way things were supposed to be, but also felt a gratitude because he'd sensed that her adoration was even more than that.

And as he'd driven slowly through the snow, thinking vaguely of their past, a peculiar movement on the D&H tracks had drawn his attention. He'd slowed the borrowed Plymouth to a crawl, and when he looked again he'd seen a man whose

bright plaid coat he thought he recognized, even through the snowfall. In another moment, his sense was confirmed. He saw that it was Broder, striding down the railroad tracks.

Ed had stopped the car and turned off the lights and watched Broder marching down the tracks. And indeed, Broder had appeared to be doing just that, lifting his knees with dress-parade flourish while his elbows, in cadence, stroked the massive flakes of snow.

Astonished, Ed had driven on ahead, then rolled down the window, looked back, and waited. And momentarily, Broder had reappeared, seeming to stride even more committedly, stepping down the tracks as if he were leading a band whose sounds inspired his gait. In absolute stillness, Broder had passed the line of Ed's sight and again disappeared into the heavily falling snow. And Ed had imagined Broder marching down the tracks to where they met the fields of his dairy farm, then marching stubbled corn rows all the way to his house.

He'd sat in the parked Plymouth until the cold began to make him shiver, then turned the car around and headed back to town, his plan to search for evidence seeming now a hopeless idea.

Ed had never told Broder that he'd seen him that night. He'd never told anyone, although his normal impulse would have been to use Broder's antics on him quickly in some loud and public way. But Ed's sense of vulnerability at the time had left him hesitant to work on anyone. And even more, he'd never said anything because he'd subconsciously sensed that Broder's foolish-looking walk was something extraordinary: the uninhibited behavior of someone numb to any thought that he was being observed. Broder had stepped down the tracks with a fueling sense of privacy, clearly confident his actions were safe from witness, would leave no trace on the memory of Myles. And to Ed, feeling the town's inspecting eye for the first time in his life, Broder's display had been in some way deeply enviable, perhaps courageous, even though the likelihood of his being

seen was wildly remote, since it had taken place late at night, along a nearly impassable country lane, while he was thickly shrouded in significant snow.

Even so, Ed had envied Broder his march of flagrant disregard. For he had seen him.

"Here," Beener said to Ed, offering him his can of beer. "Finish it."

He took the beer from Beener and drained it. He felt residually stupid, as though he were waking from a hard dream. He stretched and yawned and said to Beener, "I suppose I should, too," and got down from the oil barrel. "You won't get lonely by yourself?"

Beener remained seated on the floor. He pointed over his shoulder to the Chevrolet behind him. "I got this piece of fuck to keep me company."

On Summit Street, the light caused Ed to squint his eyes again. A small headache had started at his left temple and as he walked he rubbed its pulsing vein. He headed west along the sidewalk toward the sun, an orange dome now that had begun to set behind the hills. He reached the end of the block, turned left, and started down the hill toward his house.

As the months had passed, he'd gradually regained what felt to him like a full sense of ease among the people of the town, was once more in possession of his considerable skills at living in it. And this was fundamental to him. For what had once appeared to Ramona to be Ed's own aloofness from Myles was actually his embrace of it. He had always appeared to stay above the life by being able to coolly direct it and he could only live in Myles as he did, and as he wished to, by knowing it intimately.

But as he neared his house, the soles of his boots slapping the sidewalk with a clown-walk heaviness, his mood was morose after the memories of last winter. He looked down the hill and drew a long, frustrated breath. If he'd come to feel again his old

controlling knowledge of Myles, the daily life inside his house remained full of rancorous surprise.

He reached the grassless yard, its dirt damp with the day's humidity, a few mutant weeds sprouting in the tremendous shade of their red maple tree. He felt more exhausted now, his T-shirt showing muddy rivulets where his sweat had wet the work dust, and he reached for the screen door, eager for a beer to help his growing headache.

In the kitchen, Ramona jumped as she heard the screen door slam.

Three

The last time they'd fought, four months ago, no more than fifteen seconds passed from Ramona's throwing the can of baby formula at Ed to her fierce kick which caught him squarely on the thigh, instantly numbing it, sending him backward to the floor in a corner of the bedroom. No more than those few seconds from beginning to end, and little more than a minute of words before the fight itself began. And through it all, Jonas had screamed in his carriage by their bed, his cries curdled with fury, as though his parents' voices, then their blows, were striking him. But however he was touched by the commotion of the heated, beating air, he cried mostly because he was hungry. He was red-faced and writhing in the carriage, but not unlike any new baby needing to be fed.

Ed's strongest memory of the fight was of its beginning, of walking into the room, the grocery sack of formula under his arm, and seeing Ramona on the bed and Jonas in the carriage beside her. He remembered blinking through the thickness of

several beers and seeing his son, full of rage and energy, bucking up off the mattress as though seized by a colicky cramp, and then his wife, lying utterly still on her side. And he'd recognized at that instant some startling displacement he couldn't reconcile. The force and frenzy inspiring Jonas seemed to Ed like the noisy, ready passion which had moved Ramona since he'd known her. But even more, he'd seen the dazed passivity of his wife, resting fetally, seemingly impervious to the sounds of their baby, and to Ed she'd looked, herself, like a dulled and sleepy child.

"Here," he said, dropping the sack of formula on the bed beside her. He'd glanced toward Jonas. "Jesus Christ. Is all that 'cause he's hungry? How long's he been screamin' like that?"

Ramona said nothing, hadn't moved. She'd opened her eyes and stared at the wall.

Ed said again, "How long's he been doin' that?"

"How long've you been gone?" Ramona could barely be heard over Jonas. She'd continued to look at the wall and when Ed hadn't answered her she'd repeated, "How long've you been gone?"

"I don't know. I don't know how long I been gone. But don't fuckin' start, okay? 'Cause I ain't interested in hearin' any—"

"Three hours," Ramona said. "You been gone three hours."

"Three hours? Okay. I been gone three hours? So what? What the fuck? I ain't interested, Ramona. I *got* a watch. I *got* a fuckin' watch."

"What do you do with it since you can't tell time?" She sat up and looked at Jonas with a brief, clinical attention. "*You* asked the question. 'How long he's been doin' that?' " She spoke softly, seemed distracted. "Three hours. That's how long. You been gone three hours. He's been screamin' since you left. *You* asked the goddam question."

"Okay!"

Jonas had paused for a breath, then resumed his even screaming.

"It ain't my fault you run out of formula. You don't wait till you're completely out and then say, 'Go get me a can of formula.' "

"Is that why it took you three hours?" She'd continued to speak so quietly Ed had had to strain to hear her. " 'Cause I run out of formula?" She'd slid effortfully off the foot of the bed, making sure the new hand touched nothing as she rose, as though its plastic fingers were also unimaginably tender in the act of healing. The result of the accident was a recent phenomenon. "I guess I don't get it. I guess I'm just dumb. How runnin' *out* makes it take three hours to get some more." She opened the top of the sack and peered down into it.

"I'll tell you how, goddam it. Sampson's closed, that's how. It's eight o'clock, that's how. I had to go to the CVS in Hudson."

"It's twenty minutes to Hudson. What'd you get lost?" Her back was to Ed and he could barely hear her. "Lemme tell you somethin' that'll save you lots of time. The Hill Top don't sell formula. You probably didn't know that, but the Hill Top just sells beer." She took a can of formula from the sack. It felt very heavy to her. "Now you know that, you don't have to stop at the Hill Top every time I need some." She glanced at Ed for the first time since he'd come into the room. "I know it's hard to keep 'em straight," she said, holding the can. "I know this looks a lot like a can of beer."

Ed had taken a step toward her. "What the fuck are you talkin' about?"

"You *stink*, you son of a bitch." Her fierceness was immediate. "You smell like a goddam brewery." She'd turned and flung the can at him, her left arm flapping weakly with the throw, but its edge caught him on the shoulder with a sharpness that surprised him. The can fell, and he watched it roll out the door; then he walked to her with a deliberate canine grace, as though he were mindful of muting any noise that might alert his prey, and slapped her with a force that sent her staggering against the wall. She caught herself, pushed away, too off-

balance to kick him, and he struck her again, his open hand against her cheek, the sound a quick sharp slap like a palm against wet mud. She grunted as she fell back heavily onto the mattress.

He'd stepped to the foot of the bed, standing over her, and she'd watched him silently from within a time-slowing calmness. She lay on her side and her eye seemed to follow his hand, grow huge, cyclopean, with a disembodied interest. Ed felt her inspection, felt its force so powerfully that when he went to strike her again he paused; he held his swing. And then he saw Ramona's eye shift away from him and appear instantly to dull as it looked again toward the wall. It was as though a cataract had suddenly covered it. Her body turned, too, and fluidly drew in, seemed in the movement to fold itself maternally around her new arm. And in that infinite instant, when he'd checked his swing and her attention had gone away, she'd kicked viciously at him. Her heel struck him on the thigh, exactly on the bone, and the leg's strength was gone. Ed lurched, staggered back and fell to the floor.

And then for some seconds the scene in the room had remained absolutely frozen. Ed sat in the corner where he'd fallen, waiting for his leg to begin to hurt. Ramona made no move to see if he was coming toward her again. She lay noiselessly on her side, just as when he'd walked into the room. All the sound, all the life, came from Jonas in his crib, crying now even more strongly with a newborn baby's unmatchable resolve. Until, at last, Ramona sat up and looked at him, then moved off the bed to the crib to scoop him up. With him finally in her grasp she'd walked past Ed out of the room, kicking the can of formula down the steps ahead of her.

So if it was true that Ed's strongest memory of the fight, his only lasting one, was that first unsettling sight of his wife and his son when he'd walked into the bedroom, he'd nevertheless seen other things which subliminally affected him much more. When he'd leaned over Ramona, he'd seen her new hand

resting prominently on the peak of her thigh, and it was as though the hand in its lifeless perfection were a sculpted carapace beneath which she lay, unconcerned. Certainly he knew Ramona was physically weaker than she'd been, but more than that Ed had sensed that she was different, and that alone gave her a power over him she hadn't had: she was now a combatant he didn't understand. And so, confused, he paused.

And then he'd seen her eye glaze milkily and look away. He had hit her twice, throwing her against the wall, then back onto the bed, and he had stood over her, poised to hit her again, and yet it was at that moment that she'd seemed to shift her attention almost casually, not so much a gesture of curling fearfully away from him, but as though she were turning with interest toward something else. Toward her pain? Toward a thought? Ed had had no sense, at the instant or afterward, of what she might have been drawn to, but though he never consciously remembered it he saw in the dismissing movement of her eye and her body the deepest evidence yet that he'd become to her inexplicably negligible. Her gesture that night had been, in a sense, the final one of the sequence she'd begun when she tried to flee.

Ed had always fought Ramona with a kind of controlled, attentive force that kept his hand open, his swing closely arced, keeping an instinctive formal border around his violence, using enough to hurt her but not so much as to keep her from responding with kicks and bites and scratches that came at him with a lashing formlessness which sometimes hurt him badly. In other words, he'd fought with his wife as he fought everyone, his brutality discriminant, keeping open a certain lively risk which depended on whomever he fought working wildly and with hope. And so, when Ramona had turned her eye from him, his interest and his strength had fallen away with her indifference.

More, that night in the bedroom had been the first time

they'd fought after the accident, and Ed had viscerally sensed as he raised his arm to strike her that he could no longer measure the proportions with his old infallibility. He could not understand Ramona's revised strength, so he could no longer sense how strong, how reckless, how violent he could be.

Ramona, just as much, had seen some things she wasn't conscious of which stayed with her long afterward. Most of all, she'd sensed in that instant when he'd checked his swing the culminative proof that he thought of her now as a cripple he had no right to hit.

Before, when she was sixteen, seventeen, her longing had been so determined that the force of the few times he'd slapped her had been immediately muted. And yet the threat of his hand had also terrified her, even if it was in some sense long familiar. She had watched her parents throw themselves at one another now and then, heard their flesh collide, the thick flat sounds of unremarkable brutality. She had heard a few of her friends speak of fights, had seen their violet and mustard-colored bruises, like splotches of hideous sunsets on their skin.

But the day, early in their marriage, after they had hit each other seriously for the first time, she had gone to Wilma Jean Robertson's house to talk about it. She was sore and instinctively sick with fear. This fight had been different, like the sudden arrival of some ugly, rumored lore. She'd eased onto a kitchen chair, opened her blouse to show the welts, and Wilma Jean had stared at her chest for several seconds before saying, in a voice that sounded to Ramona like a whisper of envy, "My God. He loves you."

Ramona had tried for a time to hold on to that idea, that their fights were Ed's needs turned violent out of love; that they were a display of his regard, which he felt for her so strongly it actually gave her a kind of power. She could direct his rage exclusively toward her. But soon she could only see it as a vicious element of her growing disillusion. And from then on, so far as Ramona was concerned, their fights were filled with no

dimension, no complexity on her part beyond the simplistic wish to hurt him.

So she began to slide precipitously toward the indifference that had continuously confused Ed. Though it was not yet indifference. She still hated him daily, sometimes from inside an almost inanimate darkness. But she no longer feared him, as she had from the beginning of her love, when an exquisite fear had been integral.

Until, that night in the bedroom, the last time they'd fought, she'd been able to look up at him as he'd drawn back his hand and her eye had followed it with a devastating calmness so free of fear it had drawn all his attention. What he saw had made him pause, and in that hesitation Ramona had sensed within everything else that she was invalided in his eye, that she was no longer enough to fulfill his old impulsive rage. And so, seeing that, the life in her eye went elsewhere, and her body curled itself protectively as she'd kicked out at Ed for seeing her as weak.

Imagine. All of that said to one another in a moment of the simplest synchrony; an arm hesitating; an eye turning away; a breath of time within a second full of permanent misunderstanding, as Ramona had watched Ed hold his swing and seen in the gesture that he pitied her as less, when in fact he'd been unable to hit her because he no longer understood the nature of her strength. She'd become to him someone who was more than she had been.

Four

It was nearly noon when Ramona—pushing Jonas in the twin-seated stroller they had bought from a classified ad in the weekly county shopper—left the house and started up the hill toward the grocery store on Summit Street. On days like this, when she had no car and needed to shop, she used one seat of the stroller to hold the groceries she bought. To keep the stroller balanced, it was filled now for the ascent with a sack of empty soda bottles.

Before she began the long climb, she looked back toward the house. Branches of the huge maple hung above the front half of its roof like a judgment. The house was low and very small and had once been exactly square, though now its wood was letting go and the whole place appeared to lean seriously to the right. Its white paint was peeling rampantly, splotching the house on all sides with long weather-gray blemishes. Black trim accentuated the two front windows flanking the door, and they looked out at the street like astonished eyes.

Ramona saw her neighbor, Mrs. Beasley, sitting on her sunken front porch, where she spent most of her day watching the street. Her eyes were round and very large, as though to accommodate her work, her face permanently ruddy from exposure.

"How's he doin'?" Mrs. Beasley called, pointing toward the stroller.

Ramona nodded. "Fine. Except he don't stay still for a second." Ramona did not slow as she spoke, meeting Mrs. Beasley's eye only partially.

"That's how you was, too," Mrs. Beasley called. Her head owled left to right as she watched Ramona pass. "And so was your brother. Don't forget that."

"I won't," Ramona said. Mrs. Beasley had been a friend of Ramona's parents until they'd moved to North Carolina. When she was a little girl, Ramona had liked to play beneath the kitchen table, pretending that it was her secret cave. She sat among the legs and feet of her mother and her friends while they sat for hours eating sweet rolls and drinking scorched coffee. She remembered Mrs. Beasley's short legs dangling above the floor. The more she talked the more wildly she swung them until she'd inevitably kick Ramona and cry, "Jee-zuz H," causing Ramona's mother to say, "Git out from under there, Ramona. I swear to God I could wear you for shoes."

"Come visit!" Mrs. Beasley shouted to Ramona's back.

"We will," Ramona answered, still looking straight ahead.

"You never do."

"We will."

Halfway up the hill, Ramona felt better than she had the past few days. The morning was another bright and terrifically hot one and she was sweating freely, heat reaching into the tips of her fingers. But as she neared the top, the bottles clanking in their sack, and had to lean more into the stroller, Jonas began to pound his fists and squirm and she imagined she felt the stroller slightly sway. It was really in no danger of tipping, but even the

threat of such a thing inspired Ramona's great fear: that it might slip from her grasp and fly down the hill.

"Stop it, Joe," she snapped, then added more quietly, "Take it easy now, okay? That's it. Take it easy."

In the grocery, Jonas sat propped in a corner of the shopping cart among canned vegetables and frozen dinners. His hands pawed at the cans and cartons and closed on their colors, which he tried to lift and put in his mouth. When she'd finished, Ramona wheeled her cart to the counter and took out the food-stamp booklet.

The checkout woman said, "I'll give you a hand, Ramona." She reached into the cart for groceries, smiling at Jonas, whose eyes belatedly followed the movement of items being lifted from all around him. "How we doin' today?" the woman asked him. "Who's he look like, Ramona? I think he looks like you."

Jonas smiled at the checkout woman.

Ramona had made a fan of food stamps and dollar bills on the counter. She shrugged. "Most people say Ed," she said. "His eyes, anyway." She looked past the counter, through the store's plate-glass window. On the opposite side of Summit the row of shops was broken by the huge lots, still vacant after the fire four years before.

The hill dropped steeply beyond the other side of Summit Street, so that the shops appeared to sit on a horizon. As she stood at the counter, Ramona walked, in her head, out of the store and across the street and stepped calmly into a vast square of sky.

"You goin' to Engle's funeral?" the check-out woman asked.

"Ed is," Ramona said. Lawrence Engle had been a friend of Ed's Grandfather King. She nodded at Jonas. "I ain't about to chance this one at a funeral." She continued to look at the sky across the street. "We went down to see him after supper last night."

"We did, too," the checkout woman said, punching cash-register keys. "He looks real good, don't you think?"

"I think he looks real dead," Ramona said.

"Well, of course he looks dead," the woman said. "I just meant he looked real good, for *bein'* dead. Real natural, like himself." She waved her hand. "Oh, hell, you know what I mean."

As she counted Ramona's change, the woman looked out the window. "Oh, Lord," she said, "there he is. He usually, if he ain't come by this time, won't at all."

On the plate glass, a brown shape appeared and spread. It might have been a piece of fruit someone had thrown which had splattered and stuck to the window. Ramona saw a nose, broadly splayed, then cheeks and lips, and all of them rolling on the pane. "He'll be on you as soon as you leave, Ramona. Want me to get him away?"

"It's all right," Ramona said. "He's harmless." She raked her change along the counter until it fell into her open purse.

"Sure?" the woman asked. "He's impossible to get rid of once he sees you got a sack of groceries."

Ramona smiled. "I'm used to him. He was in my brother's class when they let him come to school that time."

Outside, she worked the stroller until it pointed down the street, and as she did Bobby Bumbry's face came off the windowpane to watch her. Then he took two long steps and met her on the sidewalk, standing directly in front of the stroller and smiling in a way that was not so much menacing as benignly out of control. He was very tall and thin and his skin was darkly tanned from a life spent outdoors. He'd recently had a severe haircut, and the closely shorn sides and back of his head appeared the shade and grade of fine sandpaper. In the middle of his face his eyes sat with a constant, dilated surprise.

But he was clean and neat. He wore a faded short-sleeved shirt, primly buttoned to the neck. His appearance alternated over time between cleanliness and filth, and when he was clean it meant he was living with his aunt. Ramona had heard that

Bobby's aunt had once more found God, Whom she regularly reclaimed, sometimes for as long as six months at a time. Whenever she welcomed the Lord into her life, she usually invited Bobby in as well.

Before Bobby spoke, he looked at the stroller. "Whatcha got?" he asked.

"What's it look like I got, Bumbry?" Ramona said, not angrily. "Every time you see me you ask me what I got." Bobby was listening carefully. "Maybe someday I'll tell you I got . . ." Ramona thought about it. "I'll say I got a pet *raccoon* or somethin', and then maybe you'll remember that and not ask me every damn time what I got."

From his seat, Jonas called delightedly. Bobby peered again at the stroller, studying what he saw. "You got groceries," Bobby announced. *"That's* what you got." He bent down to the stroller and started to reach for the sack.

"Hey, wait, Bobby," Ramona said sharply, instinctively pushing the stroller forward. He'd already put his arms around the sack and it fell on its side, cans and boxes spilling onto Jonas, and after a moment of mute shock, he released his rage.

"Shit!" Ramona said, pushing Bobby away to get to Jonas. "It's all right, Joe," she said to him over his screams. "It's okay. Yes. It's okay."

"What's the matter?" Bobby asked. "What's the matter, anyway?"

"Shut up and just hold this." Ramona had managed to get the spilled sack out of the stroller and she shoved it at Bobby. As she refilled it, she continued to assure Jonas through his receding cries. "There you go, Joe. Yes. There you go. It's all right."

Bobby watched in silence, holding the sack and rocking it gently, as if Ramona's maternal soothings were inspiring something similar in him. When Ramona had set the sack back on its seat, she looked at Bobby. She felt completely exhausted. "C'mere," she said to him. She arranged Bobby's huge hands

on the handle of the stroller and wrapped his long fingers around it. "Got it?" she asked him sharply.

His mouth hung open like a large drop of water at the end of a faucet. He nodded.

"Come on," Ramona said, and she started walking down the street, but Bobby stood where she'd left him. She stopped and turned. "Git your butt up here. I thought you wanted to carry my groceries."

"Yes," Bobby said, confused. "*Carry* groceries. That's my job."

"Well, this time you're *pushing* 'em," Ramona said. "Come on!"

Bobby leaned forward on the handle and pushed Jonas and the groceries in the stroller toward her. When he reached Ramona she looked in at her baby. He was calm again, spittle eddying down his cheek. She nodded, satisfied, and they all continued down Summit.

Ramona dropped back from her leading position and walked beside Bobby. Jonas was making serene sounds, which she always imagined as small spherical creatures which he grew in his mouth and released into the air. Bobby's mouth moved to Jonas's sounds, as if he were trying to memorize them.

They reached Ramona's street and started down the hill.

Her strength was returning. She was thinking how easy this walk home was, not having to fight the hill. She had almost come to accept the work of pushing Jonas up the hills, against the steep slopes, because the pain it caused seemed to her in some sense straightforward and legitimate—through the arm, into the shoulder, coming to rest in her neck. But guiding him down was normally even harder for her, since she had to hold on to the stroller with a desperate contortion.

But today, she could walk effortlessly toward her house and she felt pleased. She felt extremely grateful, too, not to have to fight the temptation which often formed in a corner of her mind, the other side of her fear, to simply let go of the stroller.

Ramona said, "What do you think of my kid, Bobby?"

"Kid," Bobby repeated. "I got groceries. I got a kid. I got a pet coon kid and groceries." He smiled, appearing proud of himself for having it clearly categorized. "You like the kid?" he asked Ramona. His face puckered to receive her answer.

She laughed. "Hell yes, Bobby. Everybody oughta have one. You ain't lived until you do. You oughta get one yourself. Then you wouldn't be hangin' around the store all the time, pushing your face against the window like a goddam suction cup and waitin' to carry somebody's groceries."

"It's my *job*," Bobby said.

"That's fine for now. But what about tomorrow, Bobby? You can't carry groceries all your life." She had only meant to tease him, but she realized she was feeling something meaner, too. "Now if you had a kid, you could carry *it*. Hell, you could carry it all over town, and I wanna tell you, there ain't nothin' better than getting to carry your own kid every step you take." She paused to catch her voice and when she did she heard its angry trail. She cleared her throat several times, feeling stupid after what she'd said, and didn't look at Bobby. He was studying her with a hardworking scrutiny.

The hill leveled for its final stretch. Dust from the streets and the cracked-dirt yards hung in the air, beyond the humidity's strength to dampen it, and fell, a velour, on the humpbacked shells of cars on cinder blocks.

When they passed Mrs. Beasley's, Ramona saw her straighten in her rocking chair and she smiled, as they reached her front screen door, at an image of the old woman's neck growing like a periscope while she strained to see what was happening.

"So," Ramona said to Bobby, placing her foot on the step. "What are you gonna do now?"

"Git a kid," Bobby replied. "For tomorrow."

She laughed. "I ain't givin' you a quiz on what I told ya. I mean, you goin' home or back to the store or what? We're here. This is my house."

"Is anything wrong?" Mrs. Beasley called from her porch.

"Not a thing, Millie," Ramona called back without turning around. "Bobby's just helping me out here."

There was a moment of silence. Mrs. Beasley said, "It *is* awful hot."

"Yeah, it is," Ramona said.

She shook open her purse and got out two quarters. "Here," she said to Bobby. "Go buy yourself a beer or whatever. You was a help. You was, really." She reached for the stroller's handle, easing Bobby's fingers away from it.

Bobby stood for a moment, then turned and started down the walk. As Ramona put a hip between the screen and the doorway he turned around to her and abruptly, broadly waved. She laughed and waved back and as she did she heard, then saw, the orange highway truck turn the corner and move slowly past on the street. She could see Ed and all the others staring at the sight of Bobby and her waving at each other. So, for good measure, for their sakes, for Mrs. Beasley's, she returned his wave again.

Look at them, she thought as the truck continued down the street toward the highway. Ain't one of them looks smarter than Bumbry.

Inside, she fed Jonas and placed him in his crib and listened to him fuss briefly. When he was asleep, she walked downstairs to the kitchen. The sack of groceries sat on the floor by the refrigerator. She went to the window and looked out. She could see Mrs. Beasley rocking aggressively on her porch. She wondered if her shoes touched her floor as she rocked and she remembered when she'd hidden under her mother's kitchen table, the image of Mrs. Beasley's fat white ankles rising like dough from the tops of her shoes.

When Ramona's mother had come up on the bus to visit her in the hospital after the accident, she'd arrived in a mood of

affectionate melancholy. The news had naturally shocked her, yet when she arrived she spoke softly to Ramona in a tone that was weary and withheld and had nostalgia in it, as though what had happened to Ramona was in a way the fulfillment of her mother's vague suspicions.

In the hospital, Ramona's mother—who was as small as her daughter, her skin wrinkled as a tree's—had sat by her in a chair pulled up close to her bed. She'd asked if it were true, as she'd heard, that Ramona had screamed that night to those who'd found her that she was on her way to North Carolina.

When Ramona whispered yes, that she had, her mother asked her why. She reminded Ramona that she'd spoken bitterly to them when they'd moved two years before, that their correspondence back and forth since then had been rare.

Ramona had seen her parents' moving as still another way in which the world, a year after she had married, was methodically betraying her. And after they'd left for the mill work, even though she had asked them urgently to stay, she'd written them notes on only three or four occasions.

In the hospital, Ramona had not really answered her mother's question, saying only that she needed to be with them again, wanted to live in North Carolina with them and the baby she was carrying.

Her mother's voice had grown softer but was firm. She'd said, "That wouldn't work." She'd said, "We ain't got any room where we are, and besides, we also ain't got money. Your dad makes less money than when the mills was open here."

Ramona had said that a life with Ed King was something she knew she couldn't live.

Her mother had breathed a soft, sad laugh. "I ain't surprised. He's been an asshole all his life. Anybody knows that."

"You shoulda stopped me, then," Ramona had said. "You shoulda told me."

"Why waste my strength tryin' to tell you *that?* You thought Ed King was all there was. You saw what you saw."

Then Ramona's mother smiled and touched her daughter's cheek. And she'd reminded Ramona of how she'd often lapsed, when she was a girl, into long stunned silences, her eyes watching nothing in the world that was actually before them. She'd recalled how Ramona had obsessively twirled her finger through her hair during those fits of dream, winding it around and around for however long her trance lasted. Seeing her, her little brother, James, had said that she was having one of her "twirly dreams." Sometimes, her mother had remembered, she'd daydreamed so deeply that she wound her hair into knotted coils which a brush could not untangle.

"You gotta quit that, Ramona," her mother had said. She'd stroked her daughter's forehead with the flat of her hand. "You gotta quit those kind of dreams."

Ed took a deep swallow of his beer, tilting his head to empty the can, and Ramona watched his Adam's apple jump wildly in his skinny throat.

"Standin' there in the doorway waving at that simple fuck like he's your long-lost brother, for Chrissake." He set the can down hard on the counter. "Jesus," he added disgustedly, looking away from Ramona at the kitchen shelves, where her morning's shopping sat in sloppy rows. He walked toward the refrigerator to get another beer and Ramona's eyes followed him. "What was you thinking, anyway? *That* I would actually like to know. Lettin' that dim shit near Jonas? Hell, he don't know his ass from a football half the time and you let him wheel the kid all over town like you was all out for a stroll." He leaned against the counter and tapped his fingers against the new can of beer. Two of Ed's fingernails were completely black, where he'd hit them with a hammer. Ramona watched the fingers flick nimbly against the side of the can, hating their life.

"I'm hearin' about it the rest of the day, you know. After we

saw you." Ed shook his head, looking again at the shelves. "Mitchell says, 'Hey, King, what the hell? You bein' long-cocked by a *re*tard?' " He drank three quick sips. "Then Adams, he goes"—Ed's voice rose to a girlish pitch—" 'Thanks, Bobby. You and that big thing of yours come back real soon.' "

"Don't sound to me like you're worried about your son," Ramona said finally. "Sounds to me like you're worried about the size of your cock." She got up immediately and walked past Ed to the shelves next to where he stood. With her back to him, she said, "You wanna move so I can start supper?"

Ed's anger choked him. He pulled on his long chin as if he were wringing water from it. He moved just enough to let Ramona maneuver and continued to stare at her but his anger had nowhere to fall but on her back. They stood that way, squeezed into a corner of their kitchen.

"You know what I'm talkin' about," Ed said. "You know as good as I do what that loon-ass might do. The way he followed that Musgrove girl home."

"I know what she said he did," Ramona said, turning around. She began to open cans of soup, holding them tight against her stomach to keep them from moving on the counter-top while she turned the opener. Ed watched her.

"Oh, right," he said. "You'd sooner believe Bumbry than the Musgrove kid, who wanted it all over town, I suppose, how he got her on the ground and tried to stick his pecker in her mouth." Ed shivered, as if a primness in him had been touched. "She shoulda bit it off."

"Maybe if she had you wouldn't have so much to worry about," Ramona snapped.

"Maybe if she had you wouldn't be so quick to take his side."

"May be." Ramona's mouth was a line of mean glee.

Ed came forward, then caught himself and settled back against the counter. He began to inspect the cuts and scabs along his arms. He pinched blood from an infected hair. He studied his dirt-lined nails, curling his fingers and holding them

out in front of his eyes for inspection, as if waiting for polish to dry.

At last, he spoke very quietly. "It ain't the Musgrove girl alone. You know the stories about him. That night we saw him down at the ball field, walking with his hands in his pants and askin' everybody if they wanted to see his pet."

"Oh, Christ, come on," Ramona said. "He was drunk that night and you know *that.*"

"What does that make any difference?" Ed said. He stared at Ramona, but she said nothing, watching the soup she was stirring on the stove. He continued, "I don't know what you's tryin' to prove today, but I do know this: You ain't never gonna let Bumbry near Jonas anymore. Again he paused, and again Ramona showed him no response. "You ain't never," he repeated, and there was an even more final softness in his voice. "If you do, I'll knock the livin' shit out of you, Ramona." Ed cleared his throat and drank the last of his beer. "But I'd still be curious, in fact, to know what it was you was thinkin' in the first place."

Ramona had continued to stare into the kettle, her spoon scraping metallically beneath Ed's words. When she turned to look at him she let go of the spoon to wipe her eyes. "I'll tell you what I was thinking about in the first place," she said. "I was thinking that I hurt like a son of a bitch. And that I was either gonna have to sit there until somebody come along. Either that, or I probably wasn't gonna be able to hold on to everything once I started down the hill." Her chest heaved. "And I'll tell you something else. The next time I run into Bumbry I'll bring him in here and feed him his goddam dinner if he'll wheel Jonas home for me."

Ed pivoted and walked toward the bathroom door, lifting his tar-streaked T-shirt over his head, and his turning away was the movement that sent her loathing to the surface of her skin. "You ride around in a goddam truck all day!" she screamed. Ed's face was hooded in his T-shirt. "Twirling a broom and tryin' not to

fall asleep! You sit in the back of that fucking truck, ridin' around town like you was on patrol! Like you was waitin' for somebody to escape!"

Ed's face was bared again. He stood, naked to the waist, holding his T-shirt. His eyes were very bright and a violent charge came out of him invisibly, no gesture contained it, and yet Ramona felt it as a sudden force, a slap, that stopped her. "Like I told you," he said flatly. "You do it again, I'll knock the shit out of you."

Ramona grabbed the handle of the soup kettle, lifted it from the stove, and took two steps toward Ed, drawing it back. But as she swung the kettle forward her grip failed and it clanged to the floor. Yellow broth instantly laked out over the linoleum and reached Ed's feet.

Silently, Ed watched the soup run. He shook his head, then bent to pick up the kettle. "No wonder you and Bumbry's such big buddies," he said. He wiped soup from his hand onto his pants. "You's as crazy as he is." He set the kettle on the table and stepped like a tightrope walker along the dry edge of the floor until he reached the bathroom door.

That night, Ramona woke and tiptoed past Jonas down the stairs and into the bathroom. She took a bottle from the medicine chest, lifted its cap, which she'd learned to keep loose, and swallowed four aspirin.

As she turned to leave she stopped, seeing herself in the full-length mirror on the door. For a moment she calmly surveyed the image of her body, tracing her thread-thin stretch marks, at her tiny breasts, along her stomach. She let her eyes go unfocused for a time and when she brought them back she saw in the mirror that she was leaning slightly to the right, as if trying to give one side's excess to the other. Her mind drew a bisecting line from her crotch to the top of her head. She leaned, first to the left, then back to the right, until she was satisfied she

had the tilt that would make her sides even and the notion felt to her, surrounded as she was by this floating hour of night, like a strategy.

She remembered now the self-satisfied manner of the man in the hospital. He had sounded solicitous, in the anticipatory way of one who's spoken the same sympathies so often he can't feel them freshly. "Now, Ramona," he'd said. "I'd like you to look here with me for just a minute."

"What?"

"You don't have to take all this in right now. You'll have lots of help."

"What?"

"If this looks a little frightening to you, just remember: The reason there's all these parts to it is so it can do so much *for* you." He'd shown her the hand, cradling it in his arms. He'd waited in silence for her truly to see it.

"I ain't using that."

"I know it looks forbidding. All these attachments and cables. But it's easy to use."

"I said I wanted a fake hand. That's all."

"Yes." His voice was soft. "A passive hand. I know. But this is even better. It's both. You can wear the passive hand. Or, if you detach it, like this, and attach the hooked hand . . ."

She'd looked away.

"I'll bet you, Ramona, that in a few weeks, a month—"

"Keep your hook."

"For now, just wear the passive hand. I'll show you how you can make *it* open and close a little—"

"I said, no hook."

He'd paused. "The thing is, Ramona, your insurance won't pay for just a passive hand. They call it 'cosmetic.' If you want your passive hand, you have to take this attachment, too."

She'd said, "Give it to somebody that wants to play pirate."

*　　*　　*

Back in bed, Ramona slept for an hour and then seemed to be awakened by the flatness of the night. Her eyes darted about the room. Ed turned in his sleep and his arm dropped onto her chest. She lifted it off, listening for his breath. Ed never snored and sounded in sleep like a rhythmic breeze. Ramona sat up and put her palm to his mouth, as her friend Wilma Jean did to know the breath of her baby.

She lay back and several seconds passed before she realized what she'd unthinkingly done and when it came to her she felt her chest bloat to hold her fear. For a time she couldn't think at all and finally she decided simply to repeat it and if the same thing happened she would know. Once more, she carefully lifted her arm to Ed's mouth and waited and again, in the full sleeping blackness, she felt his breath blow against her palm. Her palm. Her dead, lost palm. She stopped breathing and held her hand as still as she could and . . . *again*. She felt his breath again—light, even breath heating the lines of her palm.

She sat up and hovered her hand above Ed's mouth and tried to make a plan. She remained confused with doubt even though Ed's breathing had proved the hand's return and she knew, before she did anything else, that she must somehow convince herself she was not feeling a lie as large in its pleasure as it sometimes was with the floating pain. But how could she be sure? She knew she did not want just to reach with her left hand and feel for it. She could not stand the thought that her fist might simply close on a palm of bedroom air. Then Ed's breath blew into her hand once more and the sensation of it touching her skin suddenly gave her a clear answer. Very deliberately, she lowered her hand to Ed's lips, innocently parted in a way that might make one think his mouth was open for a lover's tongue. Yes. Ed would be her test.

She placed her hand firmly over Ed's mouth and now she felt a technical efficiency as it spread liquidly over his face in a search for leaking breath. Ed turned his head for air and her hand went with it, growing larger and stronger as he began to

move. She felt him awaken. His body surged and he shook his head fiercely to throw the hand off, but her fingers dug into his face and returned his struggle with something stronger of her own. She felt her fingers reaching around to the back of his head and up over his skull. His thrashing only fed her hand, masking him so tightly it completely stopped his sounds. She waited, her hand patient, supple, pressing, through Ed's climactic effort. His body arched desperately and held itself, then fell to the sweat-drenched sheets. Ramona felt him soften beneath her grip.

She got out of bed, dressed, and walked quietly past Jonas's crib, pausing briefly and without conscience over her son, and even as she felt her guiltlessness she said to herself that her mood was strange and new. Outside, she settled into the seat of their rusted Dodge, stretching her fingers and spreading her palm wide as it rested on the manual shift.

The Dodge crept up the hill, reached the top of the town, and followed Summit Street as it dropped toward the edge of Myles. Ramona's touch was deft and experienced and when she reached the highway she pressed the accelerator steadily toward the floor. She passed the town's last houses and then the land was flat and clear.

Behind the wheel, she bounced in her seat and sang country songs and, deciding she wanted to sing along with the radio, reached to the dashboard, but when she closed her fingers on the dial she felt her index finger painlessly snap and fall to the floor. She gasped and bent as best she could while she drove to fumble for her missing finger. But then her other fingers fell, and after them the rest of her hand dropped from her wrist.

She screamed, and when she straightened in her seat and held her arm up, she watched a baby's head, perfectly round and tiny as a fist, appear and grow quickly from the stump. Ramona screamed again, but the louder she cried the faster the head grew, pink and throbbing and healthy as birth. She felt her

grip on the steering wheel weaken and then she saw her other hand fall away and again at the wrist a smooth ball instantly formed and grew and shaped eyes and mouth and nose and both heads screamed. Ramona held the heads up to see them in an approaching car's lights and the Dodge veered toward it and she turned the heads to face each other. She shook them viciously to fling them from her wrists and the baby heads screeched and both the heads were Jonas—

Ramona jumped straight up, off her pillow, and out of bed, listening to Jonas cry in his crib. She shook violently, as if from exposure, while her baby brought her back. She glanced toward the bed and watched Ed turn in his sleep. For a length of time she had no sense of she stood between the bed and the crib, trembling.

She moved to the crib and knelt. She was too weak to lift Jonas but reached through its slats to stroke his head.

She looked at him through first light coming through the cracks of the window shade.

"Joe," she whispered. "I can't do it." He had turned his head toward her voice and she stroked his hair again. "I can't do this, Joe. I didn't know it would be this way. How could I? See, Joe?"

Ramona's whisper grew fainter. "But I wasn't runnin' from you. You was *in* me. We was together and it would've been all right then. It'd be all right and I could love you easy. I could, with my hands."

She fell back on her heels and looked up at the ceiling angling down toward them. She was not crying, though, and neither was her son, although he was awake and expectant and hadn't yet begun to make his loud morning sounds. And from the bed, Ed, too, was perfectly quiet, as he had been.

In the morning, Ed put on his suit and left for Engle's funeral. After Ramona had fed Jonas and given him his bath, she

dressed him and took him in the stroller for a walk behind the house.

The land sloped gradually behind the houses on Ed and Ramona's street, becoming, after the backyards, a low-weeded field that ran for some distance before it met the highway. Ramona often walked through the field, stopping to turn and see the back end of the town.

Pushing Jonas out of her yard and into the field, Ramona felt the surprise of a gusty wind carrying the strong late-morning heat. She stopped and bent down to Jonas, loosening the top button of his shirt. She noticed a faint rash, a pink necklace, where his collar had rubbed his skin.

Jonas liked the field, too. He usually chattered happily in the stroller as it bumped along and this morning he repeatedly squealed like a siren, as though the expanse of the field was inspiring him to try to fill it with his voice. Ramona paid little attention to his sounds and after a few more minutes the heat of day began to dull him and he drifted off to sleep.

It was his silence she noticed. She stopped, leaned down to check him, and managed to turn the stroller around, away from the highway, so that he'd be shaded. She looked at his face, quick tremors of energy moving across it even as he slept. She watched his fingers slithering against each other in a beckoning movement.

Standing by his stroller, Ramona looked back toward the town. She saw Mrs. Beasley next door, working around the foundation of her house with a fine-pronged rake. She heard the cymbally scrape of the rake through the dirt.

After checking Jonas once again, Ramona walked on into the field, seeing on the distant highway a slow procession of cars, their headlights on, returning from the cemetery. She was tired after last night's chaotic sleep and her nerves still ran to the dream. The sight of the slow line of cars moving on the highway caused the edges of the dream to rise up in her mind.

While she walked, she watched the cars disappear one by one as they rounded a curve on their way back into Myles. When the last had made the turn, she stopped, seeing that she had reached the middle of the field. She lay down on her stomach and squirmed on the ground until its contours fit hers. Her cheek against the earth, she opened her eyes and the high grass was a forest. A grasshopper squeezed between weed stalks and began to eat and ascend. Ramona watched it angularly hump a leaf as it climbed. Ants moved past her eyes, carrying a ton-speck of black food. She watched them until her eyelids fell.

A semi truck, shifting loudly on the highway, woke her. It felt to Ramona as if little time had passed. She remembered the ants and expected to see them still working, but they were gone. She slowly rose. The day's hot wind was even stronger now. She looked down at her body-print pressed into the grass. Shuffling drunkenly, she lifted her head to squint toward the stroller. She was surprised how far away it was. She'd forgotten the distance she'd walked into the field. She listened for any sound from Jonas, but heard nothing, and as she walked toward him she remembered the scratching sound of Mrs. Beasley's rake and saw no sign of her. Ramona wondered if she'd slept much longer than she'd thought.

A car honked on the highway as it passed another one and, hearing it, Ramona stopped and turned to watch the road. Three more cars moved by in quick succession, and then a pickup truck she recognized as local, though she couldn't remember who owned it. As she stood watching the highway, the sensation of driving along it in the dream returned. Particularly, she felt the moments of her escape before the dream had turned, of reaching the edge of Myles and pressing the accelerator to the floor and the landscape flying past like so much blackly streaking scenery. She remembered the lightness, the sense of buoyancy, as she'd dreamed she was bouncing in the seat and singing to herself. No more cars passed on the highway, but Ramona continued to watch it, and it seemed to

her almost to be moving on its own, a river free of ripples, swiftly carrying away whatever joined its current.

She turned back toward the town. The stroller, shading Jonas, seemed no closer than it had been and the steps she took were aimless, circling. She sensed that ahead of her, at the stroller and on beyond it to the edge of the field that met the town, there was a silence unlike anything she'd heard. It made her nervous to recognize such an absolute quiet and when she worked to give it sound, she heard the music she'd sung as she'd driven away in the dream. Once more, she stopped and turned to the highway. The music continued in her mind, but grew no louder.

And now, as she walked toward the stroller, she felt the temptation consciously for the first time. She knew that the weeds were brushing against her legs but she sensed them only vaguely. As she walked, she felt as though she were walking toward that instant in a dream when it reveals itself. When the illusion falls away. When the dreamer wakes abruptly to the dread of actual light. And as she walked, she felt uniquely in control, as though she had the power to prevent the dream from turning because she knew its certain dissolution was up ahead of her.

So she stopped and listened again for Jonas's voice. She felt the wind blowing strongly in toward Myles, and she told herself that any sound up ahead would not reach back to her but would be carried strongly into town. And that recognition pleased her. She imagined Jonas's eyes opening, the extraordinary strength of his immediate cries. His gift. She remembered the siren squeals he'd made in the field this morning.

Yes.

She felt the hot wind gusting past her again. She imagined how clearly Jonas's cries would carry on it. And then she thought of Mrs. Beasley fussing in her yard, rocking on her porch, her eyes and her ears fanatically alert for the slightest change in the rhythm of Myles.

Yes.

It came to her now with the clarity of a result, her path as indisputable as the movement of the wind. She looked for just a moment more at the back of the stroller, the sun reflecting off its frame. It sat like an icon at the edge of the field. She heard nothing.

She turned and walked into the wind, away from the stroller, away from the backs of the houses. She lifted her legs with a high, coltish step as she hurried through the weeds and the nests of wild daisies. She stumbled as she passed the place where she had slept, looked down at the imprint of her body, and walked on to the end of the field. There she paused behind a row of sumac, waited while a few cars passed, then scrambled up the ditch and touched the loose gravel shoulder of the highway.

Five

"**Y**ou hear?" Ed asked his mother, Vera. His hands were so sweaty he had to hold the phone tightly in his neck while he wiped his palm on his pants.

"Hear what?" her voice asked through the receiver. As Ed cradled the phone, he inhaled the thick sweetness of Ramona's perfume, which scented the mouthpiece.

"I'm bringin' Jonas up," Ed said. "You still got my old crib in the attic?"

"Hear *what?*" Vera's voice was suddenly alert. Ed heard her breath, a harsh whistling through her nose.

"See if there's the crib," Ed said. "You didn't hear nothin'? What, you been inside all day?"

"*Inside* all day? Jesus, Ed, it's hotter than hell. Where else would I be?"

"Just see if there's the crib. I'm bringin' Jonas up."

"Hear *what?*" Ed sensed the stir of Vera's voice. It seemed to make the phone vibrate in his hand. "What the hell is goin' on?"

"When I get there," Ed said and hung up. Sweat had run into his eye, stinging it sharply. He wiped it away and paused for a moment. Then he lifted the receiver again and inhaled Ramona's perfume from the mouthpiece of the phone.

The sky was gold with heat and light as Ed drove up the hill. But he could barely accept the evidence that it was only afternoon, for it seemed to him the morning had begun a month ago. Beside him, Jonas fussed, a thin, distracted whine which ribboned out of him and sounded to Ed, at this point in the day, like silence. He'd been crying for two hours, pausing momentarily to gather himself for a fresh full wail, and only now, banked by pillows in the front seat of the car, was he quieting down. His face remained an angry fist and his limbs kicked and beat the air, but his sounds were exhausted.

Earlier in the day, several people in town had caught a glimpse of Bobby Bumbry holding Jonas to his chest as he hurried behind the shops, through the rutted alleys. Lovilla Adams had been standing at her kitchen window when she'd seen Bobby rush through her yard. She'd heard Jonas's frantic screams and it had looked to her, as Bobby carried him, almost as though the sounds were being made by Bobby's huge, enfolding hands. Lovilla had rushed outside and called to Bobby and he'd stopped momentarily, giving her time to see Jonas more clearly. Then he'd scampered on toward his aunt's abandoned barn, where Ed eventually found them.

When Ramona had pushed Jonas in his stroller down her backyard slope and out into the field, she hadn't noticed Bobby watching them from the street. She hadn't seen him, either, when she'd paused, before she turned toward the highway, and felt the force of the wind she knew would carry her baby's calls. And so she couldn't have imagined that she'd unwittingly set the circumstances of Jonas's rescue the day before she'd left when she'd urged Bobby Bumbry to get a child of his own.

When she'd assured him that he needed one for the future; for tomorrow.

No sooner had she climbed the ditch and started down the highway than Bobby had hurried to the stroller and lifted Jonas free.

After Lovilla had seen Bobby running past, she'd driven immediately to Ramona's empty house, then quickly decided she must find the highway crew.

Raymond Adams had seen her pull to a stop behind the orange truck and naturally assumed she had come with news for him. They'd leaned against the truck as she told him what she'd seen. They'd spoken in whispers, Adams glancing every few seconds over his shoulder at Ed, who'd appeared not to notice them but whose mind had been a smile as he'd planned his words to Adams. He would tease him loudly of lamentable pussy-whipped behavior. Ed felt the hours among the crew as privileged, so Lovilla's presence amounted to a kind of trespass in his sense. He would ask Adams, in effect, how he could allow his wife to glimpse this treasured life of work and air and insults, allow her near the sacristy of tools atop the flatbed.

Ed had seen Lovilla nod her head and walk back to their car, watched Adams turn and shuffle toward him, seemingly reluctant, a gait of sheepish guilt.

"Well?" Ed had said to Adams, "Mother gonna let you stay and finish—"

"Hey, Ed," he'd said. "Listen just a minute."

Adams and Mitchell had gone with Ed to Bumbry's aunt's barn, a few hundred yards from the eastern edge of Myles. As soon as they'd gotten out of the truck they'd heard the baby's screams. Inside, they'd climbed the ladder and lifted themselves up onto the loft's plank floor.

Bobby had placed Jonas in a square of sunlight coming in from a window near the apex of the roof. Loose nests of hay

were scattered in places. The floor was spattered with purple coils of birdshit. Jonas's cries were his breath, rhythmically pure and filled with a rage so large it seemed that his sobs could not release it quickly enough, that his heaving indignation would bloat and burst his tiny body. Bobby had been mutely circling him, almost at a trot, moved to frenzied ceremony by the size of his fear of the child. The heat of the loft was a weather.

"Jesus Christ," Mitchell had growled.

"He's too scared to hurt your kid," Adams had said.

Ed had walked to Jonas and picked some strands of hay from his sweating forehead, then lifted him up. Like Bobby, he'd said nothing.

He saw Vera fling open the door and stand, her arms crossed, as he reached the gray gabled house at the top of the town. She was a tall and very wide woman, nearly filling the doorway. Ed's father had died four years before, burned to death in the epical fire. He had been the plant's night watchman, and he was far from consciousness, in the swaddling folds of an alcoholic sleep, at the time the fire broke out. He'd sat slumped in his chair, his chin on his chest, and the reverberations of his snores might almost have been heard as a sad bravado against the fire's sonic detonations and the roar of its flames. He'd sensed through his stupor only a sudden corona of heat, which he welcomed—it was winter—and which had shaped his mouth into a quick, coy smile, as people's faces do when they're pleased with the climate they're inventing in their dreams. He'd burned in his chair with pleasure on his face.

Since his death, the King house had rapidly begun to subside; but it had always reflected the family's fertile poverty, so its easing into ruin seemed less a matter of neglect than hurried biological decay—a piece of fruit rotting obversely from its core toward its skin.

Ed reached across the seat for Jonas. The baby cried softly in

hiccuping breaths and squirmed in Ed's hands, strength rippling ligamentally through his body with an urgency Ed noticed. For a few seconds in the car, as Ed held him, almost at arm's length, Jonas drew his father's focus and the air was briefly still.

Ed hadn't until now paused to sense his son. All afternoon, he'd been moving dumbly from moment to moment. There was an odd clarity to his mind, really, but nothing that was thought. He'd been given, in that instant when Adams raised his eyes to meet Ed's and conveyed Lovilla's news, far too much to solve at much too quick a pace, and a natural, saving numbness had immediately settled in. In his head the day had become a list of chores—find the kid; get him home; call the old lady; drive him up to her—while a single idea formed and prodded him with the lure of reward: simply to be *finished* with this day, in his blue chair, drinking beer.

That was as completely as Ed could view his trouble and it had let him disconnectedly tend to Jonas; he felt no anger or impatience with his unremitting screams. He'd sensed Jonas as the problem's inconsolable shape and sounds, and as little more. This denied many things, not entirely a bad result, for he didn't for a moment at a juncture in the day see his son as incarnation of Ramona's mocking flight.

So the muscular coiling of Jonas startled Ed, cut through his preoccupation the way a prick of pain gets your attention. He looked at his son and his pause was open tolerance. Suddenly alert, he sat, quite willing to see why Jonas had called, shivering his sadness down his back and through his thighs, life Ed felt as he held it in his hands.

What? Ed's mind might have said. *I'm waiting. What?* It was as though someone in the Hill Top had shouted his name from the end of the bar. Ed couldn't sense that Jonas, with his hitching cry, his snaky twist, had explained himself entirely, that the response was Ed's to make, not his. And when the baby only repeated himself—kicking the air, letting Ed's hands feel the scissoring twitch of his hips—Ed blinked and went no further.

And by now Vera had reached them, leaning her head into the driver's window.

Ed handed Jonas through the window to Vera. As she took him, her look remained on Ed.

"You find the crib?" he said.

"It's in the attic," Vera said. "It's took apart."

Vera's head was the archetypal Indian's on the face of a nickel. Her short hair was still completely black and she combed it straight across her forehead in a way that made it look like the line of a cheap toupee. She focused her eyes on Ed's left ear, since that was all he gave her. "You wanna set it up, go to it. I'll even give you a wrench to do it with. Shouldn't take you long, and you oughta be quick, since it's hotter in the attic than it even is out here. Course why you wanna spend the afternoon in the attic puttin' your baby crib together is another thing altogether. Maybe you just wanna take a trip down memory lane, or maybe, Ed, you wanna tell me"—her voice flattened now, each word snapping at the one ahead of it—"what the hell is goin' on?"

Ed sighed, still looking through the windshield at the slack hulk of the house. In his head he heard himself explaining the day to Vera, but there seemed no way to know what should come first, how to tell the story at all. Each aspect, by itself, was enough to assure his mother's thrilled scorn. He imagined himself beginning, "Bumbry swiped Jonas," and seeing Vera's eyebrows shoot up like arching inchworms.

But that was where he started, for he had no idea what to say about Ramona to his mother, since he had no idea what to say about her to himself.

Vera let him speak. Sweat ran down his nose and cheeks, tiny creeks through the work grime on his face. As she waited through his words she absently bounced Jonas on her hip. The baby's cheek, wet with heat and fear, was deep against his grandmother's side, his fussing a steady scratch of sound.

"Where is she?" she asked when Ed had finished.

"I fucking said I didn't know."

"What'd you do?" Vera asked. Her voice was quick, regiminal, prosecutorially bored. "What'd the *two* of you do?"

"What'd we *do?*" Ed flared. "What the fuck do you mean, what'd we do? We didn't *do* nothing."

"So why's she gone?" Vera asked.

Ed wearily shook his head.

Jonas squirmed on Vera's hip and she shifted to accommodate him. "So why'd she leave again, if you didn't do nothing. If nothin' was wrong?"

"Tell you what—"

"*Leave* this time. *Try* to leave before," Vera interrupted to clarify history.

"Tell you what," Ed repeated. "Next time I see her, it's the first thing I'll ask her."

"When'll that be?"

Ed said nothing.

"When'll that be?"

"She'll be back tonight," Ed said. "What's she gonna do, on foot, at night, like she is?"

Vera said, "You think I'm keeping Jonas till that little bitch decides the party's over and she comes waltzing back home, you're wrong."

"Got a better idea?" Ed said. "Wanna give him back to Bumbry?"

"A day," Vera said. "I'll keep him till tomorrow."

There was nothing to argue about, in Ed's view. The way he felt right now, tomorrow was a rumor that, if true, was surely someone else's work.

"Where's his bottles?" Vera asked. "And some milk. I ain't got any milk in the house."

Ed looked at her vacantly.

"Jesus," Vera said.

Ed wiped his face with both hands. The back of his shirt against the seat was completely soaked with sweat. "I'll go get the milk."

He needed three trips from his house to his mother's. When he came back with Jonas's bottles, he'd neglected to bring diapers. And on his next return, Vera asked him where Jonas's sheets and blankets and pajamas were. So it was well after six o'clock, the sun touching the top of the Catskills, sending out a luminous rose, as though the mountains' peaks had pierced it, spoking color through the sky, when Ed fell into his soft blue chair and opened his first beer.

He drank it in four long swallows and felt a deeper exhaustion spread immediately through his limbs. He couldn't believe he'd been carrying still more that hadn't yet been released, and cursed himself for bringing just one beer into the living room since he knew he was too tired now to leave his chair for hours. He stared through a window that looked west, behind his house, to the Catskills, gray and final. Beyond trees and the neighborhood's debris—piled inner tubes, the doors of cars and pickup trucks primed a shade of dead maroon leaning against a shed—lay the pasture which Ramona had crossed to reach the highway. Ed hadn't yet discovered the empty stroller in the field, hadn't yet, from there, traced the route of Ramona's flight, so the view of the pasture wasn't painful for him. He didn't even see it, really, since it was merely what his window gave him every day—the trucks' doors and the mound of tires as permanent as the Catskills.

As he sat, the moment of Ramona's return flickered in his mind. Images competed. He saw himself striking her, the force of his blow snapping her head against the wall. He saw her naked, on her hands and knees, weeping hysterically as fear flowed through her and made her bony back, her small ass, tremble. It was morning when he hit her; it was dark when she crawled, sobbing. Yet, violent as these pictures were, they seemed to Ed to hover in a dimness, far away, unable to arouse real venom or even hold his interest.

Instead, he simply sat, a weary sentry, observing the basic shapes of Myles outside his window, but listening attentively, expectantly, at some moments assumedly, for the quick soft scuff of her footsteps coming up the walk.

Many people in town waited as Ed did, and nearly as interestedly. Some, with windows in their homes that looked toward Ed's street, found themselves that evening held especially by the sunset and stood for minutes at a time admiring their view. Others were seized with the need to take a walk and strolled past Ed's house to the end of the block, then turned around and headed back, passing it again in the opposite direction, lingering in the heavy heat as though they were meandering through a spring night's fragrant stillness.

Like Ed's, the mind of the town had been so occupied with the pressing business of Jonas's rescue and the way to find him comfort that only now—with everyone home from work and families beginning the long hours of summer night—could people see past that immediate alarm. But since Jonas was safely at his grandmother's they could start to live with the even richer substance of the day—the dazzling fact of what Ramona had done. What she'd done *again*. People sat with it at supper, passing it back and forth like a special dish they liked so much they didn't want to finish it. They inhaled it with their cigarettes, holding it, strong smoke, inside their lungs as long as possible. They took it from their tables with a beer to their front steps where they sipped it in the twilight while they slapped at huge mosquitoes.

"I told you twice already," Adams said to Lovilla. "I told you—nothing. He didn't say nothing." He sat at the table in their tiny kitchen, smoking, while she stacked the supper dishes.

"He said *somethin'*, Raymond," Lovilla insisted to her husband. "He had to say something. You was with him two hours. He had to talk. He had to say 'Shit,' or 'I'll kill the motherfucker,' or 'I'll strangle the bitch.' "

"You just about got it," Adams said.

"He said 'I'll strangle the bitch'?" Lovilla spun around from the sink, her eyes round with alarm.

"No," Adams said. "What I'm saying is, he said about three things the entire time. But he never said word one about her. And I know that's true. Me and Mitchell talked about it afterwards, after we dropped him at his car. Mitchell looks at me and says he was thinkin' all the time the three of us was in the truck how Ramona's got her ass in some kinda sling this time."

"Yeah?" Lovilla asked.

"And that he's waitin' for Ed to say *some*thin' about it, somethin', anything, just to, he don't know, take the pressure off or something. And I says to Mitchell, 'Christ, I know what you're sayin', 'cause I'm thinking the same thing.' "

Lovilla frowned, confused.

"It was weird in that truck," Adams explained. "It was like ridin' in a goddam funeral parade, in the car behind the casket. Nobody knowin' what to say. Think about it, I mean, what do you say? 'Your wife's a cunt, Ed'? Is that what you say? Or do you say, 'She's probably home already, Ed'? 'She probably just went walkin' and forgot the time'? And especially 'cause *he* don't say a word, not about her, anyway. He mumbles, you know, 'Fuckin' Bumbry,' and 'Take a left up here—it's a short cut to Bumbry's.' And that's about it.

"Me and Mitchell, all we're thinkin' to ourselves is, "What's he gonna do when he gets his hands on her?' So of course you notice that he ain't saying a *word*, 'cause you gotta wait for him to say it before you can know what to say. Especially fucking King. I mean, it's true for anybody, a thing like that, but especially fucking King."

"And?" Lovilla asked.

"And we're waitin'. And he ain't sayin'."

"God," Lovilla said quietly, shaking her head.

"You see now what I'm saying? You see how it was weird?"

Lovilla wiped her hands on a dish towel and sat again at the table.

Adams shook his head and drew on his cigarette. Reliving the events for the sake of his wife had brought them vividly back to him. He'd been filled as they drove with a teeth-chattering nervousness, as though taken by a chill, which he'd had to hide as he sat next to Ed. He'd sensed several reasons to be worried—on the child's behalf; on Ed's; even, somehow, on his own in a way he couldn't fathom.

Finally, he said, "Well, I'll tell you one person I'm glad I ain't tonight, and that's Ramona King."

Lovilla looked at her husband. "What do you mean?"

"What do *you* mean, 'What do you mean'?" Adams asked. "Because I think he's gonna knock her into next week. That's what I mean."

From the moment Lovilla had left the Kings' house earlier that day, she'd been sure that Ramona was not coming back. Nothing she'd seen, no signs of planned departure, had given her that certainty. There was something simply so vacated about the feel of the house, as though every trace of Ramona had been lifted from the rooms. Especially those things that were specifically hers, that she had touched that day (Lovilla had paused to notice Ramona's lipsticked coffee cup and her hairbrush on the kitchen table), gave Lovilla the sensation that Ramona's life had left them. They'd reminded her of her grandmother's possessions, which had seemed—when Lovilla had helped to sort them out after her death last spring—somehow also dead, as though they'd actually had lives dependent on her grandmother's.

That was how Ramona's cup and brush, how the Kings' whole house, had felt to Lovilla—permanently empty of Ramona. So her husband's idea that Ramona would return to meet

Ed's vengeance could not have seemed less likely as she tried to think of it, which was why she'd asked him what he meant, and why she now said, "Maybe."

Ed sat up in his chair, immediately awake. The room was dark, and for a moment he couldn't get a sense of the direction he was facing. He thought he'd been startled by a noise, and waited for it to repeat itself. He heard nothing, but in trying to he remembered why he'd awakened in his chair in the middle of the night, what he'd been listening for when he'd fallen asleep.

He sighed hard through his nose and blinked. A tremendous headache had formed where he usually felt them, behind his left eye, and his throat was very dry. His shirt and jeans were damp with sweat. The air outside his opened windows still held a midday heat. He sat, listening again for the scuff of her steps, and the quiet he heard suddenly seemed to him a game she was playing, as though she was, of *course*, returning at this instant; was stepping, terrified, up the walk toward the house. But she'd learned somehow to move in absolute silence. She was out there, surely; outside; waiting to slip past him.

He heard nothing.

He stood, the pain behind his eye pulsing as he rose, and walked toward the kitchen. The moon shone through windows on this side of the house, lightly chalking the air.

He turned on the kitchen light and opened the refrigerator for a beer. As he sipped it, he leaned against the counter, the habitual spot where he drank beer after work. His eyes were drawn to her cup and hairbrush on the table, but, unlike Lovilla, he did not sense they were dead. Instead, they gave Ed a jolt which stirred the nausea he'd awakened with. He belched to try to ease it.

His anger was working solely on the astonishing fact that she hadn't come home, that she wasn't here now, slumped in shame at the table with her eyes fixed to the floor. He didn't

think about her trying to leave last winter, or about the months before that, about her steady decline into distracted sullenness. His mind made no effort to trace patterns, feel the escalating cadence of the baleful heat they'd traded.

Instead, he instinctively directed everything toward this moment, making her failure to return tonight an encompassing act. It was all there was to know, to feel the shock of. He drank his beer and stared at her hairbrush while his nausea churned at the top of his stomach just behind his rib cage. It was a simplistic sickness, eager as a flu. He listened to his headache's growing noise.

Thinking nothing, he moved away from the counter and walked into the bathroom. He ran cold water into the sink and bent to cup handfuls to his face, then toweled his forehead softly.

A mottled shower curtain was drawn its length across the tub. He stared at it as he dried his face and was suddenly certain she was hiding behind it, standing dead-still in a corner of the tub with her newfound gift for quiet. He flicked the light and flung back the curtain, and the empty tub's reflection hurt his eyes and made his head pound. He saw a nest of her hair that had collected at the drain.

He left the bathroom and walked through the house, turning lights on as he went. He climbed the stairs and opened their closet, staring for some seconds at the scant row of dresses. Moving methodically, he inspected every corner of the house, and finally, back in the living room, he pushed the couch away from the wall to look behind it. He was held in a fueling delirium, and the extent of its notion was to search the house with care.

When he'd finished, leaning against a living-room wall and staring down at puffs of dust collected behind the couch, he pictured again her strands of hair wreathing the drain, and a sound came out of Ed for the first time in hours. It was a hoarse moan, threaded with violence too weak to make much claim.

He hurried back to the bathroom, knelt to the floor, and scooped her hair from the tub into his palm. As he turned, still on his knees, he saw a few more strands beneath the sink, and with the edge of his hand he swept them up as well. He made sure he captured every hair, working with his customary thoroughness, for Ed was a fastidious man, and had been even as a child. Some of his almost legendary slowness, in fact, was a function of a constantly meticulous regard.

When he stood, his headache beat wildly against the back of his eye. Back in the kitchen, he put what he'd collected into a washed jar in the sink's drying rack, and picked her brush from the table, his fingers raking free the snarls of hair between its rows.

And so he moved once again from room to room, often dropping to his hands and knees to reach into the corners, soundless, sweating fiercely, suspended in obsession. His eyes adjusted to detect the finest strands among tufts of dust. And while he worked, two words formed in his head. He said them silently again and again. *The bitch. The bitch. The bitch.* They took on a mantric insistence, their rhythm that of the beat of his pulse, as though his heart were making the words and pushing them out within his blood. *The bitch. The bitch.* And yet, if you were watching him sweep the house for his wife's hair, you'd see or hear no evidence of that rage, nothing but a labor of compulsive, mute routine, a charwoman's automatous calm.

He moved last into the bedroom, beneath her side of the bed, and when he threw off the top sheet and began to sweep the pillow the first shades of morning helped the lamp to light his work.

Six

After Ramona had scurried up the ditch and started down the highway, she walked along the roadside with a quick and natural step. Fields of hay and high corn, rising and falling picturesquely, ran back on both sides of the road, leaving it shadeless under the sun. Sweat ran down the back of her neck and continued down her shoulders, dampening the straps of her harness. But the sun on her was blissful, her sweat an easing ointment, and she felt herself growing strong and loose beneath it. She walked on, mindful of the blessing of overwhelming heat. The rubber soles of her thongs slapped the bottoms of her feet.

Held inside the certainties of the field behind her house, she now imagined Jonas as still safely asleep in his stroller, waiting for her. She believed that she had all the time she needed and that she was becoming stronger and more limber with each step, each slap of thong. And she knew that the stronger she became, the easier her mothering life would be, and so, for Jonas's sake,

too, she should walk as far, get as strong, as she possibly could. She had no notion of time passing. Time was like the heat and the heat was omnipresent. The same heat she was moving through was waiting down the road, where the time would be the same as well.

It was nearly noon before she started to tire and then, as the sun finally began to work logically on her, she became instantly aware of all the strength she'd spent. She stopped, bent over for a few seconds, then left the road and walked through the ditch into a bordering cornfield.

Entering the field, she heard the clumsy panic of hidden deer feeding on the corn. They thrashed through the field as they fled, the loud clap of toppled stalks held in the rows of air. Ramona unbuttoned her jeans, heavy with sweat as she pushed them down, and squatted. The pocketed heat between the rows was airless and extraordinary. She closed her eyes and tried to breathe. Gnats whined at her ear.

When she emerged from the field, the air in comparison felt almost cool. Her hand trembled as she placed a cigarette in her mouth and lit it.

She was sitting in the ditch, not remembering having decided to, but when she lay back against the bank, the weeds scratching her back below her pushed-up blouse, she began to feel steadier. She smoked and listened to the occasional traffic passing above. She imagined water, saw herself lowering her head to slurp water from her cupped hands. Two hands, holding all the water she could drink, not a drop of it seeping through the tight seam where the malleable flesh of two hands joined. She was so thirsty that she felt her throat catch, her tongue stick, as she tried to swallow.

And yet a charged tranquillity held her. Her mind was floating now in even less specific pleasure. It was as though

she'd done something very well earlier in the day, perhaps even something dangerous, because what she felt was the sweet self-satisfaction of bravery's aftermath. She could have recalled the field behind her house; the back of the stroller, its handles gleaming in the sun; the gusty wind giving the field its only sound. But all of that simply lay small and quiet in her mind. Her thirst and exhaustion covered everything else. Still, a vague contentment remained, and Ramona let it have her while she closed her eyes and smoked.

The sun was lowering as she walked toward it, a reddish color bloating it, and then she saw ahead of her the finger of a brook running alongside the highway over water-polished rocks. She hurried forward, down the ditch and through high brush. Her throat moved instinctively, trying to swallow. She rolled up her jeans and stepped into the water, a chill rushing up her legs. She walked carefully over its pebbled bed, and when the water reached her knees she made her way to the bank, squirmed out of her jeans, and returned to the stream, holding them and her thongs. In a few more steps it had risen to her thighs and she bent over and placed her face into the current. She held herself still, feeling the life of the stream moving against her face, then rose up and, puckering her lips exaggeratedly, sucked the running surface, slurping loudly as she drank. The water had a faintly siltish taste. It took some time in this way for her to quench her thirst, but the water, not time, was moving for Ramona.

The brook curved quickly away from the road and ran back between maple and chokecherry trees, bending sharply again and disappearing. Ramona moved slowly along, nearly stumbling now and then as her foot slid against a stone. The water was not too cold and with the slippery feel of a lake's between her thighs. After ten or fifteen yards, she could barely hear the

highway, and when she followed the brook's sharp bend it was entirely gone, as though lifted out of the world.

Here the water widened and became a natural pool. Denser woods surrounded it and its banks were steep, smooth rock, a tannish brown the shade of a hide. Ramona sluffed forward, her feet sliding along the pebbly bottom. She looked ahead where, farther down, the bank rose vertically, the rocks in narrow shelves, perhaps twenty, thirty feet. When the water almost reached her waist, she stopped, let her head fall back, her chin to the sky, and thought again of her good fortune. She'd been desperate for a drink of water only minutes ago and now she stood waist-high in it, felt it moving against her with a sense that it would hold her if she suddenly went limp.

Already, the highway seemed a finished episode.

She made her way to the edge and struggled up, settling into the rocks, facing the sun and the steep distant bank. She placed her jeans next to her and leaned back. The sun sat just above the trees, its heat still strong but softer now on her face and legs, less aggressively medicinal. She lifted her wet hair away from her neck and felt the heat of the rock on her nape and shoulders.

And then, across the water, where the bank rose high, two teen-aged boys came out of the woods and walked to the edge, peering down into the water. Both wore cutoff jeans, slung low. One of the boys was dark-haired and heavy, rolls of fat above his cutoffs, his chest puffed fleshily with a girlish pubescence. The other was fair and thin, his hipbones jutting out like weapons, skin stretched tautly over his long sunken stomach. They moved back and forth along the ledge of rocks with an air of knowledgeable inspection. Neither of them thought to look to see if someone else might be anywhere near.

Ramona heard their voices floating over to her. She sat up, startled; she'd been feeling in her own way that this hidden place was hers. She shielded her eyes as she tried to see them, for their voices were coming out of the sun. With her eyes nearly

shut, she could silhouette their figures. Their muffled voices sounded serious as they paced back and forth in a preparatory way.

She reached for her jeans next to her and slipped them on, moving cautiously in an effort not to draw their attention. She felt slow in her mind, puzzled and disoriented. It was as though she were peering out from a dream into a threatening daylight.

The heavy boy walked away from the other one, out of the blinding glare, and Ramona's eyes followed him.

The boy pointed down into the water. "Here!" he yelled. "Right here!" He pointed down again and held his stare on the spot in the water he'd selected.

From the sun, the other boy shouted back at him, "Bullshit! I'm lookin' right at it. Here's the rocks that marks it, right? Like the three tits stickin' up?"

But the first boy had not lifted his eyes and he shouted back, "C'mere if you don't believe me!" He stood with his legs crossed at the ankles, his arms folded across his soft chest.

"Don't need to. I'm fuckin' *lookin'* at it!"

The heavy boy shouted, "You wanna dive from there, go ahead. Dive. Split your head open!" He'd dropped his arms to his sides and stood now with his feet planted. "I'm lookin' right exactly where we always dived."

"Then *you* go."

The first boy took a step back and looked away from the water. He said something too softly for Ramona to hear, and the other voice answered, "Hey! What's the matter? You said you was sure!" Squinting, Ramona could see the weed-thin figure turn, profiled now in front of the sun, and drop to a crouch on the ledge. "So go on! Dive!"

Again the heavy boy's response was too low, but she saw him lean forward, his hands behind him as though feeling for something to hold on to. He held this pose for longer than

seemed possible while his jittering feet searched the rocks for a better purchase.

"*Go on!*" The voice from the sun was a shriek, alive with gleeful mischief, and hearing it, Ramona gasped. "*Dive, you chickenshit!*"

The heavy boy fell, unconnected shudders running down his body, as though the shout had pushed him off while the rocks grabbed at his feet. He stayed bent in the air, his thick legs flailing, angling crazily in no way that could help him, and Ramona either heard him scream or heard her assumption he was screaming and he hit the water flatly with a crack.

His head broke the surface and he came up, spewing and coughing, his hair wet-slick as otter fur. He spit and shook his head, flinging water, and shouted up, "*Okay?* You believe me now?" His tone of vindication was enough to keep him buoyant. He bobbed and laughed. "Whaddaya say now, asshole?" He choked and spit. "I told you I knew. I found it in the first place." He lay back, stroking casually. "You gotta start listenin' to me, man." He leaned forward in the water and moaned softly. "So? Whaddaya say now?"

Ramona could barely see, through the glare of the sun, the thin boy rise, his hands on his hips.

"I'd say you found *another* place." Ramona thought she could see that he was cocking his body for a dive.

"*What?*" The boy in the water came alert. He looked up, his hand hooding his eyes.

"Must be two places deep enough, 'cause *I'm* lookin' at the one we knew before."

"Don't!" His chest ballooned and he rose up higher in the water as he watched the boy above him. "You crazy bastard! Don't!"

It looked to Ramona, as the boy began his dive, as though an arm of the sun had flung itself toward her. Sunlight yielded him, falling assertively, a true line toward the water, and his hands cut the surface with a soft insuck of sound.

He reappeared instantly, gave his head a single fierce shake, and swept his hair from his eyes.

"Whooo!" his friend shouted, swimming toward him. "Je-sus Christ!" He was laughing wildly as he came near, and making drawn-out sounds of agony, his relief turning him briefly crazy in the water. "You stupid asshole! Woo-ooo! I can't believe you fucking *did* that. Oh, my God! You scared the *shit* outa me."

"I guess you was wrong," the thin boy said. "I knew I had the spot." He dipped below the surface and came up again, the water parting his hair down the middle of his skull, and he was looking, for the first time, directly toward Ramona, twenty yards away.

A wide smile filled his face. "Hey!" he called to her, raising his arm. He spit water and smiled again. "What's goin' on?"

The heavy boy now saw her too. He shouted, "What's the matter? Can't you talk?" Then he said something Ramona couldn't hear to his friend, who appeared to shake his head in disagreement and, with a languid kick, stretched in the water and began to swim toward her.

It's impossible to say exactly when the thoughts of Ed, before he'd changed, had come into her mind, but at some point as she'd watched this boy they had, brought to her mostly by an intense sense of touch. Certainly, when she'd glimpsed him against the sun as he turned his body to the side, she'd also seen the line of Ed's long, loosely slouching figure. She saw the boy's arms poised at his hips and her fingers remembered tracing the cabled muscles from Ed's shoulder to his elbow. She saw, in profile, the caved grace of the boy's stomach below his ribs, and her fingertips recalled their amazed explorations of Ed's smooth skin curving up and over the frame of his hips, the cage of his ribs.

His manner, too, was Ed's, and at some point within an instant she'd recognized it very well. But just as the boy's body had brought Ramona memories of the Ed she had worshiped, so

also did his sense of immune superiority, something so complete that he judged long dives into unknown water to be free of risk, so did that same sense reach Ramona across the water inside flares of orange sun.

And the flooding-in of Ed brought the truth of the morning back to her, her mind suddenly alive with flashing fragments swiftly ordering themselves. So, as she watched the boy gliding the short distance toward her, she began to hate him, both for who he was and for who he'd seemed to be. As he reminded her of Ed, it was as though, with each reaching stroke, he was moving from the person she'd adored at this boy's age to the man she'd fled this morning. Looking down into the water, seeing the knotted rope of his sleekly arching spine, it once again did not occur to Ramona that Ed was no different this morning from what he'd been at eighteen.

The boy stood up and walked toward her, sloshing noisily, water dripping from his face, from the fringe of his cutoffs, his smile the same sure grin he'd flashed the moment he'd spotted her, as though it were the calling gift he'd thought to bring to her.

She also hated the boy simply for being here, now that the reality of her flight was clear to her. It was so huge and sudden a discovery that she was desperate to see it whole. But from this place on the rock, she felt as though she were sitting in its midst. She needed to step back from what she'd done and sit with it alone for as long as she needed to. But here he stood, too close, like her realization itself.

"How long you been sittin' here?" he asked. He set one foot forward in the water to steady himself against the drifting movement at his knees.

"Just a while," she said flatly, putting nothing in her voice that he could use. Over his shoulder, she could see the perched figure of the other boy, who'd swum back to a rock on the opposite bank. "I wanna be by myself," Ramona said. "So either you go away, or I will." She reached for her thongs.

He looked quickly behind him and turned back to her. He nodded, and the look on his face was amused, as though he understood the game, as though there was no doubt in his mind that Ramona meant just the opposite of what she'd said to him. From the edge of the water he looked up at her. Ramona's wet hair was pulled back and lay flat against her head, giving her face, without the softening help of hair, a look of bony adolescence.

He extended his left arm and rolled it in toward him so that the muscles in his forearm pushed up against his skin. His fingers ran absently, lovingly, over them. "What's your name?" he asked, still looking at the muscle in his arm, and when Ramona drew her legs in he stepped indirectly toward her, letting the water move him circularly, as though he wanted to surround her at the same time he drew closer.

He cupped his hand to his ear, and said, smiling still, "I didn't hear ya."

"Look," Ramona said. "Go back and get your friend and the two of you splash around in the water some more." In her awareness of where she was and what had happened today, she was growing very frightened, especially as she looked into the gift he'd brought for her—the smile of a boy who's smiling at himself. She sensed some stir of interest in his loins telling him what to do. It seemed to her the way things were with boys who loved themselves. She was past any patience with his preening and his smile, feeling the press of its smothering nearness.

"Hey," he said, "you hurt my feelings." His smile fell to show this to her. "Come on." He was walking out of the water, holding his eyes on her as he stepped over small rocks at its edge. "What's your name? Who are you?" He leaned his chest against the flat face of the rock she sat on and looked up at her. "Help me up?" He raised his arm, his long-fingered hand reaching toward her. "Whaddaya say?"

She looked down at his fingers, wiggling up at her like worms in just-turned earth, and suddenly her fear and her anger

turned mindless. From somewhere, one of the lessons in last night's dream—the hand's aloof utility as it had quickly smothered Ed—came suddenly to mind. She rose up on her knees.

"Here," she said, and leaned down and offered him the hand, thrust it, a stab of silent violence, toward his outstretched fingers.

Looking into her eyes, the boy reached up. His fingers closed on the hand and then he jerked away, as though burned, from its doll-rubber hardness. He stared up at Ramona with a stupid frown.

"What's the matter?" Ramona said, her voice at a level of unexcited menace. "Don't you wanna come up?"

The boy stepped back, stumbled on the rocky bottom and caught himself.

"You wanna know who I am?" Ramona said. She raised her arm and pulled the sleeve of her blouse up past her elbow, showing him the plastic shell, the connecting straps. "You wanna come and sit beside me now, you little shit? Here, I'll help you up." She pointed her hand toward him and he seemed instinctively to suck in his stomach.

Looking past him, Ramona saw his friend push off from the rock toward them. He turned around to the paddling sounds, then faced her again and shrugged his shoulders weakly. He started to speak, but Ramona stopped him.

"Now leave me the fuck *alone.*"

"Okay, okay," he said, holding his palms up to her. "Okay," he said again, and turned, taking giant laboring strides. He called to his friend, who pulled up as he neared.

Ramona saw the two boys meet in chest-deep water, their heads nearly touching as they whispered, saw the heavy boy's snap around in her direction when he heard whatever he heard, and then the two of them made their way toward the high bank. She watched them climb quickly up the rocks, knowing without pause where the footholds were.

On top, where they'd first appeared, they seemed to dawdle, pacing the ledge again, as though pondering, from safely beyond the range of this woman's craziness, whether they were going to let themselves be run off. The thin boy looked over in her direction a few times, once staring for several seconds. He reached down and picked up his shirt and shook it out elaborately. Finally, they turned toward the trees and the thin boy stopped again, faced Ramona's way, and waved back across to her with an exaggerated sweep of his arm, then stepped into the woods.

She stretched her legs out in front of her and eased back against the rock again, feeling her heart beat slow. She was listening to the water, calming now that they had left it, and she was listening as keenly to the wordless air. For a while she aggressively listened, her senses roaming, scavenging the quiet.

She was once more acutely aware of time. From the moment she'd remembered Ed, the world had again been passing before her, keeping time. And now that she was alone and could sit with the idea of what she'd done this morning, her impressions could finish arranging themselves: some of them in dreams, some in the recent past, many in the hours since she'd left her bed this morning. This was nothing she enjoyed. Her hours of confusion, when the oppressive heat had nourished her, had been a long sublimity; now, her awareness brought a deepening alarm, but she was powerless to stop it once it had begun, once the boy had dived out of the sun toward her.

She took her cigarettes from her jeans and lit one and listened. She heard the water slapping softly at the bank, but even that seemed to her an active kind of silence. She decided there should be the sounds of birds in this woods-surrounded place, but she heard nothing from the trees, so she put her own sounds in them. Birds' wings flapping as they moved from limb

to limb. Leaves rustling. Then the fussy scratch of squirrels' claws over bark. Yes.

But thoughts of Ed were in every sound. Not of Jonas, who she knew was safe. But she sensed Ed's thorough infiltration of the sounds she'd made up. The impression of Ed was in them. And also in what her eyes were taking in as they scanned the top of the water and the plaited wall of trees.

For some time she sat and smoked, picturing herself opening the rust-holed screen door. She wasn't sure how far she'd come today, so she had no idea how long it would take her to get back. Would it be dark? Early morning? As she thought, she hoped that there'd still be some light in the sky. It seemed very important that it not be dark when she opened the door. It seemed safer, somehow. She imagined Ed's anger might be slightly softer if there was even a last sheath of twilight.

As for what he would do, she had no certainty of that either. As she tried to imagine a scene that seemed most likely she found that she really didn't care. Her heartbeat neither rose nor fell to the thought of any particular confrontation. The idea of taking the slap of his words disgusted her as much as a memory of the flat of his hand. She realized that it was not really so much the moment of her return which filled her with a sickness that she felt might split her chest. It wasn't that at all. It was imagining the days of their virulent life to follow. And now she'd given them something else they would use on one another.

She wondered how long it had taken Mrs. Beasley to hear Jonas crying in the field, but she was certain the old lady had and that he had suffered only moments of discomfort in the heat.

Her body suddenly noticed that it hadn't had food. And then she thought back to the early afternoon as she'd walked along the highway, hungry only for the heat. Confused as she

had been, she knew there'd been some purpose moving her. Gradually, she began to feel again a hint of what she'd felt on the highway. With her mind clear she felt a vivid separation from the life she'd left this morning, as though with every step she'd taken away from the field of low weeds and daisies she'd made *something* like an ever longer length of light and air.

How different this was, she realized, from the first time she'd tried to flee. How absolutely different. Then, as she'd lain in a frost-crusted field, she'd screamed, not yet out of pain, but with the more terrifying sensation that she was awake inside a nightmare. From childhood, she'd lived through many scenes as unfathomable as the one she lay in then, but she'd always awakened from them, her heart wild and her concentration holding on to anything—the thick stitching at the edge of her blanket, the soothing flesh-knot of her navel—until the nightmare faded. But as she'd lain in the field, hideously awake, she'd been aware of two things too horrible to be anything but a dream. She'd felt the cold of the ground ice moving into her body and spreading steadily down her spine. And she'd felt herself awash in blood, lines of blood over her body and pooling in the frozen snow beside her, blood that she could see if she moved her head at all.

Now, instead of winter night, and blood, and ice inside her spine, she sat on a summer-warmed rock, sensing heat and light and air. Everything now was the opposite of then, and she saw that she'd been picturing her return home, feeling her hand on the screen door's frame, assuming the best she could hope for was the last hour of twilight, simply because she'd come back to her senses. Having admitted to herself the truth of what she'd done, it had briefly felt to her as though she'd been found out somehow, captured, just as she'd been found before, bleeding in the snow. But no one else had found her here; she'd only found herself.

She wiped sweat from her face, raked her hair back off her head, and found that her fear now felt cooperative, as though she were enjoying a decision's after-calm. Her stomach growled, but even her hunger felt serviceable in some way.

Then she looked below the sun and when her eyes paused on the ledge where the boys had appeared she pictured them readying to dive and she remembered what she'd thought of as she'd watched them in the air. How the elegant power of the thin boy's dive had reminded her that she hated Ed because he'd changed. Yes, that. But that had been no real surprise. No, more clearly she saw again the panicked struggle of the fat boy as he fell, his limbs beating at the air. The quick cut of terror she'd felt at that instant returned and she said, aloud, "Joe." For the boy had performed for her the picture she held in her mind of her child slipping from her grip and falling, his eyes huge with awe, his arms two flapping half-curves as they frantically squeezed the air.

She nodded slowly, watching the fat boy dive, watching Jonas fall, and thought that she could get away from *that* if she didn't go back. She could get away from having to face every morning what she already knew. Hearing him in his crib and thinking she just couldn't do it. Thinking every time she held him that he was going to fall. Every time she gave him a bath that he was going to slip and drown. If she didn't go back, all that would be gone.

She looked down at the hand. Last night she had dreamed that it could kill her husband with a fluid immediacy, and she'd just now seen that it could make an arrogant boy suck in his stomach when she pointed it at him. These were the sorts of things her hand could do. She'd learned at last what her recent life had been trying to show her: that there were no soft and cradling uses, no curved, receiving tasks; nothing for a mother in the hand's efficiency.

She breathed deeply and realized that she could get away from standing at the top of Summit with Joe in the stroller and

looking down at the house and actually thinking the thoughts: Let go. Go on, take your hand off the handle.

She wondered if she could even forget the picture of her hand coming down over Joe's mouth. Maybe, in a while, she wouldn't see that in her mind. Sweat ran down her face, hung in drops, like clear warts, at her chin. She nodded again. The drops clung.

Maybe, in time, she could even get away from that.

Seven

The flatbed swayed and dipped above its creaking springs, a barge in easy-lapping water, and Adams shifted to its rocking as he stood near the front of the truck. He heard, from inside the cab, the familiar murmurs of Bill March, the foreman, at the wheel, and Waycross, seated beside him. Adams smelled the acrid smoke of Waycross's cigarette, which the bent-backed old man rolled himself, using Prince Albert pipe tobacco. Mitchell and Day rode with Adams in back, as always. They sat on the floor at the rear of the truck, their legs lazily paddling the river of warm air, and stared at the span of hot, dew-surfaced dawn. Minutes before, when the truck had stopped in front of Adams's house, the two of them had extended a hand as he'd approached and offered his, boosting him up past them, a daily routine they'd perfected long ago. Habit and momentum had carried Adams forward to the front where he stood each morning, gazing out

over the rust-pocked orange roof as though alert for signs of trouble specking the horizon.

And yet, true as this morning was to the start of every workday, Adams's heart was beating hugely with the sense of its difference. He'd crouched slightly, readying his balance for the truck's lunge forward, but instead, March had opened the driver's-side door and stepped out of the cab, standing on the running board as he turned to speak to Adams.

"I'm askin' everybody what they think," March had said. His morning voice was its customary whisper, as though he were concerned he'd wake the town. "Whether they think we oughta stop for King."

Adams had said, "Oh." He'd cocked his head, surprised. He hadn't considered for a moment that they might not pick Ed up, anticipating only what they might find when they did, what King's mood or face might say; which, of course, was the reason for Adams's uniquely eager tension.

"Well, I see your point," Adams had said. He'd felt sharp disappointment move through him.

"I'm askin' everybody," March had said. Adams heard Mitchell and Day rustling behind him. He glanced back to see they'd partially turned to listen. "I figure," March continued, "I mean, who the fuck knows what happened? She probably came back, for all I know."

"Right," said Adams. "For all I know, she prob'ly did."

"Or . . ." March said.

"Right," said Adams, nodding.

March's fingers had lightly raked the deep seams of his forehead. His hair was thick and long, and he wore a heavy beard that nearly covered his face, so that his forehead appeared to be a summer-brown bandage of skin over a nest of thick black hair. "So I was sayin' to everybody, I thought it makes sense to drive by, like always, and if he's out front, fine."

Adams had pulled on his lower lip, considering the dilemma.

He'd felt a sudden gravity of responsibility. "If that makes sense, it sounds all right to me."

"Does that sound all right to you?" March asked.

"Fine," Adams said. "Like you say, we could just drive by, and if he's waitin' . . ."

"Right," March said.

"Otherwise . . ."

"Right," March said. "We can just drive on. That sound all right to you?"

"Fine," Adams said. He'd turned to see Mitchell and Day nodding their agreement and he'd nodded with them.

Now the truck turned a corner toward the tiny house and Adams leaned farther forward, looking for Ed. Adams heard March and Waycross's talk suddenly stop. He felt March shifting the truck and Adams, holding the slatted sides as the truck grabbed its lowest speed, assumed the foreman wanted Ed to have the longest chance to see them. He tightened his squint even more. Ahead, three houses down, Ed's dirt yard looked empty, softly edged to indistinction by the maple's heavy shade.

Over the years, there'd grown a sense in Myles that Ed and Adams were somehow complementary. Particularly to the others on the crew, the two of them had at some point seemed to fuse—Ed's lean ease to Adams's short, thick-chested urgency; Ed's black-haired paleness to Adams's weather-reddened skin. Working side by side, the two men did, in fact, often seem to form a kind of composition that sometimes caught the attention of the others—Adams bending to blend tar into road cracks and making, with his pose, an angle that held the vertical line of Ed's steady pressure of boot to spade. But beyond the supple meshing of their labor, outside the purer world of work, something larger bonded them, and Myles had simply come to assume its low, allusive strength.

Adams felt it himself and had most all his life, but for him

their pairing was a hold Ed had on him. He'd known Ed King since the first grade, and it seemed to him that the nature of Ed's presence in his life hadn't changed in all that time. To this moment, as he rode the creaking flatbed toward the shaded front yard's mystery, Adams could closely recall receiving Ed's earliest mischief. He could remember times in adolescence when the boys would grow restless as they slumped against the chain-link fence in a corner of the schoolyard and, discarding their cigarettes with a practiced finger flick, would decide a few of them should fight. Or Ed would decide, and turning predictably—his smile the only hold he really needed to throw his victim to the ground—would point to Adams. Always. You and me. Or so it seemed to Adams.

He could, then, pause at almost any place in his life and find Ed near and agitative, and though Adams was certainly not the only one in Myles Ed's bullying found attractive, he had been, outside Ed's family, perhaps its longest focus. And for his part, Adams had finally acquired a complicated acceptance of Ed's attention, had come to feel it as a central feature of his days.

His attitude had settled over him one day when he'd looked up from his work and seen, through the heat clouds of cooking tar he was readying to spread, the new man on the crew, just reporting to Bill March.

Jesus Christ, Adams had whispered to himself, it's fucking King.

And there Ed was, tall and pale and snake-muscled, beginning his first day, having quit the garbage truck two days before. Adams had stopped his work, stepped away from the tar smoke, and his eyes had followed the flow of Ed's lithely corded arms, bare in a sleeveless T-shirt. He'd also envisioned, beneath Ed's chest, the hills of muscle at his chest and clustered at his stomach. For Adams knew the feel of Ed's body intimately, after all the years of struggling in its grasp, wiggling beneath it while Ed sat on his chest, knew its privacies as one knows the

body of a lover. He knew the smell of his breath, something damply mineral, like the rain-stirred smell of rust, which Ed had panted into his face while he'd wrapped Adams in a grip.

And when he'd seen that Ed was now going to be working beside him on the crew, as he'd felt again the low suffocation of being surrounded by Ed, something in Adams simply gave in to the idea that it was meant for him to be. Shaking his head slightly, he'd smiled. Hell yes, he'd thought. I shoulda known. Hell, yes, he'd turn up here.

"I'll be damned," Adams said aloud as the truck approached Ed's house, its motor quieting so that you could hear the slowly rolling tires crunching sedimental gravel. "I'll be damned," he repeated as he viewed the empty yard. He'd been so sure that Ed would be there, waiting, that his absence was nearly a delineated shape which Adams had to blink to erase.

And because this took an added second, Adams was just beginning to sense the questions forming in his mind when he glimpsed what looked to him like a sliver of the tree as tall as a man step away from its trunk. Another second passed before he saw the form was Ed, now ambling toward the truck.

As he'd leaned against the maple Ed *had* stood so still he'd made himself virtually impossible to see. But that was simply a coincidence of his exhaustion, which, like a kind of idea, had sprung up in his brain and in a moment filled his body.

He'd been waiting at the end of his walk where he stood every morning when the full effect of the previous night had descended and he'd moved to the tree and collapsed against its trunk. He'd flipped his cigarette away and breathed as deeply as he could, thinking he might faint. He was suddenly covered with a sweat that had nothing to do with the morning's incredible heat and he looked overhead for a V of branches that might, like the sight of his rifle, hold his eye.

In a while, the dizziness had calmed, leaving him merely, elementally, tired. He breathed regularly, feeling his shirt wet

against his skin, and had thought of going back into the house to change it, but it felt so good just to lean against the tree.

In that calm, while he'd waited, more of yesterday returned. Nothing whole, only irregular pieces of the day, had floated through his mind: the first few words of Adams's news; syllables of a shouted curse—"-*ing Christ!*"; pulses of his headache on waking in his chair.

Then the three trips to his mother's, and her words, had come back to him. Not so much the words themselves as Vera's familiar tenacity, which Ed felt as something almost physically competitive.

The truck's high squeal, as it braked to make the turn, had cut through Ed's brief pause. He'd continued to lean against the maple for as long as he could and only pushed himself away as the truck rolled to a stop.

Walking toward Mitchell and Day, then looking past them to Adams standing in the front near the cab, Ed still carried the single thought he'd held when he'd emerged from his house for another day of work: that he must show them nothing, give them nothing, offer nothing. He must act as if he'd passed the night in fortifying dreams and everything inside his house was just as it had been when he'd waited on the curb for the truck the day before, nodding to the sky as if it met his stipulations.

He reached the rear of the truck and slipped the toe of his boot into a steel loop of its frame that hung below the flatbed, while Mitchell and Day offered him their hands, thrusting their arms toward him too eagerly, like saluting Nazis.

Ed nonchalantly took their grips and lifted himself up. Mitchell and Day merely grunted, showing Ed that they were sleepy and surly and not the least interested in what his mood might be. There was a silence on the truck as thick as high humidity; no radio from the cab, no profane meanderings from Waycross as he licked a cigarette paper. Mitchell yawned elaborately, again showing Ed his indifference.

Ed walked toward the front, and when he'd settled into his usual corner, he reached forward and slapped the roof of the cab with the palm of his hand. "I'm on, Billy Goat!" he shouted to March, behind the wheel. "Give me a ride."

Then, as the truck pulled away, he lifted his eyes and smiled at Adams. "You sure are ugly this morning," he said, nodding.

Like the rest of the crew, Adams had strained to show Ed that his presence on the flatbed was no more eventful than the tools'. But mostly, when he'd seen Ed come away from the maple and walk toward the truck, Adams had felt a great happiness run through him.

Something terribly important had been confirmed for him when he'd spotted Ed waiting in his front yard after all. For if Adams had been surrounded by Ed's strength all his life; pinned in the mud beneath Ed's body; clamped in his seemingly effortless grip; then he'd also been the one whom Ed had immediately released once Adams had surrendered. He'd been the defeated schoolyard wrestler whom Ed had helped up from the mud and asked if he was hurt, if he was mad, if he understood for sure that they'd just been having fun. For as long as Adams could remember, Ed had been the one who'd brushed the dirt off his coat; returned his cap; offered his body as a crutch if Adams came up limping. Bought him a beer; given him a lift; driven him home. It was as though Ed had always needed to reconcile, exactly and at once, everything he did to Adams with something he did for him. And as a result, Adams was suspended in Ed's behavior, leaving him finally to feel a certain status of his own that depended on Ed's.

On the flatbed, Adams saw out of the corner of his eye that Day's and Mitchell's backs were bent nearly into parentheses as they leaned back to hear Ed say, "You sure are ugly this morning."

Adams smiled and shook his head. "Well, Ed," he said, "folks say I look like you."

"Nah," Ed said. He rolled his toothpick in his mouth, a habit

that seemed this morning to use a second hand's full rotation of a watch face. "I decided what *you* look like, Adams," he said. The toothpick rolling. "Those big lips of yours, you watch you keep your mouth shut, or a dog's liable to fuck it."

Laughter filled the flatbed. Mitchell and Day spun around in unison, their gazes locked as though in some fierce contest. And Adams's body was curled nearly fetally as he pushed out his own laughter, while Ed leaned into the corner and looked toward the treetops, resting his arms on the side gates of the truck like a boxer winning easily being tended between rounds.

Eight

Ramona saw, above the hill line, an enormous fan of shining silver feathers sprouting tall as saplings from the curve of the earth. Following the road up, she kept her eye on the feathers, recognizing them as the top of some sort of sign just over the crest, and it helped her as she climbed to imagine what the sign might be. She pictured a prehistoric bird from the Saturday-morning cartoon shows she still watched sometimes, a flying lizard with membranous wings hovering over the road. She was panting hard, needing more from her lungs than was in them. Looking down, she saw her ankles ringed with dirt and the raw rim of blisters where her thongs had rubbed between her toes.

At the top, she stopped, and now she could see that the feathers were the metal headdress of an Indian chief in noble profile. That the sign sat atop the Chief Tah-Kah-Nic Diner just ahead of her, shining low and silver in the late-morning sun, at

the intersection of the highway she'd been following and the busy Taconic Parkway. She'd passed the diner a few times in her life, the chief highly visible on the parkway, though it was some distance south of Myles, toward New York, and nearly all her travel had been north, to the towns of Hudson and Chatham. She was farther from Myles than she'd imagined.

She reached into her jeans for all the money she had and counted it, a dollar and sixty-seven cents in change, for the fifth time this morning. She hadn't eaten since she'd left her house with Jonas the day before.

When she eased into a booth, a sense of fatigue instantly spread through her, but there was no pain in her neck or below her wrist, and she decided she was simply too tired to make any pain. She'd spent the night, near sleep, in a woods beside the highway. She'd wanted to stay on the rocks above the pool of water, but feared the boys would come back, maybe with friends, and so she'd made her way out to the highway again and walked on until nightfall. She'd sat in soft leaves against a tree, listening to the night-rustle of the woods and fighting mosquitoes. At dawn, she'd dreamed she was trying to fall asleep.

The longer arm of an L-shaped counter ran beside her, the door to the kitchen behind it. Two men sat on stools, talking to the waitress. They'd spun around as Ramona entered, watching without any expression as she passed a glass-cased check-out counter and a cigarette machine and slid into the first booth. Both men wore caps, T-shirts, and jeans. The smaller man's arms were thin and long, tanned the shade of stained mahogany.

The waitress sat a glass of water and a menu in front of her and Ramona asked for coffee.

A dollar and sixty-seven cents. She'd decided as she'd walked toward the diner that she would order only toast and coffee, but as she read the menu and smelled the grease smoke from the

grill, her hunger filled her. When the waitress brought her coffee, she looked at the menu and, without hesitating, ordered bacon and eggs and hash brown potatoes. She knew she couldn't pay for the food and it simply didn't matter; her hunger was an addict's. Watching the waitress retreat, Ramona noticed the surprising breadth of her hips in faded jeans. Behind the counter, from the waist up, she'd looked almost thin.

She felt one of the men watching her, quarter-turning on his stool to sneak a strenuous glance. She looked out the window to the lot and the highways, and as she drank her coffee she began to feel a lightness, a freedom in her situation. She'd just ordered food she couldn't pay for, so her concern for how to stretch a dollar and sixty-seven cents had been answered in a way.

Behind the counter, the waitress moved an ashtray in front of her. "We saw Willie Nelson last night in concert up at Saratoga," she said to the men. "He was fabulous. He did four encores." While the waitress spoke, Ramona could peripherally see the man, the sloping outline of his pear-shaped body, lazily spinning on his stool toward her.

"It musta been hot as hell up there last night," said the smaller man.

"It was," the waitress said, "but once he got started nobody cared. When he sung that one he does with Waylon Jennings? The audience went wild. It mighta been hot, but it sent chills up through me."

"Chills went up ya?" said the larger man. "That sounds pretty interesting. Anything else go up ya last night, Christie?" He giggled.

Ramona couldn't stop herself from glancing at him and when she did he gave her an exaggerated wink.

"You're disgusting, Lester," said the waitress. She continued, "We hoped he'd come right out into the audience and sing. He does that sometimes. But Lloyd said he must've figured it was

too dangerous. Some nut or somethin' in the crowd. Who knows what could happen?"

Ramona needed a cigarette badly and thought of turning to ask the waitress for one, but she didn't want to give the man a chance to speak to her. Then, without consciously deciding to, she simply slid out of the booth and walked to the machine and dropped coins into the slot.

Returning, she kept her eyes fixed on the smaller man's mahogany-colored arms folded on the counter.

The waitress brought her food and Ramona told herself that she must eat slowly, not call attention to her incredible hunger. She broke off a small piece of bacon and placed it on her tongue. The salty pleasure of the bacon filled her mouth, and her thought was a sadness at how soon it would be gone.

She watched a gray-haired couple climb slowly out of a long green car and come into the diner.

She'd nearly finished eating when, looking to the back at the rest-rooms sign, she pictured a possible escape, and she felt pleased with herself for having stayed calm and inconspicuous. She sponged up the last bits of egg with a corner of toast and said, "Sure," when the waitress came back with her coffeepot again as Ramona was preparing to slide out of the booth.

"How ya doin'?" said the pear-shaped man as she stood, almost beside him. She was surprised to see that he was young, her age, perhaps. His face was densely stubbled.

"All right," she said and, wanting the moment to pass in the most ordinary way, she smiled as she slipped by.

At the end of the counter she pushed through a heavy door and through a second on her left into the bathroom. It was surprisingly dark, but she saw the window near the ceiling and felt a moment of elation as she fumbled for the light. Then, flicking the switch, she saw why the room had been so dark. An exhaust fan filled the window, firmly screwed into its frame. She leaned against the door, studying the way the fan fit the

window, actually trying to imagine somehow squeezing out between the blades.

She locked the door behind her, then turned to the mirror, and the sight of herself made her swallow. Her hair was snarled and matted flat against one side of her head, where a leafy twig was held. Her face was filthy, warrior-streaked, and rings of dirt, dark and neat, seeming drawn, circled her neck. Oily dirt filled the dip above her breastbone like a smudged neck clasp, a cameo of gray sweat. In the spectral light of the bathroom her blouse was a print of overlapping stains.

"Jesus," she whispered, pulling the twig out of her hair. Her fingers moved over her cheeks and chin as though they were testing the tenderness of bruises. She thought of the great care she'd taken in the booth to draw no one's notice, counting to ten between forkfuls to steady an urge to lick the lovely grease.

Suddenly, it all seemed hilarious, and she watched herself in the mirror start to tremble with laughter. She laughed at the picture of herself in the booth, picking daintily at her eggs with a twig sticking out of her head, sitting there with the belief that she was keeping a secret. She looked away from the mirror toward the window near the ceiling and laughter tremored through her as she thought of her scheme of escape. She laughed until it had all come out of her and when she was empty nothing replaced it, no fear or despair. She felt only a pleasant sense of weakness and the need to get clean.

The two men and the waitress turned their heads toward her as she came back into the room and Ramona sensed from their attention that they'd noticed how long she'd been gone. She felt their eyes on her hand and knew they'd seen it from the start.

She sat down and took a drink of her cold coffee, her face and body still somewhat wet, and watched the waitress out of the corner of her eye. When she stepped back into the kitchen to

speak to the cook, Ramona slid out of the booth, past the men, toward the door.

She got to the checkout counter before she heard the waitress shout, "Hey! Where you goin', honey?"

Ramona turned and tried to look puzzled. "Me?" she said. "Goin' out to get my purse." She pointed through the window toward the old couple's long green car. "I left it on the seat."

"What seat?" the waitress said. "What purse?" She nodded to the window. "I watched you walkin' down the road to get here, sweetie. You looked like you fell off the Good Will truck."

Ramona turned to the window, imagining how she'd appeared as she'd crested the hill. She looked at the waitress and shrugged. "I ain't got money to pay the check."

"You ain't?" the waitress said. She'd come around from behind the counter. "Well then, we got somethin' in common. Isn't that ironic? You can't pay your check and I can't neither." She held her eyes on Ramona, arched as though amazed at life's unaccountable coincidences.

Ramona looked toward the old couple, seated in a booth on the other side of the diner. They'd paused to watch, spoons of rice pudding trembling above their goblets.

"I'll do some work if you want," she said. "Wait tables, whatever. But I ain't got the money." As she'd washed herself in the bathroom, she'd decided what to say if she was stopped at the door and once she'd settled on the simplest fact—that, indeed, she didn't have the money—a sense of immunity had calmed her.

She raised her eyes and saw the faces of the men. The expression of the smaller one was terribly sad and he seemed to be following with an attentive regret.

"Great," the waitress said. "That's great. You had money for the cigarette machine but you can't pay for breakfast."

Ramona said, "That's right." She was aware of her calm as she stood there. She felt as though she were observing herself, just as the men on the counter stools, the couple in the booth,

were observing her. She felt somehow complicit with them. She wasn't frightened, not even particularly embarrassed. Mostly, she was interested.

The waitress said, "You wanna wait tables? Well, check it out. Does it look like we need another waitress?"

Ramona glanced again at the old couple, the only other customers. They dropped their heads and spooned their puddings.

The cook, a tall, cadaverous man in a dirty white T-shirt and apron, came out from the kitchen and leaned against the doorway.

The waitress said, "You got the job a little confused, honey. I'm the one that serves the food. You're the one that pays for it." She shook her head. "Look, I'm sure life ain't easy for ya." She nodded almost timidly toward Ramona's hand. "But—"

"Jesus H., take it easy, Christie." The small man rose from his stool as he spoke, walked to Ramona's booth, and picked up the check. "You act like she robbed the cash register, for Chrissake." He gave Ramona a moment's look, an eye-flick of shyness. "I got it," he said to her.

So, Ramona thought, watching him fold the bill in half and sit down again beside the other man. This is how it's getting settled.

He looked up at her again, as though checking to see if she had gone, and smiled quickly, then his expression fell once more to a kind of warm sorrow.

"Thanks," Ramona said. "I . . . I can't pay you back."

He waved his hand.

The waitress turned to him. "Goddam it, Donnie, now you make *me* look like an ass 'cause I asked her to pay for her breakfast."

The cook went back into the kitchen.

"What the hell you want, Christie?" said the pear-shaped man, grinning even more. "First you cuss *her* out and now you give Donnie hell for pickin' up the check. You got your money. What the hell you want?"

"That's not the goddam point!" the waitress shouted. "He comes on like Mr. Hero: 'Hey, I got it. I'll buy your breakfast.' Like I'm a jerk for not just lettin' her skip out. Like it's a goddam fifty-cent cup of coffee or something and what's wrong with me for making a *thing* out of it?"

She'd turned her back to Ramona, who stood in the doorway, completely ignored.

"Well, guess who has to cover if we're short at the end of the day?" The waitress pointed at her chest. "Guess whose ass they take the skin off?" She slapped the back pocket of her jeans stretched across her ample width.

The pear-shaped man looked at Donnie and said, "I ain't gonna touch that one," and the two of them burst into spittle-spraying laughter.

Ramona had reached the door and now she opened it and was outside, hearing the waitress's muffled shouts. She walked past the windows where the old couple sat and they both waved surreptitiously.

At the intersection of the highways she stopped and looked down the Taconic, ribboning south. She watched its regular stream of traffic and turned to look down the road she'd been following, where nothing passed or approached. Ed was surely searching for her by now, late in the morning of her second day away.

Then she smiled as she thought, He ain't been on the parkway five times in his life. He always drives the country roads, talks about them like they was his.

On the parkway's grassy shoulder, she felt stronger and alert, having eaten and washed. The day was as hot as yesterday but she gave the heat little notice, though she'd felt when she'd washed a sunburn's serious sting. She was also glad to know that she was heading in a true direction, no more meandering along roads that might turn back toward themselves.

Until now, "south" had meant only one thing to Ramona:

North Carolina, where her parents had moved. For a few moments, she fantasized walking straight to North Carolina, one highway yielding to another, directing her down an obliging landscape to her mother and father and the bony press of her mother's embrace. But imagining the warmth of her mother's body folding around her caused Ramona to feel the edge of a sorrow that nearly made her falter, so she forced herself to listen to the traffic's even whoosh. And to stay outside feeling, she told herself the truth: that her parents would be anything but welcoming if they knew what she'd done now, even if there were not already an unsolved bitterness between them.

So she walked south and tried to think of nothing but the fact that she was walking south. She'd realized, in the diner's bathroom, that the nature of her hope was incredibly simple. The only thing that mattered was that she not be back in Myles. Everything would pass, anything could be accepted, so long as she wasn't there. It was as though she wished to work toward an emptiness, to return to the blameless grace that dream awarded. Yet she knew she couldn't simply will her mind to drift. The closest she could come would be to think and feel as little as possible and remind herself repeatedly that at least she wasn't *there*.

As she'd soaked the neatly folded skin that ended her wrist, squeezed a paper towel of water down the trough of her spine, she'd reasoned that if she let herself think or, worse, go deep into her feelings, she'd be surrounded by her hatred of Ed, by her failure to love Jonas, and most of all by her knowledge of what it was she'd done. And none of that could help her. She sensed, in fact, though not with detail, that any one of those sensations might somehow lead to a moment that could kill her.

Still, she'd paused, arguing that unless she let herself think and feel she couldn't make a thorough plan, then decided that she didn't need one if all that mattered was that she not be back in Myles.

The rusted station wagon pulled off the road ahead of her and

she abruptly stopped, winced as her thong cut into her blisters, and hoped as she continued that the driver had simply heard a flapping tire or become suddenly sleepy. But no one got out and she was nearly to its rear fender when she recognized the man's mahogany-colored arm hanging out the window, his palm lightly patting the side of the door. She could see his narrow eyes, framed in the outside mirror.

His arm came up, as though signaling her to stop. "Hello," he said as she drew even. Ramona squinted past his face into the car. The front seat was layered with papers, hand tools, three or four caps. She saw two large holes in the cushion, pellets of foam rubber spilling out of them.

"Hi," she answered, still looking past his eyes. The thick smell of engine grease, heated by the sun through the windshield, came from the cushions. It was the way her father's car had always smelled.

"If you want a ride, I can take you a ways." He spoke loudly over the noise of the traffic for the first few words, then finished as softly as he'd spoken in the diner.

Ramona looked into his eyes for an answer and when she did he glanced away. Why? she asked herself. He knows I'm alone and he knows I ain't got money. Why's he doin' this? Or, why *else*? Why else would he be doin' this?

"No thanks," she said. She took a long breath and tried to let her fear out silently. "Thanks anyway. Guess you're just the Good Samaritan this morning, huh?"

He didn't look at her but smiled, then the lines of his face fell to sadness again. "I guess." She could barely hear him.

He turned to her and the sudden boldness of his look had a force that Ramona unconsciously leaned away from. "It don't take a genius," he said flatly, "to see you been walkin' for a while and that you ain't dressed for a hike. You forgot to bring your food, for one thing, and your shoes for another."

Ramona's anger flared. "Mind your goddam business," she snapped. "Thanks for the breakfast."

She stepped back from the window and began to walk away and she'd gotten twenty yards when the car pulled up alongside her again.

"I'm gonna drive down there and turn off to the right." He was pointing down the parkway to an intersection a quarter mile ahead. "You want a ride, get in when you get there. If you don't, walk past and that'll be that. I can take you down to Malvern on the parkway, or I can watch you walk by. I got some stuff I need to do up around here. It don't matter to me."

He leaned back to see around her, and when a car had passed, he pulled onto the road and gunned the engine.

Watching him drive away, she thought at first to turn around and head back, then knew if he wanted to he could easily overtake her. She saw the station wagon slow, its brake lights blink, and take the right-hand exit.

She'd walked halfway, hoping that for some reason he'd let her go by, when she felt the resolve she'd come to as she'd soaked her limbs: the only thing that mattered was that she wasn't back there.

Up ahead, she saw him get out of the car and walk to the front, spread a blanket over the hood, and ease himself up. He swung around in her direction and sat, dangling his legs like a man on a dock. She remembered, as she walked, not to think and not to feel. Her foot glanced the edge of a rock and she stumbled into the road, and a car swerved as it passed her, honking angrily. She'd taken her eyes off the ground to watch him as he sat on the hood in the day's highest sun. She saw him lean back now, his arms braced behind him, and lift his face to the heat-bleached sky.

Ramona dreamed of snow, huge soft flakes in several colors. The snow fell with a calm ferocity outside a window where she stood. When it struck the ground it gave off tiny sparks and

melted instantly to a viscous silver, running through the streets and rising in seconds to the doorways of the houses.

She'd been assigned to watch the children who lived on the street as they came outside to see the building silver current, which reflected a sun shining through the snowfall. She saw the children running from their porches to wade, dipping cupped palms and splashing one another, shrieking with pleasure. The sun, off the silver, hurt Ramona's eyes but she held them on the children because it was her work to do so.

Now more children ran from their doors and squealed as they plunged into the stream. Several of them stretched their arms and locked their hands above their heads and pushed off, swimming easily past her window. A tiny boy, an infant much younger than the others, crawled naked out onto the porch to watch them swimming by. At the sight of him, Ramona stiffened with even greater interest, for she felt she'd seen him somewhere, several times in fact, and the sense grew immediately to an agitated certainty because she couldn't remember where or imagine how she'd known him.

Then, incredibly, with a strength he shouldn't have had, he suddenly stood, his naked body wobbling, and leaped headfirst toward the stream, his bent arms flapping in a way that seemed to beat the air in joyous flight. He screamed delightedly as he hit the gleaming surface and began to swim, but after a few flailing strokes he appeared to catch on something underneath and sank for just a moment and when his head popped up again it was completely coated with silver. His bright white smile was crescented inside his glimmering face and seeing it stirred Ramona's conviction even more: she felt the smile had begun its life afloat in the blood of her heart.

The other children began to struggle, too, laughing fearlessly all the while, their predicament a welcomed escalation of their play. One by one their heads also dipped and resurfaced, silver-coated. Then they all began to sink again in an unprotest-

ing sequence, and Ramona at her window stood sickened by her inaction and wondered why her duty was to watch but not to rescue.

The flow of the silver was soundless and smooth, so the world grew increasingly quiet with each child's drowning. And then the baby, giggling, began to sink, his body turning in the stream so that his head rolled left to right. As his smile revolved, Ramona caught its whiteness, like none other, so uniquely his it sent its ripe-milk breath to her, and then she knew.

She screamed, and her fists, like a prisoner's, beat the window frame as his small head disappeared. For an instant everything was absolutely noiseless as the silver river roiled and eddied past bungalowed fronts and lapped easily up hills with flood-released speed.

She broke the silence with her screams and finally they woke her. She screamed again through sobs, shaking with a convinced terror, the way, as a child, she woke from nightmares and remained inside them because they'd taken her to a province truer than life. Shaking still, she sat up in bed, surprised when she looked down at the twisted sheets that they were not the braided current of a silver river. Then, remembering where she was, she sat back against the wall behind the bed and lifted up her arm to try to make the pain leave her wrist. She was lying with her arm raised as though she were asking a question of a teacher when Donnie stepped into the doorway. She quickly dropped it and pulled the sheets up to her neck, although she was only naked below the waist.

"You all right?" he asked.

"Yeah," Ramona said weakly. "I was havin' a dream." She was trying to keep her body still. "What time is it?"

"Late," he said. "I just got back." She saw his shape leave the doorway and heard him fumbling in the kitchen just a few feet away. He came back in and sat on the edge of the bed and Ramona felt herself draw in against his casual entrance. He'd not come near her bed until now.

"Here," he said, and offered her a glass.

She sipped the whiskey and was able to relax a bit, though he made no move to leave the edge of her bed. Through the tiny window, she heard the river moving, and she reasoned that its softly constant sound had, after two days, finally gotten in, flowing silver in her dream.

"Better?" Donnie asked.

She nodded and took another drink, feeling the whiskey's heat slide into her.

"I'll get some more," Donnie said, reaching for her glass. She felt the bed spring up as he got to his feet.

By the time Ramona had reached the intersecting road where Donnie had waited on the hood of his station wagon, she'd realized the chance he was offering her, risky as it seemed to her. And she'd told herself again, as she walked toward his car, that no matter what might happen she should place it next to the fact that she wouldn't be with Ed and the resumption of her failure. So she'd walked up to Donnie and asked to be driven as far south on the Taconic as possible and he'd said, his eyes still closed and his face tilted to the sun, that he could take her eight miles, as far as Malvern, where he turned onto a local road toward his trailer in the woods on the Kinderhook River.

She'd ridden a few minutes in the heat and sweet grease smell of the station wagon before falling asleep, and when she'd wakened she was in his bed, alone, still wearing her clothes, the moon making a thin, milky seal on the night-glint of the river outside the trailer's window. She'd listened to a fish slap the surface, then walked into the tiny kitchen, where she found his note, which explained, in a penciled scrawl, that he'd gone to tend bar in Malvern and would be back at two o'clock. She couldn't believe she'd slept so long and so deeply, the idea of her hours of utter vulnerability frightening to her, and then she'd realized that Donnie's behavior, in the face of anything he might have done, had been to give her his bed and leave her

alone. She'd decided she could safely stay a day, to sleep, and instead had drifted senselessly in and out for two.

And now she thought, as she watched him come back into the room with a glass in each hand, that her nightmare had told her she'd gotten enough sleep.

Donnie gave her a refilled glass and sipped from his own. He drew his fingers across his nostrils, an unconscious habit, inhaling the lubricant smell permanently in his hands from years of fondling the mysteries of small engines. He'd spent his usual afternoon, repairing one for a man from Malvern, after a morning on the river fishing seriously for trout. When the man had come to pick up his engine, Ramona had hidden in the trailer. Donnie had watched her hurry inside when the car appeared on the muddy, rutted lane that led down to his trailer.

He glanced to see that her stump was still hidden beneath the sheet. "Feelin' better?" he asked, taking another drink.

Ramona nodded and stared straight ahead through the window at the river. Part of her calm was the clarity of knowing—from what her dream had shown her—that she'd be leaving soon. It was not that she wanted to go, but that any movement toward decision, any sense of certainty, was enough to lift her spirits.

Donnie glanced again at the sheet where her hand would have made a small mound. Its absence had intrigued him from the start, made him curious about the way she looked there; about how she'd lost her hand; he was interested to a degree he had never experienced, for he was not a curious man.

It was not curiosity but a kind of uncomplicated kindness that had caused him to pull to the shoulder of the parkway. He'd hoped for nothing from her, expected nothing, and would have let her, as he'd told her, continue on alone. But driving down the highway and recognizing her, he'd responded just as he had when he'd paid for her breakfast. What Donnie valued in life was an unabrasive ease, a certain simple geniality, and when he'd spotted Ramona walking effortfully along he knew, after

seeing her in the diner, that she was feeling the day as neither easy nor genial. So he'd given her a ride, then placed her in his bed, then let her stay through two days of food and sleep and easy exchanges of mindless talk—not once getting near the question of what she was hiding from—as she watched him fish the Kinderhook and bend like a worried surgeon over his motors. And all of it was guided by the same instinctive consideration of a man who found it easy to be kind to people because he'd never in his life thought very much about them. He felt no necessary connection with another human being, wished to arouse no particular response from anyone. So distant from concern, his abiding attitude could as easily have been ugly or dismissive, but Donnie's impulse, as it happened, was to kindness; the sincere and shallow kindness of a man who loved the embedded scent of engines in his grease-etched hands more than any human odor.

But now he glanced again at the sheet and felt the wish to draw it back.

With her eyes adjusted to the darkness, Ramona could see his face, the pouches beneath his eyes and the droop of his mouth that made him look to her inside some deeply private mourning. "I'm full," she said, confusing him. She was still a bit disoriented, slightly groggy, the dream leaving her so slowly she was having a difficult time speaking logically. She'd meant to say that she'd caught up on her sleep, but Donnie naturally thought she was referring to food.

"Good," he said. "It's about time you ate somethin'."

In fact, she had eaten little in the time she'd been here, her stomach a tight knot. But that hadn't concerned her. She'd passed most of two days in a working dreamlessness; sleep that had no time or strength for a nightmare's thoughts and sights.

She smiled and thought to try to explain to Donnie, then decided it didn't matter and sipped her whiskey.

But tonight she *had* dreamed, which she sensed meant that her sleep was now beyond the function of necessary nourish-

ment; that it now had time again for its terrible frivolity; it could play.

She looked at Donnie again, and, though she knew better, his face still appeared sad to her beyond the simple fall of its features, sad in response, a rooted sadness which began beneath its surface. "How'd it go tonight?" she asked. "You busy?"

"Real," he said, and began to talk about the night in the roadhouse bar he tended. She listened to him describe a regular drinker he'd mentioned once before, whom everyone called Jesus Christ, in part because he wore a full beard but mostly because he usually passed out three or four times over the course of a night, each time waking quite refreshed, lifting his head up off the bar and beginning again with a new and eager thirst, prompting someone to shout, "Jesus Christ just rose from the dead!"

She'd liked hearing about Jesus Christ and a few other memorable customers Donnie had described these past two days. It had made her feel secure, wrapped like a child in the protective warmth of stories. But now, as he spoke, pictures from her nightmare again claimed her attention—the children laughing as they drowned; her baby leaping from the porch, his sweet arms flapping wildly. Since she'd been here with Donnie she'd been able to stay for the most part inside the emptiness she sought. She'd slept. She'd watched him fish, watched him work, bending with loving concern over his engines while he told her roadhouse stories. And whenever her mind had moved toward thoughts, she'd fought them back with incantation: that she was here and not back there.

But now Jonas had found her, inside her dreams where she was helpless, and as she tried to listen to Donnie it occurred to her that she should have something, a weapon, something strongly charged to take with her when she departed the trailer and his company. She sensed a need for something haunting enough that she could let it loose inside her mind at times, driving thoughts of Jonas out.

She looked into Donnie's face, watching it as he talked, and its sadness seemed to be offering itself to her. She sensed that she could take *that* with her, a substituting sadness. Maybe she could make Donnie's sadness strange and real and use it as her weapon to confront the power of Jonas.

She leaned forward and touched his arm, stopping his talk. He looked at her, surprised, and his face seemed to say, Here. Take it. Use it any way you want.

She reached to touch it, to feel sadness's skin, and ran her fingers along the line of his jaw. "Fuck me," she whispered, and a shimmer of greater surprise lifted his eyes. "Fuck me, Donnie," she repeated and lay down in the bed, drawing the sheets aside as she slid forward, opening herself to him.

He rose and undressed quickly while she watched his grieving eyes and when he moved toward her she lifted her legs, asking for his face, for his mask of sorrow. He knelt to taste her. He knew that her stump was free, sensed it roaming erratically outside the sheets as if it were a freshly headless creature moving to the pulse of severed nerves. But now he felt he had no right to see it—his lust mindful and considerate in a way he'd never known—while she could not control the way she wished it shown.

She moved against his mouth and he murmured pleasure into her, the air of his voice like a word that found her everywhere. He pressed against her and Ramona closed her eyes as she felt his sad face fuck her.

Nine

he river was shallow and flowed rapidly past Donnie's trailer. A breeze ran with it, moving just above the water. On the flat, weeded bank, Ramona leaned forward and smiled as she felt the river's air on her face. She looked across the water, past sprouting rocks, to the woods. The low morning sun hit the leaves it could reach, pocking them with light. She sipped her coffee and leaned forward again to let the breeze touch her skin. A flannel shirt of Donnie's hung loosely on her.

"So that's why they call me Jew," Donnie said, speaking in a loud whisper over the river. Standing in the water, he flicked his rod forward, the line taking the time to draw a curl on the air, a whip of impossible thinness. Its fly nicked the surface like a feathery apostrophe.

Ramona watched him gather the line and cast again. She drew her knees up to her chest; her breasts felt the warmth of

her thighs. The baggy shirt covered her body like a smock. She shifted her feet to find a new coolness in a patch of damp packed earth among the low weeds. The morning's air was still, held closely by the woods, except for the small steady breeze the river made.

"Jew," she said, shaking her head and giggling. "I couldn't figure what he was talking about."

From where she'd listened inside the trailer yesterday, she was sure she'd heard the man who came to pick up his motor call Donnie Jew, seemingly with affection. And now Donnie had finished explaining that one night in the bar, some months ago, a stranger had listened to the regular customers calling to him, hailing him for refills, beckoning his attention; using what had been until that night his nickname. Knowing of his love for the river, of the hours he spent fishing it, many of the men had long ago begun to call him Fish Man.

"Another one here, Fish Man."

"I got a joke for you, Fish Man."

After a while, the stranger quickly stood to pay his bill, his face bright pink with distress, and said as he turned to leave, "I never thought I'd see the fuckin' day a Jew'd find his way up here and tend a decent bar." Donnie said he'd looked at him in complete confusion and then the man had said, "I may not be no genius, but I know for damn sure that there ain't a whole lot of Methodists named Fishman."

And then Donnie had laughed softly and said, "He just threw his money down and stomped out of the place. My mouth fell open so wide I coulda rented it. And then me and everybody else started laughin' like crazy. Well, you can imagine."

He'd shrugged, then turned and winked at her, and said, "So that's why they been calling me Jew."

Donnie dropped the fly onto the surface, its feather dancing brightly for trout, then quickly flicked it up, off the water.

"I ain't gonna call you Jew," Ramona said, laughing.

"Not everybody does," he said. "Just some of 'em at the bar."
His tone sounded almost reassuring, apologizing for any com-
plication he might be presenting her.

She smiled and drew her body tight, flexing it inside Donnie's
shirt. She felt a pleasurable exhaustion run through her limbs
and shoulders. She watched Donnie working the river, his
motions with the rod fluid and economical, metronomically
exact, and she had the sudden urge to touch him, to place her
palm on his hip. Though he was standing close to her he was
well beyond her reach, and yet she felt for a moment that she
might be able to touch his skin if she stretched her arm toward
him. Such a thing seemed almost possible this morning; seemed
very much worth trying.

Last night, she had lain next to Donnie and felt his body go
slack and then twitch viciously as though sleep were a charge of
electricity sent through him. She'd felt his chest grow and fall as
his breathing became deep and precise. She had planned to
move down into a heavy, mired sleep, holding as she fell the
gaze of Donnie's sadness; some first, harsh consequence of
asking him to fuck her. Instead, she had lain beside him, wildly
awake, and everything around her—the rush of the river; the
soft, vagrant ticking coming from the woods; the star-smoke
paleness of the sky shafting in through the window—all seemed
to rise and fall, brighten and dim, in time with Donnie's
breathing. Far from sinking gravely into the new and freighted
images she expected to take away with her, she'd been held in
the fever of a thrilling illicitness.

In the days with Donnie, before last night, she'd felt dreamily
grateful, insulated in a life that had no references she recognized. She'd felt so safely hidden that she'd been able to let
herself sleep. But last night, as she'd lain beside him after
making love, that sense of enveloping newness grew almost
minute by minute until finally, some hours into the night, she'd
felt it so intensely she began to laugh softly to herself. The grain

of her pillowcase and the shapes of the shadows, the sound of her pulse as it beat inside her ear—all these things astonished and beguiled her as she lay beside Donnie. It was as though in fucking him she had fucked this transporting newness as well. And though she sensed that the details of her distraction were absurd, were comic, they didn't lessen for her knowing so. She felt the soft bellows of his breath surrounding her, and then she remembered the light, lovely play of his air against her lips when he'd murmured his pleasure as he began to lick her. And once she'd felt that, she'd held it somewhere inside her, where it moved like a breath between her mind and her thighs, and then she'd wanted the charged exhilaration of that illicitness again.

Near dawn, she'd moved her head on her pillow, freeing his arm, and he stirred in reponse, turning over on his side. She'd felt his movement beside her as something no one had done in quite the same way before, and she'd placed her hand on his thigh and moved it down his leg. He'd stirred once again and turned obediently in his sleep toward her. She'd cupped his balls, had felt their warmth, their dampness, and heard him groan as she drew him toward a pleasure begun in quickly lifting sleep.

Standing in the river, Donnie arced the line forward, the fly settling delicately. "Hey," he whispered brightly as his rod quivered, then bent severely toward the water, and with a quick, clean twitch he sank the hook. The trout stood up on the river and skimmed along the surface, its tail swishing water in a violent sashay, then plunged again before Donnie brought it smoothly in. He netted the trout and walked to the bank, his waders shedding water.

Donnie reached her and knelt down, placing the trout in front of her. Ramona watched the fish; its back caught the sun, winking light.

"Ain't she gorgeous?" he asked.

Ramona studied the trout. She was surprised at its beauty, spots of yellow and red appearing almost painted to her. Its gills opened. It seemed to sigh melodramatically.

"It *is*," she said. She looked up at Donnie and ran her hand lightly down the length of his thin, mahogany arm. His eyes squinted in the sun. His hair, cut close, lay damp and crinkled against the side of his head.

Donnie guided the hook back through until it was free and carried the fish to the river and slipped it back into the water. It lay for a moment, then slithered away.

"Why'd you let it go?" Ramona asked. "It wasn't too little, was it? It was big, it looked to me."

Donnie walked back and sat down beside her, pulling his waders off. "Not too little," he said. "Too pretty."

Ramona smiled. "So you don't ever keep one?"

"Oh, sure," he said. "I have. I do."

"When they ain't as pretty?" Ramona asked.

"When I get hungry for trout," Donnie said.

Ramona looked into his face and again felt she had no idea what she was seeing in it. Was he showing her a permanent memory? A mournful glimpse of something he knew about his future? Or just the cast of his expression independent of a mood? It was still sometimes impossible for her to believe that he could look so sad and not be. She turned and looked over his shoulder to the pale green trailer. It appeared weightless to her. She imagined a strong breeze pushing it up the bank.

"So your dad never took you fishing?" he asked. He followed her fingers as they traced the top of his thigh.

"Nope. Never did," Ramona said.

Once again his curiosity about her was an impulse so strange to him he felt it as something almost physical; a kind of virus. Hearing himself asking her if she had fished, he felt the question leading to a dozen more. If there had been a river or a lake where she'd lived. If she'd continued, until now, to live there and if she had, what had made it such a life that she was

running from it. He felt, as he followed her hand down his leg until it rested on his knee, that he could simply begin, could ask her a question, and that another would follow and another after that.

He looked down and saw her small white feet pat the ground in a quick, rhythmic way. It seemed to Donnie a lighthearted gesture, and perhaps it was his certainty that her heart was not light that made it something which stirred him.

"Come here," he said and reached for the collar of her shirt. He loosened the first button, his eyes on her neck, her white skin spreading as the shirt parted. He ran his finger along the ridge of her breastbone. Her paleness amazed him, her skin so white in the sun as to make it appear more delicate than skin, some vulnerable tissue that skin protects. He moved his hand down to open the shirt more and instantly felt her body tense beneath his fingers.

"No," she whispered, barely shaking her head.

He rested his hand at the base of her neck. "It's fine," Donnie said. "It's fine." His fingers felt her swallow.

She leaned forward and kissed him. When she sat up on her knees, she felt the warmth of the weeds along her shins. She wanted to move more deeply down into the place she had found since she had fucked him, to once again misplace her life, and as she edged closer to him she glimpsed the sense that, not merely had these days taken her far from what she'd known, but she, herself, was someone else as long as she was in them.

She felt his fingers drifting downward again. She heard him say it would be fine. She couldn't think of the possibility of his seeing her harnessed; her straps as they ran over her shoulders and crossed behind at her shoulder blades; the coil and cable of the hand.

"No," she whispered again and she moved on her knees in the riverbank's warm grass, lifting the flannel shirt up over her hips, wanting to move his interest there. She kissed him again

until he lay back and then she raised her leg and slid it over his chest. Straddling him, offering him everything else.

But as she bent to kiss him she felt the shirt fall forward like a gift and again he reached for her and said it would be fine. She closed her eyes and felt him opening the shirt. Her body coiled. She felt his fingers moving as though each button were a thing to devote his time to. And then she looked at him, tried to bring him into focus, and she believed she was seeing his sadness lifting, though in fact Donnie's face was simply rapt, almost clinically alert.

The warmth of the air found her stomach, her breasts, and then his hands were on her shoulders, resting on her straps. She closed her eyes again and felt the shirt fall away. Her body tightened as the sun touched her neck, spread over her back. Yes, she thought she heard him say. She felt his hands move to her breasts. She tried to know only that his hands were lightly cupping them, so she wouldn't see a picture of herself in her mind. But the sun on her back was strong, telling her that she was naked. She wanted him to understand that she knew she was ugly, that her body in the harness was even more disgusting than when she was without it. She didn't open her eyes.

The touch of his fingers moved into her breasts and through her; and then his hands moved upward and slipped beneath her harness straps. She felt them pulling. Her eyes were closed and she swallowed with some effort.

But her skin beneath his hands felt almost to be flowing, like the river, and she found she wanted him to touch her in any way he would. She moved her shoulder, a languorous reflex, moved it in a slow, circular cooperation to help the harness strap slide down her arm, as though it were the thin silk strap of a slip she was shedding. As though she were letting herself be undressed, the harness a light and filmy garment women wore for a lover to remove. "Oh, God," she breathed. She moved her other shoulder in the same slow circle to let Donnie's fingers under the strap, and felt it fall, felt it all being eased from her

back, from her arm. She began to rock slowly, free in her new nakedness.

Donnie looked up and saw her head fall back. He felt her ass gently rise and fall. The muscles of her thighs flexed as she moved. Her tiny breasts trembled. He watched her reach back, as though to steady herself, and felt her hand opening his jeans. And then he reached for her other arm and held it at the tip of its rounded, sculpted bone. His fingers touched the pattern of its healing, a fold of skin like lips primly pressed. He felt her touching him, but his response seemed somewhere far away on his body, dim and distant from the secret he was holding, and he moved beneath her, sliding down in the grass to draw her toward his face.

He held her wrist again, and ran his tongue along the line of skin. And as he kissed it, Donnie sensed that she was answering his interest beyond anything he'd dreamed, letting him touch her in a way that made last night's love—with his face wet against her lips and his tongue inside her—seem a formal moment; as though she had only now let him into her deepest intimacy, her true cunt.

Ramona watched him kissing her. Sweat was running down her cheeks, in lines between her breasts. The sun on her spine was once again lubricant, her mind inside a pleasure as dimensional as thought. She leaned down to his face and moved her arm away from his mouth so that she could kiss him. Then she gave it back to him and his tongue anointed it; then she took it away once more and kissed him. Then gave him back her stump, his saliva a warm unguent; then lifted it away and kissed him. . . .

They sat at the window, looking out at the night. The sound of the frogs was almost a braying.

Ramona said, surprised, "I thought you'd been here for a long time. It feels like you have."

"Not *here*. Not *this* spot," Donnie said. He leaned forward toward the window, as if to get a better angle of the darkness. "But on the Kinderhook, yeah. I been on the river . . . forever. Last year, over by Hillsdale." He smiled. "Before that"—he tilted his head—"up by Malden Bridge." He laughed. "It's a long, skinny river."

"How long you gonna stay here?" she asked.

Donnie shrugged. "I don't think about it till I leave." He smiled and sipped a beer. "After I been some place awhile, I catch a fish, and I swear it's the same damn fish I caught the day before." He laughed again. "I swear I know it. Then it's for sure I need to move."

Ramona shook her head. "But don't it *always* seem the same? You're always on the river."

"When I first get a spot, it feels like I never seen a river in my life . . . every time. And it feels like that for a while."

"How old was you?" she asked.

He shifted in the bed and looked up at the ceiling. "Twelve, maybe. Thirteen. I can't remember." He laughed. "It was February third. I know that, anyway."

"You know the date?" Ramona said. "That's amazing."

"No it ain't. It was my birthday."

"No shit?" Ramona said, delighted. She turned onto her stomach and propped herself on her elbows to look at him. She said teasingly, "Some little sweetie's birthday present? 'Happy birthday, Donnie'?"

Donnie chuckled softly, still looking at the ceiling. "Sort of," he said. "Except it was my aunt."

"Your aunt?" she said. "What'd she do?"

He laughed. "What do you mean, 'What'd she do'?" He ran his fingers lightly down the furrow of her spine. "You tryin' to pretend you don't know how it works, you're talkin' to the wrong man."

"Come on. How'd it happen you got fucked by your aunt? What'd she say? 'Look here, Donnie, I got a present for ya'?"

He looked at her and smiled. "You ask a lotta questions." His eyes moved down her body. His hand rested in the small of her back.

She swung her legs in the air. "Come *on*," she said.

He smiled. He completely understood Ramona's asking him questions. Curiosity was a new language he was also restless to speak. And more, he sensed that she had answered—on the riverbank the day before—his most delicate question, so she had the right now to ask him anything.

"Tell me what she did," Ramona teased.

He laughed. "Like you said. She took me upstairs and said, 'Come here, Donnie, I got a present for ya.' "

Ramona squealed and kicked her legs. "Really? What'd you think?"

Donnie said, " 'Think'? *Thinkin'* didn't have much to do with it."

"Your mom ever find out?"

"Not unless my aunt told her." Then he said, "I never had much to do with my folks." He heard himself saying this, voluntarily. A quick simple sentence that seemed a full invitation.

He looked into Ramona's face with that abrupt directness which still surprised her, the sudden cutting of his focus through a soft bleak gaze. He said, "What about you?"

There was no urgent sequence to his interest in Ramona. But given what he might have asked, what else he wanted to know, the question was almost circuitous.

She looked away from him, at the wall, then nodded slightly. "I like my folks all right," she said. She was amazed to feel that she wanted to say more. "They moved away a few years ago." She was silent for a time, her eyes still on the wall. She said, "My mom came to visit when I was in the hospital."

Donnie glanced at her wrist, her word "hospital" having

touched his reflex. Her hand, cupped into a shell, lay over it. He'd noticed, when she was naked, that she often covered it in this way. Having seen it, now knowing it, Donnie wanted to learn how her wrist had been made. For that was how he thought of it, not as an absence but as something that had been made.

They lay beside each other, he on his back, Ramona on her stomach. The inside of the trailer was dead with heat. The temperature tonight had dropped only slightly and there was little air coming in through the tiny window. Outside, on the river, the frogs decried the steamy night.

She came up from the riverbank and saw him, a motor's parts spread before him on the long wooden bench he kept outside. He always worked in early afternoon when the sun was high in the sky, providing him with light that shone directly into a motor's niches.

Walking toward him, she thought again of Donnie's life, up and down the Kinderhook as it wound through the woods. The idea had come to seem almost magical to her. A life of flowing rootlessness, rooted to the river.

She reached his side but he didn't look up. She picked up a small oblong part which lay drying on a cloth. It gleamed preciously after soaking in a can of oil. "Oh," she said, a play of gravity in her voice, "this here is the trouble."

Donnie grunted absently.

She turned it in the sun. "Yeah," she said. "Anybody oughta see that right away. I'll just throw it in the river."

Still looking down into the motor, Donnie reached for the part and took it from her.

She sat on one end of the bench, dangling her legs. She said, "You had a lot of women, Donnie? You musta. Drivin' up and down the highway lookin' for 'em, like you do."

"Umm," he said, barely audibly. He closed the jaws of his wrench around a bolt.

"Hey!" Ramona said, giggling. "Driving up and down the highway, lookin' for women. It's like fishin', ain't it? It's the exact same thing!" She picked up another part. "Oh, shit, you must have had a *lotta* women. How many, do you figure?" She leaned over the motor, and he moved her back with his arm.

"You're makin' shadows," he mumbled.

He straightened up, squinted fiercely, and reached for a cloth. Drying his hands, he looked at her and said, holding his smile as best he could, "A hundred eighty."

"What?"

"You wondered how many women I had." He took the part from her. "You're a hundred eighty-one. But there ain't many on the highway. Most of 'em come in the bar."

Ramona laughed and kicked at him. He caught and held her foot.

"Well, what the hell?" she said. "What goes on there, anyway?"

"You just have to come some night," he said, letting her foot slide through his hand. "See for yourself."

She slipped quietly out of the trailer, making sure the flimsy screen didn't slam and wake him. The shade of dusk was a filter on the woods. She walked to the edge of the river, then got out into the water. Its chill was instantaneous.

The river seemed to pull at her ankles as it twined over her feet. She stood for just a moment, the cold climbing her legs, then hurried out and walked along the bank to sit on Donnie's workbench. She lit a cigarette, swinging her legs absently as she sat and smoked. The cricket sounds of listless dusk were louder than the river.

Part of her was still inside the trailer and the hour of languid

love they'd made, her mood a mix of that and this airless afterward. In her mind, she still saw Donnie's hard, dark body over her. Crouched on his hands and knees, he'd made a cloak of shadow over her, and she felt again the delight of being draped by it.

She relished the eagerness with which Donnie explored her. She'd felt from him no moment of hesitancy; only a keen and open wanting, yet with his particular calm as part of it. And as she smoked and heard the pulsing of the crickets, it occurred to her how grateful she was that he'd not known her before her accident, had no memory of her to place against the sight and sensation of her now. And from this thought, she remembered her conviction that Ed had constantly made just that comparison. They had fucked in awkward silence from the moment they'd resumed, and that had been her way of knowing. *He* had never touched her scar with his hand or his mouth. She'd been as sure of Ed's revulsion as she had been of her own.

She felt a vague revenge as she saw in her mind some of the ways their bodies, hers and Donnie's, had joined. Revenge had run mutedly through much of what had thrilled her here. She thought again of Donnie's mouth moving everywhere on her, then of Ed comparing her with the way she had been.

She flicked her cigarette away and lit another.

Donnie woke to her absence and rose groggily in bed. He listened, heard silence in the trailer, and leaned toward the window. The sky was getting dark and he could just see her shape perched on his bench.

He turned and looked at his bed. The past few days ran unspecifically through his mind. He pictured again the first night, when she'd reached to touch his face, then lain back and raised her legs in invitation. He thought of other women he had brought to the trailer. Very few had stayed past the following morning. One, the schoolteacher from Hudson he'd brought

home after work on Friday night, had stayed a week. She kept saying she found the way he lived "a revelation."

From the night his Aunt Ellen had guided him, hard and bewildered, into his gift, Donnie had fucked women eagerly and attentively, but with a narrow range of afterthoughts, none of them lingering concern. And now he looked out his window to where he knew Ramona sat and thought how pleased he was to know that she was there, in the dark, swinging her legs as she sat on his bench. And once more he asked himself why. He sensed that the birth of curiosity in him had much to do with the way her toughness came out of her small, child's body. She looked so young, often seemed to him incredibly fragile, and as soon as he'd begun to think of her that way, she somehow showed him a strength or an anger that were old and full. He was continually surprised when it happened. He thought again of her turning to the waitress in the diner that first morning—exhausted, her clothes filthy, looking like a helpless orphan—and saying calmly and firmly that she couldn't pay the check.

Ramona held her legs out in front of her and watched them disappearing in the quickly growing darkness. To her distress, she began to feel that her mood, after her thoughts of Ed, was darkening similarly. She tried to stop it by thinking of Donnie's mouth accepting her, but now the thought of him was leading to a regret that he *hadn't* known her before. If he could fuck her so eagerly now, she thought, imagine how he'd have wanted her if he'd known her before. She sat, the night settling over her until she couldn't see her body, and began to try to imagine how much more he would have felt.

At the window, Donnie watched her blending into the darkness. He reached for his jeans, his T-shirt. His grogginess had lifted, and night heat never dulled him. He remembered the surprise he had for her and moved toward the door. He stumbled in the dark against a chair and switched on a light.

Ramona turned as the window behind her yellowed suddenly

with light. She watched Donnie step out and walk slowly toward her.

"Hi," she said, trying not to let him hear what her mood had become.

He paused only briefly beside her, then continued toward the river. "Stay there," he said over his shoulder.

"Where you goin'?" she asked.

"Right here," he said. "Stay there."

She heard him reach the river, heard his hands in its current change the rhythm of its ordinary splashing.

"What are you doing?" she asked. She was intrigued, because she couldn't see him, but still her mind was mostly on her wish that he had known her before. She saw him making love to her an hour ago. And now she found herself suddenly uncertain that his eagerness was real. She asked herself how it could be. She'd been remembering how Ed had wanted her before.

As he came up to her in the dark, she heard the faint jingling of a chain and a soft flesh-slapping sound. "Look," Donnie said.

"What?"

"Use your lighter."

She sparked its flame and he brought them under its weak light.

"Ain't they somethin'?" he said, laughing. Four lovely trout hung from the chain, their dead-bright eyes perfect beads. She looked up, but she couldn't see his face at all. It was beyond the cast of the lighter's narrow flame. "Supper," he whispered.

In the flame of the lighter, she saw their bellies flash metallically. They looked to her like slices of the silver river in her dream of Jonas drowning.

"Jesus," she said, as Donnie pulled into the parking lot. "Is anybody left at home?" Cars and pickups ran in careless rows to the edges of the lot. Dozens more lined the sides of the intersecting highways.

"Friday night," Donnie said. "I told ya. It's the only game in town." There was affection in his voice, for her and for the scene he'd assured her they would find.

He found a spot where the lot became open field again and squeezed the station wagon between two pickups. As they walked toward the bar their shoes crunched the gravel. Ramona heard the faint, even beating of the jukebox escaping through the walls. The building seemed to squat as though in hiding, its roofline dipping shallowly against the summer sky. Several additions branched off the low main room which faced the highways at an angle.

She felt jumpy with excitement and tightened her grip on Donnie's hand.

"Remember," he said, looking straight ahead. "When the women start comin' after me, you gotta save me."

"Hell no," she said, laughing. "That's what I come to see."

Inside, he led her through a cluster of men standing near the door for the air they could get when someone opened it.

"Hey, Jew," one of them said. "You workin' tonight?"

"All I ever do," Donnie said.

"My ass," the man said and laughed, slapping Donnie on the back.

They reached a stool near the end of the bar. Donnie stood beside her, nodding to the bartender he was about to relieve, nodding to the row of regulars.

"How's it goin', Jew?" the bartender said.

Ramona looked around her. She was bathed in buoyant noise. Country music. Women's whoops. Trills of laughter cutting through the steady low-smoke clamor.

"Get to work." She smiled at Donnie. "I'm thirsty." Because the bar was huge, and the sound flowed easily into all the added rooms, its general noise stayed just below her voice.

He looked past her shoulder to a clock on the wall. Then his eyes brightened as he saw, one stool away, a man slumped on the bar, his head buried in his arms. Tapping Ramona's arm, he

pointed at the man. She turned and saw a head of thick brown hair and, running from his sideburns, the evidence of a beard.

Donnie said, smiling, "You're in luck. It's Jesus Christ." He shouted to the bartender, "He went down earlier'n usual."

The bartender nodded. "He got a big raise at the plant. Been celebrating."

Donnie moved past Jesus Christ to the end of the bar and stepped around behind it. "How many times is that so far?" he asked.

"First time he's died tonight," the bartender said.

Donnie opened a cooler and set a beer in front of Ramona. "Here you are, ma'am," he said, then someone down the bar called to him and he winked and moved away.

She drank from the bottle, keeping her hand in her lap beneath the bar. This morning, the sense of the hand she'd lost had been so strong that she'd opened her eyes as Donnie kissed her stump, in part surprised to see his tongue not sliding over fingers.

Jesus Christ slept beside her. She turned her head to watch him. He was quiet and his shoulders barely rose and fell.

She watched Donnie move unhurriedly up and down the busy bar, his motions as precise as his graceful casts for trout. He reached without a pause for liquor on the shelves behind him. He opened the beer coolers with a smooth, slight bump of his hip against the handle as he took someone's money, drew a draft, wiped the bar. All the while, he chatted easily with several men at once, listening and nodding with a democratic dispensation of interest and advice.

He gave Ramona no more or less attention than anyone else, but he frequently caught her eye. It made her feel he hadn't lost the sense of her nearby. She watched him, happy and impressed. He seemed to her a celebrity.

She spun around to watch the crowd. Unlike the bar, where the only other woman sat next to Ramona, the huge room was filled with couples eating and drinking. People spoke back and

forth from table to table, a network of shouted talk. On the small wooden floor in front of the jukebox, dancers moved, embracing stiffly, determined as wrestlers, the men stomping the floor as if it were a layer of ice they were trying to break up with the heels of their boots.

"I hate it, too."

Ramona turned to the woman beside her. "How's that?" she asked.

"I hate drinkin' with a crowd behind my back," the woman said. "I saw you jerk around on your stool." She nodded, her thin, tired face all empathy. "Somebody standin' behind me. It makes me nervous as hell," she said.

Ramona smiled. "This ain't the place to come if you don't like to drink with a crowd behind ya."

The woman shook her head. "Where else is there?"

Ramona shrugged her shoulders.

"Ancram? Millerton?" She snorted, disgusted. "Where a woman can go, I mean, and have a few drinks. You got some place in mind?"

"I don't," Ramona said.

"You're damn right you don't," the woman said. "Because there ain't no place else." She finished her drink and pushed her glass forward on the bar. "Where a woman can go and have a few drinks, I mean."

"I guess you're right," Ramona said. She took a drink.

The woman ground her cigarette into an ashtray, then whirled around and watched the room.

Donnie reached them, picked up the woman's empty glass. "How's your beer?" he asked Ramona.

She smiled and nodded. "I'm fine." She rolled her eyes toward the woman. "This what I'm supposed to be savin' you from?"

"You got it," he said. "You see the problem." He shook his head, pretending exasperation, as he mixed the woman another drink. He saw a customer waving money at him from the

middle of the bar. "I appreciate your help," he said, stepping away to take the man's money.

"Mellenville?" the woman offered as she spun around again. "You know a place in Mellenville we could go and have a few drinks?"

Ramona shook her head. It was the first town the woman had mentioned that Ramona knew well and in her mind the main street of Mellenville came into focus. She asked herself how far away Mellenville was.

"That's because there ain't none," said the woman. "Just the Legion Hall. But hell, that makes this place seem like a church."

She drew her drink toward her and shook her head at it. The woman said, "There's that place in Myles. Myles ain't all that far. But who wants to go to Myles?" She took a drink and set it down. "I was in the bar there once. Christ. *That* ain't no place to go."

Ramona hadn't listened after hearing the woman say that Myles was not that far. Her impulse had been to disagree, to insist that Myles was nowhere near. She smiled faintly at the woman, nodding agreement with whatever she was saying now. She looked up and down the bar, glanced at Jesus Christ beside her. As if on cue he stirred a bit and made a muffled noise, a shudder moving across his shoulders. She turned around again, watched a couple hopping awkwardly around the dance floor. And everything she saw was filtered through the woman's words—that Myles was not that far.

She realized that the woman had stopped talking, was sipping her drink in a fidgeting silence. "How far is it?" Ramona asked her. "Myles. How far is it from here?"

The woman shrugged. "I don't know. Twelve, thirteen miles, I guess. Fifteen, maybe. Less, if you could drive a straight road, which you can't." She pointed to Ramona's pack of cigarettes on the bar and raised her eyebrows. Ramona pushed it toward her. "But I'm telling you, honey. Weren't you listening? The bar there is a pit. I was in it once."

Twelve miles. Ramona asked herself how long the drive would take. She thought to ask the woman, then realized she didn't want to know, and she tried to take some comfort from the notion that the roads snaked inconveniently.

Donnie moved past, setting a fresh beer in front of her before he noticed how little of her first she'd drunk. "C'mon," he said. "I can't make any money off you at that rate."

She stared at him and smiled belatedly.

The woman turned and began to talk forcefully to the bald man on the other side of her. Ramona saw the man spin around and inspect the crowd and say he'd never really thought about it before.

At a table in a far corner, a group began to sing "Happy Birthday," to a record on the jukebox. The men at the table howled like dogs as they sang the word "you."

Ramona turned and watched the men competing, their baying rising ever higher whenever a "you" came around. One of them began to yip like a puppy as he held his plaintive ". . . ooooo!"

It suddenly seemed to Ramona the sort of drunken play she'd seen all her life. She knew this very scene, knew she'd been one of those women at the table laughing drunkenly. It was not illusion, no *déjà vu*, that held her; it was memory, all too clear, and the nearness of Myles was encompassing her.

She turned her attention to the bar, eavesdropping on the pockets of overlapping talk.

"Man, I'd crawl six miles over broken glass just to smell the ground where she pissed six months ago." . . . "That Steve. He's a goer, that son of a bitch is, I'll give him that." . . . "Fuck! I'd crawl ten miles over broken glass just to sniff the mud flaps on the laundry truck that's haulin' her dirty skivvies." . . . "Yeah, he's quite a Steve."

She was hearing Myles. She wondered how she could ever have been feeling far away, safely distant. The sensation, as she'd walked through the door with Donnie, that she had never

seen festivity in quite this way before came back to her. She'd felt as though she were watching something absolutely new, a foreign ceremony. And now she scanned the bar, watched the people, and recognized them all.

"You all right?" Donnie asked. He was standing in front of her. She looked up into his face and remembered for the first time in days how she'd planned to use its sadness.

"How come?" she said.

"You looked like you was a long ways away."

She smiled at his words. "No," she said, "I ain't."

Donnie's eyes shifted slightly as something caught his attention. "Well, look who's here," he said. "Good morning, J.C."

Ramona glanced to see that Jesus Christ was sitting up beside her. He blinked once and looked around, and when he turned to her she saw that, just as Donnie had described, his face was remarkably fresh, no patina of sleep or vagueness showing on it. He nodded at her, clearly aware of where he was and where he'd been.

Smiling, Donnie raised his arms and shouted down the bar, "Jesus Christ has rose from the dead!"

A loud wave of *Hallelujah!* came back toward Jesus Christ.

He smiled broadly at Donnie. "Morning, Jew," he said. "I seem to need two beers." Donnie had told her he always ordered two beers at a time.

Because she'd only pictured him when Donnie spoke his nickname, Ramona had unthinkingly seen his face as the common image of the Lord's: pale and drawn; a look of sweetly forlorn delicacy. But now she saw that Jesus Christ's face was extremely wide and bright, fat as a cherub's, but tight-skinned and seamless, his cheeks swelling above his beard like a squirrel's holding walnuts.

He said to Donnie, "I ever tell you about the time I almost met Teddy Kennedy?"

Donnie said, "You almost met Teddy Kennedy?" Ramona

remembered Donnie's description of this nightly routine between them.

"I was workin' construction, out in the Dakotas."

"North or South?" Donnie asked.

"*East*," said Jesus Christ. "East Dakota. 1980."

"That was when he was runnin' to be president?" Donnie asked.

"Oh," he said, and paused, "you was thinkin' I meant *that* Teddy Kennedy."

Donnie smiled. "I'll get your beers." As he moved away to draw them, he placed his hand for a moment on Ramona's arm.

"Ah," said Jesus Christ, having seen Donnie's gesture. "So this is *you*." He drew back on his stool to take her in and when he smiled his cheeks ballooned. "Good God, you're a baby. Jew's robbin' the cradle on us." He smiled more. "No offense."

Ramona reddened immediately, nearly all of it anger. "Donnie talked about me?"

"You kiddin'?" he said and waved his hand. "If he'd talked about you, that'd be talkin' about himself. Right?"

He continued, "No. Billy Schuyler come in the other afternoon. He'd been out to Jew's to pick up a motor and seen you was there. Bill used to be the best snoop around here until his arthritis got so bad. Can't cover the territory he used to."

She remembered the man's stiff, hitching gait, one hip cocked, as he'd moved slowly toward his car past the trailer, where she'd sat back from the window in what she'd thought concealing shade.

Donnie brought two bottles of beer. He said, "I hear you got a raise."

"I did for a fact," Jesus Christ said and pulled a swollen wallet from a pocket in his jeans. "Lookit." He opened it to show Donnie a width of dollar bills, thick as a book. He said, "I cashed the whole check just to see how it would look." He stared into

his wallet and angled it toward Ramona as though sharing a photograph. "Ain't they beautiful?" he said.

Ramona only nodded as he closed the wallet and sat it on the bar. She heard Jesus Christ tell Donnie of a new place on the Kinderhook where he'd caught fish last Saturday. On the other side of her, the pinch-faced woman stood unsteadily to leave. The legs of her slacks were wet from sweat and she pulled them away from the backs of her thighs. The bald man she'd been talking to stood too, ran his palm over his head, and gulped the last of his beer.

The woman turned to Ramona. "He says he knows a place where there ain't a crowd behind our back." One of her eyelids fell, like an owl's. "I'll let you know if it's any place a woman can go and have a few drinks." She waved at Ramona as they worked their way toward the door.

The smoke and heat and music had seemed to merge, like a climate. Ramona looked along the backs of the drinkers at the bar. Down at the other end, she saw for the first time a German shepherd sleeping obliviously. She wondered if the dog had been there all night long, and suddenly the story of a dog that lived in a bar as its lumbering mascot seemed very familiar to her, something she'd been told about. But where and by whom? Had it been Ed who'd come home one night and told about a dog that was owned by the regulars in a bar? An empty coffee can kept on the bar for change to buy its food? Had Ed been in this bar, seen the dog she was watching? Or had it just been that a dog had strayed into the Hill Top and stayed for a while?

She thought of Ed, only twelve miles away, and she vividly imagined, for the first time in days, his certain pursuit of her. *I'm coming for you.*

She heard Ed saying, "I'm coming for you." She turned and looked through the thin drift of smoke to the front door and pictured him entering, threading his way through the crowd, his eyes finding her immediately. His index finger pointing and his smile breaking whitely. The same angled smile, the smile

he'd flashed when he was eighteen, leaning from the window of Luther Sherrill's pickup; meaning nothing it had meant then; meaning many things it hadn't.

Ramona was aware of her fear sending coldness through her in the bar's stifling heat, a malarial chill too full to be prepared for.

"That's what makes him such a good fucking bartender." She realized Jesus Christ was speaking to her. She looked at him and saw him nod emphatically, then take one of his beers and drink half of it. "You get drunk—and it can happen—and say somethin' to Jew you maybe should have kept to yourself? It's like you never said it." He swept his hand in front of him to show how the words disappeared without a trace.

"Yeah," Ramona said. She thought of how she had foolishly pictured Donnie's life, tucked into the woods, always on the move. Of its inevitable secrecy. "Yeah," she repeated, "I guess that's right."

Jesus Christ finished his first beer and began the other. His face appeared to be growing puffier, looking even more cherubic, and she remembered Donnie telling her that, in fact, he was mildly allergic to beer and that his face swelled up in response, sometimes looking badly bee-stung by the end of the night.

"It *is* right," he insisted seriously. Ramona saw that his focus was failing again. Donnie had told her that he passed out more quickly each time as the night went along. "And that's the funny thing."

"What?" Ramona asked, feeling cold. She couldn't believe he was still talking to her, wished he'd hurry to his second death.

"Well," he said, slurring in a way that gave his speech a slow effeminacy, "here's a guy that don't tell nobody nothin', but everyfuckingbody knows Jew. Some people, he's the Fish Man. Or just Donnie. Or Jew. But you go in any bar in three counties, they know who you mean." He put his beer to his lips and finished a good deal of it.

"You know," said Jesus Christ, turning still more serious, "you're very important. Jew's never brought a woman in, any place he's worked. I know that for a fact." His manner was gravely confidential. "I've drunk beer with Jew for years and he *never* brought a woman in. And now, by God, here you are!" She watched his eyes begin to deaden.

Ramona turned to Donnie just as he looked at her. He seemed to think she was signaling Jesus Christ's fall from consciousness and he nodded knowingly.

She saw Donnie's pattern clearly now—working here and there throughout the country as he changed his trailer's location. He had lived around here all his life and he'd tended bars up and down a local river. How many bars over the years? She realized that his life on the river might have been hidden, but his amiable work was open and public.

She heard Jesus Christ mumble, "Jew's a mystery man that everybody knows." She watched him laboriously withdraw bills from his wallet to pay for his beers. "Hey," he said, delighted, "that's pretty good." He looked down at Donnie and shouted, "Hey, Jew! I just told her you're a mystery man that everybody knows! Pretty fuckin' good, huh?"

Donnie shook his head. "Good night, J.C.," he said.

Ramona tried to think of the lovely invisibility that had seemed to settle over them in the trailer in the woods. She glanced down at the hand in her lap and thought that if everyone knew Donnie, she'd quickly become known if she was with him.

"The mystery man, the mystery man. Oh, do you know the mystery man?" Out of the corner of her eye, she could see Jesus Christ's body starting forward. She turned. His profile was pinkly bulbous. She watched him pick up his wallet where it lay beside the money he'd withdrawn and reach around to put it away, but it was so thick with bills that he could force it only partially into his pocket, and he was too drunk to feel it slip out onto the floor.

She saw Donnie walking toward her, pointing amusedly, and she continued to watch him even as Jesus Christ fell forward onto the bar, his face burrowing into his arms.

Donnie was smiling, much too brightly to be of any use to her. She tried to recall the sensation of his fingers on her shoulders; of her feeling, as she'd let her harness straps slide down her arms, that she was letting filmy silk fall seductively away. She pictured the trailer and the woods, to see if she could take with her something from the river. But she saw the silver-sharded fish, and the river, too, was gleaming, Jonas's smile floating in it.

"Gone, I see," Donnie said, shaking his head fondly at Jesus Christ. He took his empty bottles and the money he needed from the pile of bills.

"Yeah," Ramona said, as she eased down off her stool and swept the wallet toward her with her shoe. She tried to make her voice sound light. "How many times a night does he get born again?" She had the wallet now between her feet.

Donnie wiped the bar and emptied an ashtray. "Sometimes three, four times maybe." He shrugged and laughed. "Sometimes he never does."

Ten

The Dodge raced down Summit, wisping dust into the air. Its tires shot surface gravel toward the sidewalks as it passed, *pinged!* hubcaps, motorcycle rims, the front of the ice machine by the door of the Hill Top. A sound of high, torqued injury from its engine filled the street, and the men in the Hill Top spun around on their stools to glimpse the Dodge's white tail as it hurried on toward Ed's mother's house, three blocks up the hill. The sound of the Dodge had become instantly recognizable in Myles and people jerked attentively, on the streets or in their houses, whenever they heard it.

"Hear that goddam car everywhere I turn," said Broder, in the Hill Top. He continued to stare out the window, the torpor of Saturday afternoon a kind of finish on the defeated expanse of Summit Street framed in the tavern's window.

"Everywhere," agreed Moon, behind the bar. "You look up,

don't make a shit where you are, here's King haulin' ass down the street." Moon was fat, completely bald, no more than five feet tall. His name was Leonard Umble, but he was called Moon by all his customers, because, as they stood opposite him, his huge round head made them think of one, increasingly so as their drinking nights progressed. Moon's face gave off the reflected glow of the beer signs around him and was lit to an opacity, hovering always above the line of the bar as if it were about to set.

Moon continued, "Son of a bitch come near running me over, when was it, Wednesday maybe?" He shook his head. "Took that corner by his mother's. Leaped right up on the curb."

"I seen that," Broder said. "He just about lost it, looked to me. I was meaning to ask you what that was about."

"About my *ass*," Moon said. "That's what it was about. He's drivin' the sidewalk maybe twenty, thirty yards. I just got out of the way."

"Looked to me like you just got out of the way," Broder said.

"Just," said Moon.

"I was meaning to ask you what that was about," Broder said.

People were especially surprised by Ed's recklessness because they remembered so well how he'd always driven around town, the mannered crawls of motor-screaming serenity, and they all agreed that the change in his style had to do with Ramona's flight. No one knew why one could cause the other, but everyone was absolutely certain that it had.

Lovilla Adams stood at the plate-glass window of Dee's Luncheonette, holding her eyes on the street, as Broder did from the Hill Top on the opposite side of Summit. In the five years since she had stood with Ramona in the gas station's lot and watched Ed ride away in Luther Sherrill's pickup, Lovilla's

body had become square, and her arms were shaped like hams, narrowing from the elbow to slender wrists and hands.

She turned away toward the table where Wilma Jean Robertson drank coffee.

"You see him?" Wilma Jean asked.

Lovilla shrugged, dropping into her chair. "I saw *it*," she said, meaning the Dodge. "He's scrunched down so low. Wearin' that hat pulled down over his eyes . . ." She shrugged again.

Wilma Jean nodded, drew deeply on her cigarette, then put it out in the ashtray with a series of quick stabs. She was tall and as thin as she'd been at sixteen. She took a stick of gum from her purse and began to chew it so fiercely her nose moved. "You was *quick*, Lo," she said admiringly to Lovilla. "You jumped outa your chair like you was bit."

Wilma Jean was the youngest member of a local women's social club, the Myles Matronettes. She was proud of the fact that she'd been invited to join, of her status as the only Matronette under thirty years old. The Matronettes were devoted to improving the quality of life in Myles. They tried, for instance, every spring to grow gardens in the meager soil of the lots on Summit Street. With spades and hoes, they hacked at the cracked, gray dirt. Their tools clanged against bits of brick, square-headed nails. They spent a full weekend chopping up the earth and cursing the idea and setting beds of flowers that lived through some of June.

Lovilla said, "Remember the talk the day she took off? That she left Jonas layin' in the grass? Even after I told everybody I seen Bumbry had him."

"God it was hot," said Wilma Jean. "I was in the store, back at the meat counter, and Don was tellin' me not to buy anything, the cooler wasn't right and all the meat was goin' bad. Then Ewel Chesley come in and said the kid was missin' and she was who knows where."

Lovilla said, "I wonder why the talk was she took off in the Dodge?"

"I don't know," said Wilma Jean. "I remember thinkin' to myself, how'd she *shift* it, with the hand, I mean? I was standin' at the meat counter with this picture in my mind of her in the car, leaning over the shift and gettin' it into gear with her *teeth* somehow."

In the Hill Top, Broder turned back to face the bar and shook his head at Moon.

Moon said, "I heard he's been sittin' out in back of his house every night. He's made a little shanty, like a lean-to, out of them car doors piled up back there. He comes home from work, picks up the paper on the sidewalk, got a six-pack in his hand, goes straight out back. Don't even set foot in the house. Reads the paper, drinks his beer, propped up in his little lean-to like he's set in bed for the night. I don't know. That's what I heard."

"Where'd you hear that?" Broder asked. His wide face grew more detailed with his attentiveness.

"Somebody," Moon said. "I can't remember. I know I heard it."

"What's goin' on in the house if he's out back?"

"Nothin'. Nothin' goin' on in the house. What is there could go on? She's left, the kid's with his mother. The house is total dark."

"And he's out back?" Broder asked.

"Sittin' under these car doors he's got, you know, arranged, I guess," Moon said.

"Readin' the paper?" Broder asked.

"Like he's propped up in bed waitin' for Johnny Carson to come on."

"And you seen this yourself?"

*   *   *

Lovilla asked Wilma Jean, "She ever say anything to you?"

Wilma Jean knew Lovilla's reference. "You mean about leavin' again?" She popped her gum loudly and glanced at Lovilla in a blink-quick furtive way. "No," Wilma Jean answered. She paused. "Did she you?"

Lovilla nodded slightly. "Yeah. But I never figured, after the first time . . ." She looked at Wilma Jean. "You think he's been lookin' for her?"

Wilma Jean stiffened undetectably. "I don't know. Do you?"

"I guess not," said Lovilla. "I ain't sure why I think that. I guess 'cause you figure, if he had've, he'da found her." Lovilla shrugged again, a slow movement of ursine heft.

"I know," said Wilma Jean. "Ed's real good at that."

Lovilla frowned at her, as if to say, At *what?*

"I mean," Wilma Jean sputtered, "like at trackin' things. Huntin' things. You just figure, Ed's smart like that. That he'd know how to find her. Ain't that what you meant?"

Wilma Jean was flustered. She feared she'd given Lovilla a glimpse of her secret sympathy. For she'd privately resented Ramona since their years in school, when Ed had first turned his interest toward her, an attention Wilma Jean had found unaccountable. To her, Ramona's dreamy withdrawal from the town's banalities had always seemed nothing but a self-important posturing. Whenever, as girls, Wilma Jean had offered gossip or asked for some herself, Ramona had wanted none and had none to give. She didn't seem to care if Alice Camper was fucking her brother. She apparently hadn't noticed Mary DeHaan's face after her father's latest beating. It was as though Wilma Jean could never get Ramona to see the exhilarating despair surrounding all of them; as though Ramona, by holding her eyes on a point somewhere above the tidal serrations of the distant, looming Catskills, could keep sharply in focus the world inside her head.

Then, in high school, Ramona's look had narrowed and drawn in, but only to see Ed. And Wilma Jean had resented that even more, for she also had admired Ed's smooth and lofty confidence, and for a time, before Ramona, she'd had it inside her. But then Ramona had wrapped him in the seamless heat of her imagination and, to everyone's surprise, Ed had seemed to feel no need to cheat it.

Wilma Jean smoked and asked Lovilla again, "Ain't that what you meant? That you figure Ed could find her if he'd tried?"

Lovilla nodded. "I guess." She shook a cigarette from its pack. "Oh, Christ," she sighed. "What a life."

Neither woman said anything for a while. Lovilla's cigarette smoke hazed around their heads. Then Lovilla said softly, "Sometimes I think if I could get me Ramona's Dodge, I'd be out of this town tonight."

Not long ago, a group of the town's older men had stood outside the doorway of Squeaky Frye's Sunoco station, loosely slouched in a line of desperado contemplation, and heard the car's reverberations drifting through the town. "The poor son of a bitch," one of them said. "Couldn't keep her in line. Sounds like he can't hold her Dodge down, neither."

So, as Lovilla's comment also suggested, the car had become Ramona's Dodge in the mind of the town, even though it was Ed who sat behind the wheel. And its lawless haste through the streets unconsciously reinforced the notion, first offered as a joke, that Ramona was somehow influencing its actions.

Ramona and the Dodge had in a way first been thought of as complicitous when she'd tried to flee before, so there'd been much confusion about its latest role. Some of the rumors assumed she'd used the car again, though no one could explain how Ed had gotten it back so quickly.

"He must've found it ditched somewhere?" Broder offered in the Hill Top.

Now that she was gone, many in town were eager to bring back to their conversations her first attempt, on a night of ice, as opposite as could be from her leaving in the oven heat of open August daylight. Now it seemed that nearly everyone in Myles had found his way to the pasture that night last winter and remembered the Dodge, curved neatly around the elm. Almost everyone had seen the hole in the windshield, could describe the pattern of cracks, a web crocheted to the edges of the glass. And everyone vividly remembered seeing the hand itself, sliced at the wrist, the clean work of a cleaver's stroke, as it lay on the blood-pink snow. Someone, only last week, in Sampson's grocery?—in the Hill Top?—recalled that it was like the hand was the only thing that had got out unhurt.

Ed sat on the ground inside his lean-to, finished with his weekly delivery of baby supplies to Vera.

Parallel walls, three car doors each, had been sunk into shallow trenches so that they stood securely. A back wall, founded in the same way, also three doors wide, rested lightly against the sides. A canvas, retrieved from the pile and smeared with grease and oil, roofed the structure. The front was open to the air and to the sloping field, then the highway, then the dappled drop of mountains; the same view Ed had from his blue chair inside.

The doors had first been dumped with other debris behind the house so long ago that no one could remember who'd begun the pile, which lay at a point where Ed's backyard and Mrs. Beasley's met the town's neglected field. It had seemed to grow on its own, flourishing as certainly as the Matronettes' flowers on Summit Street died, as though the soil of Myles contained minerals more hospitable to the life of inner tubes than tulips.

He sat in the lean-to, drinking beer, and saw in his mind the memory of Broder marching absurdly through the snow down the railroad tracks, his drum major's gait showing with each

step Broder's conviction that he was entirely safe from scrutiny.

An hour ago, Ed's mother had said to him while she was feeding Jonas, "She thinks she can fly the coop and no harm done, she's wrong, Ed. She's *real* wrong. She's dumber even than I knew if she thinks she's got away with this." And looking at Ed, she'd said, "How much longer you think I'm gonna keep him night and day while she's off on her little vacation? How much longer you think I'm gonna sit here, just thrilled to be woke up at goddam dawn every day?"

Ed had said, "Yeah, I know it's put a cramp in your social schedule. I know, otherwise, you got all kinds of things to do."

"Me?" Vera said. "Things *I* gotta do? Whoah! Things I gotta do? Think a second, Ed. Concentrate real hard. We ain't talkin' about things I gotta do. We're talkin' about what you gotta do. We're talkin' about you goin' out to find her and gettin' her ass back here."

Ed glared. He'd heard this from his mother at least once a week since Ramona had been gone.

"When you goin' after her?"

"Shut your mouth," Ed snapped. His cheek muscle moved.

"When you goin' after her, Ed?" Vera asked.

"I mean it. Shut up! Not another word. Not one."

"When?"

Vera hadn't yet heard about the lean-to. Few people had. He hadn't planned to build it; the whole thing had happened spontaneously, as he'd sat on the ground behind his house.

For weeks, he'd been spending nearly every night outside, sleeping on a blanket. He'd always moved his sleep outdoors on the hottest nights, as did many others. Viewed from overhead at twilight, the village in summer might have looked like a camp of wounded soldiers, people sprawled on lawns all over town to get the niggardly breeze. So, at first, Ed's behavior differed little from his neighbors, except that he sometimes walked directly to

the backyard after work, ignoring the inside of the house (Moon's information in this case had been correct). But now the air was crisp by nightfall and Ed had dragged his sleeping bag out back, keeping it neatly rolled in a corner of the lean-to during the day.

In truth, the heat had never had much to do with his behavior, although he'd consciously explained it to himself as that. In truth, he avoided the house because he often felt throughout it the clear sense of Ramona.

The first night she was gone, when he'd searched the corners and the closets for her, he'd been startled when he saw her cup and hairbrush on the table. But unlike Lovilla Adams, who'd seen them too, and felt them empty of Ramona, Ed had spotted the brush and the cup and they had seemed to him alive, components of her.

And by now, many other objects often held her within them in the same way as her cup and her hairbrush had to him that first day, so that he sometimes felt Ramona virtually everywhere in the house. Which is not to say he conjured her in a mourner's conventional way—looking out a window and imagining you see her walking up the steps; being startled from your daydream-grief by the image of her coiled matter-of-factly in her favorite chair. No, it was not like that. His was not a lover's sweet-suffering mirage. He did not, in weakness, glimpse her briefly in her chair. She was, instead, all through its wood and fabric; the chair itself held the sense of her, as the cup and the hairbrush had been of her that night.

Some mornings, when Ed bent to the bathroom sink to wash his face, it was as if he were unwittingly immersing himself in the deep white basin of Ramona, and as he washed he would suddenly sense the vulnerability of lowering his head into her. He would feel the porcelain begin to close and he'd jerk his head up just in time, sloshing water wildly. At times like these, to live in the house was to live inside Ramona, the whole place vibrant

with her presence. Or not her presence, really, but the specter of her absence, and he'd increasingly avoided it, on a blanket in his yard.

Then, one night last week as he'd sat on his blanket reading the *Columbia County Mirror*, he'd sensed Mrs. Beasley at her window. He'd looked quickly toward her house and was sure he saw her curtain fly shut, and that was all the evidence he needed.

He got up and walked to the pile of parts and, as though following a plan, he'd dragged the doors in all their uncooperative weight away. As was often true of Ed, the nature of the labor immediately drew him in. He decided three doors defined the space he wished, dug his trenches with precision, set the doors, troweled the soil around them with his hands, tamping it firmly.

He'd stepped back, surveyed his work, the doors rising from the ground like a crop. He'd roofed it two nights later when a sudden shower struck.

He sat now, drinking beer and staring at the Catskills. An easy wind was blowing toward him and the lean-to held it like a pocket. He lay back into its shade and rested his head on the tightly rolled sleeping bag.

"When you goin' after her, Ed?"

As he had last winter after Ramona's accident, Ed again believed that people—not just Mrs. Beasley—were watching him from their houses, from shop windows, when he passed. And, of course, he was right, though not to the extent he imagined. He even sensed their attention as he drove through town, and so, distracted, confused, Ed had become a driver who wanted to get where he was going as quickly as he could. All his life, he'd driven slowly and deafeningly through Myles in the hope of drawing people's interest. Now, seeking to become a moving blur no one could catch a satisfying glimpse of, he drove at dangerous speeds.

His understanding of the town was so keen because his was its quintessential mind. Had this happened to somebody else, Ed would have had more to say about it than anyone in Myles. He'd have relished the rumors. He'd have wondered, in the Hill Top, if the poor bastard's wife had left him because she kept forgetting just which one he was and had decided the fair thing to do, for all the men in town, would simply be to leave. He'd have offered several thoughts on who might be the baby's father. He'd have turned, his eyes twinkling, toward Moon behind the bar and observed that the kid—bald, round-faced, shaped like a stump—looked exactly like Moon. He'd have loudly concluded that Moon must have somehow found his own shriveled stem hidden in a crease of his thighs and remembered he could use it for other purposes than pissing. And through it all he'd have been urged on by the vocal pleasure of the Hill Top's other customers.

But now, that very affinity was working against him. In a way, Ed was watching himself when he felt the town watching him; he was the victim of his own sharp scrutiny. And no one else in town, except his mother, Vera, could speak of Ed's dilemma as inventively as he could.

So he drove maniacally through Myles, calling even more attention to himself, while the women watched bemusedly and held invested secrets and the men imagined that the car was somehow powered by Ramona, not knowing in their easy jest how near the truth they were; how fully Ramona's absence drove the Dodge.

Ed lay in the lean-to, the rolled sleeping bag his pillow. The incoming breeze was growing stronger, whistling around him. But within it, Ed's ears cleared a soundless place where he would be able to hear the scuff of her footsteps if they came.

He felt no need to defend himself against his mother's charge of gutlessness. He knew it was futile to explain to Vera that he couldn't leave town in search of Ramona no matter what. How could he? If he were to do that, he'd be admitting the possibility

that she was not coming back. If he left Myles to look for her, he'd not be standing at the door at the moment she appeared. In his mind he held a picture, sensuous as memory, of him watching her return through the mesh of the screen, watching as she moved slowly up the walk; beaten, delirious, frantic with remorse.

Eleven

Lovilla stood at her sink, dish-water nearly to her elbows, groping among the supper silver-ware for the paring knife floating near the drain. When Lovilla was ten years old, her mother had cut herself badly on a knife one night while she was washing dishes, her suds turning a pale pink foam before she realized what she'd done. She'd screamed and cursed as the soap began to burn. Lovilla's father had looked up from the table and said that a hand cut always bled worse than it was. The knife had severed nerves with a long clean slice, and Lovilla's mother now had no feeling in the tips of three fingers.

Lovilla thought of this every time she washed dishes and she always found the knives first, keeping them out of the soapy water.

The small square window above her sink was black with night, but Lovilla stared into it as though its view were intricate.

Just a few feet away, in a corner of the kitchen, her son, Brett, crawled soberly about on the floor, a dew-clear thread of drool hanging from his lips, as he played with a yellow plastic truck.

Outside, in the damp cold air beyond the window, her husband leaned against his pickup fender, loudly slurping coffee. Now and then, Lovilla noticed shapes in the darkness shift as Adams changed his posture, raised his arm to lift his cup, but she couldn't see the wisps of his breath and her look was not on him or anything outside.

In her mind she was speaking to Ramona. She was trying to remember if Ramona had ever looked at her and said directly, "I mean it—I'm goin' again," and she convinced herself once more that she had not. Certainly, Ramona had talked and talked. Lovilla had often said to Ramona, warmly, "Christ, your mouth's a motor, woman." But she was sure Ramona had never looked right at her and said, "Listen. I know you're sayin' to yourself that I took off once and I'm too scared to go again, but I *am* goin'." She was sure Ramona had never said anything like that, because those had been Lovilla's thoughts exactly—that she *had* tried it once; that she was surely too scared to leave again—every time she heard Ramona talking. Lovilla was certain that if she'd heard Ramona say anything so firmly she'd have stopped what she was thinking and truly believed her and would've told her . . . what? Well, something, she was sure. Something that would have made her stay.

Outside, Adams finished his coffee and set the mug on the fender. He glanced to his left, where his wife's head was framed in the window. Inattentively, he watched her for a few moments, her mouth puckering limply like a fish for breath, which he knew was what she did when she was lost in thought. He moved away from his pickup and walked past the window toward a darker corner of the yard to take a piss. Knees slightly flexed, he spoke aloud while he watched the arc of his urine glisten in the moonlight.

He said, "Not really, we ain't. We work together, sure, but what the hell, I work with Al Day and Billy March, too, and they're a coupla good fucking guys, too, so what I'm sayin' is just because I work with him, that don't mean we's really that close."

Adams imagined himself speaking to no one in particular. But for weeks now, he'd periodically been stopped on the street, or eased aside in Sampson's Grocery, or furtively turned to as he drank in the Hill Top, and as he'd encountered these stealthy approaches he'd become able to anticipate their intentions without fail. Last night, in the Hill Top, had been typical.

Marvin Broder had pushed his stool close to Adams's and asked softly, below the talk, "What's goin' on with King?"

"What do you mean?" Adams had said.

"You know what I mean. The way he just keeps bein' weird. Does he know where she is? He seein' her or what? You know. You talk to him."

Adams had shrugged. "Your guess is as good as mine."

"Bullshit," Broder said. "Don't gimme that. He tells you stuff."

"Hell he does," Adams said. "He don't tell me nothin'. If he's talkin' to somebody it sure ain't me."

"All right," Broder said, "you don't wanna say, that's fine."

"Ask Mitchell. Ask Bill March. Ask them if he says anything to me."

"Don't shit a shitter, Raymond. If you don't wanna say, just say you don't wanna say. Just say it." Then he'd moved away, with a parting look that made Adams feel Broder was certain he'd been lied to, though Adams had told him the truth, truth more frustrating to himself than to anyone else.

He'd been receiving small variations of Broder's questions and his doubting look often enough to set him talking to himself.

He finished, zipped his jeans, and walked back toward the truck. "No, really, like I said, I mean I can see where it might look like we was." He could see his breath as he spoke. "But he never talked to me about nothing private and he sure ain't said nothin' about any of this." He looked to the face of his wife in the kitchen window. "And, too, since the wives was real close."

Lovilla watched the bottom of her sink as the water drained and spied an overlooked knife beneath the suds. She was doubting now what she'd been certain of a moment ago, thinking that maybe, in some way, Ramona *had* told her. Because the second she'd seen Bumbry running past with Jonas, she'd known, immediately. Known not just that there was something wrong, but that Ramona was gone. She'd felt certain that she was already miles away, and she'd unthinkingly assumed she'd taken the Dodge again. That was the picture Lovilla had had as soon as she'd seen Bumbry running through her yard holding Jonas to his chest. She'd been standing right where she stood now, at her sink, looking out the window. She'd been wrong about the Dodge, but right about Ramona, and now Lovilla wondered if she'd been so quick to picture Ramona already miles away because she *had* told her somehow. Not directly, but maybe she had and her message had just been lying there, waiting, in Lovilla's mind. Maybe, Lovilla thought, that was why she'd been so quick to make conclusions when she'd seen Bumbry carrying Jonas.

Lovilla's son raised himself up, teetered momentarily, and pushed off toward her, his arms flapping busily ahead of him as though the air were a curtain he was trying to part. Reaching her, he collapsed into her skirt.

She remembered how frightened she'd been when she'd seen Bumbry holding Jonas. All she'd been able to see of the baby was his head sticking out and his feet paddling frantically. Lovilla had thought for sure Bumbry would accidentally smother Jonas or break him in half. Then she'd instantly thought of

Bumbry's hands, which were sometimes cut and filthy, after his aunt had kicked him out and he was living mostly outdoors. And as Lovilla watched Bumbry dart away down an alley, she actually remembered one time when she was selling red paper poppies for Veterans Day and Bumbry had come along the sidewalk and she'd given him one to stick in his shirt. While she was fixing it for him he'd tried to help and his hand had wrapped around hers and it had shocked her to feel it, so rough and callused, as though it were scaled. That's what she'd thought of when she'd seen him carrying Jonas. Those big, dirty hands wrapped around the baby, scraping his skin raw. And she couldn't believe Ramona had actually done it, no matter how bad she was feeling.

Adams was cold, and looked around for his coffee cup to carry back inside. He saw Lovilla's face drop briefly out of the window frame and reappear along with Brett's.

For the most part, the town had shown at first only slightly more than a small village's exaggerated interest in Ramona's leaving and Ed's reactions. Because Ramona had been seen, especially after the accident, as notoriously unpredictable, and because Ed had fashioned his own reputation, the attention of Myles was understandably lively at the start. But what had kept it high, and raised it, was Ramona's continued absence. It was as though a silence in the shape of her were moving about Myles; as though that world beyond the range of what you see as you look to the Catskills from the top of the town had swallowed her whole. It was that sense which had held the town's fascination; that and Ed's actions and his impenetrable silence on the subject. Had someone—Lovilla, Wilma Jean— heard from Ramona, the curiosity would have eased considerably. Had Ed spoken to someone about his wife's departure, had he not begun to behave so strangely, then interest would have turned to other matters, with an eye occasionally cast on their badly sagging little house at the bottom of Myles.

Had any of this occurred, the only people in the village, beyond Ed and his mother, still preoccupied with the whole affair would have been Lovilla and Raymond Adams. Lovilla, bonded by the intimacy of one who'd heard a friend's extreme complaints and fantasies. And Adams, enveloped by Ed's assaultive spirit in a way he'd come to need.

But what Adams had seen in Ed lately made him wish he could get free. As the time had lengthened, one plain thing had held astonishingly true: Ramona had not returned. The power which Adams had always assumed Ed held over everyone had not been strong enough to bring Ramona back, and that fact alone had shaken Adams's understanding of Ed King's personality.

Like everyone else, he'd also watched Ed's growing strangeness. He'd sneaked into Ed's backyard to see the lean-to for himself. He'd been with him at work, where Adams saw in Ed a new-angled darkness out of which he'd begun to keep watch on several tools he'd determined were his alone to use, especially a sledgehammer he let no one else touch. And which, last week, had stopped him as he'd unscrewed the mug from the top of his thermos. He'd paused, taken a deep smell of the coffee inside, and accused someone on the crew of pissing in it. Then, cursing their denials, he'd flung the coffee, thick mud-dots in the dirt, and heaved the thermos into a field.

Seeing all of this, Adams's confusion had only increased. He had no idea what to make of Ed these days, but he was sure that Ed's strength was changed and still immense and was nothing he could be comfortably close to any longer, certainly not as its victim and not even, as he'd often been, its beneficiary. In the past, Adams had come to feel Ed's attention as his way of singling Adams out and warmly drawing him in. But not now. Ed's new power seemed to Adams just the opposite—a freezing kind of strength he was using on everyone.

"No, no, we ain't," he said and looked up again to see Lovilla's bubbling lips.

Lovilla held Brett in one arm, bouncing him lightly on her hip as she rinsed the sink. She wished, as she often had lately, that she'd taken something from Ramona's house, something to have, as she'd taken some of her grandmother's things after she'd died. At times, Lovilla would be thinking of something else entirely and suddenly picture the coffee cup she'd picked up from Ramona's table. And she'd wish she had it. She could've taken it, easily, that day. When she'd seen it, and her hairbrush, she'd known how far away Ramona was.

Now she wished she'd taken the cup.

When she saw it in her mind she thought of the day several women had come to visit Ramona after she'd come home from the hospital. They'd sat in Ramona's living room drinking coffee, and Ramona, propped up on the couch, had said, straight-faced, that the first thing she'd had to do when she got home was go out and buy a set of left-handed coffee mugs. And Alice Camper had blinked and looked at her own cup and asked Ramona if the one she was using was a left or a right. And everyone had laughed, Ramona most of all.

Lovilla couldn't remember another time when she'd heard Ramona make a joke about it. Talk easily about it. Just that one time right after she'd come home. And now Lovilla wondered if that was why she wished she'd taken the cup when she'd seen it. The cup instead of something else . . . the brush, or whatever.

She didn't know. But she wished she had something of Ramona's.

Lovilla felt her son's weight in her arms softening toward sleep. She wiped bits of food from the drain and threw them into the garbage pail. From the drying rack, she lifted the knife and held it in her hand, turning its blade back and forth to make it wink in the light. She put it back in the rack, point up. Then she held her index finger over it and suddenly, to her own surprise, tapped the point, a light flick, and felt the quickest

prick of pain. She held her finger stiffly as fine threads of blood ran from its tip.

Through the window, Adams watched his wife's lips moving again, differently than before, forming words.

Without thinking, he said to her in a natural voice, "What's wrong?"—as if she could hear him and see him through the window, as if he'd be able to hear her reply.

Twelve

he laundromat sat at the end of Summit, just before the street abruptly curved and began its steep three-block drop toward the highway. Especially at night, when the Hill Top Tap was Summit's only other lighted building, the laundromat appeared to be perched at an edge, an isolated lookout filled with dirty yellow light, made more lonely still by the stretch of brick-strewn lots beside it, their air—a breadth of rooted sky—the great fire's architectural contribution to the town.

Ed waited in the dark across the street from the laundromat. He watched Luther Sherrill's wife, Karla, carry a basket of folded clothes to her car and hold its door open for her three small daughters. They emerged from the laundromat, each of them crying primally in impressively individual styles. Ed watched the wailing children file into the back of the car, saw Karla slam the door. Then she moved around to the driver's

side, and when she opened it her daughters' screams again flew out into the night.

"What'd I tell you!" Karla shouted as she squeezed in behind the wheel. "All of ya shut up right now or I'll rip your goddam arms off and beat you over the head with 'em!" She slammed the door, and drove off.

Ed waited, as if for the air to subside, then crossed Summit, carrying his laundry in plastic garbage bags. It was nearly ten o'clock, past the hour when, according to the laundromat's hand-lettered sign, customers were allowed to begin their washing. But Ed always waited until now, because it meant he'd be alone, and when Squeaky Frye came up from his Sunoco station at the other end of the street to close for the night, Ed met Squeaky's annoyed look with a shrug and said as he nodded toward a load tumbling in the dryer, "Nothin' I can do about it now but finish."

The only thing he didn't like about coming to the laundromat late at night was the condition of the place after a long day of use. Otherwise Ed enjoyed the task, its organization into colors and fabrics, which he paid religious mind to. He liked the sperm-smelling astringency of bleach in churning water.

After starting the machines, Ed lit a cigarette and stepped outside into the cool night. The town was typically quiet. Dogs barked irrelevantly from various yards. The tire-whine of semis on the highway drifted up. Now and then a motor, customized for rich effect, rippled through the streets. He heard none of these noises; they were the sound of every night.

He walked a few steps into the empty lot nearest the laundromat, stumbling in the dark over pieces of bricks. When he reached the middle of the lot, he dropped to his haunches and smoked his cigarette in a contemplative way.

Though he'd never tried to imagine precisely where his father had been sitting that night, Ed was in fact crouched twenty feet from where he had died, the factory sentry, passed out in his

chair as the fire climbed and leaped and sheets of massive flame billowed out at Myles.

The fire had begun in the first morning hours of an early-winter blizzard. It had started to storm sometime after supper, the snow falling solidly, like stippled walls. People had gone to bed after giving the weather an affectionate glance, seeing the town already blanketed, pleased with the certainty there'd be no work or school to wake up for in the morning.

Deep in sleep, Myles was awakened by great, percussive blasts. Houses near the factory trembled, as from the earth's anarchic play. Windows blew out into the night. Glass fell silently, a kind of gleaming snow. People hurried to their doors, confused and terrified by this exploding blizzard.

Outside, behind the snow, the sky was bright as noon in the middle of the night, and through the howls of dogs and the first calls of human voices there was a steady, building roar, like a huge imploding wind, perhaps the sound you'd hear as you were being sucked into the sun.

"Ed?" The voice was quick, timid, apologetically aware that it would startle him. "Hey, Ed. Whatcha doin'?"

Ed turned, still crouched, and saw a woman's thin figure stepping lightly through the lot toward him.

"Hey, Ed," Wilma Jean Robertson said again as she reached his side. He'd not moved from his crouch. "You drop something?" Wilma Jean asked and knelt to help Ed peer at the ground.

"What the hell you doin' here, Wilma Jean?" he asked.

She laughed nervously. "Laundry." She shrugged.

Ed stood and so did Wilma Jean. She pulled her coat more tightly around her. "So . . . how you been, Ed? Haven't talked to you in a while."

Ed smiled. "A *while?*" he said. "No more than, what? Four, five years?"

She laughed again. "Oh, come on, Ed. Don't be ridiculous."

Ed drew a line in the dirt with the toe of his boot, invisible in the darkness. He was in no rush to say anything but was feeling a slow gathering of control he sensed his silence would enhance. The impression was only that, but he relished it as something he hadn't experienced for weeks.

Wilma Jean looked up at the sky. Her long thin throat arched from her collar. "I come up here at night every once in a while," she lied.

"Is that right?" Ed said. "You like to stand out here in the dark, shiftin' through the rubble? I never knew that, Wilma Jean." He was watching his boot move; it made another line paralleling the first. "How come you do that? What'd you lose somethin' in the fire or somethin'?"

Wilma Jean laughed nervously and said, "Quit teasing me." Then she softly gasped and, with a sudden, urgent sympathy, said, "The fire. Of course: the *fire*. Oh, Ed, shit, I'm sorry. I shoulda thought."

Ed had no idea what she was talking about.

She continued, "Was you . . . was you payin' respect to your *dad* just now?" She pronounced the word "dad" as though to speak it with normal emphasis would break it in half. "That's why you was crouched down like that? And I come chargin' in on you. Oh, shit. Wilma Jean, where is your brain? Jesus."

Ed sighed. "Yeah, well, you know."

"And I just now thought: This is really, like his grave, ain't it. All the times I go past these lots and I never once looked at 'em like that." She looked to the ground. Her eyes followed Ed's boot as it drew in the darkness. It seemed to Wilma Jean to be making an X. "Is this where you figure he . . . was?" she asked.

Pleasure was growing in Ed. He wasn't sure where this was leading, though already he sensed an edge of sex on Wilma Jean's eager solace. But he felt, even more surely now, a kind of leverage which he'd been accustomed to in his life, and that was

sufficient, was itself close enough to sex to inspire a similar stirring.

He said, "You can't know for sure, but yeah. As close as I can remember the layout . . . where he usually sat."

Wilma Jean nodded, reverent with understanding. "And you was thinking about him."

In a way, Wilma Jean was right. His father had been on Ed's mind when she'd arrived, though he hadn't been performing anything so elaborate as kneeling to the lot's trashed earth to call his father's memory. But as Ed had been growing more and more obsessed with his suspicion of the town's interest in him, he'd been repeatedly drawn to thoughts of his father, especially the sound of his voice, a low mushy run of fragmented words bitten off before completed or begun a syllable too late.

Yet, more than just the reminiscence of a snarling mumble, Ed had been hearing that voice as it contested with his own. And what he'd been yearning for these past several weeks was the marvelous comfort of a reliably inferior opponent. He'd been turning in his mind like the pages of an album countless splendid episodes in which his father began to move forward on his chair to curse Ed, the way he appeared to lurch about involuntarily at such moments. And Ed had early learned to recognize these warnings his father's body provided, so that by the time he'd actually formed his words, Ed was ready, had been ready, and smothered his father's lumbrous obscenities almost before they'd left his throat.

"Lissenuh me, you flukey little cocksuck. You ever—"

"Listen to you? I'll listen to you after I ask Tommy Beener's dogs everything they know."

He'd been remembering all the times his father, in a stuporous fury, had tried to knock him to the ground and he'd stepped away from the fist, leaning with a matador's contemptuous grace just out of its reach, then had dropped his father with a finely aimed elbow to the side of his head.

As easy as it became for Ed against his father, he remained

merely the retaliator. For his life outside his house was of much more interest to him, and he gave his attention and his energies to it. Still, doomed as they were, Ed's father's assaults never lessened, his drunken rages never quieted, making easy victory an almost daily pleasure Ed came to take for granted.

So he'd been wistfully recalling his successes against a man he'd hated and who'd deserved his hatred. The father had been finally a resource to his son, giving some of Ed's emotions equable definition, and there was nothing at all like that in Ed's life at the moment.

Wilma Jean said cautiously, "I remember, at the fire, how they told you to go home, not to watch. I remember how Bud Myers took your arm and sort of tried to lead you off, and you jerked your arm away and it looked to me like you wanted to run in and try to save him." Wilma Jean shook her head. "Christ, that was *some*thing. I was standin' just down from you. Did you know that? With Lovilla. And I kept sneakin' looks at you, like everybody else was, too, of course. Bud Myers took your arm and you jerked away and I said to Lovilla, 'God, Ed's got guts to stay.' " She said this with a tone of remarkably fresh awe, then put a stick of gum into her mouth and began to work it rapidly. She hugged herself tightly and when she spoke her voice fluttered. "You was hopin' against hope, wasn't ya," she said. "You was hopin', somehow, your dad'd come walkin' outa there."

Ed had stood with most of the town on the slope of the hill across the street, as close as anyone could get to the heat and the smoke, a full black fog, and the falling bricks and wires. His look was alert, his head thrust forward. The blizzard, as though fighting for preeminence, seemed to intensify at the same pace as the fire, the falling snow a shade of orangy pink from the light of enormous fireballs. Sparks from the blaze were a storm of their own and as they hit the drifts of snow they sent geysers of steam hissing into the air, then turned black, peppering the drifts.

But hard as it was working, the blizzard's phenomenon was losing to the fire's. Heat was melting the snow in an ever-widening circle and water flowed in the gutters, steaming like a monstrous temper a hundred yards from the blaze. The local firemen had arrived, having finally navigated the trucks four blocks through the blinding snow. They shuffled frantically about, taking pratfalls on the ice and crawling away with painful sprains. To try to ease the heat, they hosed themselves and then their trucks. Several fainted from the heat, their toes and fingers frozen.

Wilma Jean's memory was a camera. A thoughtful man named Bud Myers *had* seen Ed and assumed, as did everyone else, that Ed's father had been inside the factory. He'd hurried to Ed's side and taken him by the arm and urged him not to watch. But Ed barely shifted his attention, had pulled his arm from Myers's grip and said flatly, distractedly, "No. Hell, no. I'll stay."

Now and then another explosion had rocked the town as the fire found more chemicals the factory used for curing rubber. But the constant sound which the blasts interrupted was that steady, sucking roar which seemed behind the people now and overhead and on all sides.

Wilma Jean remembered vividly what she'd seen, but her understanding of it was romantically flawed. Actually, Ed had insisted on staying for reasons which were not much more complicated than those of the several hundred others spread out along the hill. He was riveted to the performance of the fire, the most astounding event Myles had seen, or would see, a scene of lavish ferocity beyond the scale of richest dream—frozen heat and orange snow, fire and ice and sound and color at their fantastic extremes—promising as it flourished only to grow larger, to go on and on and on. (Which it had, for in destroying Myles's last hope of even marginal sufficiency the fire gave the town in return its own extravagant myth, which lived and grew, in talk, in minds' eyes, in ever-building memory.) And Ed had

also wanted to watch because the fire was demonstrating to him in a spectacle of confirmation that his father—the night watchman who should have seen the fire's beginnings and signaled the alarm—was a figure of incompetence even larger than Ed could have imagined.

Ed looked at Wilma Jean. She was staring high overhead, her long sharp nose seeming to sniff for the past. She snapped her gum and smoked a cigarette, seemed lost in reverie. For the first time in weeks Ed saw all the way to the end of the moment he was living. Hearing Wilma Jean, he was sure he knew what was going to happen, and the return of his wisdom was for Ed a pull, like lust.

He exhaled loudly. "It's true. It wasn't easy, makin' myself watch."

Wilma Jean continued to stare at the sky. "I said to Lovilla, 'God, Ed's got guts.' You wanting to rush in and save your dad, forcing yourself to stay there." She swallowed audibly.

"And," Ed added, "like you just said, havin' to 'hope against hope.' "

Wilma Jean nodded solemnly. She tried to move her head slowly, but she was so serious it appeared to catch and snag. She started to speak, cleared her throat, and tried again.

Ed saw all of this and waited happily.

She said, almost tremulously, "One thing I always wondered about that night. I always wondered, where was Ramona? Why wasn't she with you?"

No one but his mother had spoken Ramona's name in Ed's presence since she'd been gone, and hearing it all of a sudden, moving in the lot's night air, greatly startled him.

"No, no. She was there," Ed said quickly. He was flustered, feeling somehow obliged to defend Ramona.

"Not at first she wasn't," Wilma Jean persisted. "She come up eventually and stood with you, but not for a *long* time."

Ramona's movements during the fire's early hours were an unimportant detail in Ed's experience of it, and he had to think

with some effort to account for them. "Ah," he said, "I remember. She's with her mom. Her mom was scared to death and her dad couldn't do a thing with her. She had to settle her old lady down."

"Hmm," Wilma Jean said in a way that made it clear she wasn't satisfied. She said, "Seems to me her place was with you. Seems to me her mom's nerves coulda waited. Her mom didn't have nobody caught inside the fire."

As she heard herself say these words, Wilma Jean realized she'd stumbled on a way to condemn Ramona and she was thrilled with her discovery, her confidence growing. So she said, looking into Ed's eyes for the first time, "I think she shoulda stayed with you the whole time."

Ed said, "Is that right, Wilma Jean?"

"Yeah," she said. "I think a woman's got no right to be off worrying about her mom's bout of nerves when her husband needs her."

Ed smiled. He felt things moving recognizably again. "We wasn't married yet, then," he said.

Wilma Jean threw up her hands in a quick, dismissive flapping. "Oh, come on, Ed, you know what I mean. You sure as hell was goin' together. You was engaged, or something, wasn't ya? You was with each other night and day. Everywhere you went you was wrapped around each other like goddam Siamese twins. I—" Wilma Jean heard her voice rising with an energy that she feared was giving things away and she cut herself off immediately.

Ed watched, pleased. When she spoke again, her voice nearly broke with nervousness but she managed to say, "I woulda, Ed."

"Woulda what?" he asked.

"Woulda stayed. Woulda stood with you all the time the fire was goin'."

"Is that right?" Ed said.

"Yeah."

Ed nodded and smiled again. "Well, thanks, Wilma Jean. But it wasn't like I . . . It was fine."

She looked behind her, left and right, and was satisfied they were quite alone and wrapped in darkness. She reached for Ed and ran her hand down the length of his forearm, then moved even closer to Ed, like a volunteer stepping forward, her gum snapping, and said again with the gravity of a pledge, "I woulda stayed with you." She cleared her throat again. "You get what I'm saying, Ed? I woulda stayed with you."

It seemed to Ed just then that the past year had been in an instant lifted from his life and he was amazed by the air and the lightness which he felt come into him. He said, "Why don't we go somewhere in your car?"

"I ain't got my car," Wilma Jean said.

Ed frowned. "What'd you carry up your laundry?"

Wilma Jean giggled shyly. "I ain't got my laundry either." She breathed a softer giggle. "I just sneaked up here to see you."

"You knew I was here?" Ed asked.

"I drove past with the kids and saw you in the laundromat," she said. "I been watchin' you for weeks, Ed, waitin' for a chance."

Ed laughed. "Is that right? You been trailing me for weeks?" He was too pleased with this news to be alarmed by the fact that he'd had no sense of it.

Wilma Jean said, "Yeah." She stroked his arm again and looked toward the street. "Let's go somewhere in *your* car."

"I ain't got mine neither," Ed said.

They both looked around them. Ed stared at the lot's rubble-crusted surface of the earth and said, "The ground's hard as a bitch. All kinds of shit stickin' up."

Wilma Jean took Ed's hand. "I got an idea," she said. "C'mere."

"Where you goin'?" Ed asked, in tow.

"Over here," she whispered, moving deftly now on tiptoes.

"Where?" Ed asked again, stumbling over bits of brick.

"Here," whispered Wilma Jean, the youngest Matronette, as she reached the larger of the flower beds she'd helped the club create last spring. On her knees, she'd worked the soil at the spot she stood before, her fingers raking earth—catching pieces of glass and rusted metal and crumbled brick as fine as gravel—clearing an ample square of burned-out lot and leaving flawless soil disinclined to let life grow.

"Here," she said to Ed, and she dropped once again to her knees, her springtime pose. She said with satisfaction, "All that work went for something after all." She still held Ed's hand and looked up at him, smiling. She said, "I am here to tell you, this is the cleanest piece of dirt in Columbia County. Come down here and test it out." She patted the flower bed affectionately, as though it were a mattress, and looked up at Ed again. She could barely see his face, so far above her in the darkness. "Come lay next to me," she said, her voice shaking. "Like old times."

Yes, Ed thought. *Old times.* And then he eased to his knees to join her, a smile on his face. His mind was limpid, thoughtless strength. He had no recent past at all, only lovely life before it; only Wilma Jean's old times.

"See?" whispered Wilma Jean excitedly, patting the earth again. "It's crusted over, but there ain't a thing that'll jab ya." Her teeth began to chatter.

"Yeah?" Ed said. He took off his jacket and spread it out, a sweep of tidy chivalry. "Let's see how good a work you done." He pulled her into him and together they lay back in the combed dead soil of the fire.

Thirteen

At shortly past five, Ramona turned off the lights of Claring Florists and walked to the shop's front window. Outside, cars moved up and down Strait Street, which, contrary to its name, wound tributarially through the center of the village. She watched three men enter the Claring House, a popular steak house directly across the street.

She stood at the shop's front window for several minutes every night at closing and glanced to the street constantly as she worked through the day. She felt that the flower shop was an ideal place to watch for anyone who might be looking for her. Mostly, she imagined the possibility of Ed, although frequently she also saw in her mind Donnie's station wagon moving down Strait. But she reasoned that no matter who was coming, he'd have to enter Claring on Strait Street and she could spot him easily through the large front window. All she had to do was vigilantly watch the street, and so she did; her darting looks had become a tic. She'd also imagined her escape, out the back into

the alley, and she made sure that door was left unlatched, checking it several times a day.

It was as much as she had planned.

After she'd closed, Ramona liked to claim some moments as her own among the red and pink roses, the garish carnations, the deep blue iris, all the symmetrical arrangements that she imagined as outrageous women's hats.

Ted Van Nostrand, the owner of the shop, didn't share Ramona's pleasure in a closed-up store, a silent phone. He always hurried out the back as soon as he'd locked up.

Van Nostrand was a short fat man who appeared to teeter above his tiny feet even if he stood still, so when, some weeks ago, he was balanced perilously on a ladder while he turned the wall clock back to standard time, Ramona had been sure he'd fall any second. Looking up at him, she'd thought, Humpty Dumpty sat on a wall, and then she'd had a moment of detailed memory—hearing the sound of three rocking motions and the creaking springs of the chair she always sat in when she held her sleepy son and whispered nursery rhymes into his downy ear.

Thoughts of Jonas often came to her in this way now, triggered by some immediate sound or glimpse. They came frequently and exactly, without the slightest premonition, breaking into her mind with an overwhelming clarity. Sometimes she was able to absorb his comings and goings almost familiarly, regarding them as like the sensation of the hand when it arrived below her wrist, moments when she was also uniquely and wildly alive. And just as she'd often thought of that pain as floating free, as living stubbornly, Jonas's visits told her he would inhabit her mind whenever he wished, that he had not at all been severed.

Standing in the darkness of the shop, she looked up to the brightly lit second-story windows above the shoe store next to the Claring House. She'd begun to watch with a growing fascination the woman who lived in these rooms. She was an

artist, a painter, who usually worked late at night, and Ramona
felt grateful for the lights in her windows; for the woman's busy
movement through her rooms; for knowing there was someone
else on Strait awake so late. It felt to her like company.

She couldn't see the woman now.

That night, when she'd left Donnie's trailer, Ramona had
waited until he'd begun his regular breathing, then eased out of
bed. She'd picked her clothes up from the floor, feeling in her
jeans for the money she'd taken from Jesus Christ's wallet, and,
after pausing to hear that Donnie's breath hadn't altered, she'd
slipped out the door. Naked, she'd hurried in strong moonlight
down the rutted lane, getting some distance from the trailer
before stopping to dress.

It had taken her four days to walk forty miles south, to end
here in Claring. Because she'd wanted to keep a true direction in
mind, she'd stayed close to the parkway—walking its shoulder
now and then for an easy few miles; buying some food when
she reached a crossroads store or coffee shop; then moving back
into the cover of the landscape, through the edge of woods and
the end rows of fields. She'd felt that the countryside and the
smallest dirt roads were all that were left to her. If she'd walked
the local highways, she'd have been on Ed King's roads. She'd
imagined Donnie's station wagon driving up and down the
parkway. All the while she'd walked its shoulder, she'd kept
turning around to the sound of the cars coming behind her.
Each time a car flew past, she'd been almost surprised it was not
his station wagon.

No one stopped to offer her a ride while she'd walked along
the parkway and after a time she'd begun to believe that she
could continue in this way, moving south in a camouflage of
corn and woods, for as long as she wished. But by the time she'd
reached Claring, she was too tired to walk farther, so she'd
cleaned herself up in the bathroom of a gas station just off the

parkway—smiling ruefully as she washed at the memory of the Chief Tah-Kah-Nic Diner—and walked on into town to find a temporary room.

Before Van Nostrand had hired her, she'd been coming down in the late afternoon from the apartment he'd rented her above his shop to look at the flowers in his front window. Her rooms lost the sun around three o'clock, causing their musty smell to thicken almost instantly. No one had lived in them for nearly six months.

Focusing on the flowers in the window, Ramona could lose herself temporarily and she'd been standing on the sidewalk, staring at the displays and feeling gratefully adrift, when Van Nostrand placed a help-wanted sign in front of a row of potted geraniums.

For Ramona the sign had been incredibly well timed. The money she'd stolen from Jesus Christ's wallet was running out, but she'd given little thought to how she would get more. She was thinking no farther than the end of each day. Vaguely, she'd decided that when the week ended and more rent was due, she would wait until dark before sneaking out of Claring.

And then she'd seen Van Nostrand's sign and, impulsively, walked in to talk to him. They'd spoken awkwardly of the coincidence of her renting his rooms and now asking him for work in his shop. She'd assured him that her hand wouldn't keep her from carrying, wrapping, doing anything manually necessary, although she didn't know if this was true. As she spoke to Van Nostrand, she felt herself working hard to persuade him. To her own surprise, she grew desperate to convince him. She tried to speak calmly to disguise her sudden sense of need.

Van Nostrand said she should have told him that she wanted work. She said she hadn't thought that he would have some. She'd watched Van Nostrand nod and rock slightly on his feet,

and she sensed he was pleased for the chance to hire her, assuring him more rent. It hadn't occurred to her that Van Nostrand had been intrigued by her from the start and had become increasingly so as he'd watched her regular afternoon appearances outside his shop. And so, acting also on impulse when he'd seen her standing on the sidewalk staring in at his flowers, he'd placed the sign in his window in the hope that she'd come in.

For the past couple of weeks, Van Nostrand had begun to stay most days at his larger shop in Rhinebeck and leave the Claring shop to Ramona. Her mood brightened considerably when she knew she was going to be alone and could look forward to the pleasure of closing up at night, an act that had become more and more invested with a private pageantry. As the day neared its closing hour she grew impatient to lock the front door. She welcomed her high spirits at the end of the day all the more for the distance they'd traveled, since Ramona opened her eyes most mornings after sleeping fitfully if at all and wanted only to stay in her bed, sure that now, within the safer shapes of daylight, she could fall to the very bottom of sleep. She often persuaded herself to get out of bed in the morning by reciting a kind of lyric, a deliberate ceremony, she'd been groggily revising a little each day.

"I am breathin' deep blue air," she'd murmur tunelessly as she sat on the edge of her bed. "If life is weather, then it's 'fair.' And there ain't a hill of con-se-quence in this entire town." It seemed to her a way of rephrasing her resolve and—until she could figure out where she would go next and how she would decide—of holding on to the belief that this place, this life, was better than the one she'd left. She'd substituted the word "consequence" for the phrase "that matters" a few days ago, after overhearing it spoken by the painter who lived in the apartment above the shoe store. Ramona had stood next to her at the A&P deli counter down the street, enjoying the quick assurance of her manner, the woman tossing orders to the man

in his silly paper hat as he rushed back and forth from the meat case to the slicer.

She turned to the back of the shop and thought that whatever else you might say about Van Nostrand, it was clear he knew his business. He'd recently told Ramona that he dreaded November more than any other month; it contained no holiday that really helped a florist. ("The best you can expect for Thanksgiving is some ghastly corsage for Grandma.") He told her that it was also historically slow for both weddings and adultery and that, for some inexplicable reason which held true year after year, very few people died in Claring in November.

There'd been only two telephone orders and three or four customers in the shop all day.

Ramona walked to the back and knelt before the flower case, its light a bluish sheet angling to the floor. She wiggled on her knees until she felt entirely within it and she flushed with appetite. Since she'd sold so little today there was nearly a full stock to choose from. Bunches of iris. Three colors of rose. Carnations. Her glance refused only daisies, which grew wild in the fields where she'd last slept in Myles. Recently she'd dreamed of walking through an endless lawn of daisies which tugged at her skirt as she stumbled along and coiled themselves as snakes around her struggling ankles.

She opened the case, felt its cooled air on her face, and reached for three pink rose buds.

"Hello?" called a voice over the clang of the front door's bell. Ramona flew up to a crouch, the case door slamming closed, and sneaked behind a shelf of plants, looking toward the alley door.

"Hello? Are you open?" And now she heard that the voice, sounding nearly irritated, was a woman's. "I saw your little light in the back."

Ramona slowly straightened and squinted blindly toward the voice; the figure remained a shape in the dark near the door.

"Just closin'," Ramona said weakly. She couldn't believe she'd forgotten to lock the front.

"Closin'," the voice said, deliberately affecting Ramona. "Well, does that mean I can buy flowers or not?" Her manner was not so much abrasive as impatient, someone suddenly advancing the metronome to which a room's been moving.

"Have anything particular in mind?" Ramona asked.

"Yeah," the woman said. "Flowers. If you turn a light on I'll buy some and you can finish closin'."

Ramona walked around the shelf to the switch by the front door. She blinked in the full light and now could see that her customer was the painter who lived across the street.

"Thanks," the woman said and headed immediately for the case as Ramona, thinking clearly again, had a chance to take her in. Her pace and brusqueness reminded Ramona of certain weekend residents who came up from New York on Friday nights and often stopped in the shop on Saturday to buy flowers for their dinner parties. She wondered if the woman had moved to Claring from New York. Whenever she waited on them, Ramona tried to feel a hostility for the city people, because it was clear from the local attitude that you were supposed to. But they were a species she'd never encountered, and she was too curious to be able to dislike them. No one from New York owned a country house near Myles, sixty miles northeast of Claring and deeply isolated in the hills by its moat of spilling poverty.

The woman's jeans and boots were splotched and streaked with paint; yellow, blue, several shades of brown and orange. She was large, though not fat at all, and beneath her down jacket she wore a loose white cotton blouse, its intricate lace front reminding Ramona of her grandmother's yellowed doilies pinned over holes in the arms of her living-room chair.

"Oh, I don't care," she said, peering into the case. "I'll take the lilies there and the iris—wow, look at those iris! They're

terrific! And . . ." She noticed the pink roses on the floor. "And give me those, since you were chucking them, anyway."

Con-se-quence, Ramona thought.

"Yeah," the woman said distractedly, "that'll be good." She picked up the pink roses.

Ramona tried to envision the woman's lover receiving so many flowers. Watching from her own windows, Ramona knew that he came to see her most evenings, arriving at dinnertime in an old blood-red Toyota. But he rarely spent the night, and the woman usually turned her lights on again and began to paint after he'd left.

"Okay? Are we all set?" The woman smiled reflexively. "I'm in a hurry to get back." She nodded to her building across the street.

She started to hand the pink roses to Ramona, who felt the gesture for a moment as the offering of a gift. But her hand was holding the door of the case. And then the woman noticed Ramona's other hand, the anomalous elegance of its mannequin's curl. Her mouth made an O of flitting surprise and, seeing the distraction, Ramona instantly used it. "You know," she began, "I can't do this to ya."

The woman looked confused.

Ramona said, "See, these flowers has had it. They been in the case at least four or five days and I was tossin' them out when you came in."

"No shit?" the woman said. She looked into the case, then at Ramona.

Ramona nodded. "You was thinking they looked okay."

"They look fine, actually," the woman said.

"They ain't. It's just the cool in the case that keeps them up. They wouldn't last till you got your coat off," Ramona said.

"Perfect," the woman said sarcastically. She continued to study the flowers.

As Ramona saw her lie working, she began to feel sad for the woman, and also for her lover. She imagined him being so

touched by the gift he would throw the woman to her couch as soon as he saw them while she laughed and squirmed and pretended to worry that the flowers needed to be put in water right away. Still, Ramona thought, she needed them more than he did.

Ramona looked at the woman. She said, "There *is* the daisies. The daisies isn't old like the others. In fact, I was leavin' in the daisies."

The woman squinted in at them, white-and-yellow daisies, their centers pregnant as egg yolks. "*Just* the daisies?"

"We get daisies more often," Ramona lied. "I think the owner cuts a deal with a special daisy guy."

The woman smiled and suddenly she spread her arms, a pulpit pose, the down jacket whispering silkily. "All right! Give me every daisy. I'll turn the place into a fucking pasture!" She held her arms spread. " 'Meadows trim, with daisies pied. Shallow brooks, and rivers wide,' " She laughed and raised her eyebrows as she looked at Ramona.

"Whatever," Ramona said, smiling herself, though the meadows haunting her these days were anything but trim. She removed the daisies quickly, as if their stems were hot.

The woman helped her carry and wrap them, as customers often offered to do when they noticed Ramona's hand. She usually resented and refused their aid, sometimes punishing them for asking to help by being deliberately clumsy as she handled the flowers. But at the moment Ramona felt pleased, felt a sense of reprieve. She watched the daisies disappear beneath green tissue paper and thought of them as children someone else could freely love. Such visions—a bunch of daisies finding love; a rheum-eyed dog that roamed Strait Street which she thought of as an orphan—were another way Jonas found her now.

"Here's a card so you can write his name, and something else if you want. Maybe that rhyme you just said."

"Okay," the woman said, blurting a giggle, "why not." She

took the pen and wrote on the card. "To David," she spoke as she wrote, then paused and continued, "A good man for these troubled times." She signed the card "Goliath" and turned it to Ramona. "What do you think?"

"Goliath?"

"A private joke," the woman said.

Ramona shrugged. "Sorry there was just daisies."

"*Hey*," the woman said. "This has been the best damn daisy experience of my life to date."

Ramona laughed.

"Really. They're terrific. What I needed in the way of flowers was a *lot* of them. What kind was of no consequence." She walked to the door and paused, then turned back to Ramona and shouted, "Ah-hah! I *got* it. It was driving me crazy, frankly, where I'd seen you before."

"You seen *me*?"

"At the A&P one morning." The woman smiled. "You were studying that deli case like everything in it was going to be on the final. And then you looked up at the kid helping me and said, 'What the hell is lox?' " She laughed deeply at the memory, but Ramona felt embarrassed, her question sounding nakedly stupid to her as she heard it repeated.

The woman said, "You were so *serious*. 'What the hell is lox?' Terrific." She looked at Ramona again as though taking her in for the first time. "Actually, who are you, anyway? My name's May. May Monaghan."

"Ramona King." She pronounced the name almost as one word, a habit she'd originally worked to perfect.

"It's a pleasure, Ramona King," May said playfully. "You run a damn fine flower shop here, even if you sell only one flavor." She nodded. "*Ciao*." And she was gone.

Ramona watched her run across the street, the flowers to her chest, and through the street-level door to the right of the shoe shop. "Whew," she said to herself. She smiled. "Meadows trim and daisy pie." She walked once more to the flower case.

At last she was able to assemble her bouquet, and as she did her thoughts turned to these increasingly frequent thefts. She argued that she deserved the flowers as a bonus, since she suspected—had from the beginning—that she got less money than Van Nostrand usually paid his help. But this sounded unconvincing even as she thought it.

She stepped through the shop's back door and started up the steps to her apartment. Railroad tracks paralleling the alley began to hum and she rushed to get inside before the train arrived. At the top of the steps she heard its whistle and she was standing in her kitchen when the next blast came. Ramona jumped despite herself. She'd been trying to learn the timing of the train's approaching sounds but its noise remained pattern-less and immense. She stood, propped against the roar, a sound not nearly so loud to her as the slam of the screen door of her house in Myles.

The kitchen swayed from the force of the passing train and Ramona lit a cigarette and wrapped her sweater more tightly around her.

She put her flowers into a big glass jar and took them, as always, into her bedroom and set them on the orange crate next to her bed. Back in the kitchen, she watched the caboose pass her window, a delicate clattering fading eastward, then opened the refrigerator for the delicatessen cold cuts she ate every night. Ham, salami, chicken roll, and, most of all, lox, which she bought rarely, in tiny quantity, because it cost so much. She loved its velvet pinkness; it seemed the softest underside of some exotic animal.

She carried her plate through the bedroom to the front room, its two tall windows facing Strait, and turned on the radio by the couch. She'd found a country station and she always played it loudly for the first minute or so to sweep the room of silences that collected like dust balls in its corners through the day. She listened as a woman with a hitch of grief in her throat sang of swinging through the air on the high trapeze of love while her

lover, placed to catch her, preened for women in the crowd. "Don't let go," Ramona said to the singer of the song. "Hold the bar with both hands, honey." She seated herself at the window. Across Strait, May's second-story windows were tall panes of light. Ramona saw no sign of her, though, only the shelves and furnishings of her studio, the easel near the windows holding a canvas of bright blue and yellow shapes she couldn't distinguish.

Ramona leaned farther forward to survey the empty street. Like the flower shop below, her front room gave her the view of Strait, of Claring, that she needed to have.

The woman on the radio slipped from the high trapeze of love and was spinning like a wheel, screaming "Help," her mind areel, needing lovin' hands of steel, to snag her as she fell.

Ramona imagined the tumbling woman, her body splayed by her terror against the flat blue wall of air. "Hope you got a net," she said to her. "That asshole ain't gonna catch you."

A car door slammed. Below, Ramona saw the old Toyota in front of the shoe shop. She watched May Monaghan's lover move quickly through the outside door.

The singer reached the end of her song, spinning forever in a tent-covered sky, the trapeze high above her, her lover down below, the swinging bar and his hard heart stamped from the same cold steel.

Ramona held her eyes on the windows, and finally May's lover walked into the studio and came near the window. He held the daisies in a vase, looking around the room for where he might put them down. Finally he set the vase on the floor and dropped into a large chair with swollen arms, the studio's only piece of furniture. He was short and stocky, yet he seemed to Ramona whenever she'd watched him almost to float when he moved, to skim the floors and sidewalks. He held a beer. Ramona liked to watch him drink; his sips were almost dainty.

May came into the studio now, wearing a nightgown with a border of lace at its neck which caught Ramona's eye. It was

scalloped, like the crust-webbed doilies on her grandmother's armchair; like the spread of May's white cotton chest; like the lapping white of daisies.

May settled onto an arm of the chair and swung her legs into his lap. Her slender feet were bare. Ramona watched his hands slowly stroke them and slide up along her legs. She took his beer and drank thirstily. Ramona ran her finger over her lips and felt them absolutely dry. She worked some saliva forward and applied it like lipstick with her finger.

David reached up to kiss her and appeared to be lifted from the cushion by the force of her mouth. Again, he seemed weightless, rising with a helium ease to the chair's opposite arm. Their arms reached across the space between them. Ramona saw May's left hand knead David's shoulder, and then her right hand came around to join it and Ramona was briefly startled by the sight of two hands, the aberration of a pair, roaming in unison over his back, cupping themselves as if in search of octaves. Some nights, sitting in the dark at three o'clock, at four, and watching May paint, as though peering over her shoulder while she worked across the street, Ramona had become fixated on May's hand moving over a canvas.

She'd never seen May and David behave so recklessly, though she'd often watched them touch and lightly kiss one another as they moved about the rooms and, from across the street, catching moments between them as they passed May's windows, Ramona wondered if her memory of the days with Donnie could possibly be true. For she remembered having moved just that way through Donnie's trailer and out along the river—with that same lightness and with a sure, responsive ease—and what she saw across the street seemed to her now a kind of framed dream, behind windows and separate from anything like life.

For weeks after she'd left Donnie, the sense of him had stayed strong. Feeling Ed's hate coming toward her, feeling fearful, feeling light-headed with guilt as she was abruptly

overwhelmed by thoughts and sounds of Jonas, she tried to remember the pleasure of those days with Donnie, and she could hold him in her mind like a vivid, lesser grief. At night, she saw Donnie's face floating above her, a nearly weeping moon in the black sky of her room. But as the weeks passed, her feelings settled gradually into an abiding melancholy, the brief life with him seeming at times almost illusory.

Now Ramona watched May's legs open and David's hands go to her thighs. Her nightgown lifted as she wriggled forward on the chair arm to open herself more. Her calves were as taut as an athlete's. David's fingers played her in a lightly brushing circle; he seemed to be slowly and with awe solving the most delicate lock. May's eyes were closed, and she let her head fall to one side.

Ramona wet her mouth again and bent over her plate to lick a slice of lox, and its taste took her back until she felt her lips against the ridge of Jonas's salt-damp ear. The taste of her child shocked her. She picked up the lox and rhythmically began to swallow it. It appeared to climb into her throat. She closed her eyes and chewed it slowly.

When she turned to look across the street again there was no light in the studio, only a gauzy circle on a wall of the bedroom behind. Some nights she'd seen their shadows fleetingly cut this circle of light while they sought some particular pose. But there were no shadows tonight, and Ramona knew somehow there'd be none.

She listened to the radio for a minute more. She felt at the same time full, her belly distended, and yet as though she were carrying nothing inside her.

A man on the radio sang of betrayal; he'd smelled the musk of infidelity cutting through the scent of his wife's brand-new perfume.

Ramona rose and walked toward the kitchen, leaving the radio on.

She claims she changed her brand for me, but I know better still.

It's true she smells all new, but it's the "him" on her I smell.
Some nights, having seen May and David move through the
most routine domestic evenings, Ramona lay in her bed inside a
thrumming heat, seeing Donnie, his face floating above her.
Sometimes Donnie became Ed; Ed before he'd changed; rising
toward her, his ribs against his skin like a spread of bony
plumage. And some nights, even if her eyes had followed May
and David arm in arm toward their bed, Ramona dropped into
her own feeling numb, her mind kaleidoscopically distracted.

She felt tonight in a floating middle place. She walked from
the room to the kitchen and put her plate in the sink. She looked
out the back window at the night, so dark it hid even the sense
of the railroad tracks. The darkness gave her nothing to see and
an image of May and David in the chair filled her mind. She
thought of the last night she'd spent with Donnie after they'd
returned from the bar, when she'd lain beside him, held by her
fear and her need to leave, as she waited to hear his long, tidal
sighs.

Standing at the sink, looking out at moonless darkness, a
heavy tiredness settled suddenly over her and she wanted just
to sleep.

Fourteen

Ed eased himself off the truck and watched Adams push a roll of snow fence from the front of the flatbed toward him. The fence sagged as it was rolled, its wooden pickets creaking agedly.

"Okay, drop it," Ed said. Adams kicked the roll off the truck and went to get another.

Ed turned to the field beside the highway and squinted into it, his gaze traveling back toward the town. Especially, he tried to make his eyes detail the back of his own house, to see if he could trace its features from where he stood, the field's full length away. He was not surprised to see it as merely a squat white cube at the bottom edge of Myles, but a sense of disappointment passed through him, nevertheless. When Bill March had told the crew they'd be spending the day running snow fence along the edge of this field, a span notoriously prone to drifts that spilled onto the highway, Ed had felt a lifting hope,

in spite of himself, that he'd be able as he worked to keep his house in view, to see it well enough to spot her at the moment if she returned today.

Adams dropped another roll of fence off the truck, watching Ed furtively all the while. Ed had seemed to him this morning even more preoccupied than usual and Adams had thought that hardly possible. Except for his recent outbursts of accusation, Ed's attention, Adams felt, had been turning ever further inward to concerns which Adams couldn't possibly imagine. Despite his conscious efforts and his private rehearsals of disavowal, Adams had been unable to be free of Ed. If anything, his interest had been heightened even more by his sense of Ed's withdrawal.

But not until the truck had pulled to a stop was Ed's mood this morning made suddenly clear to Adams. Only then did he realize, as he told himself he should have immediately, that they'd be working along the edge of the field through which Ramona had walked to reach this highway.

Mitchell and Day began to set out orange warning cones behind the truck. Ed heard the ceaseless voice of Waycross as he and March climbed out of the cab. "Most amazing damn thing I ever seen," Waycross was saying. He moved with his bent-backed step, surprisingly quick for a man who tried hard to be old in every other way, as though his nimbleness were a habit he'd not been able to break.

"This was when Everett Van Zandt owned the Hill Top, years before Moon bought it," Waycross said. He was supposedly speaking to March, who received the flow of his talk as he sat beside him in the truck through the day, but for all Waycross cared he was speaking to the air, to the fields. Waycross simply needed to talk, as one needs to exhale, and it was possible to imagine that, deprived of the ability, he would die within the minute.

Dead leaves covered the roadside, hiding the lay of the ditch,

but Ed shuffled through them without looking down, knowing, as he knew the features of so much of the roadland in Columbia County, that the leaves hid no tricky fall of landscape here, nothing but a smooth and shallow dip. He knew that a hundred yards north the ditch grew steep. As he walked, he kept his eyes on the white speck of his house. He carried pointed steel stakes in the crook of one arm. They looked like a collection of hideous spears. He held the sledgehammer he now refused to let anyone else use. It swung pendulously with his step.

"When Van Zandt seen this guy—guy's name was Gimpy Neal—coming down the street he'd draw three beers and set them on the bar, in a row like." Waycross and March helped Adams empty the truck. Mitchell and Day rolled fence through the ditch leaves toward Ed, who had dropped all but one stake and stood, his back to Waycross.

As he often had, Ed tried to imagine her as she'd walked through this field. He wondered again how she'd looked that morning. Had she taken slow, even steps, so as not to draw suspicion from anyone who might see her? Had she raced through the weeds, thrilled in her escape? Had she lurched between those extremes, checking her impatience for a few slow steps, then bursting forward, unable to hold herself in?

"So when Gimpy Neal come in the door, there'd be the row of beers waitin' for him and he'd drink one in about a second and a half and give it to Van Zandt and Van Zandt'd draw another glass and set it down at the end of the row and by that time Neal woulda almost drank the other two and that's the way it'd go, Neal drinkin', Van Zandt fillin'."

Ed decided, as he always did, that she'd moved haltingly, stumbling, often pausing, looking back.

"Neal drinkin', Van Zandt fillin'. Neither of 'em sayin' a word, like this was business. And I one night watched him drink *eighteen* glasses of beer like that, never stoppin', drinkin' beers like he was a goddam machine somebody had invented to

drink beer, before he stopped to blink an eye. Eighteen draws. Now, is that a-fucking-mazing or not?"

"Not," Mitchell said, scowling. "That is bull-fucking-shit." When Waycross told these stories of the past, Mitchell and Day, for different reasons, were always held by them. Mitchell ran his fingers through dirty blond hair that hung to the top of his back. He shook his head disgustedly. "Eighteen draws, my ass."

"By God, I saw it," Waycross said. "I'll bet you a dollar to a dog turd and hold the stakes in my mouth he did."

Ed set the point of a stake in the ground and gave it three strong blows. It sank into earth not yet too firmly frozen. He sited down the field's edge, anticipating the line of evenly spaced stakes he would set to hold the fence, and then a new thought came to him: that if such a fence had been up last summer, it might have been obstacle enough to have kept her in the field. In his mind's eye, he saw Ramona trying to climb over a snow fence, one that didn't stop, as this one would, but ran the field's entire width. He saw her, robbed of the power and balance that two hands would provide, working futilely to push herself over and clear, then surrendering, glancing around to see if anyone had observed her, and heading back toward the stroller.

"What'd he do then?" Day asked Waycross, his eyes magnified through thick glasses which were held in place with an elastic band behind his head. All but the foreman, March, had reached the ditch. They gathered near Ed, whose driven stake claimed the spot where work would start. March was walking the roadside to remind himself where the ditch became deep enough to hold the drifts and snow fence would no longer be needed. Reaching that spot, he sank an orange-flagged wire into the ground.

"Whaddaya mean, what'd he do?" Waycross asked Day.

Day was Mitchell's temperamental opposite. He believed everything anyone said. He read the newsstand tabloids

devotedly, relaying their contents in a tone of airy Scripture-citing awe. "You said he stopped after eighteen. What'd he do then?"

"Well . . . he just stood up, let go a belch that, if it'd been a rope it woulda wrapped twice around the room, and said, 'Hot out. I was thirsty.' Paid Van Zandt for his beers and walked out the door."

"Oh, God, go fuck yourself, old man," Mitchell groaned.

"Je-zuz," whispered Day. "That *is* amazing."

Adams laughed and shook his head and flittingly glanced at Ed, whose gaze into the field with his back still to the crew had been making him nervous, even a little angry. That part of Adams which was deeply invested in Ed's behavior felt oddly responsible for him at moments such as this, almost embarrassed by him, as though Ed's actions reflected on him.

Now Ed moved to face them, and his turning around, like a healer's sweep of hand, eased Adams's tension as they all paused to hear from him. As remote and unpredictable as he'd become, as wary of him as they'd all grown, there was a pattern working now which was so well established that no one except Adams gave a thought that Ed might not respond as he always had, after waiting in silence until Waycross had finished.

Sometimes, in these moments, Ed gave another version of Waycross's story, one he'd heard and stored among the Myles lore he loved. Sometimes he told them a contradictory anecdote. And sometimes, when he was tired or hungover or just fed up with Waycross's bullshit, he'd simply ask three or four questions, a kind of cross-examination that immediately showed whether Waycross was building on memories or lies. Ed always endorsed an improved fact, so long as it could be traced, but a moment of the past that turned out to be pure fantasy threatened something he simply sensed as elementally important: the history of Myles, which gave the town its language and required the root of truth. His interest in Myles's past, his avid seeking of

it, was the sort of eager turning toward reminiscence which usually preoccupies men three times his age.

The others had always heard Ed's words as a verdict on Waycross's tale, while the old man himself would bristle and curse but never appeal and, soon afterward, simply launch another story.

Now they all waited. Ed stared into their faces, and Adams could see, from Ed's eyes, that he'd been watching more than the fields while his back had been turned. Their cast seemed to Adams to be aberrantly angled, like headlights out of line, high and to the side on a fully private world.

Ed had paid no attention to what Waycross was saying, his voice mere droning noise. And now he saw that they were waiting for him. He blinked and cleared his throat, as though stalling until a flicker of senility had passed, and said at last, "I got work to do." Then he reached down to pick up the pile of stakes and called to March, "How far apart you want 'em?"

He drove a stake with his sledgehammer, walked a line of carefully measured steps, boot heel against toe, then drove another, progressing toward the orange flag that Bill March had set. It was the sort of chore Ed loved, could normally lose himself in, the precise recurrence of the work enfolding him as he saw in each repetition the chance to duplicate exactly the sequence just completed. Adams did the work across the road in the opposite ditch; the rest of the crew mended cut and crumbled roadside. When enough stakes had been set, they'd all unroll fence and attach it with wire.

But today Ed's concentration wasn't on his work. He stopped, picked up a stake, looking not ahead toward March's orange flag, but through the field toward the tiny square of his house. His eyes left it only as he drove a stake; otherwise he held them on the house so strongly that he caught himself walking a

crooked line, drawn into the field by the pull of his focus. And the harder he looked, the larger the house seemed to him to grow, the more finely its lines showed.

He thought he could make out a smaller pale shape next to the house—the low sweep of the Dodge. The thought of the car made him wince, reminding him of last night, when he'd fucked Wilma Jean in its tight backseat. For Wilma Jean had become nothing more than another source of trouble for Ed, constantly telling him things he had no wish to know. Every time he saw her she talked of high school days, her memory and impressions incredibly fresh, scenes involving her and him and Ramona in which Ramona hadn't been as good to him as she would have been. He could hardly get her to be quiet long enough to fuck, and as soon as they'd finished she'd resume her memory where he'd stopped it, her anger at Ramona in his behalf at precisely the pitch she'd left it when he'd begun to peel her jeans down her legs.

Behind him, Day and Mitchell shoveled loose chunks of highway onto the back of the truck and spoke of a waitress at the Legion Hall in Mellenville. Mitchell said, "I think she wants me."

"How do you know?" Day asked, pausing with his shovel.

" 'Cause Tuesday night, I was in there, she come over and whispered in my ear, 'I want you.' "

"Really?" asked Day.

"No," Mitchell said.

They hooted in unison, and their laughter seemed to Ed to be purposely interrupting him. He concentrated even more on his house, trying to bring it closer so he'd be able to see her if she came around to the backyard. He narrowed his eyes and the view seemed to tighten and he stopped, holding for several moments the conviction that he *had*, by the force of his will, drawn his house toward him.

"Anyway, she ain't the only one," Mitchell said. "There's so much ass in that town, all you gotta do is show up."

Ed tried to fight off Mitchell's voice. Wouldn't it be something, he thought, if Ramona appeared right now? His eyes
burned fiercely from his effort to hold them on the house.

"That is true about Mellenville," Waycross said. "It's always
been that way. I remember once—"

"No, old man!" Mitchell shouted. "Don't remember nothing.
Don't remember another fucking thing!"

And then Ed saw . . . that the enormous maple tree which
towered above his house was a featureless twig from this far
away. And he saw that the length of his backyard was no more
than a faint brown thread.

Jesus Christ. Of course.

He let the sledgehammer slide from his grip and placed his
hands over his eyes. He began to laugh silently, his back still to
the others. Jesus, he thought, what'd I *think* I could see? His
laughter was growing but he kept it soundless, letting it escape
through the side of his mouth, his body quivering like a dog's
passing dreams.

He asked himself how he would know when Ramona returned. How would he know if he wasn't there, inside the
house? She would sneak back in and he wouldn't fucking know.
He felt his body shaking and fought to still it with the strength
he would use to subdue another man. Christ, yes, he thought,
that's what was going to happen. She knew when he'd be
working, and that's when she'd come back.

As he'd imagined her return, all his thoughts had been of the
instant itself, of the sight and especially the shoe-scuffing
sounds of Ramona making her way up their walk, while he
stood motionless at the door watching her approach. He'd
glimpsed in his mind countless versions of his response, a range
of behavior showing him how soon he would be violent, how
violent he would be. Ramona, on the other hand, was unvary-
ingly the slumped defeated figure pleading forgiveness on any
terms he chose.

And every impulse depended entirely on that scene. Ed had

no imagination for the day afterward, or for any kind of life they might resume. Nothing had mattered in his mind but that satisfying moment, and now he was struck with the certainty that she would easily avoid it. A sourness filled him. He couldn't believe he hadn't seen something so obvious until now and the fact of it ran through him, leaving him weak inside a silent fit of acid-tasting laughter.

Day, who habitually did even less work than Waycross, ate enormous lunches. He sat on the floor of the truck with his legs extended, a banquet of sandwiches and packaged desserts fanned out in front of him. The others were scattered near the truck, taking late-autumn sun that kept the chill in the air at their perimeter.

From the edge of the ditch, where he sat, Ed watched Day, whom he'd always dismissed, for his careless work, for his gullibility, and because he ate so much, a kind of unearned excess to Ed's way of thinking. In the past, from high school on, he'd mostly ignored him, but watching him now, his anger moving immanently after the revelations of the morning, he wanted to hurt Day badly.

"I was readin' about this woman?" Day said as he chewed. "She was runnin' in one of those marathons? And she give birth to a baby about halfway through the race and still finished second."

"Jesus," Mitchell said wearily, gnawing a chicken bone. Day did not irritate Mitchell as Waycross did. He knew Day made nothing up, telling only what he'd heard or read. "Why do you *believe* that shit, anyway?"

Day asked, defensively, "So why do they print it then, if all it is is bullshit?"

"So dumb fucks like you will buy it," Ed said. His words were quick and in pursuit. The others raised their eyes uneasily,

recognizing the new sound they'd been hearing in Ed's voice. Adams felt his stomach tighten.

"What else'd you read, Day?" Ed said. He lay on his side against the ditch, propped up on one arm. "Tell me some more news."

"Jesus, Ed, forget it," Day said.

He seemed to Ed a pouting child and when he said nothing more and reached in front of him for a fruit-filled turnover Ed's anger cohered as many whorls inside his head.

"Forget it? I don't wanna forget it, Day. I want you to tell me about that woman havin' a kid while she run in the race. That musta been something to see, huh, Day? How'd she do it, anyway? She run kinda spread-eagle, so the kid could just pop right out while she's waddlin' along?" Day no longer seemed to Ed too worthless for his fury. Nothing did. "Did she carry the kid, Day, or what? Or did she bring a knife along to cut the cord?"

Bill March put down his mug of coffee and stood up. "Okay, Ed. Okay."

Ed stood, too. The whorls were making a quick-beating hum and a luminous red tint like the chroma of a lens was on everything. "Shit, March. Don't you wanna know the news? Ain't you interested in this amazing goddam woman Day's tellin' us about?"

Adams watched, unable to speak, wanting more than anything to stop him. But though he sensed Ed losing control, and was hearing again the pitch of Ed's new abuse, Adams could not step into its way. He'd always received whatever Ed gave and it was all he knew how to do.

Waycross sat on the ground, hunched and cross-legged like a shrunken Indian, sprinkling tobacco into his cigarette paper. "Come on, King," he said. "Sit down, why don't ya?"

Ed spun toward Waycross. "I don't need your shit, old man." The red tint was deepening. "I do *not* need your shit." He

looked into Waycross's wrinkled face. "If I want any shit outa you, I'll squeeze your fuckin' head, Waycross."

Waycross looked at March, then shook his head and licked the cigarette paper.

"Come on, Ed," March said. He glanced at his watch. "It's almost one. Let's all get back to work."

Ed pointed at Day. "Day can't go back to work. He ain't finished with his lunch. Lookit! You got three, four pieces of pie still, right, Day?"

"Jesus Christ, Ed," Day said softly. "What'd I do to you? Just leave me alone, okay?"

Ed started toward him. "You're right," he said, speaking with an abruptly turned softness. The red-tinted world was pulsing. "You're absolutely right, Day, and I'm gonna apologize by giving you a hand." He walked calmly past March and reached Day, on the truck. "I'm gonna help you eat your lunch so nobody's waitin' on you and we can all get back to work."

Day looked dubiously at Ed.

"Gimme one of them pies," Ed said, pointing to a turnover wrapped in waxed paper. "Come on. I wanna help you out. I'm apologizin', see?" He continued to point. "Gimme that one there."

Day tried to look for help, for some signal of advice, but Ed stood directly in front of him, blocking his view of the others. Ed's face was solemn charity.

"You heard March," Ed said. "He wants us back to work."

Day reached slowly for the turnover and handed it to Ed. "I'm helpin' you, Day," Ed said again. "You ain't got *time* to eat all you got there."

As he walked away his fingers closed on the turnover. He looked down at it in his hand, feeling some of the rage move out of his head and down his shoulder as he squeezed. Bright-red fruit filling burst through its package and ran between his fingers. He watched it eddy thickly, coagulative with sugar, at the base of his palm. He thought obviously of blood.

When he turned back to Day his arm felt separate and bloated with strength. He aimed at nothing in particular, wanting to be rid of everything inside him, and flung the pie past Day; it splattered against the end slats of the flatbed.

Ed breathed deeply three times; he had nothing in his chest. Nobody moved or said anything, so the sound of his breathing was an exhalant breeze. He walked toward the ditch and along the edge of the field to the last stake he'd driven before stopping for lunch.

Adams watched him, feeling in a way he couldn't name a sickening sense of loss.

Everyone worked quietly, moving about with a quick constricted step. Low murmurs drifted among them. Adams glanced frequently across the road, nervously conscious of Ed in the opposite ditch.

Ed was furious now at several things, at Day for provoking him, but chiefly at the certainty his morning's thoughts had brought. What returned now was the picture of her leaving and he began to imagine it with a gift for details he'd never had. It was nothing he was trying for, they came on their own, but he had no trouble whatsoever feeling the sun of that morning. Suddenly, he was breathing August heat, inspiring him to sweat, and he saw Ramona's face, beads of sweat on her forehead, sweat blisters above her lip, her neck slick and glistening. He unzipped his hooded sweatshirt and tossed it on the ground.

The mood among the rest of the crew began to loosen. March told Waycross, Mitchell, and Day to get in the back of the truck while he drove it forward several yards to the next bad patch of highway. Day climbed up onto the flatbed and Mitchell goosed him with the handle of his rake. "Oooh," Day cried, "that felt good."

Seeing Mitchell goose Day inspired Waycross to memories of

the Army, barracks life in Oklahoma, where he claimed a Pfc
from Georgia used to regularly masturbate the camp's pet dog,
a skinny mutt who stood on his hind legs in obedient ecstasy
while the private held his front paws in his left hand and
worked him rhythmically with his right, as though coaxing an
udder.

Hearing the story, Mitchell shrieked and threw a glove at
Waycross, but not with any anger, as the truck pulled to a stop
twenty feet from Ed and Adams.

Ed again heard their voices distinctly. They'd been talking
about him since lunch, he was sure. He'd heard their laughter,
and even though they spoke softly he'd caught a few words
now and then that he was convinced had his name in them. But
now that they were close he was sure they'd be quiet.

The Ramona he was picturing could barely lift her legs
through the field's high grass. The heat and the weight of the air
were stopping her. He heard the voluminous sigh of the weeds
as she shuffled through. He heard her panting.

Waycross leaned on his shovel, moving his toothless gums
back and forth against each other. Waycross didn't know what
Ed's mood was now but he had no interest in testing it, so he
spoke in a very low voice.

"You guys heard about Bob Petrie, didn't ya?" he asked,
almost whispering.

Day raised his eyebrows in cordial invitation.

"You ain't? I thought everybody'd heard about it." A sibilance drifted. "Well, you know Petrie took in the Tabler kid
after Tabler's old man kicked him out."

Day said, "He's livin' in Petrie's basement, right?"

Waycross nodded.

Ed pictured Ramona walking directly toward him. She was
near enough to show him the expression on her face, a grimace
of exhaustion. He listened again for the labor of her breath but
heard instead Waycross's whisper carrying his name.

"Everybody's just a happy little family at the Petries' house.

Petrie and his old lady, Connie, and the Tabler kid, snug as fucking bugs." The pitch of Waycross's sarcasm was perfect, enticing even Mitchell.

Ed heard *happy little family* and *his old lady*. He tried to act as if he didn't know Waycross was talking about him. He started to measure his steps to the next stake, but lost the count and had to start again. He felt suddenly surrounded: Ramona inching toward him through the field, showing him how much she was willing to hurt to get away, while Waycross and the others were having open fun with him.

He tried a third time to walk thirty steps but stopped, mindless of the count.

"So one day," Waycross said, "Petrie comes home from work and calls to Connie, but he gets no answer. He figures she's gone somewhere, which is strange since she don't leave no note like she always does."

The others snorted delightedly, knowing now what was coming. Adams stopped his work, too, and walked up to the truck to listen.

Ed heard *lady . . . gone . . . leave no note*, and the smothered snickering of the others. The anger was sounding again, the same hum before but softening beneath Waycross's whispers, as though its deft accompaniment. He heard Waycross say something more he couldn't quite identify, but now his voice had become the same as Marvin Broder's, speculating in the Hill Top how limply Ed must hang.

He looked into the field and imagined Ramona coming to a stop as she saw a span of snow fence at the end of her path. He saw her bend over, her hand on her knee, to get her breath. He felt a pulse of hope.

Waycross began to make a cigarette. "So Petrie calls toodle fucking loo again, and still don't get nothing back, except he hears some funny rustling from the basement." March and Day were already laughing. "You ain't heard about this?" Waycross said. "So he thinks, 'What the fuck?' and tiptoes down, and it's

just a damn shame, really, for all of 'em, that there ain't no way to get outa the house from the basement except the stairs Petrie's standin' on."

Ed picked up a stake and drove it, not caring where.

A damn shame, really . . . no way to get outa the house . . .

He imagined Ramona straightening up and looking directly into his eyes. He picked up his stakes and hurried to set another. Then he saw her look to her right and immediately head off again, angling through the grass toward March's orange flag, where the ditch became steep past the end of the fence.

His panic bloomed as he saw her moving toward the end of the field where there was no fence. She walked through the weeds with energetic confidence. She lifted her legs high. Her walk was all her own, then became Broder's flaunting march through the snow, then again Ramona's own in the radiant heat of August.

Ed managed to choke his scream; it came out as a thin, high sound only Adams picked up and when he heard it he turned from Waycross to watch Ed.

Ed kept himself from running through the ditch. He imagined cutting her off, driving stakes as he ran, all the way to the field's end. Somehow he'd move quickly enough to get the fence set in time. But he stayed where he was, shutting his eyes against the vision of anything more, and it worked. With his eyes closed to the field, he saw only soft bleached light.

"And there they was, Connie and the Tabler kid, naked as jays in the Tabler kid's bed. And you know what she says? She stammers around and kinda whines, 'Oh, Bob. I thought you was goin' to Chatham today.' Like the whole thing's really Petrie's fault for not goin' to Chatham!"

Ed felt their laughter engulf him. He picked up the sledge-hammer, aimed it at the stake he'd just set, and brought it down with all his strength. A resonant clang filled the air. He raised

the hammer higher and brought it down again. The stake descended in deep eager jerks.

He beat it again and again, the clanging regular, the ring of a vicious bell, and it stopped the others' laughter. They turned toward Ed and saw the hammer lifting above Ed's head, rising with the ease of a limb. It flew through its arc, struck the stake once more, and drove it almost flush with the ground.

Ed dropped to his knees to give it still another blow.

"Ed!" Adams shouted. "Stop it!" He broke away from the others and started down the ditch.

Ed heard enough of Adams's cry to make him pause as he started to swing down and he struck the stake with the neck of the hammer just below its head. A dull splintering sound reached the crew as it watched him. Ed felt the pain of his miss, slivered steel flying up through his forearms, before he looked down to see the hammer's shattered handle. It seemed to him wounded, a horribly fractured bone. He felt a sudden deep grief.

Still on his knees, he shifted around to see Adams coming toward him and he knew that Adams, in calling to him, had wanted this to happen. He'd tried to guard the hammer from all of them with just this fear in mind.

He got to his feet as Adams approached. He looked up at the others' faces, the pleasure of Waycross's story still holding their expressions, and saw that they were no longer even trying to hide their laughter from him. He picked up the sledgehammer as an impulse went through him which made him smile.

Ed's crooked grin stopped Adams, made him stumble, but it filled him with the warmth of a longing being touched. He saw Ed's smile as something once again affectionate, a sly show of their conspiracy restored, and Adams instinctively smiled in return and walked close to Ed, feeling eager and secure, ready for whatever Ed had in mind. He'd missed Ed's old strength so much he thought he recognized it.

Ed saw Adams walking toward him through the pulsing red screen. He said, "Laugh at me, you motherfuck," and Adams heard then he'd been mistaken, heard it quickly enough to see the sledgehammer moving. He lunged and grabbed it at the top of its swing and the two of them held its handle, held each other through the wood, stumbling in the ditch through a barbarous dance, spitting wet hissing noises through their teeth, the hammer high above their heads in brutal equipoise.

Fifteen

Her kitchen was soft with late-afternoon shade when she came in the door and Ramona turned on the light to cut what felt to her a gloom. She walked to the sink and turned on a second light, then into the tiny adjoining bathroom, flicking on its wall switch, too. She took off the heavy tweed coat, which was too big for her, an old one of Van Nostrand's daughter's, and threw it on a chair. Her cheeks felt cold to the back of her hand. She'd walked slowly from the church at the edge of the village through the cold gray day. Meandering, she'd stopped to watch a group of small boys playing football in a long brown-grassed yard, had followed from a distance two girls in parkas as they headed toward the dairy bar on the highway. She'd noticed before that only children ventured out on Sunday afternoon once the autumn chores were done, the leaves raked, once the weather had turned.

The funeral today was the second she'd been to in Claring.

Contrary to pattern, the month of November was busy with death in Dutchess County: these two; four in Rhinebeck; even two in the tiny settlement of Holliston. Van Nostrand, buoyant with business, had supplied the flowers for all of them and a week ago he'd asked Ramona to help him deliver several arrangements for the especially large service of a woman, much beloved in Claring, who'd raised eight children and, after them, two orphaned grandsons.

After she and Van Nostrand had finished at the church and he'd driven her back to Strait Street, Ramona had paced through her apartment, unable to quiet her curiosity about the old woman. Helping Van Nostrand place the wreaths and sprays, she'd read their satin sashes: Mother. In memory of Aunt Sarah. Grandmother Sarah. She'd never seen so many flowers, their sweet odors collecting about the altar to form a kind of tropic of sorrow, and finally she'd put her coat on and hurried back, slipping into a pew at the rear as the service was beginning. She'd sat in a row of six old women who watched and listened keenly, their eyes darting about the church for every detail, while the minister warned all those gathered that they would have to begin immediately to lead much more worthy lives if they held even a glimmer of hope of seeing Sarah again, so near the top of heaven was she living now, so selflessly had she lived on earth.

This afternoon's funeral had been smaller and seemed much sadder, but then she reasoned, as she walked into her bathroom and stood before the mirror, that perhaps it had felt that way because she'd sat only three rows behind the family, had peered between the heads of those in front of her to glimpse the beaked and powdered profile of the dead man in his open coffin, and had watched his teenage daughter weep uncontrollably throughout the service, her shoulders hitching through convulsions of grief even as she was helped down the aisle at the end in the arms of a man Ramona took to be her uncle.

She walked into the front room and turned the radio on

loudly, looking down at the empty street, glancing across to see if May was at her easel; her lights weren't on. When she'd first lived on Strait, especially when she stayed in the room above the Claring House, she'd looked forward to Sundays. With the bar and all the shops closed, the people gone, she'd felt that Strait was hers. But she'd come to dread its deserted quiet and some Sunday mornings, standing at her windows, seeing May and her lover climb into his car for what she feared would be a daylong trip, she imagined opening the window and calling down to them, asking them not to go.

The radiator clanged with the flow of air-pocketed water, but she was grateful for the noise, any noise. She walked back down the hall; in the bathroom again she turned the tub's faucets as far as they would go and it was as though the roar of the water were somehow animating the tub and making it seem like company.

She hadn't thought to question the pull the funerals had on her. She'd simply gone on an urge to the first one, drawn in part by the flowers' promise of a tribute on some unusual scale. And then, with the experience still fresh, had gone again this afternoon, once more feeling something, some deeply satisfying diversion, as she'd sat among the mourners.

It would be easy to assume that Ramona had gone because she'd found at the funerals a way to sit inside her own despair, even to ceremonialize through the deaths of strangers her feelings of loss, which were so precise to her now—of Jonas and, more vaguely, of all that had been familiar. And surely that was some of it, some of the allure. When she'd begun to weep today in quiet cadence with the dead man's teenage daughter, the woman sitting next to Ramona had placed her hand on her thigh and gently patted it.

But she'd felt, both last week and today, something else, a simple human heat, which she needed more and more as a tremendous loneliness had begun to gather in her. She'd sat in her pew and heard all around her deep quivering breaths, sobs

and whispers, heard people blowing their noses and clearing their throats. And she was able to take in all of it anonymously, since no one at a funeral found it especially odd that you were a stranger to him. Maybe you were a niece from the Midwest, or an old friend's daughter, and you explained yourself only if you wished to make a special effort through the murmurous solemnity. It was this sense of plain companionship that Ramona greedily took in at the funerals, the pleasure, and it *was* that for her, real pleasure, of sitting among people as they gave off their participant sorrow and made their homely human sounds.

In the bathtub, she leaned close to the mirror, the filling tub roaring like a waterfall, and saw that her makeup was badly streaked from her crying in the church. She ran water in the sink as well and roughly scrubbed her face. She dried it and then stared into the mirror, which contained two distorting vertical bands, flaws in the glass, causing Ramona's face to pulse and ripple when she moved it back and forth. She held it between the bands and reached for her makeup on a shelf below the mirror. All the lids and caps were opened or off.

She rubbed foundation into her cheeks, over her nose, flushing life into her face. The man's rouged death-face came into her mind. She reached for her eye shadow.

As a young girl, she'd spent hours before the mirror, trying colors and washing them off, passing the tips of brushes and sticks over her face and around her eyes with a breath-held virtuosity, losing all sense of time, at play in a daze until her mother or father yelled at her to get out of the bathroom. When she appeared, her lips a bright waxy red, her eyebrows winged, her black-lined eyelids garish domes of green or blue or purple, her mother would tell her she looked like a clown and her father would ask her if she wanted the town to think she was a whore. She knew her mother wasn't serious, and when she was old enough for her father's alarm to have meaning she'd given no mind to what the town might think because she was making herself up for Ed.

She thought, as she finished shading her eyes, that Ed had most liked blue.

"Why?"

" 'Cause it makes you look scared."

"Scared?" she'd said.

"Yeah. When I'm fucking you, your eyes shiver. 'Specially when they're blue. Like you're scared."

"You like me lookin' scared?"

"Yeah. It's like you turn blue from bein' scared."

"I do."

She picked up her eyeliner and carefully began to draw. She'd learned to use her left hand, slowly and nearly adequately, although the man who'd fitted her said she could more easily use her right, as before, if she'd only learn to let the hook's deft touch work for her. But his suggestion, the idea, of applying makeup with the monstrous metal claw seemed to her beyond mere ignorance. At first, for some months, she'd again stood before the mirror just as she had as a girl, lost not in play but in a deep daze of work, her weak left hand soon spastic from unaccustomed use, her lips and eyes smudged like those of a face in a coloring book that a child has exuberantly smeared.

Before, she had loved to make her eyelids blue and walk up to Ed, in the halls of school, in front of Dee's on Summit, and as he'd turn to look at her she'd drop her lids to show him, saying, "I'm scared, Ed." It became their way of knowing how much she wanted him.

"Are you scared?"

"A lot. I'm really scared."

She brushed black into her eyebrows, the bathtub roaring. "You scared?"

They lay naked, where they often hid, beneath two spruce trees in the beginning heat of spring, the low, intertwining branches making a natural cave. Her eyes were closed. Ed lay on his side, his hand moving over her skin.

Her blue eyes closed, she nodded. Beneath her she felt the

bed of fallen pine needles, felt them prick her as she shifted.

"Come in me now," she whispered, breathing the curative scent of pine.

"I will," he said. "You scared?"

"Come in me," she said, too lost now to speak their code, moving more insistently, sixteen and spring-white in the season's first warm days, floating on a private pillowed lust yet burrowing at the same time deep into the earth, her body implement and seed, as if she planned to plant and bring to flower a flourishing bed of sex.

At the mirror, she passed her lipstick over her lower lip, pressing hard, and stepped back to judge her work. Her face was a mask, thick and glossy with crude patches of color. Unthinkingly, she raised her right hand to a lipstick smudge and when it passed through the mirror's distorting lines its molded fingers moved, the slightest rippling wave, a coquette's dainty tease. She moved the hand across the mirror again, watching the fingers flicker. The subtlety of the gesture amazed her and she moved the hand again, making the fingers nod in elegant sequence.

The sound of the water in the tub was suddenly irritating. She reached to turn the faucets off, leaving no sound except the faint strains from the radio playing in the front room. The silence bothered her even more, so she turned the water on again, paused at the door, spun around and turned it off, leaving the bathroom and hurrying into the kitchen.

She was surprised to see through the back window that the sky was dark. She stood in the middle of the kitchen. She thought that if she just stood there for a while something would present itself to her, some chore, something that would take her mind off the silence. She listened intently for anything, footsteps in the alley, the hum of the refrigerator's motor, the preliminary rumble of a train. If only a train would pass, she thought, it would leave enough noise in its wake to last her through the night. She stood in her kitchen, not wanting to move and make

some noise herself which might cover a better one, but there was nothing to hear and it felt to her like a conspiracy.

She looked around, her eyes drawn to the refrigerator door where she'd taped a chart she'd drawn last week, figures she'd memorized from the book Lovilla had loaned her. 1–2 months: baby responds to human faces. After 3 months: notices world around him. 7 months: first teeth. 8 months: stands. 1 year: sounds that mean something.

She hurried to the front, turned the lamp on, and stood next to it, repeating in her mind the phrase on the baby chart: sounds that mean something. The radio blared a song, a man's high whine, and she sat down on the bare wood floor inside the cone of lamplight. She tried to listen to the song and as soon as it ended she heard the radio's unusually long pause—perhaps the disk jockey had been caught away from his microphone—and Ramona quickly stood again and moved away from the spread of the radio's room-filling silence. She could not stay still and she couldn't think of a way to make a noise that would mean something.

You scared?

A lot. I'm really scared.

Show me you're scared. Make your blue eyes shiver.

I'm so scared, Ed. Look how scared I am.

Then you stay right there. I'm comin.'

All right. I will. You promise?

You stay right there. I'm comin' for you.

In her head, Ramona heard Ed say these words and she felt weak with relief. She stood, nearly crouched, in a corner of the room, as far as she could get from the radio's silence. She wanted only to be found, allowed to surrender. She tried to imagine the extraordinary bliss of her loneliness lifting. She heard him say, "You stay right there. I'm comin'," and a warmth passed through her as from the descent of grace.

She heard the radio begin to play another song.

She walked to the phone in the corner of the room. No one

but Van Nostrand, who paid the monthly bill, had called her since she'd lived here and it had been at his insistence that she had the service. She dialed, as she had several times in recent weeks, the number in Malvern that gave a long recorded description of the Hudson Valley weather. The man's voice was low and calm as he told the day's high and low temperatures, the chance of the year's first flurry on Monday afternoon. Ramona paced with the phone to her ear, listening to the end of the report, then letting it play through a second time. "Thank you," she said at the end of the message and let it start again.

With the voice at her ear, she looked across the street and saw May in her studio. She was painting, her back to the window, sitting as always on the edge of her tall stool like a woman riding sidesaddle. Still holding the phone, Ramona walked to her window and stared for a moment, then hung up, and her eyes found the phone number she'd written on the windowsill weeks ago; she'd copied it from the charge slip the night May bought her flowers. She dialed, and as she heard it ring she watched May put down her brush, wipe her hands on her jeans, and walk quickly out of the studio.

"Hello?" Ramona heard. She stared across the street at the easel, the stool, the scene, now without May, framed in the window.

"Hello?" May repeated more strongly.

"I hope you don't leave," Ramona said, speaking to the figure still perched in her mind's eye on the edge of the high stool.

"Hello? Who is this? Laurie? What's wrong, is that you?"

"I hope you don't move away," Ramona said. "It helps, havin' you live there."

"Who *is* this?"

Ramona tried to think of something to say. "You don't know me or nothin'." She heard in her head what she'd just said and realized it sounded crazy but she couldn't think of what else to say.

Now May was speaking irritatedly. "Who is this?"

Ramona knew she must say something immediately. "If you'd . . . if I could know about you some."

"*Know* about me? Who are you? Why'd you call—"

Ramona hung up, set the phone on the sill, but she couldn't take her eyes from May's window, and when she reappeared Ramona jumped out of sight as May looked out, looked up and down the street, as though she might spot the caller running off into the night. She continued to peer out for a short while, then turned again to her easel. Her stepping back from the window seemed to release Ramona from hers and she nearly ran from the room, to the kitchen, put her coat on, and hurried out the door.

She headed toward the train station, her mind rushing now. She felt humiliated, heard the echoing harshness of May's voice. She closed her eyes, filled with disgust; she was nearly running. She needed to get away from the room where she'd done that, and where she'd heard Ed's words and believed them a solution.

The street sloped slightly toward the station, a small white building at the edge of Claring where the Hudson River passed, wide and aloof. All the way from New York, the tracks ran with the river like its hem and then, at the finger of marshland where Claring began, one section of the tracks peeled inland—leaving the other to continue north—and cut through the heart of the village and past Ramona's window and eventually to Boston.

She hurried through the brightly lit parking lot. A small crowd was milling near the platform. She'd been coming to the station, mostly Friday evenings when it was busy with arriving weekend residents, pleased with the chance to mingle unobserved, as at funerals. Sometimes on Sunday she sat with the crowd in the late afternoon as it gathered in the waiting room on the long wooden benches, smoking and glancing at the clock, acting eager for her train. She imagined herself in the crowd's very center and a lovely sense of insulation settled over her. Once she'd stood in the line of people purchasing tickets,

moving with them toward the agent until there were four ahead of her, and then she pretended to have suddenly remembered something urgent and rushed out of the station. Once she'd brought a prop, an empty suitcase she'd found in the alley behind her apartment.

She'd discovered the station by simply following the tracks one evening after a train had crawled past her apartment, sounding its horn unremittingly as it passed. The tracks had led her to the asphalt-covered waiting area where several people stood in small huddles, ringed by luggage. Then a train had arrived, people hugged each other in greeting or farewell, and Ramona, standing in the shade of the station's overhanging roof, had been taken into the scenes, found herself smiling, some part of her joining the pleasure she watched.

She stood now in the same place, leaning against the station's brick wall, and saw a small boy break toward the tracks. "Here it comes!" he shouted, looking northward.

"Gabe!" a woman shouted. "Gabriel! Get away from the tracks! Come over here now."

He trotted back toward her. "It's here, Mom!" he said, sounding thrilled. The hood of his dark jacket was tight around his head so that the smile on his pink face appeared to Ramona to be floating disembodied in the night. She thought of her dream, of Jonas's silver-coated face revolving up to her as he drowned, smiling widely, in the swift and gleaming river.

"You can't see the train at night," the boy's mother said, grabbing his hand. She told him that if the train were coming they'd first hear its whistle.

Ramona's deep indecision was often palpable to her when she came to the station. Watching the trains as they sighed to a halt, watching people boarding or descending the steps, so sure of themselves, she usually asked herself, again, when she would leave and where she would go next. Every time she visited the waiting room she picked up pocket-sized schedules in a rack by the agent's desk and studied their timetables and

destinations, but they suggested nothing to her. The names of the cities themselves were somehow meaningless, foreign, as though unconnected to any language she knew. Over and over, her thoughts ran to one of two places, usually to North Carolina, which appeared nowhere on the schedules so far as she could tell; and every now and then to Donnie's trailer on the riverbank. Sad-faced Donnie, who'd murmured pleasure into her. But she knew very well she couldn't travel back to Donnie, and knew it was a trip she didn't need a train for.

Mostly, she sensed that her trip was one she knew nothing about.

Ramona watched the little boy, Gabriel, tug his mother's hand.

"Mom," he said, frustrated, "I didn't *see* the train. I just *know* it's coming."

Her thoughts of leaving were always woven through with Jonas. Not of returning to him, for she clung to the certainty that she simply couldn't do the work of mothering. And she also held the memory of her occasional impulse—to lower her hand over his mouth, to let go of his stroller at the top of the hill. No, not of returning, but of feeling some strict sense of limit, of a tightly measured distance she couldn't extend any farther. She sensed that she was, right now, in her rooms above the flower shop, as far from him as she could get, could ever be, as far, somehow, as she was allowed to be. It was as though she felt a deep and absolute umbilical insistence, but with her child holding *her* as she'd tethered off from him; just so far and then no farther; ever.

"Did you hear the whistle?" the boy's mother asked. "I didn't hear the whistle." She spoke loudly, for the crowd.

Ramona suddenly began to walk toward the boy.

"Nooo!" he said to his mother, exasperated, stomping his foot. She held his hand tightly. "You don't understand, Mom. I can just tell."

Ramona reached them. "Me, too," she said, and the boy

turned and looked up at her. His face inside his hood twisted with puzzlement. Ramona smiled and nodded her head vigorously. "I know you're right," she said. "Sometimes you can just *tell* when the train's coming, can't you."

The boy stepped shyly back and Ramona, as though tied to him, moved a step closer. She said again, "You're right." Something like a pure pursuit was guiding her. She didn't notice his mother's arm swing protectively around him. She bent down to meet his eyes. "You're absolutely right. It's amazing, ain't it, how you can sometimes tell."

The boy turned sideways, pressing into his mother's coat, but kept his eyes on Ramona, peeking out from the edge of his hood, his face still screwed tight with a kind of fearful interest. "Why is your face like that?" he said to Ramona.

She stood up, alarmed, and looked into the boy's eyes for an explanation. He seemed slightly emboldened after his question, simpler interest taking over. "How come you did that?" he said, turning slightly, giving her a little more of his face. "Are you playing Indians?"

Ramona touched her cheek. Her glove came away with dark rouged fingers and she remembered the makeup, the carnival splotches she'd given herself as she'd stood at the mirror and colored her face with a thick and messy urgency.

She looked at Gabriel's mother for the first time and began to say she was sorry.

The woman was watching Ramona with her own wary interest and she shrugged her shoulders. "That's not a nice thing to say," she said, addressing her child but looking at Ramona. "You should tell the woman you're sorry." Still she held her eyes on Ramona and was knocked a small step backward as her son turned, embarrassed, and slammed his body into hers. He said something more, his protesting tone muffled in his mother's coat.

"I didn't mean to make him shy or anything," Ramona said and the mother smiled tightly and assured her that Gabriel was

just tired and wound up. She patted his back with her mitten. "We're waiting for his father and he gets very excited."

A voice through the loudspeakers announced the train's arrival and the two of them moved away toward the platform, the woman smiling at Ramona again, the boy still burrowed in the safety of his mother's coat.

Ramona stood, watching their backs as they waited for the train's doors to open. The boy had lifted his face free and stood apart from his mother, still holding her hand. Ramona, self-conscious now of her heavily made-up face, knew that she should leave, and knew that she would, just as soon as he had turned to look shyly back at her, as soon as he had let her see his floating face again.

Sixteen

When the weather began to turn seriously cold in Myles, the very air which filled the empty lots appeared to harden into frozen silver-blue blocks. Perhaps the value of the light, penetratingly clear at this time of year, influenced the illusion, but it was easy to imagine the lots as solid squares of sky, joining with the stores on Summit to form an impregnable fortress.

Like the sky, the people also seemed to thicken with the winter. Men sat, barely moving, around a huge fume-leaking kerosene stove at the back of Squeaky Frye's Sunoco station, sucking loudly through their teeth. Women stayed longer and longer around kitchen tables or at Dee's Luncheonette, drinking endless cups of coffee to which their nerves had grown inured.

Every year, Myles officially celebrated the days leading up to Thanksgiving. No one remembered when or why the custom had begun, but it had recently become a project of the Ma-

tronettes, which at least explained why it had stubbornly endured. Since they knew no real model for a Thanksgiving festival the Matronettes had pieced together a series of events that took something from several genres, so "The Plenty of Myles: Thanksgiving Thanks" began one full week before the holiday when a huge tattered banner with faded orange letters was lifted above Summit.

The Matronettes had also raised money to buy orange plastic turkeys which squatted like nesting gulls atop the streetlights on Summit, though they grew fewer each year, shot from their roosts by teenagers with rifles cruising up and down the street in early-morning darkness, a kind of renegade midway game.

When they'd taken on the planning of the week, the Matronettes had persuaded the city council to hire a carnival. But for what the council could offer, only the most marginal troupe, willing to come to the late-fall cold of Myles when any respectable show was touring the hot and humid South, could be lured. So, beginning Thursday morning, a merry-go-round sat next to the laundromat on Summit, revolving with great effort and sending out an eerie steel-scraping sound of elemental complaint, while its owner huddled in his ticket shack drinking apricot brandy and pondering the fact that the romantic allure of circus life had weakened significantly for him.

The grocery store always held a drawing for a free twenty-pound turkey. It was generally understood that Millard Sampson, the owner, used the drawing to give a turkey to whoever needed it most, never an easy decision in Myles. There were many years when no one indisputably deserved the turkey and then it was somehow always won by Bobby Bumbry, although everyone assumed he couldn't write his name.

This appeared to be such a year, though there was as always some discussion.

"Might go to the Barretts," Abel Autry suggested one night in the Hill Top. "They had that chimney fire, gutted the house."

Moon shook his head. "That was his own dumb fault. They say he hadn't cleaned that chimney since he moved in. Besides, he built his stove out of an old *oil* barrel he picked up somewhere, for Chrissake. Imagine the fumes."

A few people suggested Mabel Flowers, whose husband had died in the spring, falling down their stairs. But he was not well liked in Myles and no one had seriously mourned his death, least of all Mabel herself, by the measure of her own lackluster grief at the church-basement luncheon following the funeral, where she ate the portions of a stevedore and insisted people sing several choruses of "Bye Bye, Blackbird," in rounds.

On the Saturday before Thanksgiving, at six o'clock, when the drawing took place at the back of the store, Don McKay, the butcher, reached into the box for the winning name, then stared in a kind of shy silence at the slip he held until someone in the small encircling crowd growled, "Come on, McKay. Just say it's Bumbry and give me the turkey. I'll drop it at his aunt's house on my way home."

But Don McKay shook his head and said, at last, "No." His voice was as small as a boy's. "It says here 'Ed King' on the slip. It's Ed King gets the turkey."

As always, Moon had opened the Hill Top from nine to ten A.M. for the Thanksgiving morning parade, offering a free double shot to anyone who wished to warm himself against the cold. The morning was raw, tented by a deep gray sky, thinly streaked with white. Seventy or eighty people lined Summit's three blocks, everyone tucked tightly into himself, mumbling curses into his chest and sometimes turning his back against the wind. Now and then there were primal howls back and forth across the street from the men in the crowd, and above their laughter the women's keening calls of greeting carried out into the day.

The high school band labored past, sulking regimentally, then a row of antique tractors. Here and there along the sidewalks, people raised their necks up out of their collars and looked down Summit in the vain hope that there might be a surprise this year, but, seeing only the familiar flow, there rose within them all an urge for an immediate sweeping of the street—everything erased.

"*Move* it, will ya?" someone shouted at the American Legion. "I'm freezin' my butt standin' here."

Someone even ordered the Ford sedan carrying the king and queen, who were chosen on a rotating schedule among residents of the nursing home on the north edge of town, to speed along.

"Who *is* it in there, anyway? You can't ever see their faces, tucked in the backseat like they are."

The royal couple, sharing lap blankets, slept in the Ford's backseat, their heads leaning lightly against each other's, looking like love-floating teenagers on a double date.

"If they can't stay awake for three goddam blocks, I say the hell with them."

The annual ugliness was settling over Summit.

Then came a line of pickups, driven by local hunters who'd taken deer on Thanksgiving morning and strapped them to their trucks, and the men in the crowd stirred with interest at the one thing in the parade they genuinely enjoyed.

"Looks like Art Deeter got him one again."

"He's a shooter, that son of a bitch."

The hunters drove down Summit, each man behind his wheel prepared to acknowledge the applause. Arthur Deeter, in the lead, raised his hand and barely moved it, the minimal, palsied wave of a tolerant monarch.

But after a few moments the crowd again began to feel a kind of subliminal agitation. Here, at the point in the parade where the men, at least, had always watched willingly, the morning's sullenness only deepened. There was a bizarre beat of silence,

broken by an irritated voice: "Yeah, yeah, we see you, Averill. Big goddam deal, you shot a deer."

Inspiring someone else to shout to the next hunter in his truck, "Whaddaya want, a medal, Mallory? I seen bigger deer than that in the Catskill Game Farm, Mallory."

In fact, enormous deer, their coats the shade of wheat, lay draped across the trucks. Thin lines of blood ran like freed pinstriping over fenders.

The hunters had, as always, expected to glide magisterially through whoops of commendation and several seconds passed before they realized that the mood, instead, was one of some hostility.

"You call that a kill? Anything that small, you're supposed to throw it back."

No one in the crowd could have explained what was going on; no one was even truly conscious of the change, of the edgy frustration that something was wrong, was missing this year.

What was missing, in fact, was Ed King, for here was the moment in the parade which had prominently included him, displaying more often than not the day's most stunning kill. In recent years, the procession of hunters had come to be defined by Ed, so his absence was as felt as his presence had been.

Some sensed it as another bit of his bewildering behavior, like his crazy driving, his backyard lean-to, his loony workday violence. Some asked themselves where he was, what he might be up to, if he was not in the parade as he had always been. And many, in truth, had grown tired of Ed's shit and saw his absence as more of it. They'd used up all their patience waiting for him to get his wife back and resume his old behavior, which was hardly endearing but was at least familiar.

Prompted by the spectacle of the day without Ed King, some of the people watching the parade spontaneously began to discuss him, using the pronoun and understanding its reference.

"You heard he won the turkey."

"Jesus, yes, I did. And I heard he swears he didn't put his name in."

"And Sampson swears he didn't put it in for him."

"He still hanging out in that lean-to? Nights're gettin' awful cold for that, the crazy bastard."

"Somebody said they heard he took it down."

And through their talk of Ed, they continued to harass the splendid cortege. People wanted the hunters gone, their slow, annoying troll for praise finished. Arthur Deeter and some others retaliated in a way, honking their horns, rigid middle fingers thrust out their windows. And the deer seemed through it all to be not so much dead as lying utterly still, extraordinarily cooperative. Against the anger of the hunters and the taunts of the crowd, the deer gave off an enduring dignity and you could imagine them, at parade's end, waiting patiently while the hunters loosened their ropes, then leaping from the fenders and bounding back into the shaded civility of their lives in the woods.

Finally, the last of the hunters' pickups passed, and a tractor appeared, drawing an empty hay rack which held the Myles cornucopia, a giant steel funnel originally used at the Mellen-ville elevator to point the flow of grain into wagon boxes and railroad cars. To simulate the shade of harvest, it had been repainted the bright official-orange of the county's trucks and tractors. The Matronettes had wanted a cornucopia but none of them had thought about filling it with anything representing the season's bounty, so it rode tightly bolted and cavernously empty atop the rack. And as it lumbered by, one of the men in the crowd, Huge Winchell, looked up into the vast dark hole and knew he was seeing, at last, the parade's ending image. "Okay," he shouted, speaking for everyone, "there's the ass-hole. Let's get the hell home."

* * *

"You had three whole days to claim the turkey," Ed's mother, Vera, said, shaking her head in disgust. As she spoke she filled Ed's plate, her spoon banging against its side as though she were ladling from a mission's vats. "You got a free turkey waitin' for you and you call me on Wednesday and say to go and buy one." She plopped baked beans on Ed's plate and took a drag of her cigarette. She slapped a mound of peas between the beans and some creamed corn.

She said, "This is the dumbest thing you done yet. It beats sleepin' in that lean-to. It beats goin' after Ray Adams at work. Those is crazy, but this, this is *dumb*. You call me the afternoon before—"

"I *know* what I said," Ed broke in at last. "I'm the one dialed the phone." He took the plate from his mother and reached for his beer. "I'm the one that called, remember? I know what I said."

"I know what you said, too," Vera said. "What you said was *dumb*."

Ed's eyes wandered, surveying the sagging kitchen. Water marks and stains of shadow mingled on the peeling wallpaper. He followed its climbing floral pattern up to the ceiling and leaned back to trace the cracks overhead. From his childhood he'd watched these cracks grow more and more intricate and his fussiness had sometimes been maddened by them as they spread, indifferent, high above the reach of his need to make the ceiling clean.

He saw the cracks tonight as the spiderweb pattern of the Dodge's windshield after the accident. Lately, he'd found it unbelievable, how many things could remind him of that span of shattered glass. Last week at work, he'd looked down into a can of paint in the warehouse and the geometrical cracks in its dried-up surface recalled the windshield instantly.

And whenever the image had recently appeared, Ed's breath went out of him for a moment and Ramona's absence filled him with a pain that was, in its way, a sharp ache of love.

Beneath the bully's fear when he's lost control; beneath the shame Ed was carrying, really a kind of cuckold's humiliation; beneath all that, there was this blade of loss that pricked him. And when it did, he remembered the days when Ramona was healthy and moved so *quickly*—God, there had been such a lightness in her movements—and when she had only adored him.

In fact, Ramona had once been a kind of mirror for Ed. Receiving her worship was like receiving an exact reflection of what he thought of himself and for him there was a sense of confirmation in it. No one else, nothing else, had ever done this for him. People enjoyed him, feared him, despised and avoided him. Women in Myles had very much liked fucking him. But only Ramona's early adoration had been as large as his own ego, so, not surprisingly, he'd grown hungrily fond of what she'd once given him and he'd settled into a happy fidelity which stunned everyone who knew him. Everyone except Ramona, who hadn't yet seen real things and had imagined there was nothing other than fidelity in love.

Now, Ed remembered well enough that the Ramona he mourned had disappeared long before she'd run away, but it was the loss of that early, worshipful Ramona that very often filled him. And when it did there was no anger in his wish for her; no flare of revenge; only a soft and overwhelming sadness.

Vera surveyed the table. "It's a good thing your old man ain't alive," she said.

"That's one thing we can goddam well agree on," Ed said.

"What I mean is, he'd shit if he saw you actin' this way." Vera smoked viciously and grasped her glass of beer. "Be damned," she said, "if I'm gonna walk past a free turkey and ask for one I gotta pay for."

Ed stabbed a fork into his soft pool of food. The sounds in the kitchen were the clank of Vera's spoon against her plate, the slush of beer and creamed corn in Ed's mouth.

"It ain't your turkey to walk past in the first place," Ed said,

and then he was suddenly furious. "By God, that's just like you, claimin' it's yours to walk past what's mine!"

Vera smiled. "I thought you said it wasn't yours."

"What I said was I didn't put my name in the goddam box. So, no, it ain't mine, but it *sure* as hell ain't yours."

When Don McKay had called Ed to tell him he'd won, Ed thought that McKay, his voice faint and stammering, had been persuaded to play a joke on him and he'd immediately hung up. Then, a few minutes later, the owner, Millard Sampson, called to assure Ed that it *had* been his name on the slip.

"Then it was you that put it there," Ed said, but Sampson insisted he hadn't. "Bullshit," Ed said and hung up again.

For a few hours that night, he'd sat fuming in the Dodge. Not only had he won a drawing he'd not entered but Sampson, whether he'd had the nerve to admit it or not, had decided Ed's life deserved the turkey. Like everyone else in Myles, Ed had always thought of the drawing as a judgment and now he saw his winning as further evidence that he'd come to be viewed by the town as pitiable and pathetic. Feeling a sudden sweep of Myles's scorn, he pounded the steering wheel so hard he sprained his wrist.

The next Monday, as Ed drove past the store, he'd seen his name, in huge hand-drawn orange letters, posted in the front window where the winner's always appeared. And that night, sometime after two o'clock, he'd driven back up to Summit and sat in the Dodge, looking at his name.

The street was empty. The Thanksgiving Thanks banner snapped like a sail in the wind. The plastic turkeys on either side of Summit stared across at one another. For nearly half an hour, Ed studied his name, his eyes moving over the curves and niches of its crude calligraphy as though searching the letters for clues.

When Ed was eleven years old, his father, seized with a rare impulse of smiling heart, had taken him to the Columbia

County fair and, without asking him, bought him a ticket for the featured ride in an aerial balloon. It remained the single time in his life Ed had been high above the ground.

As the balloon rose, the basket lurching beneath, tossing its cargo of shrieking children, Ed stood in rigid silence, gripping the top of the basket and watching the world before him alter and simplify. He was too frightened to peer down over the side, and so he stared straight ahead into the view his terror gave him. He first watched the people, then the buildings, and finally even the steep hillsides disappear. All the shapes and colors of the ground rolled slowly down past his eyes and vanished below the basket rim he held on to for his life, until all there was to see was a reachless spread of blue. While the other children sucked in their breaths and grew wild with nauseated excitement, Ed remained still, quiet as the sky. For him, there was nothing but horror in the insubstantial beauty of the air and for the length of the ride he stayed inside the wild and irrational fear that he'd never return to the assurance of his backyard's hard-packed dirt, the rise of the Catskill foothills that warned him exactly where the world stopped being flat and started to curve up like a piecrust against the side of the sky.

As he looked at his name in the window of the grocery, Ed did not think of his flight in the balloon. But if you were to compare his moments of fear, then and now, you'd find them alive with what amounted to the same vertigo, as though Ed were staring, as he had in the balloon, into a life with no horizon line to tell him what was real, what was earth, and what was vaporous sky.

Finally, Ed's eyes began to hurt. He cleared his head, cursed, and started up the Dodge. And as he drove home he once again placed every hope that he might regain control of his life in the determination to get Ramona back. He'd concluded some weeks ago that he must go after her. It had become clear to him once he'd surrendered his dream of standing at their door and

watching as she labored up the sidewalk, when he'd finally seen how stupid he'd been for holding that hope in his mind. All order had left when she had; it would return when she did, and knowing so gave him some relief, for he thought he could be ready to leave within the week.

At the Thanksgiving table, Ed and his mother were both quite drunk. They had been since noon. He sat heavily in his chair and watched Vera eat with apparent pleasure. He couldn't decide if she was somehow really enjoying the meal or merely goading him.

Ed looked to his left, where Jonas's high chair sat empty while he slept in his room off the kitchen. Ed's head bobbing, he stared at the meal before him. "Looks like supper at the nursing home. All you need is gums to eat this." He picked up his fork to make his point, smirking at the needless row of tines.

Vera poured beer into her glass. "Same meal we eat every Thanksgiving," she said. She drank and belched softly. "Except, a'course, no turkey."

"All you had to do was *cook* the damn thing," Ed snapped. "I said I'd pay for it."

"You wanna look stupid, you go right ahead. First you put your name in for a free turkey. Then you win the free turkey. Then you say you ain't gonna take the free turkey and tell me I should buy one."

Through his glare, Ed spoke very slowly. "One. It ain't my turkey, 'cause, two, I didn't put my name in. And, three, you know goddam well what it means if you win it."

"You're damn right I know what it means," Vera said. "It means if you was to quit starin' at me and look down at your plate, you know what you'd be lookin' at? Turkey!" For emphasis, she slapped her fork into her soft food.

Ed said, "If I hear 'turkey' one more time I'll dunk your head

in one of these bowls till you choke, woman, and it don't matter which one I'd pick. Corn. Peas. These runny damn potatoes. You'd gag as good on any of 'em." He finished his beer in one emphasizing swallow. Rising for another, he carelessly slid his chair over the warped floorboards, and from the adjoining bedroom Jonas answered the scraping sounds.

"Get me one," Vera said. Her eyes were blinking as if she, like her grandson, were emerging from sleep. Ed returned and they both sat listening to the child's soft, random noise. They drank and said nothing, briefly absorbed in Jonas's language, as people used to eat supper to their nightly radio serial, each living in the private drama of its evocative voices.

Ed listened with a glumly wandering curiosity. Jonas's voice now was often a dulcet squeal, round and happy, but high, in a feline range, and Ed could make nothing of it. He wondered if it was some kind of answer to him and Vera. Were these sounds what the kid was *trying* to make? Was he in control or was he trying for something else and this is what came out instead? His son screeched again, sounding even more like a satisfied cat almost capable of words, and Ed wondered which was smarter—if there was a way you could measure it—your basic cat or Jonas at nine months? Probably Jonas, but everyone said cats are brilliant and that was why they didn't come when you called them, which was no kind of brilliance Ed was interested in.

Finally, Jonas began to make sustained, wakeful sounds and Ed's mother rose, stunned by beer. "Get him one," she slurred to Ed, who looked deeply puzzled by what she seemed to have in mind. "Git his *bottle* ready," Vera said.

The three of them drank from their bottles, Jonas making slightly more noise than Ed. The baby sat in Ed's old high chair, bending the bottle's nipple expertly to get the flow of milk. Vera watched him with drunken affection. "Ya know," she said,

"when you hold him now he's like a monkey. Grabbin' at your dress. Like if you got up he'd just stay stuck onto ya."

Ed was nodding, fighting sleep. He tried to focus on Jonas's animated face as it rose and fell, working milk into his mouth. As always, Ed confronted his son with a kind of original bemusement. For someone who instinctively valued people's histories, who remembered their inclinations to use to his own advantage, Ed brought nothing of that skill to a knowledge of his son. He simply responded to whatever behavior Jonas showed him at the moment and his judgment depended mostly on his own mood at the time. And on his few rigid notions of how to raise a child, ideas based on nothing more than the things that gave *him* pleasure: order, deference, the muscles' measured exhaustion, the unremitting light of day.

Still, Ed had not come to see Jonas as a reminder of Ramona. In his consuming self-centeredness, her act had been directed solely toward him and it had never occurred to him that it was something she'd also done to her son. To Ed, Jonas had remained oddly apart from her betrayal, his presence no burden, no consequence, of her leaving.

Jonas dropped his bottle on the floor and looked down in search of it. With some effort, Vera got up and managed to lift him out of his chair. She sat down again, holding Jonas in her lap, and he snaked like a happy explorer into his grandmother's flesh. "See," Vera said, "what I'm talkin' about?"

Ed blinked and shrugged. "That's my fault, too, I suppose."

"You simple shit," Vera said. "I ain't complaining. It's nice, his snuggling. You never done that. Somebody try to hold you, you'd go stiff as a board and pull away from them." Her head fell back as she took a drink. So did Ed's, and so did Jonas's. "It feels good when a baby does that."

Ed said thickly, "How's I supposed to know? She always bitched, how it scared her when he wiggled close like that. How'd I know you wasn't bitching? It looks like it's the same wigglin'."

It was the first time Ramona had been mentioned even indirectly all day. Avoiding her name was something Ed had been determined to do as he'd thought about Thanksgiving and his mother's certain harangues. He'd decided when he woke up this morning that the day would be cleanly halved: There'd be no talk of Ramona until darkness had come; then he'd leave his mother's table and set out in search of her.

But now he'd spilled her name and he sat with a child's wild hope that ignoring the accident would make it disappear.

Vera began to feed Jonas spoonfuls from her plate. Her hand dipped and struggled in the air like a bird against strong winds, and Jonas shouted near-words to the spoon and reached for it to help it into his mouth.

"You know what all this has done," Vera said to Ed. "It's made me feel like a fool every time I leave the house. Every time I walk down Summit I know people's laughing at me."

Ed watched, disgusted, as peas and corn missed Jonas's mouth and made green and orange splotches on his cheeks. He said to Vera, "Instead of bowin' down when you walk by, like they always done before?"

Vera ignored the insult. "You got *any* idea what I'm talkin' about? How every time I walk down the street I know people's talking about me?"

Ed raised his head and held his mother in a dead-faced inspection, trying to determine if any of her words were sincere. Could she possibly mean it, asking him if he knew what it felt like? He argued with himself about this for a while and decided that Vera knew exactly what was happening inside him and was picking at it now with her sharpest mockery.

Creamed corn had found its way into Jonas's nostrils. "God," Ed said, "wipe his mouth, why don't ya?" Jonas reached onto his grandmother's plate and put his fist in her peas. Viscous greenish webs spread between his fingers.

When Ed was growing up in this house and his life was busy with furtive installments of gleaming-eyed delinquency, he'd

realized that Vera was able to know his plans almost as he was forming them. And knowing them, she used them to disarm him, as he suspected she was doing now. So he'd learned to tell her nothing he was thinking, nothing he had done, and managed now and then to hide his life from her.

Needless to say, he'd not told her, nor anyone, that he was leaving Myles tonight.

Finally, he said, "No. I got no idea what you're talking about. But tell me this, anyway. What's so awful about a kid's grandma taking him around town? Why's that so goddam strange it makes people laugh at you?"

Vera shook her head. "There ain't nothin' strange about that. I ain't talking about that. I'm talkin' about being mother to somebody who ain't got the balls God give a housecat. *That's* what people's laughing at me for." She began to bounce Jonas weakly on her legs. His sounds were softly commensurate. He moved his jaws, his mouth sawing back and forth over the discomfort of the teeth he was cutting, then sucked his food-covered fingers greedily as if he'd discovered the source of all tastes.

Vera said, "I do say this, though. It's no balls that lets a woman get the idea she can go. But it's no balls plus no guts they're fastened to that lets her stay gone."

Ed simply stared at Vera. He said nothing to explain himself, which she heard as added proof, and his silence disgusted her so she turned her head away. "God," she said. "You can't even give me an answer. Just go home, why don't you? Git outa my sight."

But Ed stayed put and a small smile broke the blankness of his face as he anticipated Vera's surprise when the news reached her tomorrow that he was gone. That would answer her; it would answer all of them.

*   *   *

After leaving his mother's house, Ed drove the Dodge through the streets at a larcenous crawl. In part this was due to his drunkenness, but mostly because he felt for the first time in weeks impervious to the town's attention, to the voices of gossip which now ebbed and accumulated at the edge of his mind.

He followed a road away from the outskirts of the village and parked across from Bobby Bumbry's aunt's high, porous house, its gray mange of dereliction almost visible even at night. He got out and sneaked through her yard to the low kitchen window. He could see Bobby sitting at the table while his aunt walked back and forth, piling dishes in the sink. Ed watched her mouth move incessantly while Bobby looked straight ahead into what Ed pictured as pale yellow space. In the middle of the table sat a huge, hill-breasted turkey. With a long knife, Bobby's aunt began to clean its carcass.

Ed let out a sigh of relief that became a quiet laugh; the turkey on the table was exactly what he'd driven here hoping he would see. For it meant to him that he'd not completely lost the sense of how life worked in Myles. And more than that, it told him he was still able to manipulate the place in some small way, something he'd accepted as a given until a few months ago.

He'd have refused the turkey in any event, but in doing so he'd also instinctively recognized a test, reasoning as he heard Millard Sampson's words through the telephone that if the world still behaved even slightly as it had, then Sampson would fall back on tradition and give it to Bobby Bumbry, via his aunt, who was otherwise too poor to buy a turkey as large as the one Ed viewed now through her window.

Seeing the splendid skeleton centered on the table, Ed went nearly limp with gratitude and fell back against a beech tree in the yard. He watched Bobby's aunt move about the kitchen. An almost sexual smile was on her face. He imagined her praying as she cleaned up the table. He bet she'd seen the unexpected

arrival of the turkey at her table as God's grace swooping down. Fine.

Suddenly the house's back door flew open and Bobby hurried out. Ed watched him lope down the road and fade into the darkness. He turned back to the window to take a final look at the turkey, then tiptoed again out of the yard.

He pulled the Dodge up to his door and hurried inside. In a few minutes he emerged carrying a cardboard box which held cans and packages of food, a pan and a skillet and his coffeepot. He set the box behind the front seat and went back inside, returning with a second box of loosely piled clothes, his twelve-gauge Remington, and a handful of deer shells. He placed everything on the seat and took his flashlight from the glove compartment. The light swept the back of the Dodge, a tidy chamber after his thorough remodeling.

A few days before, working at night while the rest of Myles slept, Ed had removed the car's backseat. In its place there sat a propane camp stove, a kerosene heater, a large bowl and pitcher, like a set one would find on an old washstand, and his bright orange sleeping bag rolled tight as a sleeve.

He'd had to work very slowly, by flashlight, to lessen any chance someone might notice him. But he'd labored peaceably and the job had gone easily, in part because it had called for his particular gift as a hunter.

Though he was a fine marksman, there were others in Myles just as accurate, and yet no one took his limit as reliably as Ed did, because no one possessed his extraordinary patience as he waited for his prey. It was a kind of intelligence, a purposeful channeling of his economical exertions. No matter how long it took, how flirtatiously the deer dawdled just beyond the frame of his line of sight, Ed held his posture of ready repose, his pulse moving his blood with a hibernative ease, a low glee in his heart.

His approach to this task had been the same—a contentment with the pace and conditions given him. And when he'd

finished the Dodge, its dimensions seemed palatial and the inside of the car felt sustenant as a womb.

He gave the new interior a quick, comradely nod and rushed around to get behind the wheel. The door of his house flapped open in the wind. Light from the kitchen poured out into the night and was diffused in the air like the spray of a wave. He started the Dodge.

He climbed the hill and drove down Summit, the route of the parade. The street was empty, no one on the sidewalks to view Ed passing, the entry everyone had wanted most to see. He drove slowly, nearing the merry-go-round, its floor tilted crazily, and he laughed out loud at the memory of the year he'd snuck up to Summit at about this hour and taped a stick of dynamite to one of the merry-go-round's horses, then lit it, expecting the explosion to spin the ride like a frenzied top.

Tonight the horses appeared frozen in their eager leaps, their mouths spread with smiles of pony-toothed obedience. And then Ed's look narrowed on the silhouette of someone sitting atop one of the horses. He slowed to a stop and, parked beside the ride, held his eyes on the figure until he could see that it was Bobby Bumbry on the horse. He saw Bumbry's long legs touching the floor and sweeping back behind him as he gripped the pole and stared straight ahead, leaning slightly forward. It was as though he were waiting for his ride to begin; or had already set off on a richer private journey.

Ed stared for a moment more at Bumbry on the pony of the sagging merry-go-round, which sat almost directly on the spot where Ed's father had died in the fire, in the lot where the textile mills began in 1820. Then he felt himself suddenly unnerved by the sight of Bumbry pitched dazedly in his saddle toward something Ed could not imagine. He tried to see the expression on Bumbry's face. He thought he was smiling, but he couldn't be sure, and again he felt chilled.

He started the car and followed Summit down.

At the highway, Ed paused at the stop sign, turned right onto the blacktop, and stomped on the accelerator. The Dodge fishtailed, then shot straight past the fields on either side, and when he pressed the pedal even harder the car nearly went out of control before it firmly grabbed the road that he knew would lead him to her.

Seventeen

$\mathbf{S}$he began to move a bit more openly around the village. Often she ate long Sunday breakfasts at The Kitchen, a large pine-paneled coffee shop at the edge of Claring, where local families arrived in shifts, before and after church, while the weekend people lingered over plates of pooled syrup, passing sections of the *Sunday Times* back and forth. Ramona liked to linger, too, eavesdropping avidly and talking to a waitress named Helen, a small and raucously cheerful grandmother with a protruding chin that tilted radically upward like the bow of a boat. The first time Ramona ate there, Helen told her she recognized her from the flower shop and asked her just when she'd started to work for Van Nostrand. Ramona paused and replied inexactly that she'd been there a month or so. But then she volunteered that it was really the first job she'd ever had.

"This is mine, too," Helen had said, and when Ramona

looked surprised, she'd winked and laughed. "My first and my only. Started working here thirty-seven years ago."

At the flower shop, she helped a big blond girl choose arrangements for her wedding. Ramona wrote down the date of the ceremony with the order and, after the girl had left the shop, decided she'd attend.

She arrived at the church and thought she'd slip unnoticed into the last pew. But a young eager usher, self-important with his assignment, greeted her immediately.

"Friend of the bride or groom?" he whispered.

Ramona blanked, then said, "The bride."

The usher thrust his cocked arm toward her and led her to a seat. She felt many eyes watching her and even when she'd sat down, already realizing she'd made a terrible mistake in coming, some of the people in the row ahead of her leaned back and craned their necks to take her in, giving her small stiff smiles.

When she'd decided in the flower shop to attend the wedding, she'd imagined feeling again the populated comfort she'd found at funerals. Writing up the huge order of flowers, she'd seen that the wedding would be held in the same church where she'd watched the service for Sarah, the saintly grandmother. In her mind, she'd reflexively seen the creaking-floored old sanctuary filled with people; had heard the organ's consoling solemnity; and so had unthinkingly pictured herself once more sitting surrounded by the low-lit diffusion of sad love which occurs as mourners give off their muted sorrow. She hadn't stopped to think that the terms of a wedding are festive and scrutinizing.

When the groom came out through a door behind the pulpit, Ramona saw that he was short and stocky, his hair sandy-colored. He looked very frightened and kept glancing at his feet. But only when the girl appeared, her skirt rocking like a bell as she hitch-stepped down the aisle, did Ramona feel the crowd's

highly pleased self-interest turn and look at the bride, and as soon as she'd passed by her, Ramona quickly stood and squeezed past four startled guests sitting in her row, hurrying out of the church.

She went one night to Van Nostrand's house for dinner. He'd asked her before, most recently for Thanksgiving, and when she'd said no he'd insisted, in that case, that they set a date. He picked her up at the shop and they drove to his Dutch Colonial house at the edge of the village. She'd passed the house often on her walks. It sat half a mile back from the highway on the outskirts of Claring behind a flat open landscape of barbered lawns and rigidly ordered gardens. There were barns and more gardens behind the house.

The whole place was maintained by a crew of four mentally retarded men. When she'd first walked past Van Nostrand's house in early fall, Ramona had seen them moving slowly in the distance over the vast lawns, two with wheelbarrows, two carrying rakes and dragging huge plastic lawn bags. She remembered Van Nostrand telling her one day how the state paid him for housing them. She hadn't understood, and he'd explained to her that the men didn't stay indefinitely. That they lived in his house for a time, doing chores, receiving food and beds, then left for other housing, their places taken by a new group of four. He'd said how beneficial the arrangement was for him and his wife, and that it was even more so for the men, who predictably responded to the relative comfort of the large country house.

At dinner, she sat across the table from Mrs. Van Nostrand, a small, quick-gesturing woman who wore large eyeglasses with blue bows which dipped to attach themselves to the bottoms of the lens. Ramona had heard Van Nostrand speak of his life enough to know that he and his wife were childless, and that Mrs. Van Nostrand's family had lived prominently for generations in Dutchess County.

While they ate, Ramona watched Mrs. Van Nostrand glance furtively at her hand while she tried in various ways to learn some things about her.

"Now, tell me about your people," Mrs. Van Nostrand said. "Do I know them?"

"My people?" Ramona said, confused.

"Are they from around here?" Mrs. Van Nostrand asked. "Does your father work in Claring?"

Ramona said that they weren't, and that her parents had moved to North Carolina. She saw Mrs. Van Nostrand's face twist as she thought of another way to ask the same question, mixing her interrogation with stories of her own father, the lumber baron of Poughkeepsie.

All the while Van Nostrand's wife was talking, Ramona could hear from the kitchen the sounds of the retarded men as they ate their suppers also. Their voices steadily rose, sounding through the wall like a building chorus of brutish grunts, as they reacted to the television program they were watching while they ate. And just when their noise grew to something which sounded almost mutinous, Mrs. Van Nostrand put down her fork and clapped three times, astonishingly sharp thunderclaps from her small, bony hands. A total calm followed immediately from the kitchen, and then one of the men shyly entered the room and Mrs. Van Nostrand asked him to refill the gravy bowl from a pan on the stove.

Some minutes later, the men's voices began to build again and once more Mrs. Van Nostrand clapped. Another man came into the dining room and was asked to fill the bread basket.

Through the meal, while the men's excited voices persistently built to an eerie agitated squeal until she clapped them quiet and gave one of them a task, Mrs. Van Nostrand continued to draw information from Ramona:

"Now where did you go to high school, dear?"

"Rhinebeck," Ramona lied.

"Do you plan to stay in Claring?"

"As far as I know," she said.

Ramona forgot for a time about Van Nostrand himself, until she suddenly realized he'd said nothing since they'd sat down. She felt unable to pull herself from his wife's strong gaze in order to look at him. But sensing his squat form next to her, she felt a wave of fondness for him; an alliance. She assumed he also saw the scene in which they sat as something too strange to be hilarious but too funny not to be. Ramona imagined that his embarrassment had quieted him completely.

Finally, she managed to turn and when she did she saw him sitting at a kind of attention in his chair, the familiar pursing smile on his face that he wore at the end of an especially busy day in the shop. And Ramona wondered if Mrs. Van Nostrand had simply been asking what he'd wanted to know, if he'd brought her here to let his wife ask all his questions for him.

At the end of the meal, Mrs. Van Nostrand clapped her hands a final time and two of the crew appeared from the kitchen. They were both tall, pale men whose horse-mouthed gums showed pinkly when they smiled. She held her breath while they slowly cleared the table, plates balanced perilously on their arms, their faces accidentally angry-looking from the depth of their concentration. She watched their mouths move as they worked, watched them cradling the dishes in their huge hands, and she thought of Bobby Bumbry.

The snow outside her window was falling casually. Now and then she shifted her attention from May, at her easel across the street, and watched a single flake descend. The snow was an addition, gentle in the way all snow should be. Not the sort of snow that could move into your body and form ice inside your spine.

She couldn't see clearly from this distance the shapes on May's canvas and their mystery deepened her interest. What could they be? Angels, maybe. The shapes seemed to Ramona

to have postures, and something about the way they were angled on the canvas made her think of angels. Celestially weightless and leaning lovingly out of the white sky, pitched forward to supervise the work of earth. Yet the colors were too bright to be angels. Ramona's mind saw angels dressed in creamy robes, holy pastels, and the colors she was watching May work against each other were so vibrant they appeared to jump off the canvas. Blues and reds and yellows floating free. Maybe, she thought, that's why they reminded her of angels— because they seemed to be floating free.

She leaned forward in her chair, her elbows on the sill, her chin resting in her hand. A cold draft blew in around the frame, rattling the glass occasionally, but she didn't notice it. She strained to see the images in May's painting. Now the power of the colors suggested royalty to her, the bold, rich fabrics of kings and queens. Looking over May's shoulder, she focused on a large swatch of blue on the left side of the painting. She imagined the form of a man beneath the swatch; the flow of an ermine-hemmed robe.

Maybe.

May's lover, David, had left some hours ago, shortly after supper. She'd watched May come all the way down to the street with him, kissing him lightly on the lips at the door of his car, waving broadly as he pulled away. Watching David leave, watching May's grand wave, as though she were bidding farewell to someone on a ship as it eased from the dock, Ramona pictured once again a version of May's departure the day she'd left New York for Claring. (After May had bought the daisies in the shop, Ramona had decided she had moved here from the city.) As she thought more and more about May, inventing her life, Ramona sometimes saw her, on the day she moved to Claring, surrounded by suitcases in the backseat of a long red car, its rear a tidal wave of chrome-trimmed fins. Sometimes she imagined May pausing on the top step of an airplane ramp, as she'd seen people do on television, and turning back into a

gusting wind to wave at her parents. Usually, though, in Ramona's thoughts, May took the train, and here Ramona could picture her arrival at the Claring station.

She'd watched as May had waved to David's car until it turned at the end of Strait, then hurried back inside. Upstairs again, she'd sat down at her easel and she hadn't left it more than two or three times. About an hour ago, she'd gone to get a beer and sat on the wooden stool in front of her painting, drinking contemplatively from the bottle, now and then rubbing the back of her neck and moving her head from side to side.

Since the night she'd called May, Ramona had been watching her more and more. Although she'd told herself it was impossible, Ramona had feared for a time that May might somehow know it was she who'd telephoned, so she began to watch for some sign of May's suspicion: perhaps a certain way she looked over toward the shop or glanced up at Ramona's windows as she walked along Strait. Once May was hurrying past the shop and suddenly waved in at her and Ramona gasped, forgetting in her edginess that May had ever come into the shop.

After a few days, she grew easier, felt her secret was safe, but her interest in May did not relax. From Van Nostrand's plate-glass window, she saw May leave at eleven-thirty every other morning in her big, dented Ford. Its rear seat was always piled to the ceiling with rolls of canvas and wooden stretchers loosely tied like stacks of kindling. She hadn't noticed before the detectable order in May's days.

May's was an ideal life to dwell on, open in its habits, moving freely above Strait before tall uncurtained windows. It was filled with repeated narrative: the arrival of David, several nights a week; their affectionate domesticity; sometimes, their shadow-play on May's bedroom wall. And yet, the structure of May's life was as spare as it was reliable, leaving so many spaces which Ramona filled with history and plot.

She wondered about David. Why he seldom spent the night.

If he was married and had to visit May when he could sneak away. Sometimes she imagined that May had been married before. Sometimes she was hiding from someone, too, and if she was, Ramona envied May's ease in moving freely about the town. She observed May's days across the street in the same way she watched the progress of her paintings—beckoned by their shadings and held by their arrangements but unable from a distance to know what their shapes made. And so, as she watched, her imagination joined in painting it—May's life.

Ramona had lost track of the time, had no idea how long she'd been watching at her window. She thought the Claring House had been closed for several hours. The snow continued as it had, faintly, benignly. She blinked, trying to focus again. The blues and reds and yellows of the painting began to bleed into the snow, giving its flakes the colors of a snow she'd once dreamed, the snow that had melted and become a silver river.

She shifted in her chair and glanced at May's phone number, penciled on the edge of the windowsill. The numbers had become dark and elaborate from Ramona's many tracings of them as she'd sat here at night watching May paint.

She heard a noise on Strait, then garbage cans rattling. She leaned forward and saw the rheum-eyed dog that roamed Strait nosing exuberantly in spilled garbage.

Trying again to see the painting, she narrowed her look, watching May's hand as it moved over the canvas, imagining it a kind of spigot through which her colors poured freely down May's arm and through her fingers to the canvas. Ramona had no idea how someone thought to become a painter. No matter what part of May's life—or anyone else's here—she dwelled on, her interest settled finally on *how* they had become what they'd become. As she invented May's life, part of Ramona always held the irrational hope that she might find something she could use in her own.

She felt her head nodding, her eyes too tired to see anything but blurs of snow. She noticed now the draft around the

window and she was suddenly cold. She rubbed her arm and shivered slightly as she rose and left the window.

In her bedroom, she undressed quickly while she smoked. She sat on her bed and placed her cigarette in the ashtray before she slipped out of her harness, then stared in a daze at the huge bouquet on her bedstand. She rarely took flowers from the shop anymore, but tonight they had looked especially beautiful in the case and she'd paused, selecting several, before she'd come upstairs.

She smiled, grateful for the company of flowers. And then a richly tinted impulse rose from her exhaustion and she felt a kind of solace as the idea held. She stood again and walked into the kitchen. It took her a few minutes to find, in the drawer next to the sink, a long length of string she'd remembered seeing somewhere.

Back in the bedroom, she sat again on the edge of her bed and put out her cigarette, then reached for the flowers, lifting them from their jar. She placed them along the inside of her arm. Their wet, slick stems sent a shiver to her elbow. With her hand, she wrapped the string around her arm several times, just tightly enough to hold the flowers. And then she eased back onto her pillow and reached to touch their petals. Colors bloomed from her wrist, spreading themselves over her white sheets brilliantly—red and pink and yellow and the several blues of jays' wings.

Eighteen

Adams stared at his glass of beer, impatiently waiting for its head to disappear. He was one of the few customers in the Hill Top who didn't drink straight from his bottle and not only did he insist on a glass, he was finicky about the manner in which it was filled, trickling his beer down the side in an effort to achieve a perfectly headless result. He believed he could taste a change for the worse when there was any foam at all that had to be allowed to settle.

But he was distracted tonight by his thoughts and the talk and inadvertently he'd just poured a majestic chiffon head. He cursed under his breath and told himself the beer was ruined. Nervously, he tapped his fingers on the bar and heard the microwave oven on the counter behind Moon make its soft binging sound.

"My cousin saw it all the way from Hudson," he heard Don McKay, the butcher, say. He watched Moon take a melted

ham-and-cheese sandwich from the oven and slide it down the bar to Marvin Broder.

McKay said, "My cousin told me later, he said he heard this rumbling, like a jet airplane flyin' real low, and he got outa bed and he said the whole eastern sky was lit up. He said it looked like there was this huge light over everything and you know what he thought? He thought the Russians'd dropped the bomb. He woke up his wife and said to her the Russians'd dropped the bomb on Myles."

McKay was speaking in his turn, on the fifth anniversary of the fire, of its compelling beauty and its frightening scale, beyond any destruction the town, the county, the state might see again. Of that, everyone in Myles had long been sure and several other drinkers in the Hill Top had already offered their memories of the night, as they often did, especially on its anniversary.

"And this was in *Hudson*," McKay said. "This was fifteen, sixteen miles away." He pointed out the window in the general direction of Hudson, using the stump of his index finger, the only digit he'd lost in twenty years of cutting meat.

Adams looked into the mirror behind Moon at the reflections of the men. He watched their heads nod in unison, their faces lost in solemn memory.

Marvin Broder said, "You could see it even farther than that." He took a bite of his sandwich. "You could see it across the river. Somebody in Catskill told me he seen it from there."

"Maybe not hear it, though," said McKay.

"Maybe not," said Broder, "but you could see that huge light sky like you were describin'. You could see that in Catskill for sure."

"I know you could hear the explosions in Hudson," McKay said. "My cousin said his first thought was they'd dropped the bomb."

"The guy in Catskill told me it was beautiful," Broder said,

and he nodded, as though in recognition of a profound liturgy. Adams smiled at the sight of Broder's winter cap—its lowered flaps like a dog's ears moving as he nodded—and the red bandanna hanging loosely around his neck. Adams remembered sitting here last winter next to Ed when Broder had first walked in wearing the cap, its ears tightly tied under his chin, and the bandanna which covered his nose like a desperado's. Ed had looked at Broder and yelled, "Look out, Moon! A holdup. It's that fuckin' outlaw cocker spaniel they been talkin' about on the news."

Adams heard Al Day, from the highway crew, clear his throat. "Why would the Russians wanna drop the bomb on Myles?" Day asked McKay.

McKay looked at him blankly. "What are you talkin' about?"

"You said your cousin thought the Russians was bombing Myles. That don't make sense to me, why the Russians would pick Myles."

"Jesus Christ, Albert," McKay said, shaking his head. "Did I say it made any sense? What I'm saying is, my cousin saw the fire so clear in Hudson it could've as easy been an A-bomb."

"And *heard* it," Moon added.

"And heard it, right," said McKay.

"Well, that's different," Day said. "I thought you—"

"I swear to God, Albert," said McKay, "you are a piece of work. We're talkin' about the fire and you're worryin' about the fuckin' Russians sailing up the Hudson."

Everybody in the Hill Top laughed except Al Day. In the mirror, the torsos of the drinkers appeared deliberately composed along the length of the bar. The back of Moon's head was a perfect pale globe. It rested in the lower right corner of the mirror, as if it had fallen from the sky.

Adams asked himself, as he often did at work, how Day could have survived in life this long without brains.

"Christ, Don," said Day, "all I said was—"

"You are one amazing piece of work, Albert."

"Fuck you. You're the one that—"

"You are about an Albert Day," said Don McKay.

"Maybe they could hear it in Catskill, too," said Broder.

"I wouldn't be surprised," said Moon.

"I'll bet they did," said Broder. "I think that's what the guy in Catskill said, now that I remember."

Thinking about Day's ignorance reminded Adams of Ed's belief that Broder, not Day, was the dumbest man in Myles. He remembered debating the point with Ed through an entire afternoon, the two of them shouting back and forth over the sonic scream of chain saws while they trimmed branches away from power lines along a highway south of Chatham. Adams believed that Broder was not really stupid at all, though he didn't quite know what else to call him, and he was sure Ed's opinion had mostly to do with the night in the Hill Top when he'd overheard Broder talking about him.

Broder finished his sandwich and drank from his beer, the loose flaps of his cap flopping as he tilted his head. Watching him, Adams was reminded to drink his own and found, to no surprise, that he could taste the sour damage the foam had done.

He smiled ruefully, recalling the night last winter when Ed had asked Broder why he was wearing the cap and bandanna. And Broder refusing to say more than that it was winter and it was cold outside. Adams remembered Ed fuming when he'd been unable to draw anything more from Broder, then falling ominously silent as though in concession.

In fact, from that first night on through the rest of the winter, Broder had continued to wear the cap with spaniel's ears and the thief's bandanna covering his nose, until they became simply what he wore and were nothing anyone but Ed noticed. And he wore them then, as he'd resumed wearing them again this winter, because he'd suffered a seriously frostbitten nose and ears from his late-night drum major's march through the snow. For Broder had been drunk, had left his pickup at the Hill

Top the night Ed had seen him striding through the storm, and, just as Ed had envisioned him doing, he'd walked the D&H tracks all the way to his farm, seven miles from the edge of the village, then turned into his fields where they met the railroad tracks and continued on toward the weak speck of light from his kitchen window, barely visible to him through the pointillist snow.

"It was Henry King that started it," Moon said as he wiped the bar. "I'll always think that, I don't care what anyone says."

"What?" said Broder, growing interested. "You think King set the fire? Why would he do that? He fuckin' *died* in it, for Chrissake."

Adams watched the back of Moon's head in the bottom of the mirror as he shook it. It winked like a star, catching the light from the bar signs. "I don't mean on purpose," Moon said. "I mean the bastard was drunk."

"Of course he was drunk," said Broder.

"I mean, does a turd draw flies?" said Moon.

"If he was breathin', he was drunk," said Don McKay. "Of *course* he was drunk."

"That's all I mean," said Moon. "He was drunk, and dropped a cigarette somewhere or somethin', and then he was too drunk to do anything about it."

"Even leave," said Don McKay.

"Proves my point," said Moon.

Whenever the conversation moved, with an always dreamy energy, to the night of the fire and its thrilling calamity, some mention of Ed's father was inevitably a part of it, and Adams had heard Moon's theory many times. He knew there were others who agreed with Moon that Ed's father had somehow started it, though he was fairly sure that most people believed, as he did, the official explanation of a furnace throwing sparks. He thought to himself, as he listened to Moon, that he'd never heard Ed say what *he* felt was the cause.

After their skirmish at work, Adams didn't hear Ed say much

of anything. March and Mitchell had reached them in the ditch, as Adams's grip on the handle was beginning to slip, and had wrapped the two of them in desperate bear hugs while Ed and Adams cursed each other and strained to wriggle free.

"I heard you, motherfuck!" Ed screamed again and again at Adams. Waycross and Day had joined them by then and sought clumsily to wrap their arms around Ed and Adams, too. "I heard you! I heard you! I heard you, motherfuck!" There was something primal and mistaken in Ed's voice that they all caught.

Adams had had a lifelong history against Ed which proved he was the weaker man, but as he'd struggled to break Mitchell and Day's hold, feeling even Ed's screams as assaults he needed his arms and fists to counter, Adams had believed at that instant he could beat Ed senseless, and he'd surely wanted to.

In the days that followed, his feelings had taken on a quiet bitterness. On the crew, March kept their jobs separated. They spoke only the most necessary grunts to each other. And while Adams worked he thought again and again—sneaking looks at him while they worked at a tacitly legislated distance from each other—of Ed dementedly pounding the fence stake into the ground, and of hurrying to help him as Ed was rising with the hammer and the clear intent to kill him. And every time Adams thought about the handle in their hands he also remembered how it had felt to struggle against a new sensation of physical purpose which Ed had never brought to anything between them before. What Adams had felt was something loose and untempered in Ed, something with no trace of his old muscular conscience.

In the Hill Top, Broder said to no one in particular, "Somebody said they spotted King in Mellenville." There'd been a lull in the talk after Moon's argument that Ed's father had started the fire, and in that pause the thinking moved naturally to Ed, himself, and his Thanksgiving disappearance.

"Doin' what?" asked Moon.

"Seen the Dodge, rather," Broder said. "Just seen it parked, I guess."

In the first days after their fight, Adams had also had to endure an extraordinary rumor that Ed had ripped Adams's left ear off. He couldn't imagine how it had started, and no one could tell him any more than that they'd heard it had happened. He decided it must have had to do with the reports of Ed's screaming, "I heard you. I heard you. I heard you, motherfuck!" But wherever he went in town, Adams met the same astonished looks and some people could not entirely hide their slight sense of disappointment as they bobbed their heads furtively left and right and saw that both of Adams's ears were clearly still attached. When he'd stopped for gas at Squeaky Frye's Sunoco, Adams had seen the look of dashed expectations on Squeaky's face.

"Hey! You still got it!" Squeaky had said as he'd bent to Adams's gas cap and peered in through the pickup's window. "That's, uh, *good!*"

Moon wiped the top of the bar with a towel. He said to Broder, "They seen the Dodge but not him?"

Broder shrugged, "That's how I got it."

"Maybe it broke down on him," suggested McKay.

"A car of King's?" said Moon sarcastically. "I can't imagine that."

"Hah!" said Al Day. "Right."

It had been easy for Adams, after their fight, to settle ever more certainly into a bitterness toward Ed. And easy, too, to keep it alive as they'd worked side by side, speaking rare grunts to each other. So that ten days ago, when Adams had heard that Ed had left town, he'd felt an enormous surge of relief, and the hope that Ed would never return.

At work, he now performed with a sense of luxurious space in every direction, an ease that grew each day, and only occasionally did he still sense himself as caught in a kind of exile by all that had happened since Ramona had left. Betrayed by Ed;

suspected by others of lying on Ed's behalf. Although no one really assumed any longer, after their skirmish in the ditch, that Ed had confided in him.

"I'll tell you one thing," Moon said. "It's a helluva lot *quieter* in this town since that goddam Dodge is gone."

Adams watched the row of drinkers in the mirror, their heads nodding again.

"That's for damn sure," Broder said.

"Safer, too," said Don McKay.

"Safer, right," agreed Moon.

No one had stopped Adams on the street and asked if Ed had told him his plan. No one had wondered if he'd gone down to Ed's house and looked around the next day; if he had been the one who'd closed and locked the door which Ed had left flapping in the wind like a hand beckoning people in. No one seemed to suspect that Adams had private knowledge anymore of anything in Ed King's life.

Al Day asked, "You think he'll be back? I mean, he went after her, right? So, what if he don't find her? You think he'll be back, anyway?"

Adams finished his beer, glad to be done with it, and motioned to Moon for another.

"Who the fuck knows," said Don McKay. "Who knows if he went after her or not. Who knows where he went."

Adams said nothing, feeling as he listened an anger coming from a place he couldn't understand.

"If he don't find her . . ." Al Day said. "I kinda hope he don't come back if he don't find her. The way he got. I mean, Jesus, if you think he was in a bad mood before he went, just imagine . . ." He shook his head at the prospect and looked at Adams. "Ain't that right, Ray?"

Adams felt a sudden deep charge of resentment against Day, his assumption, it seemed to Adams, of their alliance against Ed. He thought of the scene at lunch break when Ed, full of contempt, had flung Day's food at him. He thought of a few

occasions in high school, when Ed had asked him to help him make fun of Albert Day. Now Adams found himself unable to reply, and he only shrugged his shoulders.

"Crazy fucker." Moon laughed and shook his head. "He always was, wasn't he? You never knew what he might do."

McKay smiled and so did Day and several others.

"So nobody here seen him in Mellenville?" asked Broder.

Moon smiled. "Remember that time he taped the stick of dynamite to the ass end of the horse on the merry-go-round?"

"At the Thanksgiving thing." McKay nodded, smiling too.

"Lit that sucker," Moon said, starting to chuckle. Laughter rippled infectiously down the bar.

"Fuckin' horse blew up in a thousand pieces," McKay said. "He said he figured the dynamite'd make the merry-go-round 'go around and around.' "

"Merry-go-round never budged," Moon said, laughing.

"Fuckin' horse," said McKay, and then his laughter stopped him. "Boom!" he managed to say and grandly arced both of his arms to demonstrate the fountain spray of plaster pieces rising into the air.

"The best was in high school," Al Day said. "When he put the bull snake in what's-her-name's desk." Day turned to Broder. "What was her name?"

Broder nodded. "Lamp," he said. "Mrs. Lamp." Even Broder was smiling.

"We all knew he done it," Day recalled. "But she wouldn't open her drawer. Finally, he gets Luther Sherrill, who just come in and don't know what's goin' on, he gets Luther to ask her if he can borrow a ruler."

"Jesus H. Christ," shouted Broder over the room's high laughter now. "You never seen a woman run so fast in your life."

"And it's Sherrill's the one gets thrown outa school," Al Day added.

"No!" called Adams over everyone. "That ain't it. Sherrill never got thrown outa school for that."

Broder and Day and Moon turned to look at Adams.

"I thought he did," said Day.

"Well, you're wrong," Adams said. "Sherrill never got thrown out for that. You can ask him."

"What the fuck difference does it make?" said Don McKay.

"Anyway, that ain't the best one I heard about him," said Moon. "What's the one where he drove the car into the gym?"

"Oh, yeah," said Al Day, grinning. "When he broke the windows in the gym and Dittmer told him . . ." Day looked at Adams. "How'd that go, Raymond? I forget just how that went."

Adams watched his new beer easing in a rivulet down the side of his glass. "I don't know," he said flatly. His lips puckered along the line of his mouth like the tissue of a scar.

"You was there," said Day. "You was in the gym when Ed came drivin' in."

Adams kept his eyes on his beer as he slowly righted his glass. "I got no idea what you're talkin' about."

"You know," insisted Day. "When Dittmer told him he better not see him come in the gym again until he paid for the windows he busted?"

"Come *walkin'* in," said Broder. "That was it. Dittmer told him he better not see him *walkin'* into the gym again. So the next day King opens up the big double doors and just drives his car, that old beat-to-shit Mercury he had, just drives the son of a bitch right onto the floor."

"That's it," said Moon. "That's the one I'm thinking of."

Al Day turned again to look at Adams. "You remember, Ray. You was there, I know you was."

Adams shook his head. His eyes were fixed on his clear gold beer, an insignificant scum circling the edge. He said, "Nothin' like that happened when I was around." His mouth was tightly set. He said, "King never done that as far as I know."

They all heard the odd determination in Adams's lie, and it immediately stilled the talk. An awkwardness descended, holding everyone's memories of Ed just where they were, and they all sat silently for a few moments, referring to their thoughts, smiles of general pleasure on their faces. There were a few murmurous chuckles within the quiet and then Moon broke it. "Anyway," he said, "he's a crazy son of a bitch. I wonder what he'll do."

"Me, too," said Al Day.

"Keeps you guessin', don't he," said McKay.

"I tell ya," said Moon, "this whole thing—her going, the kid, now him—this is the most interesting thing in this town since the fire." In the tone of his voice there was a fondness for his life.

"But nobody here heard they seen him in Mellenville?" asked Broder. He took off his cap and with his bandanna wiped the sweat he'd raised in his rare fit of laughter.

Adams lifted his glass of foamless beer and as he put it to his lips he had the sudden certainty that it would taste the same as the one he'd just finished.

Ed held his flashlight on the map of Columbia County, veined with its smallest roads and lanes. Outside the Dodge, the night wind blew strongly. He felt it, icy, at his ear, coming through the crack in the window he kept open when his kerosene heater was lit. It blew again, a fierce gust that gently rocked the car.

He knew the map so well he could trace much of it in his mind; he'd used a copy of it regularly with the rest of the crew to plot their work. And he knew the features of many of the roads it showed just as thoroughly. Filling holes, sealing cracks, shoring ditches, he'd continually refined his miniaturist's eye. He'd raked gravel over the road he was now parked on early last summer and he remembered the deep gashes, after spring mud,

that chronically furrowed its surface where it dipped and held any rain, several hundred yards ahead.

The beam of his flashlight followed an overlay of new lines Ed had drawn with a ruler and pencil as he'd planned his search in the weeks before Thanksgiving. With Myles as its starting point, a neat angular web spread to the edges of the map, every town connected in a pattern of concentric precision. Then, just in case she'd traveled farther than he sensed, he'd drawn the same meticulously logical webs over less detailed maps of Rensselaer and Dutchess counties, above and below Columbia, and of Greene, across the Hudson. He'd worked several nights, a delighted draftsman, until he'd fashioned the routes he knew would inevitably yield her if he followed them procedurally from town to town, convinced that at some point he'd drawn the tip of his pencil through Ramona's hiding place.

Again he felt the wind against the car, and it made a shrilling as it blew through the crack in the window, but he didn't mind the breath of frigid air; his heater warmed the Dodge cozily. He looked up from the map and rubbed his eyes, then scanned the interior with a domestic affection he felt so sharply it seemed a kind of longing. Everything was neatly in place—the washbowl, the jugs of water in a row, the gleaming twelve-gauge Remington, the stove, the sleeping bag, the box of clothes; trig as a composition after twelve days away from Myles.

He reached for a bottle of whiskey. "Shit," he whispered through a sigh and took a drink. Ed's mood was the bottom of gloom, and had been for more than a week; the residential fondness he felt for the Dodge, felt increasingly each day, was the only aspect of his scheme that had gone favorably at all. Otherwise, the methodical certainty it was founded on had so far proved futile and for the past two days he'd abandoned it completely, driving more or less on patternless impulse, allowing the roads to dictate his path as he'd always let them do when he roamed the country for pleasure late at night.

Now he spread the map taut across his knees, determined to

record where he'd been today. He squinted and began to draw with a red-ink pen, and the route's coiling aimlessness, immediately apparent against the rigid geometry of his original plan, sickened him and made him feel ashamed of himself. "Fuck!" he shouted and swept the map off his lap. He took a drink of whiskey.

As desperately as Ed wished to find Ramona, he'd nevertheless conceived the details of his effort as though it were an assignment, something Bill March, his foreman, might have asked him to solve using his knowledge of the geography and his patient pleasure in repetitive work. Studying his maps, asking himself where she could be, he'd gotten caught up in the challenge of procedure, and as he'd drawn his artful webs he might as well have been a surveyor determining the logic of a landscape.

He had not, then, paused to think of actually enacting his journey, hadn't rehearsed himself in conversation with anyone. It was not until the first morning, when he'd sat at sunrise in front of a diner on the main street of Mellenville—the settlement closest to Myles and, so, the first stop he'd planned—that it occurred to him that he was fairly well known in the town; chances were good he'd be recognized and were almost as likely that the news of Ramona would be familiar.

A panic had filled him and he grabbed the map on the seat, quickly deciding to reverse the direction of his travel. Instead of starting closest to Myles and moving gradually away, he'd begin at what he'd originally imagined as the end, in New Lebanon in the county's northeast corner, in the Berkshire foothills on the Massachusetts border. He'd been near there only two or three times with the crew, pouring tar.

He'd started the Dodge, suddenly fearful of being spotted, and hurried out of Mellenville, feeling the stir of a perilous uncertainty he hadn't dreamed the task might contain. He flew through Ghent and Chatham and on through East Chatham on Route 295, ignoring village speed limits and without any thought

of stopping to ask about Ramona. By the time he'd reached New Lebanon Ed was furious with a sense of disorientation and, though it was still early, the feeling that he'd lost essential time on his first day. He pulled to a stop and again opened the map and studied it, working in his mind to adjust to his route's reversal, but he'd conceived it with such conviction he was unable to shake the sense that he'd be traveling backward.

The New Lebanon post office had been the only thing open when he'd arrived that first morning and Ed had decided he couldn't wait for the insurance agency and the real estate office, the street's other businesses. Besides, if the postmaster hadn't heard of anyone's seeing Ramona, it was not very likely she was hiding around New Lebanon. So he'd gotten out of the car and walked to the door, feeling distracted and unconvinced. Inside, behind the counter, a thin, drawn-looking man had looked up and said good morning.

Ed had nodded and begun to speak and felt as he had a timidity that thinned his voice to a nearly inaudible hoarseness. He'd cleared his throat and started again. "I was wondering," he'd said, "if you mighta seen my sister."

"I don't know," the postmaster said. "I don't know who your sister is."

"We just moved over here," Ed said, sweeping his arm in the general direction of the Berkshires. "She was comin' up from Hudson about a week ago, for Thanksgiving, and she never showed up." He'd cleared his throat again when the postmaster frowned with interest. "She was hitchin' rides," Ed said. "We told her it was a dumb idea. The weather. But she said she'd be fine." He'd added, "Her phone don't answer."

"What's she look like?" the postmaster had asked. "I haven't seen anybody new I can remember." He'd cocked his head in thought.

"She's real small," Ed had said. He'd held his flattened hand in the air to show Ramona's height. "Skinny."

"Hmm," the postmaster said. "Anything else?"

When Ed had composed the story he'd begun to tell the postmaster he'd assumed Ramona's hand would be an advantage to him, a feature so memorable it would inevitably announce her.

"Anything else besides small and skinny?" the postmaster had asked.

Ed had nodded. "Yeah. She's got a fake hand." Again, his voice had been thin. He raised his palm, a pose of sworn allegiance, and pointed to it. "You might not spot it right away," he added. He'd felt an impulse to apologize for something.

"Like a hook?" the postmaster had asked, growing more interested. He'd lit another cigarette and sucked smoke into his nostrils.

"No," Ed had said and shrugged. "Just like a hand." He'd suddenly wished to seem ignorant of all but the fact and tried to pantomime a confusion with how such a thing had happened. "Just like a regular hand," he'd said again. "You probably wouldn't notice it. She even wears a glove on it when it's cold out." He'd added quickly, "I *think* she does, anyway."

The postmaster had shaken his head. "Afraid I haven't," he'd said. "Haven't heard anybody say they saw someone."

Back outside, Ed had hurried to the Dodge to consult the map once more, opening a beer to quench his deep thirst. His mind had been alive in so many directions he could hardly force himself to attend to the map. He'd swigged deeply, asking himself where he should go next. If he were now intending to reverse his route, shouldn't he begin with the bordering counties and slowly home in? But how likely was it, really, that she'd traveled that far? Or perhaps she'd headed due east from Myles, not terribly far, across the line, and was hiding somewhere in western Massachusetts. A sense of flux and frightening possibility had filled him, and as he'd looked at the map the inexorable strictness his lines had drawn had suddenly seemed to Ed a hindrance, a guarantee that in following them he'd

narrow his chances of ever finding her. But if not the route he'd planned, then what? And how?

He'd finished his beer and thrown the can to the floor and decided as he cursed that he would stay with the idea to first work his own county in the opposite direction, and if he hadn't yet found her when he'd gotten too close to Myles to move about anonymously, then he would pause and consider where to go next.

As one day had followed another, Ed had grown more and more unhappy with the routine of his search. For the first few days he'd faithfully adhered to his map and his story, though he'd grown increasingly uncomfortable with both. He'd felt that he was moving against the plainly evident current; that she was doubtless traveling farther and farther away from Myles while he was looping slowly back toward it, and weeks before, as his strategy had evolved with the unspecific certainty of discovering Ramona, he'd thought of the instant itself as something that would happen when he'd caught up with her; overtaken her. He'd not formed a picture of where it would happen, had not been inspired by a distinctly etched moment in the way he'd once held the image of himself standing at the door, watching Ramona shuffle weakly toward him, her shoes against the sidewalk making thin sandpaper sounds. But he'd keenly imagined a sense of the scenario's proper *direction*, had felt its momentum, and as he'd proceeded through three days he'd tried vainly to convince himself that it was just as likely he might meet as overtake her.

He'd stopped in bars and restaurants, in various main-street stores, and soon he'd begun, even as he got out of the Dodge to enter a place, to anticipate people's squints of concern, their pauses for thought with their eyes turned ceilingward, then their regretful replies that they'd seen no one resembling his sister. By the end of the first week, Ed's faith in the wisdom of his lie had grown extremely fragile; he was like a salesman losing confidence in the persuasiveness of his pitch. Several

times, as he'd turned to leave, he'd suddenly sensed the lively heat of conversation and snickering preparing to start up behind his back, a sensation which he felt in the nape of his neck, a shaft of audible sunlight.

He'd also found himself more and more hesitant to mention her hand and though he'd continually reminded himself in the privacy of the Dodge that everyone thought she was only his sister, he'd still sensed, as he'd talked about it, an embarrassment he'd feared was visible on his face. Worse still, each time he'd given someone its description Ed's mind had bloomed with memories of the accident, of the months of vile confusion in their house before and after. And then, dependably, of how she'd been before, when the lushness of her passion had been as commonplace as air.

Whenever he'd left a place after people had told him they'd not seen Ramona, he'd carried all of that inside him as he'd driven away, and the idea of having to repeat it just down the road began to influence his route. In the past few days, without thinking, he'd avoided three towns where he knew there were several stores and shops and bars to visit. And when he *had* come into a village, grimly determined, he'd driven at a crawl up and down its central street, again and again, unwittingly recreating the Summit ceremony of his impudent adolescence. He had circled and recircled the town's most obvious places, postponing his ordeal until that part of him which honored hard and reiterative labor forced him to park the Dodge and go inside.

The wind blew against the car again and Ed heard it through the window crack as a phonic burring, as a sole's harsh scuff against the surface of a walk. He looked around the car and felt for a moment his frequent suspicion that something was missing. The flashlight's beam looked left and right, highlighting the camp stove, the heater, his twelve-gauge lying in the well of the

trunk. He couldn't think of anything that was not accounted for and tried to quiet his concern.

His eyes lingered on the muted gloss of the Remington's stock and he remembered a thought he'd had on Thanksgiving morning when he'd awakened with the eagerness to begin. He'd said to himself that this journey to find her might take some time, and then he'd smiled with the thought that it would call for the patience he used when he waited for a deer. And he'd known, in that case, he had everything he needed.

He reached for the whiskey and took another drink and when he stretched his legs inside his sleeping bag he felt an aching stiffness in his back and shoulders. Briefly, he considered trying to go to sleep, and wished that he could, but although he felt groggy he judged that he wasn't drunk enough yet. He groaned softly as he shifted his weight again, his body telling him, as the red-ink lines on his map already had, that, except for three brief stops—the last to look for soap in the men's room when he'd gotten gas in Malvern—he'd not left the spacious security of the Dodge all day.

Nineteen

Before leaving her apartment for breakfast at The Kitchen, Ramona looked out at Strait on Sunday morning. The street was typically deserted, all the shops closed for the day. The rheum-eyed dog emerged from the shade of a doorstep and moved proprietarily along the sidewalk, paused to stretch, then resumed its mincing trot. She watched the silver Christmas bell suspended above Strait rock softly in the wind, flash in the sun. She focused on the cable which held it, tracing it from her side of the street to May's. She imagined it a wire carrying voices back and forth.

On Strait, she walked past the closed shops. A few of the windows were outlined with Christmas lights, lifeless trimmings on Sunday morning. New ridges of snow edged both sides of the street. It was very cold, but cloudless, and the sun was low and full on Ramona's face as she walked toward the coffee shop. She welcomed the cold, hoping it would help her to wake up, and it bit into her skin.

Last night she'd taken a long walk through town, wandering down a street that angled off from Strait toward the high school and was lined with some of the town's oldest homes. More and more, she'd been feeling the desire to learn where people lived here, especially to know if anybody she regularly saw around town owned one of the three or four houses she most loved in Claring. One of the houses was on this street, but she couldn't see anyone when she stopped to look in its windows.

She'd come back late to her apartment, chilled and tired. She'd slept soundly for a few hours, and the first minutes of her dream were lovely. The light and the planes of its room were amber-tinted, and though she seemed to be lying on its bare wooden floor, she was incredibly comfortable, the boards cushioning her and giving softly under her weight whenever she shifted. She felt no pillow, but the air in the room itself somehow held her head, keeping it raised so that she could watch Jonas as she held him while he nursed at her breast.

She felt his mouth pulling eagerly and the color of the dream brightened and dimmed to the rhythm of his sucking. Her milk flowed easily and it felt as though it were coming from everywhere inside her, flowing not only from her breast but down her arms and up through her legs toward her chest. Its movement tingled pleasantly. She watched as he drew milk without predicament through channels of her body she'd had no reason to feel before, and the sensation grew to a prolonged release more sharply edged than orgasm.

But then, as Jonas nursed, his mouth tightened and he began to suck directly on her nipple. She tried to slip her finger into a corner of his mouth to break the suction but he held on; then she squirmed with discomfort and felt Jonas slide away. She tried to draw him back but he had somehow moved farther from her, not crawling, not walking, and lay just beyond her reach. She strained to pull him back, but the room's amber air, which had billowed supportively, now seemed to be pressing against her and holding her in place. She struggled to get to Jonas, inching

her way across the room, but he stayed always just beyond the frustrated stretch of her fingers.

Ramona had seized at the sense she'd felt of coming up through the dream toward consciousness and sat up in bed until she was completely awake. Then she'd gotten up and made a pot of coffee and waited for morning at the table in the kitchen. At some point in the night, she'd looked over at her refrigerator door where the chart she'd made, detailing a baby's growth, still hung. Once again she read the figures she'd long ago memorized—3 months: notices world around him more . . . 7 months: first teeth . . . 8 months: stands . . . 1 year: sounds that mean something.

She'd stared at the chart. It had been as though she were looking at the map of a place she'd never been but somehow knew instinctively. She'd wondered, though, if you could still look down onto Jonas's skull as you held him at the window in a particular sunlight and watch his soft spot clearly throbbing, its pulsating skin like a wall of his heart. There was no place on her chart, she'd remembered nothing from Lovilla, which could tell her that. She'd shaken her head and her thought had been why she'd made the chart in the first place, and why she'd let it hang there all these weeks.

Tears had moved down her cheeks. Lately, her crying had become silent and without gesture, no change in her voice or expression signaling it. Her tears ran almost as rumination, her guilt's oddly tranquil extreme, appearing suddenly in her eyes as the thought not quite yet thought.

Then she'd put out her cigarette and walked to the refrigerator and pulled the chart from the door. She'd torn it in half, torn it sloppily again, and thrown the pieces into the wastebasket.

The coffee shop was just opening when she arrived, and she walked past the counter to a small table in a far corner which

gave her a full view of the dining room. She heard the cook and waitresses talking behind the kitchen's swinging doors and smiled when she recognized Helen's broad laughter suddenly covering the voices. She heard the clatter of silverware being hurriedly sorted. Then Helen and another waitress came through the kitchen doors, carrying stacks of cups and plates. Helen saw Ramona sitting in the corner. She smiled, causing her bowed chin to bob, and said, "You shoulda hollered."

"No hurry," Ramona said.

Helen carried a cup and coffeepot to Ramona's table. Filling the cup, she said, "I'm tired already and the day ain't even started."

"How come?" Ramona asked. She sipped her coffee. A couple dressed for church came in, then a family with two small children, a girl and a boy of nearly the same age. Helen greeted everyone, loudly announcing their entrances like a mistress of ceremonies.

Turning again to Ramona, she said, "Baby-sat my grandkids last night." She rolled her eyes exaggeratedly as she went to wait on the family at the table.

As the restaurant filled, Ramona smoked and listened to the talk moving around her, people waving quick hellos and asking one another about the simple events of the week. Helen brought Ramona's food and she ate slowly, watching Helen hustle among her tables, keeping several conversations alive. Ramona could hear the talk at the tables close to hers, but she wasn't interested in the isolated conversations. She was held instead by the larger weave of sound, the noise of locality.

She turned to look at the sound of a noisy entrance across the room. She saw three men in bright orange hunting vests drop into their chairs and, looking at the back of the man closest to her, she felt panic move her rib cage when she saw that it was Ed. She saw his straight black hair, wet with sweat and curled around his ears. His long, milk-white neck.

But even as her eyes darted to the swinging kitchen door, her

only hope of escape, Ramona began to realize that the hunter wasn't Ed. For she felt no charge of heat or danger emanating from him and she knew she would have sensed both these things immediately if Ed were here.

She felt herself calming and after a minute or so the hunter became a figure in the pattern of the room, although the fear he'd caused her gave him a prominence. Once, when he abruptly turned to someone at the table next to him, Ramona's heart jumped, caught short by the suddenness of what seemed his pouncing movement. She watched his back while he and his friends paid their bill and left.

When Helen came to her table again the room had begun to empty. She sat down and poured herself a cup of coffee and lit a cigarette.

"I can't seem to get movin' today," Ramona said. She felt embarrassed for having stayed so long.

Helen smiled. "I thought you were hangin' around so you could talk to me." She laughed her wide cackle. "Lord, Lord, Lord," she said, "I am so tired this morning."

Ramona said, "You baby-sat your grandkids last night?"

Helen nodded and held up three fingers. "And they're all of 'em hell on wheels. The youngest is a year." She sipped her coffee. "I say to my daughter—and I tell her this, right out—I say, 'It's always great to see 'em. And it's always great to see 'em go.' " She laughed again, then said, "But that's not so true with my son's kids. 'Cause they don't live so close, I guess."

She prattled happily on. Ramona saw her mouth moving, saw her hands darting and fluttering as she spoke, and yet she couldn't pay attention to what Helen was saying because she'd begun to hear in her head what *she* wanted to say. Ramona felt herself wanting to raise her hand to cut off Helen's talk, then begin to give her some of her own life in natural trade.

She heard Helen start to speak again of her night with her grandchildren. The mischief they'd made. The saving fact that they were gorgeous, each of them. And Ramona imagined

reaching across and touching Helen's arm and telling her to stop now and listen to what she had to say. She wanted to tell Helen that she also had a life, a past, and that she was worn out from trying to live here without one.

Ramona heard herself telling Helen that she'd ended up working in the flower shop in Claring because she'd had nowhere to go and she'd been running out of money. Money she'd stolen days before. As she watched Helen talk, Ramona felt the temptation at the bottom of her throat. It made her nearly short of breath.

She heard herself saying that she'd left her husband, whose name was Ed King. She pictured Helen's head tilting with interest. And then that she had a nine-month-old son and that somehow she'd left him, also. Had turned from him as he slept in his stroller and had just walked away, through a daisy-riddled field, into the face of a fierce August wind.

The desire to tell all this to Helen made her stomach tighten, the sensation of leaning from a railing and imagining the fall. She pictured telling her, then waiting as Helen swallowed, frowned, tried to take in what she'd been told, and finally said in response whatever she would say. Ramona tried to imagine sitting quietly as she waited for Helen's reply. She felt that whatever Helen offered her would be all right. Whether disgust or shock. A gasp of surprise. Perhaps, somehow, some sympathy. She would welcome anything.

Helen paused and took three slurps from a fresh cup of coffee. She smiled. "The youngest—she's a year—just one day started talkin'. Hadn't made a sound except to cry and all of a sudden starts sayin' words: 'Mommy.' 'TV.' You name it."

Over Helen's shoulder, Ramona watched the town's policeman in his gray uniform finish his breakfast and walk with his bill to the cash register.

"Same thing happened with her walkin'. Just one day decided to stand up and walk. I used to watch her layin' on the floor like a lump an hour at a time. Hell, I thought she was feeble." Helen

laughed and looked at Ramona, then reached across and patted Ramona's arm. "I know this don't mean squat to you, at your age." She waved her hand, as though moving smoke away from her face. "It's kind of unusual, is all, a kid to just start up like that."

"I know," Ramona said quietly.

"Unusual to me, anyway. None of mine did it that way."

"I know," she said again. She was hearing Helen's cheerful dismissal of any interest she could have and she wanted to shock her with her knowledge. "You know," Ramona said, clearing her throat to try to make her voice stronger, "a baby hates to have you hold his head."

Helen looked at her quizzically.

"His head's real, real sensitive. If you try to hold it—when you're feedin' him or something?—he'll fight to get it free." She said, "I know some things about kids." Her voice was thin and dry but with a pugnacity in it.

Helen's look softened but she kept her eyes on Ramona. She said, "I guess you do."

Ramona began to think of a lie: that she'd cared for her sister's babies; that her best girlfriend had had a child she'd sometimes fed. But then she stopped and said nothing for a few moments, as though inviting Helen's questions.

Helen only looked at her, then looked away.

Ramona said, "A baby's head, it's like an egg. You think of it bein' round, like a ball, until you hold it. *Try* to hold it. But it's really like an egg."

Helen shifted on her chair. There was a perplexing edge in Ramona's voice—what sounded like anger—as she spoke of holding a new baby and the sweet shape of his head. Helen looked again at Ramona as though she knew her tone, with those words, made no sense.

Finally, Helen said softly, "For sure." She nodded. "You do know some things about kids."

Ramona had sensed a kind of surrender forming as she

talked, and now a sense of distance, too. If she'd been trying in a way to declare her past to Helen, then she'd been referring to a time she suddenly understood was finished. She felt a completed piece of her life break free and float away.

"Yeah," she said quietly to Helen, nodding. "I do." Her voice was jumpy with adrenaline. She quickly lit a cigarette, drew deeply, and sat with the sense of the piece floating free, unreclaimable.

Helen looked around the room and slowly stood. "Well, I better get hustlin' here." She raised the coffeepot to offer Ramona more.

"No, thanks," Ramona said.

Helen took a step, then came back and bent awkwardly across the table and patted Ramona's arm again. "See ya next Sunday."

She nodded and smiled slightly. As Helen walked away, Ramona glimpsed in her mind the line of a life, of Claring Sundays running infinitely.

She walked slowly back toward her apartment. The day remained as cold as the morning had been, and the sun gave the town a harsh and shadowless light that seemed to bleach the fronts of houses and press the branches of the trees into tentacled shapes against the sky. Claring felt closed as Ramona walked along; she passed none of the churches, where people were hurrying in the cold to their cars after services.

She continued a random path along various side streets, postponing Strait. Her mind held no particular thoughts but it was alive with a fear that felt new to her.

She'd told herself since she'd been here that she couldn't go back to Myles, but, caught as she'd been—feeling the umbilical hold her child kept tight, its steady insistence that she could go no farther—she'd lived day to day in a kind of inconclusive dusk and one of its effects had been to keep Myles from seeming

finished. It had continued to be her present, living unhealed like the absence of her hand.

All the while she'd been away, she'd continuously felt a fluctuating terror of Ed. She'd also thought of her days with Donnie, wondering how they could have happened so easily and yet been as real as she knew they'd been. And all this while, too, she'd been unable to forget the violence she'd felt so close to in Myles, picturing its coolly perverse forms. Imagined violence done to Ed. The temptations toward Jonas. And most of all, she'd asked herself over and over in ways that had measured the strength of her imagination how she'd ever reached the moment that had let her walk away from Jonas while he slept in the field. Or how the moment had reached her. And what had been its quality. How it had been made.

But now, as she reached Strait Street, she carried the sense of a past that was completed.

Up ahead, the old red Toyota was parked in front of the shoe store, but she walked for a block, not taking it in, until May and David stepped out onto the sidewalk, opened the trunk and tossed suitcases inside, then climbed into the car.

Ramona stopped and watched the Toyota pull from the curb and head slowly away, coughing smoke. She waited until it reached the far end of Strait and turned right, disappearing. The street returned to silence but she paused a moment more, then walked on past the darkened storefronts. When she neared the Claring House she impulsively turned into the narrow passage, a break in the facade that led to the rear of the buildings.

The picture of May's leaving was vivid in her mind.

She came through the passage to the alley and looked up at the backs of the buildings, their network of rear wooden stairs zigzagging down the bricks.

She'd seen May and David leave dozens of times, but never with suitcases.

She walked past the back of the steak house, last night's

garbage sacked in several huge cans, and stood at the bottom of May's stairs.

She knew their suitcases meant they'd not be back today. But, more than that, the suitcases suggested departure, and Ramona saw May's heading out of town in the laboring old Toyota against all the ways she'd imagined her leaving—waving from the top of airplane ramps; tucked among possessions in sleek limousines.

She stood at the foot of the wooden stairs leading to May's back door, glanced up and down the alley, then started up. At the landing, she cupped her hands to her face and peered into the kitchen through the tall back window. As she'd thought, the layout of May's apartment appeared to be identical to hers: a doorway from the kitchen leading toward the front, through the bedroom, to the studio with its windows that gave onto Strait. She tried the knob and pushed futilely against the door.

She'd turned to descend the stairs when the window reminded her that she'd once climbed through her own after locking her key inside. She saw that, like hers, May's had no storm window. She stepped to the window and pushed on the frame. It lifted easily and she crawled through and stood in May's kitchen.

The room was dark, the window the only source of light besides the small panes in the door. She stood for a moment, looking around, the sense of identicalness overwhelming to her. It was as though she'd returned from breakfast to find her walls had changed color, her buckling linoleum another pattern. She saw that the hot-water heater stood in the same corner by the doorway to the bedroom.

She was breathing quickly. The clear dread she'd carried as she walked through town, the simpleminded sense of surrendering Myles, was changed to a light and heady danger that she felt in her chest. Her curiosity was a thief's. She detected the smell of turpentine.

She walked through the doorway and stood at the foot of the

bed. The sheet and blanket were thrown aside. She turned and walked to the open closet behind her, passing her hand over May's clothes, carefully parting them like a considerate shopper. She saw the scalloped-necked nightgown hanging from a hook on the door and she brought it to her face and breathed deeply. Turning back to the bed, she looked at the shaped impression May's body had made in the mattress and walked around and sat on the edge of the bed. Then she took off her shoes and swung her legs in. She lay small as a child inside May's shape.

She looked at the wall beside the bed. It made her think for the first time of herself, across the street, watching them, sometimes glimpsing the ghostly lust of their shadows on this wall, and her compulsion grew subtly more diffuse. She was here and there at once and the complications of vantage moved in her mind. Her hand, her flesh, reached out to where he would lie, and she imagined him turning. She pictured again a particular shadow of him—crouched to taste her it had seemed— a shadow she'd seen long ago, in her first weeks here. Then, perhaps because this bed was as new with scent and touch as Donnie's had been, she remembered him, her first night there, as she'd lain beside him as he slept and felt the pulse of his breathing animate the air in the trailer, the river, and the woods. Now her mind was here and with Donnie and across Strait at her window watching their shadows.

She got up and stepped back into her shoes and walked out of the bedroom into the sudden soft sun of the studio. The quality of the light surprised her; the studio seemed much brighter than her own front room. She saw the old swollen-armed chair. A gray tarpaulin, brightly splotched with paint, covered the bare floor. May's huge easel held a large new canvas. It stood near the windows beside a long wooden bench. She breathed the stronger fumes of turpentine. A row of coffee cans held dozens of soaking brushes.

Beyond the easel, three large sketches were taped to the wall. Ramona walked to them and saw that the one on the left was the

nude figure of a man standing next to a chair among several bottles and vases. The lines of the drawing were furiously frayed, like arranged strands of black string. She knew the figure was David. She could see his broad chest, his short, thick legs. She knew it was David, though the face in the sketch was a featureless oval. She saw that the middle sketch vaguely repeated the first with none of its detail, some of the vases and bottles now as tall as David, and that the third, on the right, only suggested the lines of the original, distortedly transformed into overlapping shapes. She panned the sequence several times, left to right, right to left, imagining David and the chair and the bottles and the vases sliding over one another until they reached abstraction. She smiled with recognition at May's technique and remembered the painting she'd once sat at the window watching her make—its lengths of vibrant color that had made her think of angels.

She walked to a stack of paintings leaning against the wall and flipped through the canvases, colors fanning past her eyes. They looked too much alike for her to know which one she'd watched May paint.

She moved about the studio. She picked up tools and felt their heft. She held May's heavy stapler and it took all her strength to fire a staple into the air. She lifted a brush and watched turpentine trickle from its bristles. Her mind was occupied in so many places now that it was as though she'd forgotten in some sense where she was; she felt malleable and bodiless, like David devolving. She was interested in the balance of May's hammer and the sound of the dripping turpentine and yet finally she wasn't and she knew that, too. She began to feel restless, her inspections grew hurried and careless, as though her assignment were simply to touch everything in the room. She was aware that the studio was becoming very cold with the heat turned down.

She moved back to the bench beneath the window and began to riffle through a huge pile of portrait sketches. Most were of

David, but the rest were faces strange to her. Again she thought of herself, across the street, and imagined her there watching her here.

She'd flipped past May's sketch of her before she suddenly stopped, delayed surprise cutting through her inattention, then turned back, two, three drawings, to see that, yes, it was of her. She glanced at the bottom of the sketch, where May had written, "flower shop, november," and stared down at her own face for several seconds.

The likeness was clear. She followed the lines that made her face, traced them down her neck and shoulders, and as she pulled the drawing free from the pile she saw that May had drawn her with her arms folded on a counter or a tabletop. And that one hand lay, huge, along the surface, while the other rested, in proportion, in the crook of an elbow. The enormous hand was cleanly drawn, no loose nests of lines, May's draftmanship becoming spare and elegantly sure from the wrist to the tips of the fingers. The hand stretched almost the width of the sketch like something low and immaculate in nature.

The drawing looked at once grotesque and beautiful to her, the hand freakish in its size but lovely in the way it lay in the foreground like an undulant landscape. She stood, riveted. She felt a sense of violation mixed with fascination. She studied the way May had drawn her nose and her small, thin mouth; then she looked at the hand again. For a moment, she tried to recall just how May had reacted to her hand the night she'd come into the flower shop, what had occurred that would have made her draw it as she had. Huge, yet delicate. But she could remember nothing more than May's helping her wrap the daisies. At least she thought that's what had happened, but she found she wasn't sure.

Holding the drawing, she walked to the chair and perched on an arm. And as she looked at it, she was conscious of the notion that May knew her—had remembered her, had focused attention on her—in a way that she couldn't have dreamed.

She looked at the set of her eyes and thought they made her look like a person who shouldn't be trusted.

How long, she wondered, had May's attention lasted? For just the time it had taken her to do the drawing? Ramona hoped that that was so, that May had now forgotten her entirely. And then she hoped the opposite. She hoped that May still watched her as she moved about in the flower shop. That May perhaps caught quick looks of her as she passed her own front windows.

She wondered how long it had taken May to do the drawing. And if May had been pleased with what she'd drawn. She looked at the line of her mouth and ran her finger along her lips. No, she thought. They weren't so thin as May had drawn them.

And as she sat, feeling the room's dropping temperature and the swirling dislocation of knowing May had used her, Ramona did not quite form the thought that just as she had sat at her window and looked into this room and drawn her dreams of May, so had May drawn her.

She let the drawing slide from her fingers to the floor and, looking down at it, it did not occur to her that May's appropriation of her life, her graceful distortion, was no more fanciful, no more selfish, than her use of May's. She did not think, as she pictured herself watching May move about in this room where she now stood, that May's drawing was precise in the way that Ramona's speculations were.

Or that May's version of Ramona was as faithful and as false as was Ramona's of herself when she stood before a mirror and remembered her body. Or saw her life as it was inevitably fated to be; or closed her eyes and drew her memories of how her past, how Ed, had been.

But if she did not consciously realize all this, she felt its effects almost physically, as though she were standing in the midst of a sourceless echoing that wouldn't quiet, wouldn't fade.

She stood up and walked to the windows, but she couldn't raise either of them. Turning to the room, she saw the drawing on the floor. She eased herself up onto the stool in front of the

easel and stared at the canvas. She had an urge to paint it. To follow May's method and take her face and neck and hand to bright abstractions.

She ran her finger over the canvas, sketching the fall of her hair, correcting the set of her eyes. A thought came to her. She imagined holding the brush in her left hand, then in the right, and wondered which would better make May's shapes. Neither one could copy her likeness recognizably, but it was possible that either could give it a suitable confusion. Her left, which grew tired and clumsy when she drew her lipstick and lined her eyelids. The right, through an alien machinery of coil and cable which opened and closed it very slightly.

She turned her eyes to the window and deliberately looked across to her apartment for the first time since she'd been in May's rooms. She felt a kind of private power of knowing what lay behind the windows, who lived what sort of life there.

Perhaps it was the way the sun seemed to highlight the building as she looked over at it that made her windows appear in her mind dangerously exposed and open to discovery. Or perhaps it was the ease with which she'd entered May's apartment that caused Ramona to think about her rooms and imagine Ed walking casually through the doorway as she sat on the couch listening to the radio, as though he'd known exactly where she'd been all these weeks and had for reasons of his own chosen the moment to appear. Walking up to her, a look of condescending amusement on his face, and saying, "I came to get you, Ramona. Let's go." Laughing then, and saying, as she watched his smile, "You musta been waitin' for me. 'Cause this place was easy to find." Smiling again, and her hearing the radio play a steel guitar's loosely quavering lament, his pointing finger curling to beckon her. "This ain't no place you'd be if you was trying to hide."

Or perhaps it was the discovery of May's drawing and her sensing now that May had been watching her without her suspecting it. Perhaps it was that, as well, which caused

Ramona to view her rooms across the street as though they were perched openly above Strait.

But in any event it was at this moment she understood she must leave Claring.

She moved calmly away from the window and out of the studio. She walked through the bedroom without looking at the bed or glancing at the wall where their shadows shone like shapes on canvas. But she paused in the kitchen when she saw that her shoes had tracked on the linoleum. She wiped the floor with paper towels and stuffed them in her coat pocket.

Climbing through the window, she stood on the landing and looked out over the empty alley. She didn't hurry down the stairs, and her calmness was evidence of a clear decision. For as she descended the steps, she knew that she would not be bringing her past with her this time. She had felt it close and break free and float away while she talked to Helen in The Kitchen. Now she could hold her past and look at it, even while she fled. She could still weep for it, quite alive with guilt, but she did not have to wonder if she was going back to it.

She reached Strait and stopped to look across the street. There was no need to go up—she'd gotten paid on Friday and carried all her money in her purse—and she couldn't imagine doing so in any case.

A pickup passed on Strait, and then a car full of teenagers. She could hear its radio playing through the windows; the three girls in the backseat were swaying to the music. She thought she recognized the driver as one of the boys who worked at the A&P deli counter. He seemed tempted to wave as he passed, his eyes catching sight of Ramona and his expression lifting. She watched the car continue on, the girls' heads ticking left and right like window ornaments.

There were just a few people waiting at the station for a train. Inside, the small room felt cavernous without a crowd, and

Ramona hesitated at the door. She recognized the bald attendant behind the ticket counter. A bearded man in a corduroy suit glanced up from his magazine to look at her. She wished there were the slowly moving comfort of a line to step into.

She walked up to the counter. Her calmness was gone. She watched her hand trembling as she lifted a schedule from the rack.

"Help you?" the agent asked, not looking up.

Ramona tried to open the schedule and when she'd finally spread it out on the counter she squinted at the times and destinations. Hurrying toward the station, she'd imagined she'd decide where she should go as she inched forward in the line.

She looked up and stared at the bright dome of the agent's head.

"Can I help you?" the agent said again. He finally raised his eyes to meet Ramona's.

"When is the train?" Ramona asked.

"To the city?"

"What?" Ramona asked.

The agent said, "The train to New York left Rhinecliff fifteen minutes ago. It'll be here any second."

New York. She tried to give the place some sound, some look. She thought of May. Of the weekend residents she'd waited on in the flower shop, had listened to on Sundays after breakfast in The Kitchen. The city people.

"Okay," she heard herself say from somewhere.

"One-way or round-trip?" the agent asked.

Ramona frowned. "One-way."

As she fumbled in her purse she heard the train approaching, heard the handful of people behind her gathering their things and shuffling past her. The train gave the loud blast she'd finally grown deaf to when it had passed beneath her window and shaken her kitchen. Stepping outside, she saw it pull to a stop with a whoosh of braking air, a sudden silver wall.

Doors slid open at two places on the train. The waiting

passengers hurried forward. She watched the back of the man ahead of her. He carried a huge suitcase that made him tilt against its weight when he lifted it and for a second it seemed to her impossible, an illusion, that she was leaving if she didn't have a suitcase.

" 'Board!" the conductor shouted from the doorway.

Ramona looked behind her, struck with the thought that there must be someone here she recognized. She thought of the little boy, Gabriel, she'd seen here, and a part of her felt surprised that Gabriel and his mother weren't here now. She looked into the parking lot and thought for a moment that she glimpsed Donnie's dented station wagon. It felt possible, even likely, that Donnie would suddenly appear, walking through the lot, waving her toward him.

The conductor looked down at her and extended his hand. "Let's go." She couldn't believe that this moment was moving her so quickly, with such ease.

" 'Board!" he said again to the platform's empty waiting area as Ramona climbed past him and stepped through sliding doors into a half-filled car. She found empty seats near the rear and, slipping into one, she saw the station through the window as the train started forward, creaking like a porch swing. She turned, continuing to watch the station slide away, and then the train followed a bend in the tracks and a density of bare trees moved like a closing drapery across the view.

The train lurched and groaned as it eased around the bend, behavior Ramona recognized from the way it sometimes crawled below her kitchen window. And she smiled, thinking of her resentment of the train when she'd first sat at the table in the kitchen and heard it approaching the outskirts of Claring. How she'd tried to anticipate the sound of its horn, but always jumped in her chair when it abruptly blasted. She had thought of the train then as an enemy, and she realized now that it had been all the while the answer she'd been waiting for, screaming as it passed as though to get her attention. She closed her eyes,

listening to the moaning springs as the train came out of the turn, and imagined she was right now passing her empty rooms above the shop.

She pictured herself gliding secretly past her back stairs just as Ed was climbing through her kitchen window. She was moving past and out of town at just the moment he stood in the darkness of her kitchen, stunned to find that she was gone. Then walked through the bedroom to the front where she wasn't sitting on the sagging couch, listening to the radio. Wasn't sitting at the window, lost in thoughts of Jonas, and didn't spin around, startled to see him walking toward her. Wasn't anywhere to be found as Ed moved back and forth through the empty rooms, unable to accept the truth their quiet was telling him.

She heard movement in the aisle behind her and saw an old woman in a fur coat edging slowly past. She was leaning on a metal walker as wide as the aisle, making her way toward a seat in the front. Her loose coat swayed with each step she took. She leaned on the walker as though she were gripping the railing of a tiny private balcony to take in the splendid view. She dropped heavily into a seat.

Ramona watched her fold the walker and slide it in beside her. The whistle blew and the train gained sudden speed as it straightened. Ramona sat up in her seat, abruptly attentive to the phenomenon of movement. She looked out her window and watched the gray-white woods streaking past. The whistle sounded again and the speed built even more. She told herself that she was moving no faster than she'd be inside a car, but the sensation of the train was new and told her otherwise.

Again she pictured her hurriedly diminishing kitchen above the shop. But now she was inside it, sitting at the table, and as the room grew smaller and smaller she felt again as though she were watching herself. The train on which she rode was speeding away from the kitchen where she sat, smoking cigarettes, having wakened from a dream of Jonas falling, Jonas

drowning, Jonas moving away from her breast and floating free beyond her reach.

She saw herself at the table. She was waiting to be found. Hours, days, had passed. And still Ed hadn't come to claim her. He knew where she was but he wouldn't come for her.

Ramona leaned out of her seat on the train and looked up the aisle toward the old woman. She couldn't see her, but knew where she was; the metal frame of her walker showed above the seat beside her.

The train flew through a tunnel and out and into another; the car going black, light, black; then out again into daylight. Ramona sat formally in her seat, her arms folded across her lap, mindful of the tremorous sway and the landscape flying. She knew now that she had never moved so swiftly. She imagined she was already miles and miles from Claring. Thirty, forty miles, imagined that she had traveled farther in minutes than she had from Jonas in the months she'd been gone.

She said the numbers to herself—thirty, forty, fifty—and tried to picture the instant distances. Until now, she had moved gradually away from Jonas on foot, or imaginarily in her mind. The first had progressed so slowly as to seem an act of distance in the way that breathing was; the latter was spectral, nothing her body truly felt. But now the train seemed to be combining them. She sat, inside the fact that she was moving—she felt it everywhere in her body, but moving so uniquely it almost seemed something her mind was inventing.

Forty, fifty miles.

Sometimes when she'd read the chart she'd taped to the refrigerator she'd thought to herself how incredibly fast a baby grew. After a month he was smiling. After seven he sat strongly. After eight, or nine, or ten, he stood. She'd remembered how Jonas had doubled his weight in five months, had become almost overnight too heavy and too strong. And how she'd imagined him continuing to grow, so fast, ahead of any pace her strength could hope to meet.

The sliding doors opened and a fat conductor stepped through.

"Tickets, please," he said. "Tickets."

She thought, Seven months—first teeth. She imagined the startling needle-prick of Jonas's mouth as he sucked on her finger with his sharp new teeth.

The conductor stood in the aisle, swaying slightly to the motion of the train.

She remembered Lovilla telling her that he'd add a pound each month. Sixteen pounds at six months. Seventeen at seven . . . Twenty at ten. She felt a clenching in her stomach.

"Tickets." She watched his hand that held the ticket punch, saw it wavering over its target with the movement of the train. He reached her and held out his hand. He smelled freshly of soap. She handed him her ticket and watched him punch it several times. From the seat behind her, a woman's voice asked, "How long to Poughkeepsie?"

"Ten, fifteen minutes," the conductor said and handed Ramona her ticket.

"And the city?" someone else behind her asked.

"An hour after that."

Looking out the window, she saw the too-close wall of woods abruptly end and now the river shimmered suddenly and ran alongside; so much bigger than Donnie's; and not silver, like her dream's, but wide and brilliantly lit.

She watched the river, the cinder cliffs beyond a mournful gray. Her stomach clenched more tightly. She sat erectly in her seat with a pupil's formal posture. She was listening consciously to the clacking of the wheels on the tracks.

She felt herself moving swiftly and it was nothing she had dreamed. The river running, coils of light. She had never moved so quickly. Had never felt herself traveling, truly fleeing. She thought of the numbers and said them to herself. Fifty miles. Sixty miles.

Nine months, she thought. What is it at nine months?

Sixty miles. Truly fleeing, with the current of the river. No. Faster than the river. Seventy miles, she thought. Ten months.

A year.

Yes, moving faster than the river as it ran beyond her window.

Moving too fast.

A year. Makes sounds that mean something.

She heard the frantic clacking of the wheels on the tracks and it sounded in her ears like the metric hum of language.

She had never moved before and she was moving so clearly now, so quickly; away.

No.

Too clearly; too quickly.

She looked out to the clamorous flash of the river. She shook her head and whispered, "No."

Twenty

Although the roadhouse outside Malvern where Donnie tended bar had long been known to Ed, he had never been inside it. He'd spent plenty of time in places that were farther from Myles than Malvern was, but in the way that people's subjective inclinations turn them arbitrarily in a certain direction and not in another, Ed had driven to Mellenville or even all the way to Chatham, rather than to Malvern, when he'd felt the wish to drink beer somewhere away from Myles.

Now he sat in the roadhouse's huge gravel parking lot, which was thickly floured with snow. Snow had begun to drift against a side of the building and shoal in around the trees at the far end of the lot. There were only two cars and a pickup, and Donnie's rusted station wagon, parked in scattered fashion, and it was the pattern and scarcity of the cars that told Ed the hour was late. Otherwise, he had no sense of the time. He'd fallen asleep

in the parked Dodge at some earlier point, and although he'd remembered when he opened his eyes that it had been dark when he'd drifted off, the information had done him no good because the sky was dark by five o'clock these days. For all he could sense, he might have been asleep for three minutes or three hours.

He'd drunk a beer, to help himself either wake up or grow drowsy again. Whichever way the beer worked would be all right with him. Ignorant of the hour, deep within a snowing darkness on a trough of a lane no wider than a driveway, he would let the beer tell him whether it was nearly morning or still early on in night. But after he'd finished it he was neither more nor less awake; he was only somewhat drunker than he'd been when he'd fallen asleep. Still, he'd seen that the snow was something he should probably attend to, that he might need to find a wider and easier road in case the one he was parked on became impassable. And it was as he'd driven away along the isolated lane, another beer between his legs, that his day's accumulated indolence began to speak to him like guilt.

Earlier, at midmorning—heading slowly along one of his favorite highways that paralleled the Hudson toward Albany and looked down for a stretch on the sun-play of the river—he'd abruptly decided that he should use this day to study his maps and try again to revise his plan, that the continuing randomness of his stops had simply gotten out of hand. He'd felt, in fact, a powerful wish to return to Myles, believing that if only he were home he'd be able to step back from his confusion and see its remedy. But he'd privately pledged as he was first preparing to leave town that he'd only come back when he'd found Ramona and that promise continued to seem overridingly wise even as he felt the heady urge to go home. So he'd convinced himself that the day should be spent in strategy inside the Dodge. It would be a waste of time to stop anywhere and ask about her. He knew well enough what the answer would be, and what it

would continue to be as long as he was operating haphazardly.

But nothing had come of his day-long retreat. The maps had suggested nothing. The red-ink trails he'd persisted in drawing at the end of each day, decorative scrolls frankly charting his inefficiency, only enraged him. Twice he'd leaped from the Dodge in a rage of bitter energy and walked around and around the car, calling curses to the sky.

And so, just moments ago, as he'd come out of the lane onto a wide gravel strip that ran past the roadhouse where Donnie worked, the full sense of a wasted day had begun to weight his despondency even further. Recalling the bar at the next intersection, he'd slurred, "Goddammit, *yes.*" The determination to do some work, salvage something from his horseshit day, guided him. He'd carefully eased the Dodge into the lot (he was a driver who usually knew when he was dangerously drunk), and watched the snow for a short time while he talked himself out of simply going to sleep again in the parking lot; he sensed now that the dullness in his muscles was drunkenness combined with an invalid's torpor which only felt like sleepiness.

He sat in the parking lot, working strenuously to believe that someone in the bar might have seen Ramona. "Ya never know. Ya never know," he mumbled aloud, and suddenly he flung open the door and scrambled out of the car.

From behind the bar, Donnie looked up in surprise as Ed entered. He was readying to close. He'd been busy through the first hours of his shift, but people had spoken of wanting to get home in case the snow became a problem and the rooms had cleared earlier than usual. He'd decided he would stay here tonight, sleep in the bar, if the weather seemed risky when he stepped outside. And he was concerned about Jesus Christ, who sat across from him, alert for the moment, but who'd drunk several pairs of beers tonight, his face swelling steadily from his allergy, speaking many times of his near encounter with another

Teddy Kennedy in desolate East Dakota, and who'd risen from the dead at least three times by Donnie's count.

"How is it out?" Donnie called to Ed.

Ed nodded and weaved a bit as he made his way toward the bar. He walked past the silent jukebox and three empty tables, their wire-backed chairs of an oddly delicate filigree. He felt unsteady, felt the filmy weakness of a rushed recuperation, as he slid onto a stool next to Jesus Christ. He said to Donnie, "Whatever's cold."

Donnie reached for a beer and opened it for Ed. "Gettin' bad?" he asked. "The snow?"

Ed blinked and scanned the room, nodding to Jesus Christ and noticing his swollen face, then raising his hand to the other two customers at the end of the bar. He'd been concerned there'd be someone here who knew him and was relieved to see four strangers. "Not too bad," he said finally, telling the truth as well as he'd been able to notice it.

"Really?" said Jesus Christ. "We been hearin' how it's comin' down." Ed looked into his dark eyes, surrounded by his shaggy beard, his feral head of hair; they shone as brightly as lakes, appeared miraculously those of a completely sober man.

Ed shrugged. "That's how snow usually comes, ain't it? Down?"

Jesus Christ smiled. "Hah! Pretty good." He looked to Donnie. "Jew, hear that?"

Ed frowned. "Did I hear what?"

Jesus Christ pointed to Donnie and said, "I was askin' him."

An instant belligerence enlivened Ed's dull face. "You said, 'Did you hear that?' I figured you was talkin' to me. You just *was* talkin' to me."

Donnie said, with pleasant firmness, "He was talkin' to me." He'd known that Ed was very drunk from the moment of his entrance. Seen the deadness in his face, his pause at the door, snow clinging to his boots, as he squinted effortfully around the

room. Donnie's initial demeanor with drunken customers was easy and alert. He said to Ed, "Take your time, drink your beer. I'll be closing when you're done." He pointed to the clock.

Ed turned to look at it and when its face finally clarified he read eleven-thirty. "You're closin' awful early," he said to Donnie. He felt a sudden alarm that things were moving too quickly. He'd imagined settling in a bit, drinking some beer, floating for a while in the eddying talk, before asking about Ramona.

Donnie spread his arms and smiled. "So it goes. 'Early to bed . . .' "

Ed's eyes paused to look at Donnie, really for the first time since he'd sat down, and he received from Donnie's expression— that cast of nameless sorrow which had preoccupied Ramona, which she'd asked inside her, had tried in vain to take with her—Ed received from the expression an extravagant warmth. For the look from Donnie's eyes was exactly the disposition of Ed's heart, and it was the only expression there was to wear in the world as far as Ed's mood was concerned. It was not so much that he noticed Donnie's look as that he sensed it was fitting, was naturally appropriate. He was sure he felt a wave of commiseration move across the bar and, grateful to have it, he smiled stupidly at Donnie.

Donnie nodded.

The two customers at the far end rose to leave, waving at Donnie and pointing to the bar where their money lay. Ed stared at their backs as they walked out the door.

"You live around here?"

Ed turned his head to Jesus Christ, who'd just asked him the question.

"You talkin' to *me* now?" Ed said. "You ain't talkin' to him?"

Jesus Christ laughed. "You're about a pisser, ain't ya. Yeah, I'm talking to you."

Ed shook his head. "Last time you was talkin' to me you was

talkin' to him." He nodded at Donnie, then watched him carrying cases of beer from the kitchen locker to stock the coolers for tomorrow. In all his stops during these weeks on the road, Ed had not felt a hint of the sympathy he was sure he'd sensed coming from Donnie, and finding it here convinced him that his luck had just turned. Distracted, he said to Jesus Christ, "Yeah. In Myles."

"Myles?" said Jesus Christ. "You know Verlan Dennison? I work with Verlan."

"Sure," said Ed.

"Lazy cocksucker, ain't he."

"He was the last time I checked," said Ed. He was trying to catch Donnie's eye again. He felt ready, the nervous urgency of infatuation in him. It made his throat dry and suddenly he needed the rest of his beer. He tipped the bottle to his lips and drained it.

"He was at five o'clock today," said Jesus Christ, smiling widely. "I can swear to that. That's the last I seen him, leavin' work, and he was still a lazy cocksucker when he said 'So long' at five o'clock." There was suddenly a rambling sibilance in his speech, lightly detectable, a subtle shift of dialect, but it was the very sound that Donnie had been attentively listening for while he stocked and cleaned behind the bar.

He turned and said, "J.C. Why don't you get some exercise? Take a walk to the head and splash some water on your face. I'm too tired to carry you outa here tonight." His voice was parentally patient. He saw, as he'd suspected he would, that his friend's dark eyes were losing their light.

Ed had begun to imagine Donnie's reply—*A woman? Real small? Yeah. She was just in here a couple days ago.* Somewhere in his muddled mind he heard the conversation he was about to have with Donnie, heard it with the same haunting clarity he heard the laughter starting up behind his back when he'd turned to leave a place.

Jesus Christ smiled sheepishly at Donnie. "Am I startin' to go?"

Donnie nodded.

"Listen," Ed blurted. "I'm lookin' for this woman? Maybe you seen her." His voice was loud and imprecise with excitement. "She's short and skinny?" He held his flattened hand at the height of his shoulder. "About this tall." His eagerness for Donnie's confirming response made him forget his usual story completely. He forgot she was his sister, that she was hitchhiking to Thanksgiving.

The strange, agitative crackle of Ed's voice alone would have caught Donnie's interest.

"She's got this fake hand," Ed said, swallowing. "You might notice it, maybe not."

"Hey!" Jesus Christ said, his hooded eyes lifting. "Hey, Jew, that's gotta be—"

"Nope," Donnie said. His voice was a blade. "No, I ain't," he said. "I'm here every night and I ain't seen nobody like that." He turned to Jesus Christ and held his look on him. "I woulda seen a hand," he said to Ed. "I notice things like that."

Ed sat, blinking hard. Donnie moved a few steps away from him to wash the final glasses.

"J.C.," Donnie said nodding toward the bathroom. "Go powder your nose so we can all go home." He reached for Ed's empty bottle and held it up to the light, then dropped it into a rack below the bar.

Ed watched Jesus Christ look at Donnie, then give him a laborious salute as he eased off his stool and walked lightly like a burglar toward the bathroom door.

Out of the corner of his eye Ed caught Donnie's movement. His pacing up and down the bar was slow, the routine of closing chores, but to Ed everything seemed suddenly a swirl of confusion—Jesus Christ leaving his side, Donnie's turning away—and in his mind he shouted, No, this wasn't how it went. Not what you was supposed to say. He'd seen Donnie's

face of sympathy. He'd felt its warmth. He shook his head, trying to clear it, blinked his eyes several times, and in his mind said to Donnie what his words should have been. He leaned forward on his elbows and took the deepest breath he could. You seen her, you son of a bitch.

Donnie was turned toward the shelves and Ed watched his back as he walked down the bar carrying cases of empty bottles, then disappeared through a door to the kitchen. Ed was alone in the room but the conviction that Donnie had seen Ramona stayed, and he stared at it, squinting straight ahead at his certainty, a kind of mirage, like the shimmering that rose from the highways in the road-baking days of mid-August. For Ed was not so drunk that he'd missed Donnie's voice as it had cut Jesus Christ's exclamation.

In the kitchen, Donnie sat the cases on the top of a stack, thinking that he hoped the bastard out front was even drunker than he'd judged him to be. He doubted that Ed had believed him, that Jesus Christ's innocent outburst has passed unnoticed. Donnie said to himself that no matter how drunk someone was, he'd be alert enough to hear a lie as clumsy as that one had been. If someone was looking for Ramona he'd be especially watchful, as he asked about her, for everything about the response.

He moved quickly in the kitchen, sweeping the floor, checking to see that the grill was shut off. He wanted to get back out to the bar before Jesus Christ returned. Donnie imagined him talking on and on about Ramona, the night she'd come to the bar and had stolen his money; how he was sure she'd been the one, since she'd disappeared from Donnie's the very next morning.

For a week after the night Ramona left his trailer, Donnie had awakened each morning and told himself to move to a new place on the river. It had been his first impulse, and then his first full thought, when he'd discovered she was gone. He'd taken a cup of coffee with him to the riverbank and sipped it slowly in the sun as he thought about where he would set the trailer next.

He'd heard about a place near Stuyvesant Falls where the Kinderhook dropped steeply down a splendid wall of cliff-steps to a trout pool. The idea of a shift in the river's attitude had appealed to Donnie, for he'd wanted the look of his surroundings reordered—the lay and composition of the bank, the woods somehow altered in the way it met the river. Inside the trailer there'd been nothing except his bed that had caused him to think of Ramona, but they had lived nearly every hour outdoors during those days of stunning heat, so the riverbank, where they'd drunk morning coffee and made love, where they'd built fires to cook the trout he'd caught and where they'd tried to sleep on blankets, desperate for the slightest movement of air on the hottest nights, the riverbank evoked her, and he'd felt certain for a week that the time had come again to move.

But each morning when he'd risen he'd told himself to leave and at the end of the day he hadn't. And as he thought about it—taking a new bartending job, setting his trailer in a place where the Kinderhook boiled and cascaded, behaving as though it were a river he'd never seen before—he said to himself that he should weigh his moving against his belief that there was no chance Ramona might return. He was a man who'd left places all his life, moving and resettling under many circumstances from the day he'd run away from home at the age of fifteen. He could read a departure, the mood of its wake, as well as anyone alive, and he'd known immediately that Ramona would not give in to whatever temptation she might feel to come back. So he'd reasoned that if he left now and settled somewhere new, there was an extremely slight chance, as long as Ramona continued to run, that he might meet up with her again. But if he stayed where he was, he felt certain he would not.

The first week had ended, then a second, and each morning as he'd fished he'd seen more clearly that he was going to stay and let the sense of her fade from the riverbank and from the shade beneath the trees. As badly as he'd missed her and

wished she were with him, as much as he'd wondered where she was, he'd begun to understand that he did not want to risk ever meeting her again. For he couldn't imagine seeing Ramona without learning somehow the reasons for her leaving. And he'd found, as he'd thought about it, that he didn't want to know why she'd snuck away, a stealthy thief. He couldn't fathom why she'd done it and each succeeding morning, as he'd wondered what her leaving might reveal about himself, about the ways in which it hinted that he'd badly misjudged her, he'd realized that the prospect of knowing these things revulsed him. His curiosity, which she'd awakened, had felt boundless in the beginning, but as he'd considered what to do, Donnie had slowly come to sense the limits of its range and he'd clearly glimpsed the places where it had no wish to go.

He had reached his decision to stay, and was conscious that he had, the morning he'd caught a fine, long trout which fought him vigorously, dipped and glistened in the river. Preparing to slip the hook free, he'd been struck with the certainty he'd caught the fish before. He held it and turned it in the sun. Then, chuckling ruefully, he'd bent to the river, eased the hook out of its mouth, and after a moment felt it pulse to life as it slithered through his hands. He'd watched it glint like a present as it cut through the water.

In the kitchen, Donnie quickly sacked garbage, listening as best he could for the resumption of voices from the bar. He had no thoughts, no question of his impulse to protect Ramona now, and as he moved about the kitchen, his alarm hurried him. From the moment he'd seen her walk into the diner, sensed her fear and her almost disembodied determination, Donnie had believed she must have valid reason to be running. And her fleeing his trailer as she had, fleeing his side while he slept, had somehow only strengthened his sense. So if the man out front was that reason, or its mercenary, then Donnie's purpose was clear to him.

He took the garbage bags outside, hurried in and locked the door. He thought he heard two voices in the bar. He quickly scanned the kitchen, turned out the light, and as he came back into the room he saw the two of them, Ed still staring straight ahead. Donnie moved deliberately toward them, trying to decide how best to handle things. He not only wanted Ed out, but wanted him to believe he was nowhere near where Ramona had been. He started to speak, then saw Ed turn to Jesus Christ.

"Where you been, boy?" Ed said. There was no discretion in Ed's voice now, as though he'd been sitting out here alone just letting his frustration build and couldn't wait to use it.

Jesus Christ seemed to hear that something had changed. He shrugged his shoulders, looked defensive. "Where you think?" he said to Ed. "I took a piss."

"Took a piss?" Ed said. His incredulity was loose and elaborate. "Longest piss I ever knew. Fucking world-record piss, I'd say."

"Listen," Donnie said. "Let's take it home and—"

"Fucking *Guinness Book of Records* piss if you ask me," Ed said.

"Okay, buddy," Donnie said. "Look, we're closed. And you're drunk. Either one means you gotta go, so take your pick."

Ed looked at Donnie, his head dipping as he tried to hold him in focus, then he turned to stare at Jesus Christ. Through everything else, he felt a sudden embarrassment, Donnie's scolding the kind of reprimand he'd always watched others receive, men who hadn't learned, as he had, how to control a bar no matter how drunk they were.

"Okay, okay," Ed said. He knew he must keep his desperation inside him. The bartender's tone had been a warning of how much he'd shown them and he filled his lungs with the bar's smoke-blue air in order to calm himself. "Just a second and I'm going."

He turned again to Jesus Christ. As he'd sat at the bar, sure he'd heard their lies, he'd decided that he should work on Jesus

Christ, try to get him to talk about Ramona. Ed had sensed that Jesus Christ was drunk, though he didn't show it, and stupid as well, and that Donnie was neither. Besides, Donnie had made a fool of him already, offering his sympathy and then pulling it back when he'd reached for it.

"Listen," Ed said to Jesus Christ. He turned away from Donnie and curled his back, trying to make a private cave to talk, and whispered conspiratorially. "You sure you ain't seen that woman I was talkin' about?"

He saw Jesus Christ's eyes dart toward Donnie. "No," he said. "I ain't. When you first mentioned her I thought I did see her once, but it was somebody else."

Ed thought, You son of a bitch. Why won't you tell me? He watched Jesus Christ's eyes trying to find something to fix on. His anger, which sometimes shaded the world in sudden red, was colorless now, but sounding. It made a whine in his ears. And still he tried futilely to think through it.

"You're *sure?*" he asked. What'd I ever do to you? he thought.

"He said he never seen her," Donnie said. "And I said the same thing. Now let's go, cowboy. Do us all a favor." He reached above the liquor shelves and switched off a light, walked midway down the bar and switched off another.

Ed watched Donnie move away from him, making darkness as he walked, then turned back to Jesus Christ. He sensed a tension in the room that was vivid; molecular; that the air held the throb of his name and his life. He whispered fiercely, "I *heard* you, you bastard."

Jesus Christ tried to smile. His swollen face looked tight as a child's to Ed. "Hey, look," Jesus Christ said. "I'm drunk and I know it. Maybe you are some, too, so let's leave when we're even. That's what I always say."

Ed's eyes had come to rest on Jesus Christ's ears. He imagined plucking them bloodlessly from the sides of his head. "Is that what you say?" he asked. "Leave when you're even? Is

that what you say?" He lifted his hands off the bar, slowly, in unison. Jesus Christ watched them, but in his own clouded eyes their motion seemed innocent, seemed, even as Ed reached for his ears, too calmly deliberate to have violence in mind. "I heard you say somethin' *else*." Ed's hands cupped Jesus Christ's ears and closed on them like spiders. "I *heard* you." He pulled on them, fully expecting to pick them cleanly from his head.

Jesus Christ's shriek was equally pain and surprise, high and clear as a eunuch's song. "Fuckin' asshole! *Jew!*" he shouted and shook his head wildly, but Ed's grip only tightened. "—this son of a bitch off me!"

"Tell me!" Ed screamed at Jesus Christ. He moved his head back and forth. "I heard you, you bastard!"

Donnie had reached them and grabbed Ed from behind. He got his long arms under Ed's and up behind his head and wrestled him from his chair. Ed made a brute sound of surprise, felt the air go out of his chest, and struggled momentarily, but not with any heart, and Donnie backed him away from the bar.

"Get the door, J.C.!" Donnie shouted. He and Ed moved in a clumsy, cooperative embrace, boots scuffing the floor. They grunted back and forth, the closest they came to words, but as Donnie held Ed in his arms he felt the briefest urge to lean to his ear and whisper, "You was right. She was here." Perhaps as an impulse of verifying consolation; perhaps to provoke him further, punish him for whatever he'd done to make Ramona leave.

Jesus Christ had hurried to the door and when he opened it, Ed again fought briefly but weakly in Donnie's arms, as though only for form. Then Donnie felt Ed relax and as he guided him out the door he let go of him and Ed wobbled on his feet. Donnie reflexively offered him a steadying hand and Ed took it; he seemed about to curtsy. Then he stepped out into the snow and the door shut behind him.

He stood in the parking lot for several seconds, then bent over, his hands on his knees. He stared at the ground, a plain of

snow, and it looked to Ed to be close to his face. He noticed that the snow reached the ankles of his boots and he felt it softly falling on the back of his neck.

Straightening slowly, he shuffled toward his car. Snow covered it completely and it took him some time, using the sleeves of his coat as sweeping brooms, to clear its roof and hood and windows. He breathed heavily as he worked and when he climbed into the Dodge he felt as though he'd finished a day on the crew. But he wasn't tempted to sit and wait for his strength, for all the while he'd cleaned away the snow Ed had fought a furious impatience to get away from here. Not only for what had happened to him inside but, even more, because he now knew absolutely that he had to get home. His thoughts were blurred at best, his drunkenness surrounding them like a deadening insulation, but still he knew that he must get back to Myles and think through his search again. He cursed himself, as he started the Dodge, that he'd not followed his instinct to do so this morning.

He eased away from the roadhouse, his tires' parallel furrows the only marks in the lot, while his mind tried to compose the easiest route home. He drove very slowly; the snow was a particulate wall beyond his windshield. In his mind he made turns, was choosing roads, asking more of his knowledge than he had in his life. He knew there was no logical way between here and Myles. It was simply a matter of how to use as many of the wider, flatter gravel roads as possible. He reached the first intersection and turned left, his initial decision an easy one; turning right meant the Hudson. Still struggling in his head, fuzzily sketching and revising, he started down a white strip free of any tire tracks, its ditches defining it. He was fairly sure he knew this road.

He knew as he drove that he was drunk and that the snow was serious, but he felt that as long as he remembered these things he would be fine. He had with him his unmatchable wisdom of the landscape, and he sensed his dilemma as in fact

a kind of gift: a challenge for which he was peculiarly suited that would force him to think his way out of his drunkenness.

As he inched along, he sensed himself back in Myles, hiding out in his house, leaving all the lights dark, avoiding the windows, the Dodge parked somewhere safely distant from town. To make sure he stayed undetected, he'd only step outside in the darkest hour of early morning, the same hours he'd worked when he'd redesigned the Dodge. He'd feel no need to rush his plan, making certain this time that he overlooked nothing. And no one in Myles would know he was home.

He smiled at the thought, then felt the Dodge seem to slide out from under him and a flare of adrenaline went out through his arms. He took his foot off the accelerator and the car settled and moved again to his direction. Ed breathed deeply and told himself to pay attention, not to think of Myles until he got there. He bent over the steering wheel, his eyes close to the windshield so he could watch the road more carefully.

He felt the road's small lifts and falls, its bends of direction, and eased the Dodge through them. Yes, he sensed as he steered more attentively now, he knew this road well. And he'd decided which one he would follow next. He began to watch for a fork he'd follow to the right, half a mile or so ahead.

As he drove, he suddenly saw through his mind's thickness an image of himself wrapped in Donnie's arms, and he shook his head to clear it, for it interfered with his view of the road. He couldn't believe the events in the bar had happened just minutes before and he briefly labored to retrieve their details, feeling an old man's urge to float in youthful recollection. All the preoccupations of the moment—his plans after returning home; the deluge of snow; the strain of paying attention as he steered through it—had removed Donnie's bar to a distant memory. He shook his head again, nearly conscious of this fraudulent sense of distance, until the snow came toward him unobscured once again.

He tried to picture exactly the way the road he would follow met the road he was on, what he could look for that might announce the fork unmistakably, but it was very hard work and his mind had little strength. The snow seemed even heavier now and he told himself to drive more slowly through it. Yet he had to ascend the frequent inclines with enough speed to keep the Dodge from slipping. He still held to his confidence that he'd be able to spot the turn, but to help himself he tried to search his memory for work he'd done at the fork. Trees he'd trimmed. Shoulders he'd smoothed. If he could see himself there in the past, he knew he'd be able to sense his approach.

But as he watched and tried to think, the fall of the snow began to work on him. Instead of finding any memory, he began to sense himself moving freely, his only job to look for the turn. He tried to peer through spaces in the snow, but its movement drew him in, held and methodically dulled his attention like the impalpable hum of a lullaby. He drove, squinting, his head lolling, and he was going, feeling amazed and grateful that the car was behaving perfectly on its own, and then he caught himself at the edge of sleep and jerked his head up, the force of a seizure's spasm in the gesture.

"Shit," he said and slapped himself. The Dodge skated to a stop in the middle of the road. Ed opened his window and breathed several times. He leaned out and let the snow hit his face for a while, then wiped its water with his sleeve. He made a long "Ahh!" sound, a cantor's drunken hum, to set the sound of his voice moving inside the Dodge. "Okay," he said, "okay." He turned off the heater and started up again.

He'd driven no more than fifty yards when he sensed he'd missed the turn. He was suddenly sure that it did not take this long to reach it. He'd passed it somehow; yes, while he was drifting off. He tried to argue with his fear: The falling snow confused things and he was driving so slowly that his sense of distance was unreliable. But he couldn't hold on to these

thoughts and he knew, he sensed, he'd missed it. He knew that a mile felt like five in snow like this.

But no. Somehow he'd missed it.

And then he saw it immediately on the right, the fork climbing away, a coiling white line through the white hillside, and he quickly turned the wheel toward it. The rear end came around in response and seemed to him to pass on the left as it led the Dodge through two balletic spins, the car moving for the edge with the unhurried sureness of birth, then off and into the ditch. It settled sideways on the steep bank, nearly paralleling the road, its cargo sliding and crashing in the back.

Ed sat, stunned, behind the wheel. The car was silent and he made no noise, either. He looked straight ahead as though steering still mattered, then turned around to inspect his cherished interior. Everything had slid to one side to make a pillaged-looking heap. He stared at it for several seconds. It seemed important to him to try to identify his things. He saw the water pitcher and its bowl; the stove. He looked almost melancholically at his pile of possessions, as though he were holding an old photograph of them. Several bottles of beer had rolled out of their case and Ed reached for one and twisted its cap. Foam shot from the mouth and he quickly put his lips over it.

He sat forward again and saw that snow had covered the windshield. There was a nearly vertical bank of snow through the windows on his right; the ditch's draw and then another plane of snow through his driver's side window. He was in a white well and, sensing so, a claustrophobia started in him. He turned the key and was surprised that the Dodge started instantly. He waited through a difficult moment while the wipers cleared, then pressed the accelerator, ready to feel the world widening out again as the Dodge climbed free.

The tires spun as he revved the motor. They spun again, and the Dodge didn't move. He stomped the pedal and held it to the floor. A fog rose from the spinning tires, the sound of their

crazed whine a kind of suffering music, and then the car slid, as though losing its grip on the bank, slid in a moment to the bottom of the ditch.

Ed screamed above the clanging of his belongings and when the Dodge came to rest he smashed his palm against the steering wheel. The beer he'd opened had spilled on the seat and he could smell kerosene fumes coming from the back. He screamed again, wild with the Dodge's disobedience. Now steep cliffs of snow were on his left and his right. "Shit!" he shouted. "Shit!" He snapped his head as he cursed. He gulped the beer still in the bottle and spun around to see the mess behind him. A pool of kerosene was spreading, and he reached for his twelve-gauge to save it from getting wet. "Shit! Shit! Shit!" He beat the steering wheel each time, then opened the door against the side of the ditch and squeezed out.

Carrying his shotgun, he stumbled forward. Snow was halfway up his shins. He turned around to look at the car, unable to comprehend its betrayal. To Ed in his fury it was as though the Dodge were looking smugly back at him. He raised the shotgun to his shoulder and fired at the car, and from the hole in the windshield an ordained pattern, like a massive spiderweb, spread out along the glass, but the snow was very thick and Ed was insensible, so he didn't see clearly the design his shot had made. He turned again and started to walk away, each step a struggle. Using the twelve-gauge as a climbing stick, he made his way up the bank. On the road, he bent for breath, exhausted from his climb. The snow was more than ankle deep.

He shuffled back along the road toward the fork he'd missed. When he reached it and turned he felt its slow ascent as a shift in the surface underneath the snow that pulled on his legs, the muscles in his shins, making walking even harder. With each step, he sank the stock of the shotgun into the snow ahead of him. He struggled to think of what he knew about this road, where it dipped and climbed and how severely, tried yet again to picture any history he'd made working it, but his thoughts

were now utterly blank. His temper had moved from rage to a kind of bleak pouting that had only some harsh, unspecific revenge in mind. A gust of wind blew snow especially strongly into his face and he cursed it, its insult, and through his numbness felt its wet, bitter chill.

He was briefly able to sense being home, where he would take all the time he needed. He wouldn't even try to work, to plan, until his body was warm and dry and that might take several days for all he knew. It didn't matter. He would wait, hiding out, happy in the heat of his unlit house, until his body was ready.

He leaned forward as he felt the road lifting more steeply, and plunged the shotgun into the snow ahead of him. He grunted occasionally and felt his breath going. Finally, he stopped, panting, his hands on his hips. As he stood still, his exhaustion began to flow downward from his mind, through his neck and shoulders, and it made him lucid for a moment in his consideration of the road. It occurred to him that he'd seen no tire tracks since leaving his own. He looked ahead at the sky and asked himself whether it was snowing harder. It seemed to be when he held his head a certain way, but he didn't know any longer. And it didn't matter. He felt something beyond tiredness—a need for sleep—settling in his arms, and he sensed how sweet his sleep would be when he'd gotten back to Myles.

And sensing it made a kind of heat that moved through him, enough to start him forward again. The heat and his sense of delicious revenge mixed eagerly, became the same thing as he walked and for a few minutes he moved on its energy more strongly through the snow. His pants legs, frozen from the knees, molded scabrous leggings, rubbed stiffly against his shins. The feeling was not the chafing of his skin but the grazing of two numbnesses taking place beyond his body. Above his knees, an icy wetness moved upward in the fabric of his jeans toward his crotch, the only sensation below his waist he could still feel.

His breathing whistled in his nose, a wind inside a wind, and soon his strength fell off again. The walking became more

difficult, the snow wetter and heavier as it received and resisted his steps with a deep sand's uninterested sameness. His mind simplified still further, his fatigue and the weather taking anger out of it, and he imagined sneaking into Myles, a fugitive, imagined the joy of his hidden life inside his house, forgetting there had been anything more to his need to return. He had no picture of himself planning his renewed search for Ramona. Thoughts of Ramona were nowhere in his mind.

For a moment he heard his breath and paid sole attention to it. It made a kind of clattering sound, as if his air were dislodging crystals from the walls of his lungs, but to Ed its sound was an ordinary response to the wind's. And anyway, once he was home it wouldn't matter.

His walk became a shuffle, a lifeless, imbecilic gait.

He began to feel dizzy. He looked up into the snow. The sky was neither dark nor cut with any hint of dawn; the sky was simply snow. He looked to his right. The lip of the ditch was still barely visible, but the snow was coming down too heavily for him to see any distance ahead, whether the ditch line curved or turned or ran straight ahead. He glanced left to the hillside but saw only falling snow. He slowed his step, a fear coming at him as part of the snow, and he shook his head, fighting off the incessant throb of flakes descending into him. He tried to see the surface of the road, any feature of the landscape, worked to see where the earth met the sky, but he was floating, horizon-less, a boy in a balloon, and he stumbled, touching nothing, and sat waist-deep in a steeply angled drift.

Crystals swirled off its face and blew into him, biting his cheeks. He sat, squinting to see his trail of steps. They were nearly vertical and he could follow them back up to the road. The ditch in which he sat was deep, and wind blew through it as through a tunnel. It gusted past Ed like something frantic in escape, hitting him in the chest and taking his breath.

He screamed at the snow, a thick human sound in the air against the wind's high howl. He leaned forward to the face of

the drift to get under the wind and then, as though it were a pillow, felt the urge to place his cheek against it. Again the idea of sleep moved immediately through him, to farther places in his body now, past his arms and into his hands, even to his waist and down through his legs as they sat in the snow. It was the first thing he'd felt in his legs for a while. The heat that had come as he'd thought of sleep returned.

Now he screamed again, the same sound, a word from his lungs to fight the lure of sleep. Grunting, he pushed himself forward. He came free of the drift and with everything he had crawled back up the ditch.

On the road, he looked up at the snow and now he imagined it a storm of weightless white birds he could kill. He imagined raising his shotgun to the snow, and calmly, indefatigably, killing each flake as it fell, and it was then that he realized he'd lost his gun when he'd fallen. He glanced behind him, took a few steps back to where he'd come up. He squinted down into the ditch and saw that there was already no evidence of his fall. Blowing snow had erased it. He turned back and saw that the steps he'd just made were already nearly gone. And fear spread through him, a clear thought of fear, against everything that had been working to dull him.

He looked ahead into the same white fall he'd been seeing; it seemed the only thing he'd ever seen in his life. He had no idea of the hour. He was awake in a space irrelevant of time. He beat the front of his coat free of the snow still clinging to him from the drift, then swept his arms and legs of it. He suddenly broke into a circling warrior's dance on the road, trying to nudge his blood, until it felt as though his whole body were his heart, his toes pulsing as strongly as his chest. And then, because there was nothing else, nowhere else, he started off again.

He altered his step, spreading it to a bowlegged stomp as he tried to feel each step. Mindless, he hunched clumsily along, aged and powerful. Every now and then he yelled at the snow,

berating it now, telling it to fuck itself. Intermittently, he slapped himself and beat his thighs and pulled his ears, trying to keep a pain spinning and stinging, something on his skin he could pay attention to.

But this greater effort was tiring him more quickly and he began in a while to slow his step again. And increasingly, he watched the snow. At first as the thing to hate and keep him going, but then he unconsciously began to try to decompose it, to watch pieces of it fall into him, and though this was impossible to do, the repetitive futility of it distracted him. He chose a flake streaming in. Isolated it. Watched it come. Watched it. Gone. . . . Chose a flake. . . . Chose another.

As he watched the snow in this way, Ed began to sense that it was pulling him, an ally. His inattention grew, and grew more pleasurable, taking him farther out of himself, and then it felt like his solution. He'd simply use each flake as he sometimes used the telephone poles that ran in orderly ranks along the roadsides he worked. Telling himself just to work to a pole, then, when he'd reached it, just to work to the next, forgetting he was tired and wanted to quit for the day and drive home and drink a beer. Working just to the pole; then to the next.

He watched a flake move toward him, watched another, and another, and he was drawn effortlessly along, felt the snow sucking him forward. He sensed his expertise sharpening with each repetition and after a time he could follow the flight of a flake until it struck his face.

The snow began to accommodate Ed. The flakes enlarged and separated to help him trace them and they flew into his face, lush as petals. He became able to follow each one through his low-lidded eyes until it exploded against his cheek. He watched another. And another. He was inside the weather now, wrapped in it, snug in its fluid, and as he moved along, filled with wonder, he suddenly pictured Broder. Broder's walk through the snow.

Ed burst into laughter, mad with insight, as he saw Broder's march through the snow once again. For at last he understood what Broder had seen as he'd moved with such extravagance down the D&H tracks. He'd seen the snow in several colors falling fatly into him, drawing him along, oblivious and free. Of course. No wonder he'd stepped so exuberantly through the night, his knees flying up to his waist with each step, his head thrown back as he watched the snow descend, each flake blooming, lustrous, as it struck his face and chest.

Broder had seen the snow just as Ed was seeing it now, and he'd also felt its help. And felt, as well, the same ebullience Ed knew now he'd been wrong to fear. Broder had felt that void of pure aloneness that had stopped Ed on the road when he'd climbed from the ditch and seen his gun was gone and watched his footprints erased by the fierce new snow. Ed had thought it was a thing of horror, but now he felt it as Broder had, as a calm of thrilling privacy, vast and intimate at once. He laughed again and tilted back, like Broder, to better watch the snow, to let it beckon him more easily. He watched it coming at him, and leaning back even more he took three steps, four, before he lost his balance and fell.

On his back in a low drift, he marveled that the snow fell into his face even more beautifully. He turned his head left and right and shifted his body, and as he moved he heard the scuffing sound of his coat against the snow. He stretched fully on his back and swept his arms like a child making angels, and the drift beneath him was a bed of smiling explosions in his ears. He moved his arms once more through long arcs and they made the sound again, a gentle scratching, like the soft even scrape of a shoe against a walk. He waited, then moved his arms again, first one, then the other, a walking rhythm, and heard the sounds, the shuffling of steps. He heard apology in them.

Smiling, his body buoyant without will, he turned onto his stomach and timidly lifted his ass to the sky, then lowered himself into the snow. He repeated the stroke as tenderly,

easing into the drift as if considerate of a virgin's fear. Then again, and again, soon finding a pulse that moved him with no thought of anything but the calling of the deep and fluent heat. He groaned, his arms spread, and the cadence of his love became a frantic search for heat.

Dropping, spent, into the drift, he wept for a time as he lay in the snow and then, at last, felt the heat, and sleep, moving everywhere in him.

Twenty-One

The four-mile walk from Mellenville, where her last ride had dropped her, seemed easy to Ramona; easier than the shoulder of the Taconic Parkway; much easier than her claustral trails at the edges of woods, through the suffocating rows of high cornfields.

The snow on the roadside was level and firm, almost springy underfoot, after the plows had passed. She saw no footprints ahead of her, only the plow blade's small delta-patterned sweeps and gashes. She heard her footsteps quickening slightly as the hillside started to fall almost undetectably toward Myles and her breath came easily, became even more plentiful.

She'd drunk only coffee in Mellenville, her stomach too jumpy to let her eat, and now, as she squinted up ahead toward the back of Myles, her nervousness was also in her chest and throat; was the thing that moved her legs. It made her feel physically hollow; a cavity. And it gave her an energy that

moved cumulously inside her. She squinted again into the sun—its light was glaring off the snow—and saw the field behind the town, neatly bordered by snow fence.

As she'd sat in Mellenville, thinking through once more the order, the procedure, of her return, she'd finally surrendered the idea that Jonas was with Lovilla. All along, though she'd known it was logical that his grandmother was caring for him, she'd felt a calmness when she imagined that her friend had taken Jonas. Nothing like absolution, but a kind of fragmentary ease at the idea of her baby with Lovilla. Maybe Ramona's thin hope had had to do with her sense of talking so often to Lovilla, about Jonas, about leaving. She had shown Lovilla everything, so there was the thought that Lovilla might have been able to see past what she'd done.

But she knew, as she'd thought yet again about what awaited her, that she would find Jonas with Vera.

She walked easily, letting the long descent help her. She was warm, a light sweat on her face, and she lifted her hair off her neck, a summer gesture. The day hit her moist skin instantly, but its chill was a quick pleasant cut against her nerves. She felt the road begin to level out.

She hadn't realized until she'd looked at the wall calendar in Mellenville that it was Saturday. She'd had to wait through the heavy snow in Poughkeepsie, then waited for the plows to open the roads, and she'd given no thought to the particular day. When she'd seen herself walking back into Myles, she'd loosely assumed that Ed would be at work, that she'd have at least a brief space of time to first find Jonas.

But it was Saturday and she thought to herself—because, like everyone in Myles, she hadn't yet heard—that if he wasn't at the Hill Top, chances were he'd be home. She'd given endless thought to what might happen. But she found that she had no clearer picture than she'd had that first afternoon, when she'd sat on a rock by a wide, shallow pool after the diving boys had

left and tried to see her return through the low red sun. Her first hope then had been to beat the darkness home. It had seemed for the moment the thing that mattered most.

She followed the road around its last slow bend. The field and the fence ran along beside her. She saw the fence's pattern, its slats of wood and air. She could continue along the highway as it looped into town and became Summit for three blocks, or leave it just ahead and cut through the field. She'd already decided to follow the field to the house. She wanted to get to Jonas as directly as she could. Even on the train, when she'd understood that she was coming back for Jonas, she'd begun almost immediately to see herself returning as she'd left, through the field.

The thought came to her that if Ed was in the house, Jonas might be, too, and she felt her heart move in her chest.

If no one was, she'd call Lovilla, as she'd planned.

She stopped and looked across the field. Snow was new and hard on it, like a lustrous hide. She shielded her eyes, tried to see the back of the house. It was only a white speck against a full sheet of white. But because she knew where it was she could see it. She started into the ditch, ready to sink into snow. But the frozen crust held and she scurried easily down. Several inches had drifted up along the fence and made a kind of gradual ramp. She walked through the ditch and stepped easily over the fence into the field.

She walked effortlessly through, on top of frozen nests of daisies. Every few steps she felt the crust give slightly, her boots stamping quick, thin cracks, but it did not let go. She tried to hear what her first words would be, to whom she'd say them. To Lovilla on the phone. To Ed in the kitchen. But nothing she thought of seemed conceivable.

The first night, in the motel room, she'd imagined herself explaining why she'd left and immediately, as though Jonas had looked up at her, his eyes curious, she'd asked herself again how she'd been able to walk away through this field.

In the dark of the motel room, she'd watched the snow through the window and thought about the train. Thought of how she'd sensed her leaving as the size of what that meant, and what it would mean, had grown by the moment. An emptiness had spread in her. It had stirred in her stomach, the hint of something infinite, continuous as the river.

She reached the end of the field, where it met the backyard. She could see, ahead of her, that the street in front was newly plowed and quiet. She walked along the side of the house. She cleared her throat, her heart beating crazily, and when she came out in front she saw that their sidewalk alone had not been cleared. She looked up and down the street. At the end, where plowed snow had been piled high, children were diving from the created cliff to the softer drifts below, then climbing back up its face. She imagined holding Jonas.

Frozen snow was scalloped intricately though the tiny front yard. Here and there it swirled, was curled and held like stiff confection. The snow in the yard seemed high to Ramona, accumulated weather, but she stepped easily through it toward the door, her boots making crisp crunching noises; solid sounds atop the drifts. She stopped and watched the children at the end of the street for a second more, heard their thrilled shrieks as they plunged, then reached for the screen door's handle.

About the Author

Douglas Bauer lives in Boston with his wife and stepson. He
is at work on a new novel.